PETER TRIED TO SCREAM AS THE HEAT FROM THE HOT PLATE SEARED HIS BARE FEET....

It made small sizzling noises each time a foot landed on it squarely, and he turned his feet so the plate would hit the sides instead of their already badly burned soles. It only made the knot of the rope around his neck grow tighter. Once again he tried to scream, but the ever-tightening noose turned it into a strange, gurgling sound. Gasping for air, he managed to plead a little. Could anyone understand him?

"Jennifer! Don't do this to Jennifer!"

His body shook and twisted as the red-hot plate burned into his skin. *"Don't—not me—please...."* he cried. *"Oh, God ... please...."*

Other Books by
DAVID LIPPINCOTT

E PLURIBUS BANG!
THE VOICE OF ARMAGEDDON
TREMOR VIOLET
BLOOD OF OCTOBER
SAVAGE RANSOM
SALT MINE
DARK PRISM
UNHOLY MOURNING

THE NURSERY

DAVID LIPPINCOTT

A DELL BOOK

Published by
Dell Publishing Co., Inc.
1 Dag Hammarskjold Plaza
New York, New York 10017

Dell ® TM 681510, Dell Publishing Co., Inc.

ISBN: 0-440-16474-5

Printed in the United States of America

First printing—June 1983

*For my son Christopher's good friend Teddy,
who was kind enough to lend me his last name,
albeit outraged at how cruelly the plot treated him.*

PART I

AVANT-PROPOS
(1978)

Just as night fell, the storm that had been muttering to itself all afternoon roared out of the Delaware River estuary and hurled itself at the coast. Sheets of dark rain swept across I-95, intermittent squalls that raced across the concrete as if chasing one another to the edges of hell.

The windshield wipers struggled bravely but quickly became useless as her eyes strained to make out the road ahead; their rhythmic *pee-kwok* was almost hypnotic. The girl slowed the car even further, almost totally unable to see the edge of the road—a blindness that came as much from the hot tears behind her eyes as from the rain sheets that pounded on the windshield like tortured strangers pleading for admittance.

"How could he? Damn it, how *could* he?" the girl demanded. The question was not new; she had been asking it ever since she fled Wilmington and headed for Baltimore. Inside, she knew the query was futile; no one knew, no one would ever know. She tightened her hands on the wheel; a sudden gust of wind had almost lifted the car off the road, and she had to struggle to keep it from skidding sideways across the highway.

"How could he?" she demanded again, as if God, who had toyed with her so cavalierly, now certainly owed her an answer. There was no reply except the angry, mournful sound of rain lashing the metal roof, the *pee-kwok* of the wipers, and the distant howl of an unfriendly wind.

Perhaps five miles farther down I-95 the gale rose to a furious pitch, making the whole car lurch and tremble under its buffeting. Then, as suddenly as it had risen, it stopped—spent, postorgasmic. With the death of the wind, the rain took command, spilling in thick waves across the car. On the right-hand door, the girl could see water running down inside the glass where the window joined the roof. Softly she swore. The car was almost new, and already its windshield wipers were ineffective, its windows leaked, and the motor coughed unhappily as water splashed into the carburetor.

Rain alone, though, made the girl more confident; she no longer feared being picked up off the road and hurled into the bushes along the side. Gradually she picked up speed again. She was, she knew, still going too fast for such a night, but the compulsion that had put her in the car in the first place still hounded her to make good her escape quickly. The question returned and rattled her brain. Her driving was becoming reckless, but she seemed unable to control it. She felt unable to control anything in her life anymore. Damn, damn, damn! How *could* he?

Maybe Henry Dykes, her boyfriend and occasional lover, would be able to explain something of it to her. He had urged her to flee to Baltimore—to him.

Perhaps Henry could help her see how a man she had loved and trusted could, without warning, suddenly turn and try something so incredibly sick.

Suddenly the girl began to cry. Henry Dykes might be able to put it all together for her, or Henry Dykes might just be as baffled by the incident as she was. She didn't know. The thought of even telling him what had happened made her cringe.

Fuck her father. The statement troubled her, and the girl found herself on the uncertain edges of hysteria again. Tears got all mixed up with unbidden insane giggles, and she felt self-control slipping away. Not the best shape for maneuvering a car down a murderously wet highway, she told herself.

Like an old enemy conspiring against her, the high wind and driving rain began tearing at the car again, the water hurling itself angrily at the windshield. Even in the direct glare of her lights she could barely make out the turnoff to Route 40. To her the wildness of the downpour, the eerie lurching of the car as the wind tried to lift it from the road, capsulized how she felt about life. Why, for God's sake? Oh, Mary, Mother of Jesus, why *her*?

The tears ran down her face; her trim body was racked by sobs; the shadows of the past closed in on her—distant whispers and murmurs, cries of pain, shrieks of protest.

Her wheels suddenly seemed to leave the road, skidding sickeningly on the wet concrete. Ahead she saw more shadows, a dark kaleidoscope of bushes and fences and shrubbery, and the sudden shattering scream of metal and glass as her car ran head-on into a tree.

She struggled to stay conscious. A face appeared in the window beside her. It was a nice man's face, but it was wearing an anxious look. He was dripping water from his cap. "Is it bad, miss? I raised the police on my CB. Is it bad? What happened? Don't try to move, miss. What happened? I was driving the truck behind you and you just— What happened, miss, what happened?"

The girl stared at the nice man and tried to answer. "How . . ." she began, but her mouth couldn't handle the words. She looked at the man helplessly. His face seemed to be going in and out of focus, and the dim light around him seemed to be growing even darker.

"Don't try to talk, lady. Don't try to move. The police . . . I can hear the sirens, lady. . . . You'll be all right," he added, with an attempt at a reassuring smile.

From somewhere far away she could hear the thin cry of sirens, rushing down the highway toward her. The man was trying to be so kind, smiling at her, the water running off the visor of his cap. Suddenly she wondered if somehow he could help her. She put all her strength into one sentence. "How could he?'' she asked him in a croaking whisper, and then saw that the nice man's perplexed face was slowly melting into the darkness around him. A moment later she could see nothing at all.

The question was academic.

The girl was dead.

CHAPTER ONE
(1983)

I don't exactly remember when I first had the idea for Blossom House; the how and why are easier. My brother, Henry, you see, had cracked up, and something drastic simply had to be done. Blossom House was the answer.

Henry, the poor man. People who looked askance at him after his breakdown should remember that only the year before, he'd lost his wife, and then his favorite daughter in a freak accident. And the year before that, he'd lost his older daughter, too. Pills, they said. Suicide, they said. Henry didn't say anything; he just screamed silently in his private agony. Alone. Abandoned. Tragic for a man like him who was used to, and desperately needed, a family.

I can't pretend that Blossom House wouldn't provide me with a lot of answers, too. I'd never been married—when I was young, boys apparently just considered me too damn huge to marry—so I was left to grow old by myself. All young men are bastards, really. Anyway, I was stuck in a painful, family-less void that couldn't be filled. Until the idea for Blossom House came along.

Henry, suddenly without a family, and myself, who'd always wanted but never had one, would both be made whole. Henry was a little reluctant at first—even as a child he'd always been

*on the squeamish side—but I knew so much about him—little
things he'd even forgotten himself—controlling him turned out to
be a cinch. He gave in to the idea of Blossom House, finally,
without a murmur. Henry is always telling me I shouldn't keep
pointing out to people how right I am. Maybe I shouldn't.*

On the other hand, how can I help it?

> *Journal of Blossom House,*
> *Entry, page 3—Harriet Griggs*

"Not smart, Hil, not smart at all. You know how old Stemms
reacts to that kind of stuff."

The piercing shrillness of the voice from the phone's other end
sounded like tape running backward. Jennifer winced. Sometimes
Hillary was a pain. She tried a halfhearted defense, but gave up.

"Ummm. Well, I think she's a sexless old prune, Jen,"
Hillary announced in a world-weary tone. "Looks like Ichabod
Crane in drag, and I suppose that hurts."

Jennifer *knew* it hurt. The reality was kind of sad, when you
thought about it. Miss Stemms's problem was that she was old
and tired, ground down by a lifetime of struggling with the young
ladies of Miss Chalmer's. Not easy. For this her reward was the
enmity of the girls and, next year, when she retired, a simple
gold pin presented by an embarrassed headmaster. Jennifer felt
sorry for Miss Stemms, perhaps even liked her a little. But not
enough to try to help her; girls of seventeen are bitterly cruel to
anyone reckless enough to challenge their verities.

"Been teaching too long," Jennifer said, a reply allowing her
neither to defend nor condemn poor old Miss Stemms. She
wiggled her toes inside her Nikes and decided they were already
too small. Damn. Growing up had its drawbacks. She acknowledged Hillary's endless harangue with monosyllabic grunts and
pulled herself up a little higher in her chair, luxuriating in the
veiled sensual excitement of too-tight designer jeans. On her lap

was a porcelain paper clip dish, empty of clips so it could serve
as an ashtray. Later she would dump the ashes and butts down
the john, replace the paper clips, and put the dish back on
her desk. This subterfuge had practical roots.

"Jen," her father had said only the week before, gazing off
into space the way he always did when he had to bring up
something unpleasant. "Jen, if you want to smoke, well, that's
your business. It's kind of stupid, I think, for a kid your age, but
that's none of my business. Just please try not to rub your
mother's nose in it; she's got this thing about smoking. . . ."

Jennifer laughed lightly. Her mother had a thing about damn
near everything, but particularly smoking. Grudgingly she conceded her father was right. She'd have to be more careful with it
because, when it came to tracing the faintest suspicion of nico-
tine, her mother had the nose of a Georgia bloodhound.

"I'll swallow the butts," she'd said, giggling, making him
laugh. Jennifer had jumped out of her chair and begun spinning
in tight little circles in front of him. "How do you like my new
Edouardos?" she'd asked, rotating her bottom just the tiniest bit.
Provocative, she had supposed, but that kind of behavior invaria-
bly got to him. When she was a little girl she had batted her eyes
and curtsied a lot; these days, she wiggled her ass. He loved it.

Her father had studied the jeans's skintight fit with a small
smile, his eyebrows raised. "Very neat, certainly very tight." He
had paused, his lips pursed. "Is Edouardo inside there *with* you?"

Jennifer Delafield had laughed, and Townsend Delafield had
laughed, and she had scored another round. The cigarettes were
forgotten. If only her mother were as easy to handle, she had
thought.

Hillary Crane's voice was still pouring out of the phone when
Jennifer suddenly realized she was being asked a direct question,
something her noncommittal string of grunts was inadequate to
handle. "Can't, can't, can't, Hil. Peter's coming up from Princeton.
Daddy and the Dragon Lady will be in East Hampton, opening
up the house, so—"

Choking on her Merit 100, Jennifer broke up at something

deliciously dirty Hillary said. Looking up, she was slightly annoyed to see Ingebord slide hesitantly into her room again. This was the third time Ingebord had been dispatched to get Jennifer, and she was beginning to look a little upset. Struggling with herself, Ingebord tried to remain silent, but when Jennifer only smiled at her and went right on talking into the phone, she finally interrupted.

"Jennifer, it's dinner. They're holding it up still, and your mother's getting mad. Now she acts as if it's *my* fault."

The Delafields' housekeeper had been with them since Jennifer was only seven, and sometimes thought Jennifer was as much her child as theirs. Cleaning women and cooks came and went; Ingebord stayed, cooking as well as waiting on table, serving at cocktail parties, trying to maintain a vestige of a grander day when the household had been touched with elegance. It was hard, thankless work, made harder by trying to deal with Mrs. Delafield. Jennifer was the only reason Ingebord stayed.

Resigned, Jennifer sighed. It wasn't fair to get poor old Ingebord in trouble. One's allies have to be taken care of. "Gotta go, Hillary. Feeding time at Bronx Zoological. Mom's pacing her cage like a Bengal. Gotta go, gotta go."

Quickly she dumped the ashes and flushed the toilet. Now the arguments would begin. Who the hell invented dinner, anyway?

"We started without you," her mother said, fixing her with a steely eye. "You know what time dinner is."

Jennifer stared at her plate. She had come into the dining room, ready to apologize; her mother had just made it impossible. Across the table, her father shifted uncomfortably, not looking at her.

"It's not as if it were a different time every day," continued her mother. "Unless there's company, every night's the same."

Jennifer snorted. "We're in a rut. Wow, are we ever." Her father had been taking a sip of water. His only child's riposte produced a small explosion of air and water. He was speared by the same withering stare his daughter had been earlier; his smile vanished abruptly.

Quickly Jennifer tried to draw the fire to herself. "Dinnertime is dinnertime is dinnertime," she said vaguely. It was a ridiculous comment. Gertrude Stein could get away with that kind of doggerel; Jennifer Delafield couldn't.

"That makes no sense, Jennifer, no sense at all." Jennifer was inclined to agree with her mother, but admitting it was as impossible as apologizing. Her father tried to bring the conversation back to neutral territory. "We *are* a little early tonight. . . ."

"We are *not* early," Mrs. Delafield said firmly. Studying Jennifer, her mother appeared to notice what Jennifer was wearing. "And that's no way to come to the dinner table, either. Jeans!"

"Designer jeans." Jennifer was aware that she was expected to wear a dress at dinner and knew her answer sounded weak. She'd changed into them when she got home from Chalmer's and, talking to Hillary, had just forgotten about them.

Her mother studied her angrily, trying to figure how to handle this new breakdown in discipline. Jennifer was too young, apparently, to reason with and too old to send to her room without supper. Down the table, Mrs. Delafield saw her husband trying to look as if he were someplace else; he was never any help when it came to lowering the boom on Jennifer, anyway. That girl had him absolutely in her control—far more than she herself did. Letting her soup cool, she stared down at the rice swimming loosely around in her consommé. For a moment she wondered if she could be jealous of Jennifer's closeness to Townsend, then dismissed the notion as unworthy of herself. Jennifer was just a young girl with a talent for manipulating people—her own friends, *their* friends, the help, strangers, and particularly her father. That smile of hers—it dazzled, it warmed, it won. Even as a little girl, she'd known just how to use it to get her own way. Once she herself had shared the same talent, but as she grew older, the smile had lost its magic, and the world stopped obeying.

Abruptly Mrs. Delafield stopped staring at her soup and looked at her daughter with distaste. Damn it, she *was* jealous. In the dining room the only sound was the stirring of the soup spoons and Ingebord's muffled movements as she served the toast and poured more water into Townsend Delafield's glass.

Toward the end of dinner Jennifer dropped the bomb. It was neither the moment, nor were the conditions what she would have chosen, but tomorrow would be too late. "I can't go to East Hampton with you this weekend, Mother," Jennifer said softly, gentling the statement with a small smile. Across the table, she heard her father put down his knife and fork and raise his head to study her. She could tell because of a small sound his neck always made when he lifted his head too quickly.

"Oh. Why not, Jen?" There was an edge to his voice. The man who allows himself to be controlled by his daughter lays down certain unspoken rules. Not going where the controller had bidden was one rule that was not broken lightly.

"Well, you see," Jennifer explained, trying to make her mother feel included by looking at her a lot, "there's this really humongous paper due on Monday. 'History of Economics,' " she added, playing to her father. "And Hillary and I have been slaving over it for weeks at school, only now we have to pull the whole crazy thing together by Monday. It's going to be a terrible grind; the assignment kind of got away from us, I guess."

A new look of extreme displeasure mushroomed across her mother's face. "What you mean, Jennifer, is that Peter Owen is coming up from Princeton, and you're afraid *he'll* get away from you."

Damn her mother. She'd probably injected Peter into the matter just to upset her father. Jennifer did her best to look blank.

"I don't think so. I think the tennis team's got a match on."

"Peter Owen," her father repeated sourly. When it came to Peter, her father could be just as unpleasant as her mother. In his eyes, Peter couldn't do *any*thing right. That smart bitch mother of hers, using Peter to move her husband to her side. Damn it, the "History of Economics" had seemed such a foolproof gambit. "This paper—" she began again.

"Can't be done here," her mother finished for her. "There

won't be anyone in the place. You can't stay in the apartment all by yourself, and that's all there is to it."

"Ingebord—"

"Has Sundays off."

Jennifer was suddenly panicked. Now they were *both* closing in on her; she was a prisoner in her own home. "I'll get Hillary to come over and stay here," she said suddenly, "We'll be working on the damn paper both Friday and Saturday nights, anyway."

There was a silence while this possibility was examined. "Maybe if we checked with the Cranes and made sure it was all right . . ." her father suggested, relenting and trying to go along with Jennifer.

Jennifer's mother could sense the power shifting and maneuvered to get herself back on top again. Any mention of Peter was always useful. "You're *sure* Peter Owen isn't going to be in town?"

Even across the table, Jennifer could feel her father bristle. She heard the *clang* as barred steel doors all over the apartment slid shut. "I wouldn't think so. The tennis team—" They stared at her without sympathy. Were all kids her age treated like this? Did parents all across the country try to control their children like serfs, hold them in bondage, making them chattels to their personal fiefdoms like hers did? Abruptly she tried a new tack.

"Honestly, I don't understand why you both have this thing about Peter. He's not a monster, for God's sake."

"He's too old for you." Her mother was wearing an even more sour look than before.

"*Twenty* is too old? Oh, come on."

"Too old, and he still doesn't have the slightest idea what he wants to make of his life. Not a clue," threw in her father.

Jennifer sighed heavily. In a moment of giddiness Peter had once told her father he thought he might not go in to one of the conventional areas—banking, brokering, law, attending Harvard Business School—but make a living writing folk songs and singing in bars. That the songs he wrote were purely for fun and usually far too off-color to perform anywhere, or that he had a career in corporate law already carefully mapped out, was of no consequence. In Mr. Delafield's mind, Peter was destined to be a drug-soaked, vagabond minstrel, wandering through second-rate dives—probably somewhere in the Third World—playing his guitar and dragging his beloved daughter, Jennifer, behind. Nothing Jennifer could say ever appeared to make a dent—the reason, Jennifer concluded, her mother had shoehorned Peter into the discussion.

It was not that Jennifer loved Peter with a mad, uncontrollable passion. She loved him, yes, but she was not so blind she couldn't see that her love for Peter grew and shrank, depending on how much trouble she was having with her family.

Peter was a handsome boy—actually, extremely appealing—as well as bright, articulate, and funny. And woven through every fiber of his body was a quality of delicious sensuality, a quality Jennifer knew would finally be consummated this weekend. They had been moving toward it for months. Jennifer's own body ached in anticipation. But love him insanely, wildly, heedlessly? Jennifer didn't think so.

Rather it was Peter Owen who loved *her*—to the point of obsession. He appeared unable to exist without her, and Jennifer was not above using his love to her own advantage when it suited her. It was, she supposed, a workable arrangement: To her, Peter represented a way out of the agonizingly painful, confining limits of her life at home; an escape from the intolerable.

"Peter's going into law. Corporate law," Jennifer said wearily, for perhaps the thousandth time. "And he's not coming up to New York this weekend. I don't know where you got that idea."

"You're positive?" Her father was beginning to bend. In the end, he always did.

"Positive."

From her mother came the sound of the winning trump being slapped on the table. "That's funny. I talked to Midge Owen earlier this week, and she said he was. There isn't any tennis match this weekend.''

One of the cardinal rules, Jennifer was aware, was that the controller never lies to the controlee. Or at least never gets caught at it. Jennifer could see her father's expression change, moving inevitably toward a mixture of sadness and wounded disappointment.

Her mother remained expressionless. Calm but brutal, ''I guess that explains your sudden interest in the history of economics. It sounded out of character, anyway. It also ends that harebrained scheme of yours to stay in New York for the weekend. We'd walk out one door, Peter the folksinger would walk in the other. You're coming to East Hampton with us. I'm sorry, but that's the way it's going to be.''

Avoiding Jennifer's eyes, Mr. Delafield sighed heavily. ''I guess your mother's right, Jen. It isn't safe for you here alone, you know. And you'll have a good enough time there.''

Jennifer felt the breath go out of her. She stared at them both in disbelief. It was her mother, her goddamn mother, who'd engineered this, making the issue Peter Owen. Clever, very clever. The old lady had her own expertise in manipulation, something that Jennifer always tended to underestimate.

Everything boiled up inside Jennifer at the same time: the trapped feeling; the unfairness; the sense of being continually misunderstood—of being treated like a child, being monitored, restricted, held back; and most of all, it had struck her so suddenly—it was the interference in her relationship with Peter. The sensual ache inside her returned. Up until this moment it hadn't been anything overwhelming; now, abruptly, it was the most important thing in her life.

Jennifer wanted to scream, to throw things, to get into her car and flee as far from home as she could. Without her even realizing quite what was happening, the screaming and throwing of things took on reality.

''Damn you, damn you, damn the both of you! You don't

understand me, not one miserable little bit, you don't. You hate my friends, you hate what I think, you hate what I say, you hate what I do, you hate what I wear. You want to lock me up and let me rot in this dungeon. Well, shit. I'm fed up kissing your asses. Both of you. I'll run away. I'll go someplace where they've never heard of me and be myself. I'll say what I want and do what I want, for Christ's sake, and for just once in my life I'll be a person. . . . I'll—I'll—I'll—''

An explosion of tears suddenly burst from her. She stood motionless, the stream of tears running down her face, her fist jammed into her mouth, and shaking with silent sobs. Furious at herself, furious at the world, she grabbed her butter plate and sent it crashing into the near wall, there to slide down in a thousand pieces and clatter noisily to the floor. ''Bastards! Bastards!'' she screamed, and ran from the dining room. Her mother's icy ''Jennifer—'' spoken warningly just before Jennifer ran from the room, went either unheard or unheeded or both.

Behind her, a stunned audience stared at the empty spot where she had just been. Her mother remained motionless, studying her water glass, squeezing her lips together in a new, even more compressed expression. At the head of the table, her father sat stricken, looking at his wife, then at his plate, his eyes darting anxiously from one to the other, stunned and concerned and hurt. Close to the pantry door, Ingebord, holding a tray of tapioca she had been about to serve, seemed close to tears. ''The poor child,'' she whispered under her breath, and then, realizing the danger of expressing anything at all—it wasn't her place—managed considerable clattering with the tapioca dishes, as if trying to bury the sound of her own impetuosity.

Mr. Delafield studied the tapioca with distaste, listlessly poking at it with his spoon. He hated the stuff. His face wore an expression of unhappiness that clearly went far deeper than tapioca. Slowly he raised his eyes to his wife's. ''I guess I shouldn't have taken those pokes at Peter. Stupid. I never saw her react like that before.''

Mrs. Delafield was patting her mouth with her napkin. She wasn't particularly fond of tapioca herself, but had read somewhere it was good for you, particularly for growing children. Her eyes remained steely. "You haven't ever seen it because you haven't ever looked. Jennifer has been wrapping you around her little finger for years. Now you see the result. This time, you can't let her get away with it. She's still just a child, and a very rude child at that."

"Maybe . . . I don't know."

It was a comment open to many interpretations, precisely as Mr. Delafield had intended it to be. He was a lawyer, wasn't he?

In the end, Ingebord's sudden offer was what provided the solution. "Yes, Mrs. Delafield, I'd be happy to. I didn't have anything planned for Sunday, anyway. I'll just take some other day, if that's all right with you."

Mrs. Delafield stared at her uncomprehendingly. Somehow Jennifer had Ingebord wrapped around her little finger, too. Mrs. Delafield managed a sour smile. "That's terribly nice of you, Ingebord," she said, the insincerity showing. "I'll talk to Mr. Delafield about it when he gets home." Damn the Swedes, anyway. They'd made surrender an art.

Oddly enough, Mr. Delafield was finally left to tell Jennifer she could stay in New York for the weekend after all. His wife was still adamantly opposed but aware that further resistance was now useless. That damn little Jennifer had pulled it off again. "I wash my hands of it," she had told her husband. "You made the decision—you take the responsibility."

Jennifer took everything. She had won. She was delirious. She and Peter would be free to do whatever they wanted—as long as it wasn't at the apartment—Ingebord was pliable, but not *that* pliable. No problem. Peter's family had just flown to Hobe Sound, their apartment left unattended. The ache inside her—new, but powerful—would be satisfied.

God bless Ingebord. God bless Peter. Screw her mother. The picture this evoked was so grotesque, Jennifer broke into private laughter. She must call Peter. Call him now. Tell him. Delight him. Tease him.

Jennifer remained unaware of the ominous cycle of events her triumph had set in motion, an olla podrida of small, apparently unconnected happenings that would eventually come together to destroy her.

CHAPTER TWO

Putting Blossom House together was a lot of work, but Henry and I really put our hearts into it. Fortunately, he had plenty of cash from the sale of his house in Wilmington, as well as an income from his separation agreement with Ewing, Coxe, & Bradlee.

The house was a graceful red-brick Georgian, built in those days when people had a real eye for simplicity of line. But, my God, it was in terrible shape. No one had lived in it for years. The roof leaked, the bricks were literally falling out of the walls, and the grounds were beyond belief. Originally the place apparently had been planted with a wealth of flowering trees and shrubs, but everything had been neglected so long, the plantings had become a tangled jungle of undergrowth. It took the landscape gardeners six months just to make a dent.

The one big problem was redoing the third floor. For what we wanted built there we couldn't very well use our contractors. Too bad the people who built Devil's Island were all long dead.

Then I remembered Cousin Larry. Both Henry and I loathed him, but I knew he'd always been extraordinarily good with his hands. When I called, he turned out to be as broke as I had expected, and was delighted to come down and pick up some money working on the third floor. Creepy boy, totally dishonest, and ready to do anything for a dollar.

We bought the materials—some pretty peculiar stuff—and he did the work. Better, I confess, than I would have ever dreamed. Of course, next time he's out of cash again, he'll be back demanding a handout—blackmail disguised as charity. But we had no choice.

When you ask the criminal mind to do something for you, you know it's only a matter of time before it will try to do something to you.

Journal of Blossom House,
Entry, page 5—Harriet Griggs

The fickle sun of early morning striking hard on her face woke her. If Jennifer had been at home, she would have sworn softly and burrowed beneath her pillow, trying to salvage sleep. Today she made no effort; the excitement of being here and of the day that stretched out ahead brought her fully awake.

Beside her, a gentle snore came from Peter Owen. He lay flat on his back, his mouth slightly open, his bare chest slowly rising and falling with his breathing. Jennifer longed to wake him, to experience again what she had for the first time last night, but Peter had had too much to drink, and she supposed he needed sleep to recover. She let her eyes wander around his room. She'd been here before, of course, but never in this way—an unwitting gift of the Delafields' journey to East Hampton and the Owens' flight to Hobe Sound, and of Ingebord, the Capulet nurse.

Seen from the same bed Peter had slept in for fourteen years, the room had a mystical boyish charm. In this room soldiers had once marched, staring mournfully up from leaden bases, replaced a few years later, she supposed, by electric trains that whirled around endless ovals, and finally replaced by the blast of his stereo and the Beatles and the Who and the Stones. It excited Jennifer even to think of Peter that young. At the moment, thinking of Peter at any age brought back the delicious ache inside her.

Her eyes moved on to the trophies of his late teenage years and early manhood. Fellow members of Princeton's Cottage Club gazed confidently from one wall, casting the shadows of their virility across the gangling teenagers grouped uncertainly on the lawns of Deerfield below them. Tilted crazily out from another wall was a paper hat of orange and black; from beneath it hung a pink crocheted jockstrap, gift to the Cottage from some girl long-ago forgotten. Peter had won it in a poker game and hung it here at home, confident it would rattle his mother. It had.

Thinking of Peter's mother made Jennifer think of her own, and a sour look came over her face. She pulled the covers up further across her naked body with a slight shudder. It wasn't just a matter of her mother either, it was worse. That explosion the other evening proved that when the chips went down, her father could be just as arbitrary.

The thought cast a sudden cloud of suspicion across her assumption that all these years she had been so great at handling him; maybe she hadn't been handling him at all, but he *her*.

If he could, he'd have locked her away somewhere, frozen in time, the sweet little girl she was at eight or nine—unquestioning, accepting everything he said as truth, doing as he bade her without complaint.

No, she decided, he just wasn't that selfish. Somehow, it was all her damn mother's fault. Torturing herself, Jennifer gave a betrayed little moan.

She saw Peter's eyelids flutter. A sound—a soft sound—had intruded suddenly into his world; a breach of security. Something was wrong. Something beyond the throbbing of his head and the desert dryness of his mouth. He explored the world tentatively with one eye, and a shock ran through him. My God, Jennifer. Her eyes found his and her face broke into a smile.

Peter's first reaction was to panic about his parents, but then he remembered, and the fear dissolved. They were in Florida. Of course.

"Hi," Jennifer said, the smile widening.

Peter grunted. Her fingers were running lightly up and down the inside of his legs, tracing circles and moving slowly upward. They found his morning hardness—my God, did she think that was *her* doing?

"Hi," Jennifer said again.

Peter's answer was less than romantic. "My head hurts."

Jennifer was in a forgiving mood. "I'll kiss it and make it well." Peter was startled—Jennifer was a little startled herself by her own sudden aggressiveness—to find her pulling down the covers and kissing his body from one end to the other, exploring, probing, encircling. His body began trembling, his stomach rising and falling like the center of a trampoline. From inside him came the suggestion of a moaned dissent. He needed coffee desperately; his mouth tasted awful; his head throbbed unmercifully. He wouldn't, he couldn't, not now, he—

From the wall, the men of Cottage stared at him with reproach.

"Rah, tiger, sis-boom-bah,
  And send the backs on 'round the end;
  Fight, fight for every yard,
  Princeton's honor to defend!"

Flipping her over on her back so suddenly that Jennifer cried out, Peter Owen, of New York City, Hobe Sound, Florida, and East Hampton, L.I., defended it admirably.

In the rear corner of Mortimer's the lighting, like the wood of the walls, is dark. Earlier, Peter had told her everything today made him feel unreal—his head, he supposed. Jennifer watched; maybe a Bloody Mary would make him feel better.

Seen across the red-checkered tablecloth, Peter's blond hair appeared to be attached to the etched glass filigree of the partition behind him. She looked at him with love, but the depression about her family had settled around her again.

"Peter," she asked suddenly. "Have you thought of getting married?"

Peter Owen sat in his place, stunned, staring at Jennifer in disbelief, as if she'd just pulled a butcher knife from her purse and suddenly stabbed the woman at the next table. Of course he'd thought about it; there were days when it was the only thing in the world he *could* think about. Somewhere along the line, he and Jennifer had even joked about it. At least, he'd thought it was a joke. Jennifer would never settle for someone like him. . . .

He loved Jennifer: adored and worshipped her; considered her the most attractive, beautiful, wonderful, bright, warm, sexy, and sensational girl he'd ever known. But all of a sudden things were happening too fast. He was dizzy from trying to keep up with the changes. And the casual way she'd sprung her question about getting married—as if she were asking his shoe size or something. Today *was* unreal.

Jennifer was almost as surprised at herself as he was. *Marry* Peter? Well, she'd thought of it, of course. She was very fond of him. No, that wasn't strong enough. She loved him. But it was not the overwhelming, dizzying, blinding, sort of love she'd always imagined—the kaleidoscope of passions, murmurings, compulsions, and thrashings you read about in books and saw in movies and watched on television. Last night's sudden inauguration into sex had left her aching with happiness. Did that have anything to do with the change in her?

Her own blunt question left her staggered. She sat motionless, still staring at Peter, her mind reeling drunkenly, the kitchen noises and the dining room voices of Mortimer's growing deafeningly loud in her ears.

"You can't stay in the apartment all by yourself, and that's all there is to it," her mother had said. "We'd walk out one door, Peter the folksinger would walk in the other," she had added. "You know what time dinner is. . . . That's no way to come to the dinner table. . . . *Jeans!*'' Her mother's voice had been increasingly cold and accusatory.

From her father, suddenly peremptory: "Too old, and he still doesn't have the slightest idea what he wants to make of his life. . . . Your mother's right. . . . It isn't safe for you here alone. . . .''

The recollections of what her father and mother had said during Wednesday night's argument played against the voices and slamming of pots and dishes in Mortimer's kitchen like fourteenth-century counterpoint. She looked at Peter again. He appeared speechless. Jennifer could see a slight trembling of the smooth skin of his upper lip, like a child's attack of stage fright. He blinked at her uncertainly.

Finally he spoke, the voice strangely thin and uncertain for Peter. "My God, Jennifer. My God. I don't even know where to start. It's—it's— Christ—I've dreamed about it, I've thought about it, I've prayed about it, and all of a sudden out of nowhere you— What I mean— Jesus!'' For some reason a peculiar silence, introspective, baffled, searching, dropped over both of them.

The implausibility of their earlier conversation, when it came, surprised Peter, in that it came from him. "I don't know,'' he said to Jennifer suddenly. "There's some practical things. I mean, I've got a year left at Princeton. Not to mention law school. And you're supposed to be heading for Smith in the Fall. . . .''

Jennifer felt a surge of relief. Peter himself was going to put the damper on the suggestion; she would resist mightily, but allow him to talk her out of what she herself knew had been an impetuous idea. "I think,'' she said, "that you ought to finish Princeton, Peter. That kind of thing's important for a man. Law school, well, we can think about that later. But Smith. Smith's a crock. Lot of girls in knee socks, trying to look meaningful. We can live somewhere near Princeton and feel our way from there.'' It struck Jennifer that she was probably overdoing the positive side of it, yet the words kept coming out unbidden. Maybe marrying Peter really *was* what she wanted. No, not yet, not yet.

Peter was staring into his glass, suddenly looking quite sad. "There's other things, too. Your family—"

"Yells at me whatever I do, anyway." Jennifer could imagine their reaction to this scheme. The picture was strangely pleasing.

"I don't mean that. Of course they'll yell. I'm not their favorite young man. It's something else. You're too young—legally underage, I guess it is. You can't get married without their consent. Your old man could just come charging after you and drag you back. Christ, I think he could even put *me* in jail. 'Corrupting the Morals of a Minor Child'—you know the bit. So does he; he's a lawyer."

Jennifer sighed loudly. "Oh, shit. Then there's money. Daddy sure as hell isn't going to subsidize us."

"I have a little from a trust fund," Peter said, a little surprised that Jennifer seemed to be giving in so easily. "But I doubt if it's enough. For law school and everything."

"Damn, damn, damn."

Peter suddenly stared her hard in the eyes. "But look, in another year, Jennifer, all the legal stuff about your age goes out the window. And I don't *have* to go to law school. Then we can really talk about it seriously. Christ, you know I want to. You know how much I want to. How much I've *got* to. I love you, Jennifer. And have for years. God*damn* but I love you. . . ."

Jennifer felt better. Sometimes Peter could be as reassuring as her father.

Peter stayed downstairs in his car while Jennifer checked in with Ingebord, who must have been wondering what had happened to her by now. She'd tell her she stayed over at Hillary's— plausible enough. A little later there was that cocktail party that Muffie Sloane was giving up in Pound Ridge. She and Peter were expected. She'd change clothes, come back downstairs, and they'd hit the Ridge just about on time.

When she opened the front door to the apartment, she saw Ingebord dusting something about two thirds of the way down the long gallery. Jennifer called to her cheerfully, but Ingebord didn't answer; instead she seemed to be waving her arms wildly. It didn't make any sense at all.

Suddenly it did. Her father stepped out of the library, his face troubled. Right behind her appeared her mother, planting herself in the middle of the gallery, furious, wearing an expression like a thunderhead. What the hell were *they* doing here?

"Hi," Jennifer said, suddenly feeling her knees go weak.

"Where have you been?" her mother demanded icily.

"Hillary's. It got so late I spent the night there."

"No, you didn't. I called. Hillary isn't there, she's in Greenwich. And has been since yesterday."

"Where have you been, Jen?" her father repeated softly. "Ingebord didn't know, nobody knew." His voice had an agonized tone to it, waiting for Jennifer to say something that would make everything all right again. Jennifer knew he was hurt; she also knew her mother would take that hurt and turn it into anger if she could. Jennifer, feeling somehow double-crossed by all that was happening, couldn't think of an answer for her father. Instead she tried to turn the question around.

"I don't understand. You're supposed to be in East Hampton." The floor felt as if it were sinking beneath her feet.

"Yes, we were supposed to be, but we're not, are we?" Her mother's sarcasm was as laced with repressed fury as her face. "Henry"—the man who looked after the East Hampton house when sober—"had forgotten we were coming. Drunk. No electricity, no water, no heat. We came back this morning—to this. And you still haven't answered: Where have you been, Jennifer? *Peter?*"

"Peter." Her father repeated the word, mouthing it like it was an oath. "Peter Owen."

"That's it, isn't it, Jennifer," her mother asked, not so much as a question but as a statement. "Well, young lady, you're grounded. For the rest of the spring. We'll get to exactly what you and Peter were up to later. I can imagine. Now I think it's time—"

A dam burst inside Jennifer. They didn't understand. They

didn't *want* to understand. Peter, or anything else. The kitchen sounds and the voices at Mortimer's suddenly filled her ears again. With Peter, she was an equal. A person. With Peter, she was free. Here, she was nothing. A prisoner. "Okay, if that's the way you want it, I'll run away. We'll get married. Peter and I were discussing it at lunch. There's not a damn thing you can do about it, either. I'm sick of "

"You're legally underage," her father announced, precisely as Peter had predicted. From his tone, Jennifer knew she could expect no help from him; he was using his litigation voice. "You won't get married or anything else until I say you can. This nonsense, Jennifer, just has to stop. I don't know who you think you're—"

"It's not nonsense. And I'll damn well do what I want. You can't stop me. Peter and I talked about that at lunch, too." It was a lie, but a satisfying one. "You should have had a son. Then when you got mad at him, you could sock him. The hell with both of you."

Not really sure of how it had all happened, Jennifer turned and marched out of the apartment. The door slammed behind her with a sound as final as the closing of a coffin lid.

"You're really sure you want to go through with this, Jen? . . ."

Hillary Crane stood outside the canopy at 725 Park, helping, along with a doorman so old it seemed criminal to let him carry bags, to load the last of Jennifer's things into her car. It was two days since she'd last been home. She was staying with Tibi Clark, not really a close friend, but always reliable. Hillary, Jennifer knew, would be under constant pressure to tell her father where she was. But no one outside of her class at Chalmer's even knew Tibi existed.

Tibi's apartment, like Hillary's, was a block or two up Park. All of Jennifer's friends seemed crammed into this same tiny area. A couple of blocks toward Fifth was 18 East 72nd, where Peter's family had *their* apartment.

"You're *sure*?" repeated Hillary, opening the trunk for the doorman. Jennifer looked at Hillary as if she were crazy, taking a small case from her and putting it on the front seat beside her. "I'm sure."

Jennifer felt safe enough going home to pick up her stuff; her father would still be at the office, and she'd waited outside until she saw her mother leave about half an hour ago. Only Ingebord saw her, and she didn't argue, just cried and cried and cried.

"I'll miss you," Hillary said simply. "But Peter's a great guy; you're lucky as hell. I mean that. And I just wish I could be at the wedding."

A look of concern passed across Jennifer's face. "You're not supposed to know about that, remember? Peter made me swear on a stack of civics books that I wouldn't tell anybody. *Anybody.* If word gets around, my parents will have the police and the bloodhounds and the FBI out. You know them. But *you*—well, you know—I *had* to tell you."

"I won't say anything to anybody. Honest." Hillary picked up a Vuitton makeup case and handed it in through the car window. "Where will you get married?"

"Chivers. It's in Maryland or Delaware or someplace like that. No age requirements."

"Promise to call me afterward? I mean, after you get to wherever you're going to live."

"Peter has to finish school, so it'll be someplace near Princeton— but not near enough so my family can find me easily. And I'll call you, you know that. Thanks for everything, Hillary. I don't know what I'd have done without you."

She started the motor of the car and then, remembering something, motioned Hillary to come close to the car. "And remember, for God's sake, Hillary, don't get pissed at P.J.'s and tell somebody. That would really do it."

Hillary laughed and clutched Jennifer's hand through the window. From under the hood came a roar as Jennifer raced the motor, then let it settle into a reassuring hum. She waved at

Hillary and, trying to look casual through a scattering of tears, drove firmly off into the twilight.

For a long time Hillary stood there, staring at the spot in the distance where she had last seen the Pontiac's taillights before they disappeared over the top of a small hill on Park. She pulled the sweater tighter around her, shivering from a sudden coldness.

Like the car's taillights, it seemed that Jennifer had climbed a hill and then simply disappeared into the gathering darkness. She shivered again.

CHAPTER THREE

Five feet nine and a half is too damn tall for a woman. And ever since I was a teenager, that's what I've been. Not the lithe, willowy, elegant kind of tall, either—like Consuelo Crespi or Nancy Kissinger—but a big-boned, full-bodied, heavyset sort that made me the butt of all the other kids' pathetic attempts at humor.

"The bulldozer" was one thing boys at high school called me. "Ape-Lady" was another. Boys can be awfully cruel about things like that; they never came near me.

Never for a moment did they consider that I was one hell of a cook, or that I had a fine mind, or that I could keep a fine house and would make a wonderful mother. No, the thought of marrying me was something they hooted at, pointing at me in the hall and making ribald gestures.

"Let her get you in the sack," I can remember Barry Lombard telling a bunch of kids one day, "and she'd suffocate you—if the bed didn't collapse first." Big laugh. Very funny.

Since the girls at school always went along meekly with whatever the guys were saying, those damn snickers followed me everywhere I went—even into the ladies' room. I don't care who you are; that hurts.

*It's one of the reasons, I guess, that in my guts I hate all men,
even today. A thoughtless, cruel, vain, stuck-up, bunch of bastards. Some of those guys were damn attractive, and I ached to
go to bed with them, but Christ, not with them laughing at me.*

*I've never forgiven the way those boys treated me, and Blossom
House is my revenge. None of them would marry me, okay. Then
they won't really marry anybody else, either, I'll see to that.*

*There's a certain kind of poetic justice that the last thing they'll
see is Ape-Lady, laughing like hell.*

> *Journal of Blossom House,*
> *Entry, page 6—Harriet Griggs*

Peter's maroon Dodge Dart, its vinyl top almost white in the
late afternoon sun, hummed across the Delaware-Maryland bor-
der just south of Brookside. Jennifer exchanged a smile with
Peter when they saw the sign marking the change of states. There
was something very final about that.

In less than an hour she would be married to Peter. Something
also very final. In less than an hour—the thought flickered only
briefly in her mind before she managed to dismiss it—she would
finally be free of the prison her family had built around her. It
wasn't the sort of thing you were supposed to be dwelling on just
before you got married; she should be thinking only about how
much she loved Peter. Well, she couldn't think about that *all* the
time, she told herself.

"Maryland, my Maryland," Peter sang vaguely. For some
reason his singing annoyed Jennifer; she couldn't have explained
why in a million years.

Jennifer looked at him. "You've got a lousy ear," she noted.

"Call Pavarotti."

"I don't think he does weddings." She struggled and managed
to produce a laugh. Why was she feeling so uptight? she won-

dered. Eloping had been her idea, after all. Nerves, she supposed. But she had an uneasy feeling, a sense that something was wrong, a reaction as hard to explain as her irritation with his singing. For the first time she realized the weave of his sport jacket and his tie both carried a small maroon pattern in them, and wondered if he'd chosen them to match his car. Sometimes he did things like that. Pretty fey. She'd have to work on that side of him.

A few minutes later Peter slowed the car down and began moving tentatively down Chivers's main street. Jennifer put one hand on Peter's arm, as if frightened.

Chivers, Maryland, was not a pretty place. Once, it may have been, but its only business had given it a tacky, frantic look. Even in daylight a blizzard of neon signs blinked on and off, too impatient to wait until dark.

"Wow," Jennifer said, a tone of disgust lacing her voice.

Peter sighed. "They certainly don't let you forget what they do for a living. . . ."

They continued slowly down the street. The girl shook her head, the boy grunted, the neons blinked. JUSTICE OF THE PEACE, one sign announced in flickering, blatant purple, and then, in an orange Day-Glo afterthought, added: FREE FLOWERS FREE! —WITNESSES!—COMPLIMENTARY ORGAN MUSIC! Directly across the street, in brilliant, iridescent yellow, another establishment pointed out that along with a justice of the peace and a troupe of witnesses came a genuine embossed keepsake book and decorative scroll—SUITABLE FOR FRAMING!

Farther along Main a sign outside of one house got directly to business. In bubbling neon red and Day-Glo green, the sign informed all comers that not only was a justice of the peace, flowers, and organ music included in the fee, but that free photographs and overnight rooms were available twenty-four hours a day.

Jennifer couldn't help but giggle. "What a place to be photographed. Cecil Beaton should eat his heart out."

"Don't laugh. See, they put their camera in the ceiling right over the bed, and while the complimentary organ music is playing, they take a highly personal portrait of you and your husband for your genuine embossed keepsake album. As for the decorative scroll, well, they take that and—''

Jennifer started to laugh, but suddenly stopped. The silence was as startling as if someone had thrown a switch in the middle of a Philharmonic concert and turned off the musicians. ''Peter, look!'' Jennifer had grabbed his arm with one hand and was pointing up a narrow side street with the other. Peter looked, but could see nothing out of the ordinary. ''There! There!'' Jennifer almost yelled at him.

There were angry blasts from the cars close behind him as Peter abruptly turned up the side street Jennifer had pointed to. Halfway up the hilly, tree-shaded street, he saw what Jennifer had seen. Set back on an immaculately kept lawn stood a handsome three-story red-brick Georgian, as perfectly kept as the lawn. The house was one of the most graceful examples of its era that Jennifer had ever seen.

As with almost every house in Chivers, it too housed a justice of the peace, although only a chaste white sign—the kind you might see hanging outside the office of a New England doctor or lawyer—announced that Henry L. Griggs, L.L.B., Justice of the Peace, did business inside. Beneath the lettering of his name, in the same modest script, was the name of the mansion itself: BLOSSOM HOUSE. The sign swayed silently in the light breeze, casting strange, moving shadows on the sun-dappled lawn. ''Look at that one, Peter,'' Jennifer said excitedly. ''After all those tacky places—wow.''

Slowly Peter pulled the car to a halt in front of the house, jockeying back and forth until his wheels were tight against the curb. Together, they stared at the house.

''God, look at all those azaleas,'' Peter said, ''and the apple blossoms.'' The plantings around Blossom House *were* spectacular, Jennifer decided, and they were probably seeing them at the peak of their bloom.

''Incredible.''

"This is it, then?"

Jennifer was surprised to hear herself hesitate. "I guess. But there's something about it, you know? Like it was too perfect, almost. On purpose." A small shiver ran through her.

Peter turned snappish. "The rest were too tacky, this one's too perfect. Christ, I'd hate to see you picking out a pair of shoes."

There was an edge to Peter's voice that upset Jennifer. She was, she admitted to herself, being pretty hard to please. "I'm sorry, Peter. We shouldn't be fighting. Not today. Maybe that's why the bride and groom aren't supposed to see each other the day of the wedding. . . ." Silently she studied the dashboard, staring at the speedometer as if she expected it to suddenly show fast movement. She turned and looked at him, touching his hand lightly. "It's just that that house—there's something— I mean, it's, well— Oh, hell. I don't know *what* I mean." She looked at herself in the rearview mirror, adding some lipstick and determining to change the subject. "You ought to wear a tie, I suppose."

Peter shrugged, one hand already pulling a tie out of his pocket. "Definitely."

The trouble was Peter knew exactly what Jennifer meant, but was damned if he'd admit it. He couldn't put his finger on the reason any more than Jennifer could, but there was something about the house that bothered him. It was too chaste and elegant for this town, too tasteful to be in the business of quickie marriages. That the JP was an L.L.B. only added to the mystery; lawyers don't usually end up as justices of the peace. Retired? Perhaps. Looking at the house again through the car window as he finished tying his regimental stripe, Peter saw something—a person waving, he thought—moving behind one of the windows on the third floor, but before he could make it out the lights in the room were abruptly extinguished and the figure was no longer visible.

Stretching himself out, pressing against the seat back and pushing his feet all the way toward the motor bulkhead, he shook himself to chase away his misgivings. Nerves, he supposed. A man doesn't get married every day. Turning, he faced Jennifer. "Ready?"

She reached for his hand and smiled warmly. "I've been ready for six months."

From behind the curtain of a narrow window beside the front door, Peter's and Jennifer's every movement had been studied. As they stepped out of the Dodge Dart they paused a moment, carefully straightening their clothes, patting their hair, and stood at the end of the path, discussing something while Peter locked the car doors.

The man at the window put down his binoculars and let the curtain fall straight again, thought for a second, then walked quickly toward the rear of the house.

"Customers," he told his sister, slipping into the kitchen, where she had planted her huge bulk in front of a counter and was peeling something. "Very *promising* customers," he added.

"Ummm. Good," his sister commented, looking at him with a trace of contempt. Quickly—people of Harriet's size can be surprising in the speed with which they move—she slipped off the stool, undid her apron, and pulled it up over her head. "I just wish they wouldn't always show up right when I'm in the middle of something." Harriet Griggs stared at her brother with pale distant eyes; she could sense his discomfort.

"They're talking down at the end of the path," Henry Griggs said. "I always hate this part of things," he added miserably.

Harriet ignored his statement. "We have a lot to do. Get going, Henry. They'll be ringing the doorbell any minute."

Henry sighed. Harriet always pushed him around so. She had when he was a child, she did today. Unlike his sister, Henry Griggs was a small man, his bald head surrounded by a fringe of pure white, a complexion of glowing pink-white, and the gentle, amiable look of an English country squire about him. He seemed to shrink before the mammoth bulk of his sister as she moved rapidly around the kitchen, making preparations. She was dressed entirely in black, making her look even larger than she was.

Somehow the cathedral somberness of her clothes seemed more suited to a funeral than a wedding. So did the stern, unyielding set of her face.

"Henry, damn it, is your stuff ready? No, of course not. Last time you forgot half of it. Don't just stand there."

Moving to a cabinet below the sink, he began placing items on the tabletop as Harriet recited her mental checklist, sounding like an angry head surgeon demanding scalpel, clamp, and sponge.

"Lock?"

Henry pointed to a small padlock. "Lock."

"Regular rope?"

"Right here."

"Slip rope? Last time you forgot the slip rope, Henry."

"I have it."

"Pills?"

"In my hand, Harriet."

Carefully he shook three or four capsules out of a plastic vial and added them to the items already neatly ranged across the tabletop. Harriet looked over the array, as if to check her brother's efforts. To an outside observer, she would have appeared more to be preparing for a commando assault than a simple wedding. But then, she knew there was to be nothing simple about the ceremony coming up.

Satisfied, Harriet splashed water over her face and tucked some wisps of hair back into the knot at the back of her head. "Upstairs, Henry. Now."

Her brother shook his head and walked slowly out into the hall, followed by Harriet, who watched as he climbed the graceful winding staircase and disappeared.

Humming, the woman walked briskly toward the front of the house and peered out through one of the windows next to the front door. The couple was finally on its way up the path; they'd certainly taken their time about it. Tucking another wisp of hair into her knot, Harriet positioned herself directly behind the front door so that she wasn't visible from the outside. When the doorbell rang Harriet began counting to herself softly: "One-Mississippi, two-Mississippi, three-Mississippi . . ."

The doorbell rang again, but the woman remained motionless, still counting, now in a whisper. "Six-Mississippi . . . seven Mississippi . . ." When she reached "Thirty-Mississippi" she finally opened the door, breathing heavily, as if she'd just hurried from some other part of the house to answer the bell. "Yes? May I help you?" She adjusted her dress and smiled at them. "I'm a mess, I'm afraid . . ."

Jennifer clutched Peter's hand tighter; the woman's smile did little to soften her Goliath-like presence. Jennifer could hear Peter swallow beside her; she'd often told him he had the noisiest swallow in New York. "Well—yes." There was a shaky, uncertain sound to Peter's voice that Jennifer had never heard before. "We were wondering if the justice of the peace is at home."

"Indeed he is, dear. Mr. Griggs—my brother—is upstairs. I'll get him for you right away." She smiled at them again in an attempt at reassurance. Turning, she called up the stairs. "Henry dear. There's some people down here to see you." She gave the couple an understanding smile and guided them toward the rear of the house. Through the open French doors at the end of the hall, Peter saw something and stopped.

"My God, those trees. Those apple trees. I've never seen blossoms like that." He took Jennifer by the arm and led her closer to the French doors and the orchard beyond. "Just look at them, Jen."

Jennifer knew he was just trying to be pleasant to the lady and nodded, mumbling a handful of superlatives to disguise her utter lack of interest.

"They *are* nice this year," Harriet said, smiling again. "Henry gives so much of his free time to them, you know. To all the plantings. He seems to spend half the year out there, trimming, pruning, fertilizing, things. Those blossoming trees are quite unusual; the Garden Club did an article on them, you know. Said Henry must use magic instead of fertilizer." She laughed, transported by the pleasure the Garden Club's valedictory still gave her.

The three of them turned when a sudden voice spoke from behind them, coming down the staircase into the hall. "Hello," said the voice. "I guess I'm the man you're looking for."

When Peter saw him, he at first felt a little foolish about his earlier misgivings. Harriet Griggs might be a little overwhelming, but in spite of what his sign said, Mr. Griggs was *not* Mr. Griggs at all, he was Mr. Pickwick. The smile was warm, and the eyes twinkled. Suddenly Peter realized that his hand was being pumped. "Henry Griggs," announced Pickwick. "My, but you're a splendid-looking couple."

Peter blushed. He was beginning to relax, but a curious sound, like someone stamping on the floor and crying, drifted down the stairs. Henry Griggs had noticed Peter's eyes move upward, trying to locate the source of it. "That damn cat again. Crazy animal." He laughed heartily, *too* heartily, Peter thought. The misgivings returned.

Moving into the conversation, Harriet Griggs hurried the introductions along. Peter made their introductions, explaining that he and Jennifer were from New York and that he was a student at Princeton, while Jennifer was at Miss Chalmer's, but due to go to Smith next fall.

The sound from upstairs was repeated. Mr. Griggs this time did not acknowledge it. "Good school, Princeton," he said, turning toward Jennifer. "And, of course, for women, it's hard to beat Smith."

Harriet laughed loudly, as much *too* loudly as her brother had a moment earlier. "Henry's really not much in favor of women's rights." Both Harriet and Henry laughed this time, again too loudly, and with a visible trace of nervousness.

Abruptly Mr. Griggs turned to Peter. "You have the papers? Birth certificates will do." He studied the photocopies a moment. "One time, I even used driver's licenses. Only identification the couple had. It worked. Maryland is very benign in such matters—

including its definition of marriageable age," he added, looking up from the photocopies to smile at Jennifer.

"Do we need anything else?"

"If you'd just sign the register over here . . ." Griggs led the couple over to a loose-leaf book on a slanting stand not far from the French doors, and Jennifer and Peter signed their names and the day's date. The previous last names—on the page facing theirs, Peter noticed—bore a date almost a week old; Mr. Griggs's location on a side street apparently made business very slow.

"Good. Thank you," Griggs said. Standing at the same slant-top table, he filled out a license, referring to the birth certificates for correct spellings. He allowed a broad smile to cross his face. "Would you rather the ceremony were in the parlor or out in the garden? It's very pretty this time of year."

Jennifer answered too quickly; she realized it herself. "The parlor. I mean, the garden's beautiful, but you know—well—I'd feel more at home indoors."

"Of course," Griggs said with an understanding nod of his head. The smile never wavered, although he was unable to hide a trace of annoyance in his voice.

He was leading them toward the parlor when his sister, Harriet, suddenly stopped them, addressing herself to Peter and Jennifer. "Isn't there someone you'd like to call?" she asked them. "That is, someone special you'd just like to tell that you're—right this minute—about to get married?"

Peter looked at her incredulously. "Good God, no. Nobody knows we're even here. It wouldn't be eloping if they did."

There was a pause. The constant smile faded from "Mr. Pickwick's" face, and he allowed himself a resigned little sigh. Harriet stared hard at him, her words full of some meaning only she and her brother understood. "Then, we should get right to it, Henry. *Now*. If you'll position the people . . ." Her voice was suddenly commanding, perhaps even a little harsh.

Henry Griggs sighed again. "If the groom will come into the parlor with me. Harriet, if you'll show the bride where she is to wait in the hall, then you can come in and play the 'Wedding March.' "

Jennifer found herself being led into the hall. From somewhere Harriet produced a small bouquet, telling her to come into the parlor when she heard the "Wedding March" she would play on the piano a few minutes from now. "I'm sorry there's no one to give you away, dear, but these ceremonies are always a little less than perfect."

Waiting in the hall, Jennifer suddenly felt foolish. The tiny bouquet, walking to the Griggses' altar by herself, all of it, seemed a little like some makeshift game little girls might play rather than a real wedding. From the parlor came a buzz of voices: Henry Griggs, a.k.a. Mr. Pickwick, and his sister, discussing last-minute adjustments, consulting with Peter, at times arguing a little between themselves. At one point Harriet's harshness to her brother reminded Jennifer of how her mother sometimes spoke to her father, grinding him down, intimidating him, bending him to her will. She smiled to herself, once again pleased to have escaped her prison in New York.

Looking around the hall, she saw the registry book Mr. Griggs had had them sign when he was issuing the licenses. She walked softly over to it; seeing their names side by side in the book would perhaps help erase the sense of unreality created by the makeshift nature of the wedding. She stared down at the page. It was blank. Maybe—Jennifer flipped to the pages on either side— no, their names weren't there, either. And the last entry she could find was for over a month and a half ago, not the entry she had seen earlier, dated last week. Strange, but she was sure there was some perfectly simple explanation for it. Maybe there was one book for Maryland residents, another for people from out of state. Still . . .

Any further speculation was put to one side; from the parlor came the unmistakable strains of Wagner's "Wedding March," played really quite well, Jennifer decided, by Harriet Griggs. Taking a deep breath, she prepared a virginal smile and began walking slowly into the parlor. They were waiting.

CHAPTER FOUR

When I was in high school the only thing other kids liked about me was my piano-playing. The fact is, I was damn good. I could handle anything from swing to classical.

That piece of music I play after—well, after each incident—came out of the same period.

The piece itself was an improvisation of an old song that I started messing around with one day, playing it the way Bach or Handel or Mozart might have written it. The song is "Yes, Sir, That's My Baby," which has plenty of open space for arpeggios and glissandos. Later, I extended the tune even farther, so much so, no one can recognize it.

I still get a kick watching people hear it; it sounds familiar, sort of, but all the Mozart worked into the arrangement throws them. Sometimes I even play the piece for the boys before we give it to them. I really get a kick out of that, watching their faces and thinking what we're about to do to them.

Do to them? Hell, what we do is what I call really paying someone back.

Journal of Blossom House,
Entry, page 7—Harriet Griggs

". . . by the authority granted me by the sovereign State of Maryland, and in the presence of these witnesses, I pronounce you man and wife." The ceremony had been brief, almost hurried, as if Griggs had urgent business elsewhere. Gone from his face was the easy smile; it reappeared suddenly the moment the ceremony was over, although to Peter, there was a forced quality to it. "And now," Griggs said, tilting his head to one side, "I insist. My little wedding present to you: champagne. I always keep some in the refrigerator for clients I particularly take to. We can sit in the garden and watch the sun set. I really do insist. . . ."

At first both Jennifer and Peter resisted. Peter explained they had to get on the road, Jennifer underlining this by pointing out the great distance they still had to travel this evening. Adamant, Peter kept resisting. Equally unyielding, Mr. Griggs kept *insisting*, at times becoming almost savage in his determination.

Quickly, though, Jennifer stopped saying anything. The idea of a little champagne on the terrace while they watched the gentle spring sun go down was appealing. But even more important to her was the realization that Mr. Griggs was entirely taken by her. She could see it in his eyes. The familiar warmth of being loved and appreciated by an older man flowed through her; given time, she knew she could have wrapped Mr. Griggs around her finger just as she always had her father. She didn't know why, but proving this to herself was suddenly enormously important.

"Peter," she interrupted. "You know, it *is* terribly inviting out there on the Griggses' terrace. We can get started a little later. It really won't slow us down at all." Peter stared at her, caught somewhere between annoyance and confusion. Jennifer, after all, had originally been the one with misgivings about Blossom House. Now the doubts had been replaced with a suggestion they stay on here a little while. Sometimes he didn't understand women at all—particularly Jennifer.

"And champagne, Peter! Come on, you only get married once." She thought about this for a moment, then added impishly, "Or, anyway, you only get married for the first *time* once."

Mr. Griggs found Jennifer's remark enormously funny, and

smiled and winked at her, telling Peter he'd married "quite a girl." Grimly Peter agreed. He groused, he grumbled, he groaned, but in the end, swayed as always by Jennifer, he agreed they should stay and have the champagne.

Out on the terrace, the conversation took on a strange tone. Mr. Griggs's toast, once he had gotten the bottle open, was meant to be solemn and sincere, but full of curious, ominous overtones that left Jennifer baffled. Mr. Griggs had risen to his feet and ceremoniously raised his glass high in the air. "To Peter and Jennifer Owen. May their lives together be as beautiful and serene as the blossoms of this garden . . . and when God has called them to their rest, may they lie through eternity surrounded by such peace."

"Hear, hear," Harriet Griggs added. Peter watched as Jennifer went back to charming Mr. Griggs. As he listened—Mr. Griggs was telling Jennifer how much she reminded him of his own daughter—he felt the champagne hit him suddenly. Strange. A little champagne, and he felt positively light-headed. It reminded him of that day last week, at Mortimer's with Jennifer, when what she was saying—in fact, the entire world around him—had felt completely unreal. He shook his head, but it didn't seem to help. Across from him, Jennifer's chattering grew distant and blurred. Quietly he asked Harriet if there was a men's room downstairs.

Harriet Griggs laughed. "Nerves," she said. "We see it happen all the time. Men are supposed to be the strong ones, but we find it's always men who get more upset at their weddings. It's always the groom who asks to use the bathroom." She laughed again. "Don't worry. You'll be fine in a few minutes; the champagne will help." Then she told him where the men's room was and injected herself into the conversation between Jennifer and her brother.

He stood up and left quietly. Behind him, Jennifer watched him go, curiosity filling her eyes. His departure struck her as odd. Other men might suffer a fit of nerves at their weddings; not Peter. Strange.

Out in the hall—Harriet Griggs had said the men's room was right beside the kitchen door—Peter heard a voice coming from the kitchen and wondered how Harriet had managed to get there so quickly and without his seeing her go. He still couldn't find the bathroom and pushed open the door to the kitchen to ask Miss Griggs exactly where it was.

There was no one in the kitchen. The woman's voice spoke again, angrily, although her words were so full of echoes, he couldn't understand what she was saying. Opposite the door he had come in, he saw a half-door, with what was apparently a dumbwaiter inside. On the shelves was a pile of dishes—enough for ten or twelve people, he guessed. The voice again. Somehow it was very strange. Earlier, talking to Harriet Griggs about how beautiful their home was, Jennifer had mentioned its size and asked if they had other people—or children or relatives—living there with them.

"Heavens, no," Harriet answered. "It *is* a large house for just two people—sometimes Henry and I *do* rattle around badly in all this space—but other people? No. There's just the two of us." His head was spinning, but Peter was pretty sure that's what he'd heard.

But if there were just two of them, whose was the voice that he kept hearing? Who had eaten all the food it had taken to fill the empty dishes now sitting forlornly on the dumbwaiter? Why had Harriet Griggs lied to them about so unimportant a point? Maybe it had never been said at all—any of it.

Peter saw buttons beside the shaft marked "Up" and "Down"— the dumbwaiter was apparently electrically powered—and pressed the "Down" button to see if he could pinpoint the source of the voice. At the sound of the motor, a voice from upstairs began shouting at him, growing clearer as the dumbwaiter lift moved out of the way. Peter stuck his neck inside the shaft and, wobbling on his feet, looked up. A little girl was leaning into the shaft, looking back down at him, her face anxious.

"My God, my God, get out of here. Fast. Both of you. Don't

go back for your bags, just get the hell out of this place. This minute. While you still can. Get out of—''

Another voice from behind her sounded strident and angry. The little girl's head was yanked back inside by some unseen hand; the dumbwaiter door upstairs could be heard slamming shut. Holding onto the edge of the dumbwaiter opening for support, Peter stood up. In his ears came a sudden roaring, a distant sound, as unreal as everything else that seemed to be happening to him. He didn't know whether the little girl really existed; he didn't know whether she'd really said what he thought he'd heard her say; he didn't know whether any of this was really happening to him.

Out in the hall again, Peter went back to his search for the men's room, which he finally found. Right next to the kitchen, exactly where Harriet Griggs had said it was. He couldn't tell whether he felt better or not; blurred logic had taken over his brain. One minute he would be filled with fury over Jennifer's decision to stay for the champagne, the next he would be filled with a nameless fear. Illogical. ''Get the hell out of this place . . . while you still can,'' the little girl had said. Whether she was real or something that existed only in his imagination, the advice was sound. Maybe he'd been drugged, he told himself uncertainly, surprised to find that the idea made him giggle.

Peter Owen had no idea how little there was to giggle about in the guess he'd just made; he *did* know it was time to get out of Blossom House. There was something very wrong here.

When he was back out on the terrace again, Jennifer turned to him, all smiles, clapping her hands together in delight and exchanging a warm glance with Mr. Griggs. Peter could only see her dimly. All of them on the terrace seemed wrapped in a thick silver fog. ''Peter,'' she said, laughing at something Peter hadn't heard. ''Guess what. The Griggses have asked us to stay for dinner, and I said we would. Isn't that wonderful of them?''

Stunned, Peter sat down hard in his chair. The fury again. But fury followed, almost immediately, by fear. And a sudden indif-

ference. Who the hell really gave a damn. "Wonderful," he
mumbled. "Just great."

It was anything but.

By the time dinner was through, so was Peter. It was a
delicious dinner, Jennifer told Harriet, adding that she was appalled poor Peter had crumpled out on them like that. It had been
a long, exhausting drive, she explained, and then there were
those crazy nerves Harriet had mentioned that frequently affected
the groom. Add to all that a little to drink, and . . .

"My dear, my dear, don't you worry that pretty little head of
yours for a minute," Henry Griggs said, beaming at her. "It's
happened before. It will happen again. Some people can't drink.
Why, when Peaches was—"

Harriet cut him off abruptly, turning to Jennifer. "We have
plenty of extra rooms, dear. Give him a good night's sleep here,
and he'll be good as new in the morning."

Henry Griggs sighed, shifting uncomfortably in his chair and
staring at Jennifer in a way that made her uncomfortable. "Not
much of a wedding night," he added solemnly, "but then these
days—"

Harriet cut him off again in midsentence. "We can help you
get him upstairs, dear," Harriet suggested, looking at Peter, who
still sat in his place at the dinner table, his head lowered almost
to his chest, his mouth slightly open.

"Oh, I can manage him, I think," Jennifer said, embarrassed
by the whole thing. "I just saw him move a couple of minutes
ago."

Carefully the three of them got Peter to his feet. He seemed
two-thirds asleep, but Jennifer found she could get him to walk if
she talked to him and moved him along slowly, one arm beneath
his elbow, one of his hands thrown over her shoulder. Peter was
mumbling nonsense in a blurred voice, muttering things she
couldn't understand to people she couldn't see.

"Are you sure you don't want me to help, Jennifer?"

"No, I don't think so, Mr. Griggs. If I can't handle him, I'll holler. . . ."

Jennifer kept talking to Peter, supporting him, moving him slowly along, not paying very much attention to the nonsense he was mumbling, something about a little girl and a dumbwaiter and it was time to get their asses out of Blossom House and—

Halfway across the entrance hall, on their way to the staircase, Jennifer tripped on something. Peter's weight and her sudden loss of balance was too much, and they both crashed to their knees, Jennifer's last-minute struggle being all that kept them from being stretched out flat on the marble floor.

Peter appeared to come suddenly awake. "Ouch," he said, then: "Damn it, what the hell's happening . . . the little girl in the dumbwaiter . . . get out fast . . ." Peter looked around him, staring at her in confusion, his face slowly filling with anger. "You're selfish, Jennifer Delafield, a spoiled little brat, a—" He wobbled against her, lurching. ". . . told you I wanted to get the hell out of this crazy place . . . little girl in the dumbwaiter said the same thing . . . get your asses out of here while you still can, she said. . . . You wanted to stay . . . selfish . . . never marry a spoiled brat baby . . . my mother was right . . . little girl in the dumbwaiter was right . . . son of a bitch . . . go someplace and get the damn marriage annulled . . . get out of here while—"

"Peter!" Jennifer almost screamed. Drunk or not, his words hurt. Jennifer loved him, she was sure of that now. She really did. Maybe, somehow, all along, instead of marrying Peter to escape her family, she had been escaping her family to marry Peter. "Peter," she pleaded. "I love you. Don't say things like that. For God's sake, it's our wedding night."

Peter snorted, his head beginning to droop again as he knelt there on the floor. "Call Henry Griggs. Be happy to take care of you . . ."

Jennifer stared at him in disbelief, aware that everything was going terribly wrong. She was also aware that if she didn't get him back on his feet fast, she never would. His head was back

down on his chest, his words once again impossible to decipher.
Struggling, Jennifer got both hands under his arms and tried to
pull him upright. Heave as hard as she could, she got nowhere;
he was dead weight.

"You'll never do it that way, dear." Harriet Griggs's voice
came from so close behind her, Jennifer almost dropped poor
Peter completely. Slowly she turned around, both hands still
supporting him, to stare at her.

"Let me, dear," Harriet said with a grim smile. She leaned
over and picked up Peter, as if he were a wounded child,
carrying him in both arms as she started toward the stairs. "I've
carted a lot of bodies around in my day," she added, giving a
hollow little laugh. Numbly Jennifer followed her up the graceful
winding staircase. Maybe Peter had been right. Maybe they
should have gotten their asses out of this crazy damn place.

After Harriet had dumped Peter on one side of the huge double
bed and left, Jennifer tenderly began undressing him. The sight
of his body began the ache inside her again. She'd been feeling it
all day long. Knowing that tonight it wouldn't be satisfied only
seemed to make it grow worse.

He lay on the bed, now wearing only his shorts, one arm over
his head. Jennifer had debated taking off the shorts, but had
decided against it; he might want to go to the bathroom in the
night—she would leave the light on there, she'd decided, and the
door open, so he could find it easily—and might be embarrassed
to find himself naked. For a moment she studied him, his chest
rising slowly up and down, the sound of his breathing coming
gently from his mouth. Below his chest, a stomach as flat and
hard as a smooth pine plank, and below that—Jennifer, ashamed
as she did it, peeked under his shorts. It was not particularly
impressive at the moment, but she could remember it, turgid and
straining like a caged animal. Damn him for being asleep like
this.

God, he was attractive. She kicked herself for going along
with the Griggses and allowing this to happen. Some wedding

night. Along with the ache came a new twist inside her: fear. She couldn't explain this new addition to her kaleidoscope of emotions. There was nothing to be frightened of, she kept telling herself, but the strangeness of where she was and the so far benign madness of Henry Griggs and his mammoth sister, Harriet, kept an ominous uneasiness nagging at the front of her mind.

Undressing quickly, Jennifer slipped beneath the covers beside Peter. Quite suddenly she felt exhausted herself, feeling the darkness close in around her along with the strange floating feeling you suddenly get when you've taken a strong sleeping capsule. She was asleep before she realized she was even sleepy.

Sometime during the night Jennifer woke up and reached out to touch Peter for reassurance. He was still breathing deeply and evenly. Effortlessly she slipped back into her drugged sleep.

It can't have been later than six o'clock in the morning when something again woke her. From somewhere in the house Jennifer thought she could hear someone playing the piano. It was a weird piece, sounding like Mozart, but nothing she'd ever heard before. Yet somehow it was terribly familiar, like the fragment of some half-forgotten song. Jennifer felt her skin crawl with the strangeness of it, and again she reached over to touch Peter.

Jennifer came awake with a jolt. Her hand could find nothing to touch. She opened her eyes, unbelieving. The other side of the bed stared at her emptily.

She ran to the bathroom. It was as empty as the bed. Peter was gone.

She tore out of the room, calling his name frantically.

There was no answer.

CHAPTER FIVE

To me, Peter Owen summed up all the things wrong with young men. Just boys, really. All right, he was extremely attractive, with beautifully molded features, a sensuous mouth, and a face capped by a crown of dazzling blond hair.

But the little bastard was too damn aware of it. They always are. You could see it in the lithe, self-confident way he walked, the cruel way his lips moved when he laughed, the oh-so-careless toss of his head he gave to show what a catch he was.

All last night I could see it in him. Jennifer Delafield was all right, even though I did think she was flirting too much with Henry. But Peter—well, Peter, because he was well brought up, acted politely enough, but underneath I could sense the same contempt for me I always felt at high school. I was useful, I was necessary, but to him, something to be sneered at, laughed at, shunned, and shrunk from. Christ, but it was familiar.

Well, he isn't laughing much today.

Journal of Blossom House,
Entry, page 10—Harriet Griggs

The moment she was actually in the hall outside her room, Jennifer began feeling a little silly. Peter was downstairs, probably making himself an early breakfast. Very early. It didn't seem like Peter, but it was an explanation.

She stood, listening. Silence. Good. Her first cries of alarm, then, hadn't woken Henry Griggs or his sister. Finding her in the hall in her nightie, at barely six o'clock in the morning, yelling for Peter, who would undoubtedly turn out to be somewhere downstairs, would strike them as very peculiar, indeed. Jennifer leaned against the wall, running the points of reassurance around in her head. She should feel better, Jennifer supposed, but didn't. Somehow the same strange feeling of fear that struck her when they first parked outside the house had returned. Softly Jennifer went down the elegant winding stairs into the early brilliance of a springtime morning. For a moment the chiaroscuro of the sunlight from the garden falling across the darkness of the front hall took her breath away, and with it, the fear. But a second later the pressing dread returned, stronger than before, demanding to be acknowledged.

Jennifer looked into the first room she came to—the library. Empty. Silent. The old-fashioned dolls that filled the shelves stared reproachfully at her with their glass eyes, their china feet and hands frozen into eternal stillness. The dolls seemed out of place in a house with no children. Harriet's when she was a little girl? Perhaps.

Farther down the hall Jennifer passed the peculiar register from which their names had so mysteriously vanished the afternoon before. Across the hall from it was the front parlor, where they had been married. The whole ceremony came back to her. Miss Griggs playing the piano. Mr. Griggs reading from the Bible. The pathetic little bridal bouquet. Peter's voice, firm and clear, in his "I do." Jennifer suddenly wanted to cry; the whole thing, all of it, seemed a fantasy from another world, another time. Where had it gone? Why was she standing here alone, looking for Peter, who should still be soundly asleep beside her, breathing softly, waiting to begin another day in this happiest time of her life? Damn, damn, damn.

Jennifer wondered if his disappearance this morning had anything to do with his fury at her last night, his mumbled threats about having the marriage annulled or running away somewhere. No, that was just booze, she knew. Still, the recollection of it hurt; *in vino veritas* always comes back to haunt you when something cruel has been said.

As she neared the kitchen she heard a distant buzz of conversation. Jennifer's heart leaped in relief. Peter *had* come downstairs for breakfast, one that Harriet was apparently fixing for him.

With a small cry of happiness Jennifer shoved the swinging door into the kitchen open so hard, it crashed against the wall. She was about to call out his name and laughingly tell him how upset she had been and ask him why he hadn't woken her when he got up.

Jennifer's heart fell like a stone through space, bouncing off the jagged rocks in the darkness, thudding and crashing on its way toward infinity.

Peter wasn't there. Instead, looking at her strangely, were Henry and Harriet Griggs. They were fully dressed. Harriet was doing something at the kitchen table, and Henry was in some sort of work clothes, washing his hands in the kitchen sink. Beside him, leaning against the same sink, was a dirt-encrusted shovel.

"My, child, but you're up so early," Harriet said with a warm smile. "We were always country people, so we're up and about every morning by now. We thought you and Peter would probably sleep much later." Harriet laughed. "Honeymooners, you know . . ."

Henry was wiping his hands on a towel, drying them vigorously. His smile was apologetic. "Forgive me for looking such a mess, Jennifer. I was at work in the garden extra early this morning. It's the best time to put on my magic fertilizer, I've discovered."

"Oh, dear," Harriet added with a sigh. "We probably woke

you two young people up. We tried awfully hard to be quiet, but—"

"Have you seen Peter?" Jennifer blurted out, suddenly feeling stupid standing in front of them in her nightie. Not even a bathrobe, just her nightie and her slippers. It wasn't, she realized, even a very opaque nightie, but one so sheer, it was almost see-through.

Harriet and Henry continued to stare at her. Finally, from Harriet: "Well, no, dear. Peter isn't down here. He's upstairs in your room."

"He's not, he's not," Jennifer said, beginning to feel her self-control slipping.

"Did you look in the bathroom, dear?" Harriet insisted. "After all he had to drink last night—"

"He's not in the bathroom. He's nowhere upstairs. He must be down here someplace. Damn him, if he's hiding somewhere . . ."

"He's not down here, Jennifer. I mean, I've been all over the first floor this morning. Are you sure he's not in the bathroom?" Henry was shaking his head, as if the mystery of Peter were as much his concern as Jennifer's.

"Henry's right, dear. No place down here. If Henry hadn't seen him, I would have. I've been dusting, you see."

"The garden—" began Jennifer.

"I'd have seen him out there," Henry cut in. "Or if he were on the terrace. Nothing there but a lot of bees and a flock of cardinals eating up my seed. They're terrible, those cardinals. Keep scaring away the smaller song birds and gorging themselves on my bird feed. Why, last year—"

"Henry," said Harriet sharply. "The poor child's upset. Don't go prattling on about your damn birds like that."

Henry looked suddenly ashamed, apologizing with his eyes, abruptly turning silent. Harriet kept on trying.

"Did you look in the closet in your bedroom, child? It's a very big one. Maybe Peter's in there hiding. Playing a little joke on you."

Jennifer shook her head. She'd looked into the closet earlier, and told Harriet so. "Well," Harriet said, one hand to her mouth as she struggled for another solution, "well, let's see now . . ."

Jennifer couldn't explain it. Both of them seemed to be trying their best to help, offering suggestions, making reassuring little jokes, yet she couldn't shake a sense of evasiveness in whatever they said. As she thought about it, though, Jennifer couldn't think of a single thing they'd said that was equivocal; they'd been completely straightforward, doing their damndest to be helpful. The pair of them were a little dotty, of course, but they were trying, and Jennifer felt suddenly ashamed of her ingratitude.

"He might have slipped out to have himself a little walk. Some men love to take little walks in the morning, you know." Harriet smiled encouragingly at her, apparently proud of her latest explanation.

"Peter does look like he walks a lot," added Henry. "You can tell from how trim he keeps himself. In great shape, that boy."

"That's it," Jennifer said, forcing a smile. "Peter loves to walk." It was an outright lie. Peter Owen's idea of a long walk was out his own front door into a taxi at the curb; the trim, in-shape look came from playing tennis. But Jennifer was becoming increasingly embarrassed by the soap-opera overtones of her situation. In the *Daily News* it would be described with the headline "Socialite Jilts Heiress on Wedding Night!"

The headline was so outrageous, it made Jennifer want to laugh. She couldn't bring it off. The anxiety building up inside her was too powerful for so much as a smile. "That's it," repeated Jennifer, suddenly desperate not to look pathetic. "Peter went for a walk. I don't know why *I* didn't think of it." Smiling, she turned to Harriet. "You see, Peter and I had a fight last night, and I . . . well . . ."

"All young couples do that." Henry laughed. "It takes time to adjust to each other's habits, Jennifer. Nothing to worry about."

"Nothing at all," chimed in Harriet.

Once again the feeling of evasiveness crept over Jennifer. It was stupid, she supposed. No matter how you looked at it, neither of them had any reason to be hiding anything. "I'll just go back upstairs, I think, and—"

"No breakfast, dear?"

Jennifer settled for orange juice and coffee, which she said she'd take upstairs with her. At the doorway, she paused and turned back toward them. "Please don't tell Peter I was worried. He'd only laugh. He should be back any moment now."

"Of course he will," Harriet assured her.

Jennifer wished she was as sure as Harriet. Inside, for reasons she couldn't understand, she could feel her whole body begin to tremble.

In her room, the cheerfulness fled like a scudding patch of sunlight on a stormy day. She couldn't drink the orange juice, which was sour, or the coffee, which seemed bitter. In the bathroom, she poured them both down the toilet so that Harriet wouldn't know. Lying on her bed, Jennifer stared at the ceiling vacantly. Without meaning to let it happen the sheer wonder of Peter Owen suddenly seized her and began to take possession of her. The crooked smile. His humor. The way he kidded her, never letting himself be manipulated the way she had manipulated so many people—everyone from her father to poor old Ingebord. The lithe way he moved. The sensual smoothness of his naked body. The panting, groaning, writhing of Peter Owen in orgasm, toes pointed, head thrown back, breath coming in gasps. Her own responses—a trembling that ran from head to foot, uncontrollable synaptical quiverings, and violent thrashings of a primitive order. Even thinking of it made her skin grow hot and her body moist.

When it came, it was as if someone had just dumped a bucket of ice water on her. The fear, the worry, and the dread all rushed back in on her at the same instant. The sensual fantasy was abruptly replaced by the horrors of last night. Those cutting, terrible things Peter had said. The names he had called her. The threat to have the marriage annulled. He *couldn't* mean that. But all of the threats and insults were gathering around her like a black cloud, whispering in her ear, haunting her.

All morning long she lay on the bed, which seemed suddenly lumpy and hard beneath her. She lay there waiting. And waiting. Occasionally she would doze off for a second into half-sleep, then snap her eyes open to see how much time had passed. Not enough, never enough. Any moment, she was sure, the door would crash open, and Peter would rush in, explaining where he'd been, and throw his arms around her, laughing at her foolishness. And they would both laugh and laugh, and pretty soon they would tear off their clothes, and the bed wouldn't seem lumpy or hard anymore. Again, the fantasy made Jennifer want to cry, and she did, a little.

Every sound she heard she was sure would be Peter. Only it wasn't. She concentrated on listening, waiting for the glad sound of his feet coming up the stairs, down the hall, to her door. When you listen that hard, she decided, your mind begins playing tricks on you. At best, it was an old house, full of strange groanings and creakings that never really stopped.

Every now and then Jennifer was conscious of another sound, just as strange. From directly over her head, she thought she heard something like people moving around. Impossible. Last night, when they'd been talking about the great size of Blossom House, Harriet had made that very clear. "Sometimes Henry and I *do* rattle around badly in all this space—but other people? No. There's just the two of us."

Jennifer suddenly sat bolt upright on the bed. There had been a heavy thud—as if someone had just fallen down or been knocked off their feet—and what sounded like a woman's scream, distant and muffled, but unmistakable. A moment later Jennifer heard what seemed like heavy footsteps—then silence.

Moving softly across the room, her heart thumping loudly, Jennifer opened the door a crack and looked out. The long hall was empty. The stone bust of some long-vanished Roman stared at her, as if he resented Jennifer's intrusion into his privacy. At the end of the hall she heard a new sound, a sound like someone was crying. To Jennifer it seemed to come from behind the door at the far end, and she studied it to see if the door might hold some explanation.

It was a curious door, covered by what looked like an outer door of thick wooden planking. Beside its heavy-duty handle was a thick brass loop set into the thick woodwork of the frame, secured by a massive brass padlock that made entrance or exit impossible. A storeroom, Jennifer decided. It was hard to imagine what the Griggses kept behind the door that should call for such thick planking and such a heavy lock. More mysterious, she heard another short burst of crying. Very definitely, it came from behind the door. A shudder she couldn't explain made her whole body twitch.

Jennifer returned to the bed, preparing to begin waiting for Peter again, but suddenly she knew she couldn't. She was both curious and frightened but, thinking about it, realized she was more frightened than curious. Too much time by herself worrying about Peter. Nerves set on edge by the endless waiting. Her imagination running wild, hearing things that had probably never happened, and seeing peculiar objects—the heavy brass lock was a good example—that probably had perfectly logical explanations. The maddening worries about Peter were making her think things that were farfetched and insane. Where the hell *was* he, anyway? The strange sounds from the floor above her. *What* the hell were they? Suddenly Jennifer knew she couldn't stand being by herself another minute. Combing her hair, she sighed heavily and went downstairs.

"Oh, good, Jennifer. I was just about to come upstairs and tell you luncheon is ready," Harriet said cheerfully.

"Leftovers from last night," added Henry, smiling broadly at her. "But Harriet always does a superb job with leftovers. Sometimes they're better than the first time around."

Harriet swept them into the dining room and fussed with plates and serving dishes while Henry gallantly pulled out Jennifer's chair for her as she sat down. For the first few moments there was silence. Harriet watched Jennifer pick at her food and became either worried or annoyed. Jennifer, trying to read her face, wasn't sure which. "I'm afraid I'm not terribly hungry," she explained. "It's delicious, of course. But my appetite's, well, it's—"

"Nonsense, child. You have to eat. I know you're worried about Peter, but you still have to get something inside you. Just a little, dear. For me."

The words Harriet was using treated Jennifer so much like a child, Jennifer half expected her to add something like "Now, here comes the little potato choo-choo, so open your mouth and let the engine in . . . *whoooo! whoooo!*"

Henry tried to soothe her. "You know, Jennifer," he told her with a benign smile, "it's silly to worry about Peter. He'll be back any moment. You know that. That walk I mentioned earlier; he could have gone much farther than he realized. Or maybe he went to a bar somewhere. Boys his age are always doing that."

Jennifer was outraged. "At six o'clock in the morning?"

Henry laughed. "A taxi driver could have taken him to one of our all-night places. Illegal, but there're several in Chivers that never shut at all. If a man wants a drink, he can always get one. And, from what I saw of Peter, he loves to drink."

"Not in the morning he doesn't, Mr. Griggs. And if he'd gotten lost, well, he would have called to tell me."

Henry Griggs laughed again, reaching over and patting Jennifer's hand. "You young people worry about such tiny little things. You know, Peter could just be playing a joke on you. A big joke, hiding in town somewhere. You said you'd had a fight. . . . He'll be back any minute, he'll be back."

Harriet snickered. "Henry's right. It's probably a cruel little joke. All young men are cruel, Jennifer. Take it from me. *I* know."

Silence dropped over them again like an ominous, dark cloud. For some minutes there was no sound except the scraping of silver on dishes and Henry's noisy chewing. He must have, Jennifer decided finally, a lot of false teeth, making every bite he chewed into something that sounded like someone smacking his lips in satisfaction. Jennifer moved her silverware around on the plate a lot and did a good deal of rearranging of her food, but she ate very little. The little potato engine made very little progress.

Harriet watched her a moment and sighed. "It's silly not to *try*, dear," she said with another sigh. "Henry's probably right. A strange little joke." Another idea appeared to strike her. Along with the idea came a suggestion that gave Jennifer a sickening shock. "Or maybe he went to the travel agent to pick up the tickets. They take forever at those places."

Jennifer was bewildered but could feel her stomach sinking. "Travel agent?"

"For the tickets to Europe. In all the scrambling around this morning, I forgot to mention it, but I heard Peter on the phone very early, asking what time flights left for Europe." Harriet studied Jennifer's stricken look and suddenly blushed. "Oh, dear, oh, dear. Maybe it was supposed to be a surprise. But I just assumed—" Automatically one hand rose to Harriet's cheek in embarrassment.

Jennifer stared at her in terrible confusion. What was he doing making reservations before six o'clock in the morning? Was Peter running away to Europe without her? It wasn't possible. No, no, no. He couldn't be. A whole litany of dreadful thoughts raced through her mind, especially his drunken threat to have the marriage annulled. Each accusation seemed worse than the last, the whole lot of them running and crashing into one another as they crowded into her brain.

Jennifer was unable to keep up her brave pose any longer. A sudden sob burst from her and she raced out of the dining room and tore up the stairs into her bedroom.

As she lay on her bed the strange noises of shuffling feet and an occasional crying voice from the floor above her became loud enough to rise above her own soft sobbing. A hand of terrible dread seized her heart and squeezed it hard. She was suddenly terrified.

Peter. Oh, God, Peter, where *are* you?

CHAPTER SIX

At least Jennifer didn't scream or have hysterics or anything. A lot of them do, and it always upsets Henry so. Oh, she cried at the end of lunch and ran from the table, but that's nothing compared to the show put on by some of the others.

Breeding, I suppose. The right genes, the right environment, the right education, and superb training. When the chips go down, a lady knows how to react. I like that.

Of course, I'm aware that as we get further into things, that inbred self-control will begin to crumble quite quickly. The crumbling is a necessary part of our training, and one of my jobs is to push the girl toward her complete disintegration.

I'm damn good at it, if I do say so. That bit about hearing Peter Owen on the phone, calling a travel agent, was a nice touch. The expression on poor Jennifer's face!

A very chaste wedding night for both of them, which must have upset Peter the most. There's a hungry, sensual look to that bastard, as if he went through life with a permanent erection. Of course, most boys are like that—cruel, corrupt, spending a lot of *their time trying to think of the quickest method to get their erections to go away—if only briefly.*

And then doing it.

> *Journal of Blossom House,*
> *Entry, page 12—Harriet Griggs*

Jennifer woke with a start, unaware she had even dozed off. Before luncheon she'd had a couple of sherries with Henry Griggs, and then a little wine with the meal she hadn't eaten. She wasn't really used to this at midday and, cried out and spent, had just quietly drifted into sleep.

The fact surprised her. Worse, for reasons she couldn't explain, awareness of it made her feel guilty. As if she'd somehow let Peter down by being asleep. As though it were a mark of faithlessness. That if he'd walked into the bedroom and found her peacefully dozing, he'd have grown justifiably furious at her blithe unconcern. My God, maybe he *was* back by now, downstairs chatting with Henry and Harriet, and had already discovered—

Quickly Jennifer slipped over to the door and silently opened it, listening for the sound of Peter's voice downstairs. She could hear Harriet criticizing Henry for something; she could hear Henry's much gentler voice trying to defend himself; then she could hear Harriet again, shrill in her stridency, dismissing his rebuttals and continuing her harangue.

One voice was missing: Peter's. But that very normal-sounding bickering between a brother and sister was somehow reassuring. Softly she pushed the door shut again. Peter would be back. Peter would be back any minute, and everything would be explained, and both of them would soon be laughing at the insanity of the whole crazy incident.

She heard Henry grunt something at Harriet—from the sound of his voice, Jennifer knew it had been something cutting and angry—and then begin thumping up the stairs. Jennifer was about to pull her door closed but decided against it, stopped as if by some unseen hand. Instead, she pushed the door *almost* shut, keeping a lone eye glued to the crack.

Henry huffed into view and set something down beside the padlocked door at the end of the hall. He drew a key from his pocket and began struggling to get the lock open. From his muttered swearing, this was an old and familiar battle.

Jennifer let her eyes move to the pile of books and other things he had been carrying. The books were a curious collection, large and thin and brightly colored. Children's books, Jennifer finally realized. In itself, there was nothing strange about this, but it raised a question: Neither Henry Griggs nor his sister had any children, so why would they have children's books?

Even more perplexing was the object sitting on top of the pile. From what Jennifer could make out it appeared to be a stuffed sphere of some kind, probably fuzzy and soft, colored a variety of deep yellows and light oranges, and about the size of a basketball. Jennifer opened her door a crack wider, trying to get a better look. On the fuzzy sphere's top, she suddenly saw, was a stylized green felt stem, leaning sharply to one side. The object now made more sense, but at the same time less. It was, apparently, a giant stuffed peach, a cuddly child's toy, although a mammoth stuffed peach seemed a strange thing to give a child to play with.

Jennifer could not explain it, but there was something sinister in that crazy thing, as if it were a fuzzy space satellite transmitting waves of dark malevolence. Jennifer almost laughed. An *evil* stuffed peach? Impossible.

Down the hall the padlock finally surrendered, and Henry, still muttering to himself, picked up the pile of books and the stuffed peach and threw back the heavy door. He disappeared, but Jennifer could hear him heavily clomping up an unseen set of uncarpeted steps. For a second Jennifer wondered if she could safely creep down the hall and get a look up them—Henry had left the door wide open. She had just started to pull her own door wide when her blood froze.

"Henry! Henry! You left the door open again. I've told you a thousand times about that. Keep it shut."

Harriet had apparently come up the back stairs, then into the hall. To Jennifer it was remarkable that so large a woman could move so softly, but she remembered hearing once that fat people could be incredibly light on their feet and therefore made good dance partners—as long as you remembered to judge them by their dancing and not their appearance. As quickly and softly as she could she pushed her door shut. Through it she could hear Henry clomp down the stairs again and slam the stairway door.

Thank God Harriet had come up when she did and not a few minutes later, when she could have been caught out in the openness of the long hall. There was no real reason, but she could feel her heart beating inside her. Jennifer gave a sigh of relief. Harriet was somewhat frightening, and Jennifer knew she would not have appreciated her spying.

As she walked back across the room, still breathing hard, she passed the mirror. Jennifer was shocked. The crying after luncheon and the grinding strain of the whole day had left her face looking creased and wrinkled, a pale white prune set below a tangle of uncombed hair. My God, Peter would take one look, turn around, and run from the room, screaming. Who could blame him?

In the bathroom she painstakingly combed her hair, patted little face powder under her eyes, and screwed up her mouth to receive some much-needed lipstick. For the moment there wasn't a damn thing she could do about her face as a whole; only time could repair the drawn skin.

Sitting in a chair by the window so she could look out Jennifer felt the anxieties crowd in on her again. The possible explanations Henry and Harriet had offered earlier seemed suddenly hollow. A long walk, Harriet had suggested. No one walked from six in the morning until five in the evening, especially Peter.

Gone and gotten drunk after their fight, Henry had posited. Peter obviously liked his booze, Henry'd added. Yes, Peter did

But not at six in the morning and not all day long in some tacky Chivers bar.

The telephone call to the travel agent. Checking on flight times to Europe, Harriet had said. Impossible. Peter hated airplanes, Peter hated traveling, Peter certainly wouldn't go anywhere without all his clothes. His bags were still there; Peter would never go without *them*.

That dreadful thought that had crossed her mind this morning came back once more. Maybe Europe was part of how you got a marriage annulled; she didn't know. Oh, Christ. Peter wouldn't do something like that. Not Peter. But those awful things he'd said . . .

Inside her, the anxieties began pyramiding. Jennifer knew Peter hadn't driven anywhere; earlier she'd looked out the window downstairs and seen his car still parked at the curb. She could think of no reason Peter would be using taxis with his own car sitting right there at the house, but then, Jennifer realized, she had been able to find reasons for very few things since they had walked across the threshold of Blossom House. It was as if this place and Henry Griggs and his sister, Harriet, were in a private world where everything was frighteningly upside down. Frightening— and laced with a sinister aura. Jennifer suddenly found she was shuddering, trembling from some indefinable fear.

She went into the room and ran herself a glass of water. Running water was reality. You turned the faucet, water came out—the way it had when you were little, the way it would when you grew up. Reality. There were no imponderables, no unanswered questions, no consuming fears, no tearing anxieties to face. Turn the handle and out came water. The concreteness of reality made Jennifer suddenly feel better.

Back in the bedroom, though, the fears returned. Suppose for a second that Peter, however illogically, had been so disgusted by her behavior with old Henry last night—my God, it was only flirting, but men were unpredictable creatures and often reacted to things in very peculiar ways—suppose, just suppose that was what had happened and Peter *had* run off. She'd pushed him into

the marriage in the first place, after all. But suppose, just for
ridiculous fleeting moment, suppose that was what he *had* done
The idea of course was ridiculous; Peter would never do a thin
like that, he wouldn't, he *couldn't*. But suppose that for som
crazy incredible minute he had then—or Jesus, suppose— Wha
was she supposed to do now? My God—it suddenly hit her like
thousand speeding express trains—what in goddamned hell wa
she supposed to do?

She couldn't go home. No, never. There'd been that note.
was such a stupid note, really—she had known that even as sh
wrote it—but she'd left it there, anyway, ticking away like
bomb on her mother's dressing table, when she'd gone back
the apartment to pack up her clothes. A note that told her moth
how much she hated her and how much she'd always hate
her—and why. A cruel note that even held something hateful fo
her father. Yes, she had told him, she loved him, loved him ver
much, but he'd always been weak and ineffective with her moth
er, letting her walk all over him. Which meant walking over he
at the same time. Christ, wasn't he man enough to stand up an
fight for himself? His weakness had made her life impossible.

So, the note had finished, she was leaving them for good
Leaving them to marry Peter Owen, another of the people sh
loved but they hated. She had to; it was her only escape. The
would never see her again. She'd miss her father, but she ju
couldn't take it anymore, dying slowly in the prison they'd bo
tried to lock her up in.

Jennifer sighed, thinking sadly of how hurt her father mu
have been. Even her mother, she supposed, must have felt *som
thing*. Unlike her father, though, what would have affected h
mother most was probably what people would think. She was lil
that.

However they had reacted to the note, it made going hom
impossible. Maybe in a few years; certainly not now. Oh, h
father would forgive her quickly enough, but her mother, wel
she could put up with the screaming and yelling and bitterne
that would come from her mother; what she couldn't put up wi

would be the loss of her own pride. When you storm out of a house, leaving ugly missives strewn behind you, thumbing your nose at your family to marry the man you love, you can't very well accept having to crawl back only a week later and admit that maybe you'd been terribly wrong.

Hillary. She should call Hillary, that was it. Hillary would know what to do, where to stay, how to handle things until Peter showed up, something most of Jennifer was still sure would happen. Even as she toyed with the idea, the whole thing came apart in Jennifer's hands. Okay, Hillary Crane was her best friend, but given a story such as the one Jennifer had to tell, it would be unrealistic to expect her to keep it to herself. Jennifer was aware that by now the whole school must know about her elopement. To give Hillary this new and sensational news could only lead to its becoming a fixture in the school's already titillated picture of her. There would be whisperings in the ladies' rooms, snatches of conversation on the track field, hissed comments at every luncheon. Hillary was out. Her pride again.

Thinking about it, Jennifer felt tears welling up behind her eyes. She was completely alone in the world, unable to talk to her mother or to her father or even her best friend. Alone—and scared half to death.

Jennifer knew she was about to cry—her lip was trembling, her breath was giving those odd wheezes that were the warning of sobs building up inside her chest—when the noises from above her, the strange sounds that came intermittently from the third floor, began again. They had disappeared for a while, now they were back. Jennifer sat up in her bed, holding on to the covers and staring upward apprehensively. Now what?

This time the noises were completely different and even more curious. To Jennifer they sounded like distant singing—not the singing of one voice, but of many. Muffled and hushed as the singing was, Jennifer couldn't hear it clearly enough to make out the tune, although several times she was convinced a group somewhere was singing "Frère Jacques." She wasn't really sure the singing was even coming from upstairs, or whether it was from a radio somewhere.

Or maybe Mr. Griggs, like Mr. Rochester in *Jane Eyre,* had a crazy wife locked away on the third floor. Dressed only in a tattered and stained smock, her long, tangled hair falling wildly down across her face, laughing at the mice but snarling viciously at her nurse, the woman existed solely to escape her third-floor prison and burn down the house around their heads. The notion of old Mr. Griggs with an insane wife locked away upstairs was so crazy, Jennifer smiled for the first time that day. *There* was an idea that would make Peter roll off his chair laughing, a grotesque notion that he would appreciate in all its mad overtones, a bizarre twist he—

The smile on Jennifer's face suddenly vanished as she thought about Peter. The tears and the sobs that had been trembling just below the surface broke into the open, leaving her drained and exhausted. Looking at her watch, Jennifer Owen née Delafield went quickly into the bathroom to fix herself up for dinner.

Or was it for the reassuring reality of turning on a tap and having water come out?

". . . and blessed be the food Thee sets before us, Lord Amen." Mr. Griggs cleared his throat and looked solemnly at Jennifer, his hands still folded in front of him, apparently pleased by how he'd handled the saying of grace. As he unclasped his hands he smiled warmly at Jennifer and cleared his throat again.

Jennifer was always startled by people who still said grace before a meal, and lived in fear that they would ask her, as the visitor, to honor them by saying it for the whole family. This had happened once when Jennifer was only about twelve, and she'd never forgotten the combination of stage fright, mumbled stabs at prayer, and stammering that had followed. She'd gone through the same thing last night at dinner, trying to catch Peter's eye, not yet realizing he was so bombed, he couldn't even see across the table.

"Delicious soup, Harriet," Henry announced, and then looked

at Jennifer, apparently expecting her to add something. Jennifer remained mute. Thinking, even briefly, about Peter had set off a chain of memories from the day before—of their joking in the car, of the wedding, and even of the damn dinner itself. The dining room was haunted by Peter—his laughter, his charm, his warmth. Even when the drinks had gotten to him, he had tried to be pleasant.

"And if there's one thing better than Harriet's soup, it's her home-baked bread. Just smell it, Jennifer! Isn't it wonderful?" Once again Henry's eyes were fixed on Jennifer, his face smiling, but with an intense look boring through the small, steel-rimmed spectacles that implored Jennifer to compliment Harriet for her cooking. A stamp of approval that was not so much for Harriet's benefit, Jennifer decided, as for his own.

With effort Jennifer struggled to produce something. "Oh, my, but it does—"

Harriet cut her off with a bellowing laugh. "People who ask for compliments, Henry, don't deserve them. Leave the poor girl alone. If she likes something, I'm sure she won't be bashful about saying so. Anyway, Jennifer's all wrapped up, worrying about Peter. Silly Jennifer! He'll be banging on the door any minute, child."

Jennifer looked at Harriet curiously. She was again treating her as if she were about ten years old. Even her words—"Silly Jennifer!" and "Any minute, child"—held the same ring as the little potato choo-choo she had imagined earlier. Jennifer smiled weakly. Inside, she could feel herself growing moodier now that Peter's disappearance was there in words as well as thoughts. Struggling, she broke off a small morsel of Harriet's bread and put it in her mouth. It *was* delicious, hot and primitively simple, filled with a wonderful taste that evoked images from long ago. She turned toward Harriet and told her so.

Harriet appeared to shake with pleasure, but seemed to notice how quickly Jennifer retreated into her dark, despairing mood. "Do stop worrying about Peter, dear," she counseled. "These things happen," she added with a sigh. "It will all work out if you just give it a little time."

Jennifer began feeling acutely uncomfortable and decided to change the subject. "I was wondering, Miss Griggs. I keep hearing such strange noises from the floor above me. I didn't think anyone else lived in Blossom House—"

"Oh, no one does, Jennifer. Just Harriet and myself—and for the moment, *you*." Henry assured her, reaching over again to pat her hand as he'd done at lunch. "It must be your imagination that—"

A look of disapproval passed across Harriet's face, annoyed either by her brother's attempt at explanation or because she didn't like his patting the hand of an attractive young girl. "It's a very old house, child. *Very* old. Always creaking and groaning. Old beams do that, you know. And when the wind comes down the chimneys! Moans like a pack of banshees. Why, sometimes, it can almost sound like someone singing. Until you get used to it, dear, this house is a little eerie, I know. But very definitely, no one else lives in Blossom House. Just old Henry and myself. Lonely, I admit."

There was something wrong about what they were both saying, but Jennifer couldn't put her finger on it; she was too upset and worried about Peter. She had meant to get back to the noises later on in the meal, but somehow never did.

Henry cleared his throat, cocked his head to one side, and looked at her intently. "Jennifer," he began, "my sister and I were wondering what you planned to do next. What I mean is, until Peter turns up. I could tell you of some good motels around here, but, you know, what we were really wondering was if you might not like to—"

"Oh, for the Lord's sake, Henry, you make it sound so complicated." Harriet was wearing a warm, gentle smile as she leaned slightly out over the table to beam at Jennifer. "What my brother is fumbling around trying to say is, you know, dear, we wouldn't stand for your going to a hotel or motel; they're all fleabags and, anyway, you're our favorite visitor in years, so why don't you just plan to stay on in the room you're already in, anyway, until Peter turns up. Something that will happen when you least expect it, believe me. God knows, there's plenty of room here. And frankly, I haven't seen my brother as relaxed as this in years. Why, he's smiled more in the last twenty-four hours than he has in all the years since his own daughter died. And you'll be right here, waiting, when Peter *does* come back. Oh, please say you will, child. It would make us both so happy.''

Jennifer stared at Harriet blankly. The invitation startled her, yet there was a great deal of truth in what Harriet said. If she stayed on at Blossom House, she would be on hand to greet Peter the moment he stepped inside the front door, seizing her, holding her, laughing with her—and ready to explain where he had been. The darker side of Harriet's logic was unknown to anyone but Jennifer; she couldn't go home, her pride wouldn't allow her to crawl lamely back to her family, and the same pride was even preventing her from calling her best friend, Hillary Crane. The discussion went back and forth, Jennifer resisting, Henry and Harriet insisting. It was strangely like the original argument about their staying to have champagne after the wedding—the Griggses insisting, Jennifer's mind already made up to accept. Only today there was one missing element: Peter.

''I just don't think I could impose like that,'' Jennifer said finally, letting her vulnerability to be talked into it show. Part of Jennifer very much didn't want to accept; there was something odd about Blossom House, a sensation she'd felt from the first moment they'd drawn up in front of it yesterday. But she virtually had no other choice. All of her other options had been foreclosed. Out of politeness, she continued to say she couldn't, all the while knowing eventually she would. To wait here for Peter, she told herself over and over again, that was her first duty.

In the end she gave in as gracefully as she could. ''It's terribly sweet of you both. I just don't know how to thank you. To take in a virtual stranger like me—well, it's incredibly good of you. . . .''

Henry and Harriet beamed, Henry patting her hand again. After it was settled they went into the library and played Parcheesi. To Jennifer, Parcheesi was a game she hadn't played since she was a little girl, but Henry and Harriet both entered into it as if it were some wild species of tournament bridge, hooting and cheering each play, clapping with glee when they scored a point, groaning loudly when the board put them a step backward. It seemed a curious game for three adults to be playing, Jennifer thought, but then everything about these people and Blossom House had strange overtones to it. Involuntarily Jennifer shivered.

To take her mind off what was a growing apprehension, Jennifer excused herself for a moment, walked over to another table, and returned with an ashtray. Pulling out her cigarettes, she fumbled with a book of matches and finally had a match ready. She was startled to discover her hand suddenly in a viselike grip, and with Harriet staring at her with a grim expression of hostility. Jennifer braced herself for the standard lecture on the evils of smoking, although she found it hard to understand, if the Griggses felt this way, why there were ashtrays all over the house. And, looking at her, she remembered seeing Harriet herself smoking at the end of the meal. "I'm sorry," Jennifer began, "I didn't realize you—"

Harriet snatched the book of matches from Jennifer's hand. "Little girls shouldn't play with matches," she announced angrily. "You've been told that a million times, child."

"But *you* smoke, Miss Griggs, why—."

"Grown-ups do lots of things. But that's because they're grown-ups. I never want to see you fooling with matches again."

It all made so little sense, Jennifer didn't bother to carry the argument further. Harriet was still glaring at her, as if she'd done something absolutely terrible. "Little girls shouldn't play with matches." What did that mean? She wasn't a little girl; she was a married woman. Harriet's attack suddenly reminded Jennifer of her mother's—sometimes equally senseless, always unpleasant, and frequently vicious for the sake of being vicious. She shook her head in confusion. To ease the tension, Henry Griggs took his turn on the Parcheesi board, laughing at his own cleverness and good luck. Jennifer joined him in laughing, particularly after she made a move of colossal stupidity. Harriet just glared.

A little later, as gracefully as she could—Jennifer had always hated being a guest, even of people she knew intimately—she yawned extravagantly a couple of times and announced that she was exhausted. Would they mind terribly if she were to—

"Of course not, child," Harriet finished for her. "You've had what must have been a very unsettling day. A good night's sleep will make the whole world look different tomorrow."

Henry was less effusive this time, almost appearing to sulk a little, but managed a smile. "Yes, yes, yes, of course, Jennifer. We understand completely. And please, stop worrying. Peter is all right, believe me."

"And he'll be back, dear," added Harriet, "any moment. Then it will all make sense to you, and you'll laugh at how silly you were to fret about him."

Upstairs, Jennifer changed into her nightie and glumly climbed into bed. None of the Griggses' reassurances could handle the worry and dread growing inside her. She wondered about kneeling beside her bed and saying a prayer, something she hadn't done since she was little. But God, surely, would know she had only turned to prayer after all these years because she wanted something desperately—for Peter to come back—and Jennifer suspected God didn't work that way, granting pleas to people who turned in His direction only when they petitioned a favor.

Trying to get to sleep, Jennifer twisted and thrashed under the covers, lying listening to the wind moaning down the chimney. Every now and then she would hear the same strange sounds from the floor above that she had heard earlier, but did her best to dismiss them as the creaks and groaning of a very old house.

She had almost drifted off into an uneasy sleep when there was a tremendous thud above her head, accompanied by a muffled shriek no amount of self-reassurance could blame on the house's age. Again, Jennifer shuddered, pulling the covers tighter around her. Sleep was slow in returning. Through Jennifer's head a single sentence played itself over and over again: "Peter. Oh, God, Peter, where *are* you?"

CHAPTER SEVEN

My days as a teenager were miserable. My mother tried, but my father was cruel, saying things just to be mean. Sometimes, when he'd had a few drinks, he'd even make fun of my size, saying things like maybe I should take up heavyweight wrestling. Christ, how could anybody be that mean to his own daughter?

In a way, it was all groundwork for what I am today. And for what I'm doing with my life; paying back those horny, good-looking boys with the too-high opinions of themselves; settling a few scores with all young ladies who think they can get anything they want just by smiling a lot and tossing their hair and batting their damn eyelashes.

Be mean to your kid, and the kid learns a lot about how to be mean to other people.

Thanks, Dad.

Journal of Blossom House,
Entry, page 16—Harriet Griggs

In the very early morning—5:15, to be precise—Peter Owen suddenly came back. Although Jennifer was in a deep if troubled sleep, she woke up at the first sound of him coming into the room. She was beside herself with happiness, saying his name over and over, fumbling for the light switch, laughing, crying, and telling him how much she loved him and, my God, she'd been scared to death he'd left her and run off somewhere and, Jesus, Peter, don't ever go scaring her like that again. Cute and wonderful Peter, slipping into the room like this, struggling not to awaken her, trying to get into the bed without making any noise.

Still half laughing, half crying, Jennifer's shaking hand finally found the switch and turned on the light beside the bed. The laughing-crying was replaced by first a gasp, then a scream.

It wasn't Peter at all. It was Henry Griggs, blinking in the sudden light, both hands on the far edge of the bed. Jennifer screamed again. Henry stood up, struggling to restore his dignity. "It's all right, Jennifer. It's me, Henry Griggs. See, I had to get some things from your closet," he explained, holding one hand between his eyes and the light, "and, well, I didn't want to wake you up and, damn it, I tripped over one of the legs of the bed in the dark and almost fell." He seemed to be studying her, finally lowering the protective hand from in front of his face. "I'm terribly sorry if I scared you, Jennifer, really, really sorry, but I just had to get this stuff out of the closet in here."

Jennifer said nothing, just drew the covers up tighter around herself; she was still sitting up after her search for the light switch and wasn't sure how much of her showed. What the hell could be so important that a man would go hauling things out of a closet in the middle of the night? Harriet had said they were "country people," but even farmers didn't get up at five in the morning if they didn't have to. Henry seemed to sense her skepticism.

"I'll just get that stuff and let you go back to sleep, Jennifer." He continued to stare at her for a moment, and then, appearing almost overly nonchalant, strode into the closet, turned on the light, and fussed around inside briefly. A few minutes later he emerged carrying a small pile of things—just what, Jennifer couldn't see.

As he came out he turned once again toward Jennifer. "It was probably stupid of me to try getting this stuff in the dark, but I knocked very softly on your door, and when you didn't answer, I knew you were still asleep, and with all the worries you've had, the last thing in the world I wanted to do was wake you up. I'm sorry and I apologize—for being stupid *and* for scaring you half to death."

Jennifer remained silent, only nodding in acknowledgment of his apology. Henry tried to wave with his one free hand and went stumbling out her door, tripping over himself in his embarrassment, smiling and pulling it shut behind him.

She didn't know what to make of it. Jennifer wanted to believe his explanations, but the more she thought about it, the more trouble she had with it: the crazy hour; the things in the closet—the necessity of getting them at this very moment; tripping over a leg of the bed. Too *many* explanations, really. But, well, Henry might just be telling the truth, so Jennifer decided against mentioning it to Harriet. Damn this place anyway.

The moment she'd slid back down under the covers, Jennifer knew that, for her, any hope of sleep had vanished for the night; slipped quietly into the dark shadows that somehow always surrounded Blossom House. She could still feel herself trembling from the fright Henry had given her. Worse, her original reaction—that Peter had returned—brought up the mystery and agony of his disappearance all over again. This, coupled with worries, now about herself, crowded in on her—a writhing tableau of fears and dreads crying out to be exorcised and explained.

Henry and Harriet Griggs had kept telling her not to worry, that Peter would be back any moment, but for the first time Jennifer began to be unsure. Harriet was always smiling—as her mother did, but, like her, with thick steel armor plate just beneath the skin. Henry, well, Henry was a much gentler person, but given to creeping into your room at night for God alone knew what. How could you put any great store in the assurances of people like that?

Peter had certainly been right in his observation that Blossom House was a strange place, even from the outside. Or had that been her own comment? Suddenly she couldn't remember. Then Peter's snapped reply to her reservations came back to Jennifer: "The rest were too tacky, this one's too perfect . . ." Jennifer sighed, her face drawn long in disappointment and worry, and sat down in the chair by the window. By six she would get dressed and go downstairs. Maybe the Griggses wouldn't be up yet. A minute later she decided she would get dressed right away. She had some exploring to do, and she didn't want to run into either Henry or Harriet while doing it. Jennifer shuddered slightly at the thought and quickly began slipping into her clothes.

Downstairs everything was eerily quiet. The loudest sound you could hear was the ticking of the grandfather clock on the stairs. Jennifer smiled at her parody of the Rolls-Royce ad, but it was a grim smile. Now was not the time for humor.

Blossom House fully lived up to the word *strange*. Looking first in the library, then the living room, then the kitchen, she couldn't find a single phone anywhere. As she thought about it she couldn't remember having seen one since she got here. Nor had she ever heard one ring. At first, the fact only annoyed her, one more facet of her growing feeling that something about Blossom House was all wrong. Then annoyance dissolved into panic. Where the hell *were* the phones? How had Peter found one? That didn't make sense.

Until this moment she had had no particular use for a phone, but deprived of one, Jennifer found herself becoming increasingly anxious, like a child who doesn't want some particular toy until he finds out he can't have it. She could call Hillary— No, she had already decided that would be a lousy idea. She could call— Jennifer couldn't think of anyone her pride would allow her to phone.

But the phone, every house had a phone; this one must too, somewhere. Yes, she was sure of that.

With a sigh, Jennifer continued her study of Blossom House. There were the shelves of dolls in the library, where there should have been books. They stared at her in the pale early-morning light, their painted eyes looking at her with hostility for disturbing their privacy at such an ungodly hour. Silently Jennifer agreed with them. Ungodly was appropriate.

Wandering through other rooms downstairs, Jennifer kept running into further evidence of children. In one room, leaning against the wall, was an elaborate standing music box, brightly colored and looking quite new—as gaudy and glittering as a jukebox. But when she wound it up, the box, instead of rock, played a tinkling version of "Sur le Pont d'Avignon." Children again. Jennifer stood back, listening, and remembering the gusto with which she and the other little girls in her French class at Chalmer's had sung the song—long ago, when the whole world had seemed friendly and warm and safe, and the only anguish she ever felt was when her parents wouldn't let her do something it was absolutely, desperately, screamingly obvious she should be allowed to do. A picture of her mother flashed through her head; her way of treating her was so like Harriet Griggs's, it was frightening.

Aimlessly she moved through room after room, uncertain of what she was looking for or expecting to find. In one—a small sewing room in the back area—she came across a stack of children's games, neatly boxed and labeled in what she assumed was Harriet's meticulous hand. In the other corner of the room a large stuffed panda was propped up at a crazy angle, its eyes studying her with infinite weariness, looking as sad as she herself felt. The stuffed panda reminded Jennifer of the crazy stuffed peach with its strange overtones of dread. She left the room quickly. Christ, in Blossom House even stuffed peaches and pandas could evoke unsettling fear.

Walking briskly down the long hall, she came to the front door, the door Peter and she had used the first day they arrived there. Jesus, could it really only be two days ago? Jennifer decided maybe she should check Peter's car, still parked at the curb in front of the house. Did the town of Chivers give tickets for overtime parking? She decided she'd best go outside and see.

Her resolve dissolved. The door was locked, and when she reached down to turn the usual inner knob that would unlock it, she discovered the knob itself was missing. There was a small hole where it should have been. A small hole but no knob. Taken out to be repaired? To be polished? She didn't know. She *did* know that once again some mysterious facet of Blossom House had frustrated her. The knob was doubtless missing for some perfectly logical reason, Jennifer decided, but its disappearance added to her growing sense of uneasiness.

Jennifer's head snapped upward as she gave an apprehensive look at the ceiling. Overhead, she heard a distant alarm clock ringing somewhere, followed by the thud of someone's feet striking the floor and the heavy sound of walking. Quickly, her blood pounding, Jennifer headed for the kitchen. One of them— Harriet, perhaps—was now up, and her snooping around downstairs would not be appreciated. She'd get back to it later. The swinging door into the kitchen seemed to stick at first, only surrendering to a hard shove. As Jennifer moved inside she felt her heart give a sudden jump.

"My child, but you're up early, aren't you!" boomed Harriet, swinging around from the range to face her. "I always thought New York people didn't get up until noon. At least." Harriet was smiling broadly, but there was a thread of criticism in what she'd said that didn't escape Jennifer. The smile slowly vanished, leaving only the hard stare of Harriet's eyes to give her face expression—a piercing, shrewd, searching, one. Jennifer could feel her veneer crumbling.

"Well, I—I couldn't sleep, and when it got light I decided I might just as well get up, you see. What I mean is, I hope I didn't disturb anyone."

"No, dear, not a soul. We're heavy sleepers, both Henry and I."

Jennifer wondered how, if Henry was such a heavy sleeper, he'd wound up crashing around in her room at five in the morning. If Harriet knew about the incident, she certainly wasn't admitting she did. "Good," Jennifer said, very aware of how unconvincing she sounded.

"There's nothing worse than not being able to sleep, is there?" Harriet asked Jennifer, a vestige of the smile returning, although now it had a peculiar shadow of amused irony behind it. "Sometimes you just want to get up and wander around, looking at things, opening and closing doors, *anything*. Nerves. It can be very bad for your health, you know." The amused irony had just reshaped itself into indirect menace. Had Harriet known all along that she'd been down here snooping? Was this a warning she'd just been given? Jennifer felt a small shudder run through her.

Maybe it was time to get the hell out of this crazy house and make a run for it in Peter's car. A sudden panic swept through her. Yes, she knew she should stay, to be on hand when Peter came back—*if* he came back. Yes, she knew it was crazy to be even thinking this way; sure, they were a little odd, but there was probably nothing at all really threatening about either Harriet or Henry and, okay, it was all her stupid imagination running wild. But the whole setup—Blossom House, the people, the belongings of unknown children in evidence everywhere, the thumpings and voices and moans she kept thinking she heard from over her room, the ominous padlocked door at the end of the hall, the missing lock knob from the front door. These things weren't just her imagination, were they? No, they were as real as the floor under her feet. And, no, stupid little Jennifer, you aren't standing on a trap door.

Jennifer's pathetic effort at humor put things back in perspective, as it always did. There was nothing to be afraid of. There really wasn't. It *was* her imagination running riot.

The panic suddenly returned. Even if she decided to run off, she didn't know where the car keys were. She'd looked everywhere in her room and, damn it, they simply weren't there. It didn't make sense that Peter would take the keys with him and leave the car for her. For a brief instant Jennifer played with the idea that Harriet might have stolen them out of her room, but then remembered she was struggling to dismiss the panic, not trying to light a fire under it.

"Well, Jennifer," Henry said cheerfully as he walked into the kitchen, studying her with pleasure. "Don't you look wonderful this morning! You must have slept like a log."

"Eggs?" Harriet demanded of her with a sardonic smile. "Poached, scrambled, or fried?"

"Just toast. Toast and coffee, thank you," Jennifer answered in a small voice.

"Of course, dear."

A few minutes later Jennifer was staring at the food on her plate with consummate loathing. Harriet had put it on the kitchen table in front of her with a wide smile and the comment "That's not enough to keep a bird alive, child," but the particular bird in question—Jennifer—was almost at the point of not caring much one way or the other.

After lunch, lying again on her bed, Jennifer stared emptily at the ceiling. She had begged off, saying she wanted to take a little nap. Every few minutes Jennifer would glance at her watch.

She knew that every afternoon, weather permitting, Harriet would lie in the back garden, reading a magazine or something, while Henry puttered around his garden, spreading that damn magic fertilizer he never stopped talking about around the base of the flowering trees and shrubs. She wanted to get back to her exploration of the house. No matter how often she told herself it was her imagination, something was terribly wrong about this house and the people in it. And that somehow she and Peter were victims of it.

Above her, the strange noises started again: muffled walking sounds, occasionally the thud of something dropped. For the moment, there were no distant moans or cries. She checked her watch again. Three thirty—time for Harriet to be in her hammock.

and Henry in his garden. Jennifer opened her door a crack and listened. Nothing.

She slipped down the hall toward the stairs and listened. Still nothing. As she had counted on, Henry and Harriet must be enjoying the clear, warm weather in the garden that stretched out smoothly behind Blossom House. While listening, Jennifer's eyes fastened on the giant padlock hanging from the door at the end of the hall. What could be up there that required so elaborate a precaution? She walked softly over and took the padlock in her hand. It was an enormous thing, its brass kept bright and polished, and very old-looking, except for the locking device itself. This was a Yale double-tumbler lock of recent vintage, which had been set into the heft of the brass to add the sophistication of a modern security device to the unassailable strength of its lock and hasp.

"It's an interesting lock, isn't it?" asked a booming voice. Jennifer jumped so violently, she almost lost her balance and went teetering down the staircase. Harriet. What the hell was she doing here? She'd slipped up behind Jennifer without making a sound. Jennifer's heart was still pounding from the fright. That woman was everywhere. And right now she was supposed to be in her hammock.

Instead, she had caught Jennifer examining her lock like a second-story man caught casing a house before trying to break in. Jennifer found herself babbling almost incoherent explanations about how the padlock looked so old, and how she had this thing for antiques, and—

"Yes, it is very old, although I guess I never thought of it as an antique," Harriet said, tilting her head to one side as she appraised the padlock from a distance. She turned her eyes back on Jennifer, the smile still pasted on her face.

"You should be outside, dear. It's as warm as summer," she said. "The sun would do you good," she added. Harriet laughed and still appeared, Jennifer conceded, totally unruffled by Jennifer's examination of the lock. "The fact is, child, I had to come back in and get a hat; *that's* how hot the sun is today."

"Oh, I've been reading," Jennifer explained lamely. "And suppose it's about time I got to that nap I came up here for in the first place. But thank you, anyway."

Harriet shrugged pleasantly as she turned toward the stairs. Jennifer's eyes fell on the padlock; it was a question she had to ask. "Miss Griggs, what's up there anyway? Those noises—"

Harriet's eyes narrowed; the pleasant smile vanished; the question had disturbed. "It's a storage place," she snapped. "We have stuff stored all over the house. But *that* one's special." Harriet took one step down the stairs, then turned and came back. Wordlessly she seized Jennifer's wrists in her giant hands. "Don't ever try to open that door. Never, never go near it again, child." Harriet's eyes were thin, icy slits now, boring deep into Jennifer's whole being, her expression making no effort to hide her hostility. "The things stored up there are very personal to me and Mr. Griggs. As far as you're concerned, that door and the stair beyond it are completely off limits. It's a rule of Blossom House." She was shaking Jennifer by the wrists so hard, Jennifer could feel her whole body moving with it. Her own eyes widened with fear. At this moment this strange woman seemed capable of almost anything. "Do you understand me, child? Do you understand?" Her voice rose to an overwhelming roar.

Jennifer tried to tear her wrists free but was unable to; Harriet's grip was too strong. Numbly she nodded her head up and down to indicate she understood—perhaps too well. Her whole body trembled; her heart thudded against her rib cage; the bottom disappeared from her stomach.

Her wrists were suddenly released. "Good," Harriet said vacantly into space. "The child understands. All little girls are better behaved when they understand *why* they mustn't do something."

Jennifer watched in confusion as Harriet once again headed down the stairs. "All little girls," she said. The potato choo choo was back. It was all very mysterious. A mystery that Jennifer might have enjoyed in a book, but not when Peter's disappearance held her hostage to it. Then it became unsettling and frightening, in its implications. The book you can escape by shutting; reality you cannot.

The most mysterious part of her recent encounter didn't occur to Jennifer until she walked inside her bedroom door. Harriet had said she came upstairs to get a hat because the sun was too strong. There was no hat on her head, and Jennifer's wrists still ached where Harriet had seized them in her hands.

Harriet had not come to get her hat. She had come to spy on *her*.

CHAPTER EIGHT

Henry and I, of course, were raised together. As children, a lot of brothers and sisters fight; we had a ball. My father—so extraordinarily cruel to me—doted on Henry. Maybe it's because he was a boy; men are like that. Or maybe it was because Henry wasn't grotesque and half-giant the way I was.

Nevertheless, since Henry was on the shy side, and I wasn't, we stuck very close to each other, doing everything as a team. Even though he was older than me, I had already discovered I could control Henry completely. Control him then, just like I do today. (In those days, though, I used to let Henry think he was a little bit in charge, so that his male ego wouldn't be totally pulverized. I don't bother with that tiresome nonsense anymore.)

When his wife died, followed by one child and then the other, I guess Henry thought it was the end of the world. Anyway, he behaved as if he did. But for me, it was actually the beginning of a whole new and wonderful world. Honestly, I think he's better off with me; certainly, he's happier.

We're back doing things as a team. A lot of people might think the things we're doing here at Blossom House are a little crazy, but that's just because they don't know any better. After all, even the Bible says "An eye for an eye . . . ."

Peter Owen was one eye; the pretty little thing, Jennifer, will be the other.

> *Journal of Blossom House,*
> *Entry, page 17—Harriet Griggs*

Jennifer didn't take a nap, any more than Harriet went to lie down in her hammock. For one thing, the strange noises from the floor above Jennifer seemed to be going through one of their more active spells. Sometimes the noises would be vigorous and unending, other times almost inaudible. But almost always there. Jennifer was about to open her door and slip downstairs to continue her explorations when she heard someone walking down the hall. Pushing her door open a little, she saw Harriet, carrying a tray, walking to the door at the end of the hall. To unlock the brass padlock she had to put the tray on the floor beside her while she fished around in her pocket for the key and then began struggling to make the lock obey her.

What Jennifer could see on the tray she'd deposited on the floor only deepened the mystery of the third floor. The tray was covered with what looked like a large white napkin. On top of the napkin was a pile of additional napkins, neatly folded into squares. Beside them, and covering the rest of the tray, Jennifer could make out a small aluminum bowl and a variety of chromium instruments with the distinctive shapes only one profession on earth called for: dentistry. More things to be stored in the third floor storage area? It seemed unlikely; Henry had been described as a retired lawyer, not a dentist.

The lock surrendered to Harriet with an abrupt click; she had overcome its stubbornness far more quickly than her brother. With a grunt, Harriet reached down and picked up the tray, opened the door, then shut and locked it behind her. Jennifer retreated back into her room; there was no point trying to explore the house while Harriet was roaming around in it.

Perhaps twenty minutes later Jennifer stared upward with awe.

Someone upstairs was making an unearthly shrieking sound directly over her head. The sound was terrifying—as if someone were undergoing deep surgery without anesthetic. Jennifer shivered. The awe quickly transformed itself into cold fear as Jennifer realized there was no longer much possibility of denying it: The third floor held at least one occupant, an occupant who at the moment was suffering acute agony. Jennifer's earlier half-joking thought that perhaps there was a Mrs. Rochester locked away upstairs returned. Possibly, the idea wasn't as preposterous as she'd first thought.

Preposterous, she decided on reflection, was not the right word. Fearsome would be more appropriate. Her ear pressed against the door, Jennifer finally heard the sounds of Harriet's return—the grinding of the lock, the opening of the door, followed by the slam of the door's being shut and the lock once more being struggled with. Gently Jennifer pushed open her door to watch. To relock the door, Harriet had had to put the tray down on the floor again. From what she could see, the dental instruments and the aluminum bowl looked very much as they had before, but the neat pile of folded napkins was now a heap of bloodstained linen.

No wonder the mysterious occupant of the third floor had loosed so awesome a shriek; from the amount of blood, it appeared a tooth must have been pulled. Jesus, Jennifer thought to herself, if Harriet practiced do-it-yourself dentistry, didn't she believe in anesthetics? The thought made a shudder of revulsion course through her.

About ten minutes later Jennifer heard Harriet coming down the hall, whistling softly. Again, Jennifer's door was pushed slightly open. Harriet had come out of her room and, this time, she *was* carrying a hat with her. Listening, Jennifer could hear her open the French doors to the garden in the back of Blossom House, and still whistling, go out. To her hammock. Jennifer could now begin her exploration once more.

Downstairs, she checked the outside through a window. Harriet was lying in her hammock, reading a copy of *Child Life;*

Henry, as expected, was digging in his garden. A thought crossed Jennifer's mind. What in hell was a childless woman doing reading *Child Life*? More of that same strange phenomenon: children in a childless house. Jennifer shook her head to dismiss a mystery that suddenly seemed very secondary to her. For in the back of her head, she was beginning to plan ways of getting out of Blossom House without having to depend on the front door. Of course, she told herself, to picture it as an escape was ridiculous. If she wanted to go, all she had to do was march up to Harriet and tell her she was leaving, right? Or even easier, bat her eyes at Henry a little and tell *him*, right? Oh, they might plead a little with her out of politeness, but that would be the end of it, right?

Wrong. Jennifer wasn't in the least bit sure it would be that easy. Blossom House held too many strange things in it for a simple departure to remain simple. Without telling either Henry or Harriet, it might be wiser to slip out through one of the downstairs windows; hail a cab on the corner, and be on her way to wherever she finally decided to go. Even the prospect of facing her family didn't seem too awful just now. But that she would worry about later.

Jennifer wandered over to one of the windows and turned the small brass handle that controlled the casement window's opening and shutting. The window swung gracefully open, then abruptly stopped. Broken, apparently. Jennifer looked closer and tried another of the windows. The same thing happened. The windows would open perhaps six inches, but no further. She stared at them, confounded. The mullions were of reinforced steel, the panes apparently of Plexiglas. She tried one window after the other, all of them—not only in the library, where she had started, but in all of the rooms downstairs. All of them operated in precisely the same way: six inches of opening, then the handle would no longer turn to open them any wider. A sudden flash of something from the past went through her head, toying with her, teasing with her.

"God, Jennifer, if they catch on, they may never let you and me out of here. Try to shut up and look normal," Hillary had said, giggling.

"Normal?" Jennifer had asked. "You mean like *this*?" Jennifer had managed to cross her eyes and make her face look twisted and mongoloid. The affect was so grotesque, Hillary's giggle had turned to near hysteria. A burst of "Shhh" came from their teacher. "Yes, ma'am. Sorry ma'am," Jennifer and Hillary had chorused, until some of the fury in Miss Lane's face—Miss Lane taught psychology to the young ladies of Miss Chalmer's and was considered a total dork by her students—subsided.

Jennifer and Hillary—her whole class, in fact—had been on a field trip to the Buckley Sanitarium, studying the procedures used to care for the mentally ill with enough money to be sent there instead of a state asylum. The cost, Miss Lane had told them, was $750 a day—and that didn't include drugs, doctors, or psychiatrists' fees.

That trip was the first time Jennifer had seen the kind of windows she had just discovered today.

"You see, making the patient feel he is staying at something akin to a private club is very important to his treatment," one of the staff doctors had told them. "There are no bars on our windows to make him feel he has been locked away, yet we must protect him from the outside world—and the outside world from *him*. This is one technique," the doctor had added, striding over to one of the casement windows and turning the handle on it vigorously. When the window was opened six inches, it had stopped. "The patient has no sensation of being confined, yet he is as securely detained inside as if he were in prison. He has the illusion of being able to leave any time he wants to, you see, but this particular variety of window keeps him right where he is. No adult can force himself through a six-inch-wide opening."

"Couldn't he go on a diet?" Hillary had asked with a straight face. Miss Lane looked at her with fury. The class broke up. The doctor smiled wanly.

"You can't diet away the size of your skull, I'm afraid." The class's sympathy had suddenly shifted toward the doctor; Jennifer had been able to sense it ebbing away from Hillary. She had overplayed her hand, been too smart-alecky, and now had lost. Or possibly—Jennifer could remember thinking this even then— the reality of what it would have been like to be a prisoner there had begun sinking into the other girls as it had into her. There had been something terrifying about the thought, even when looked at as an observer.

Now, though, Jennifer was no longer just an observer. More and more, she felt like a prisoner. Why else would Blossom House have the same kind of windows as the Buckley Sanitarium? A panic began edging over her as she considered it. Ridiculous, she finally told herself. As with so many of the things she had been fretting about here, there was doubtless some perfectly logical explanation of the curious phenomenon of the escape-proof windows, too.

The one area she couldn't dismiss so easily was the mystery of the third floor. The occupant—now presumably lacking a tooth— who was she? Or was it a he? My God, Jennifer suddenly thought, it could even be Peter. Maybe for some strange, sick, inexplicable, reason the Griggses had Peter locked away up there. His teeth were brilliantly even and perfect-looking, but he was always complaining about toothaches and having to go to the dentist for fillings. Genetic failing, he had explained. ''Our kids better learn early how to chew with their gums. . . .''

That moment when Harriet had come back from the door at the end of the hall and disappeared into her own room played through Jennifer's head again. Harriet had walked into her room, carrying the key in her hand; when she emerged, she was carrying her hat in one hand, playing with its straw brim with the other. The key was somewhere inside the room. If she had been distracted at all, possibly she had left it somewhere—inside her makeup table or dresser, perhaps?—where it could be found.

Quickly Jennifer slipped up the stairs and into Harriet's room. The chamber was a large one, furnished in an odd mixture of wicker and faded chintz. On the chaise longue was a mountain of small pillows, apparently stuffed with lavender sachet, filling the whole room with the smell of another time. Walking softly over to the makeup table, Jennifer was surprised to discover what looked like the key to the padlock lying in plain sight on top of it. It struck Jennifer as almost *too* easy. She picked up the key and crept quickly down the hall to the door. The key went into the Yale lock, and Jennifer was stunned when it opened at the first turn of the key; both Henry and Harriet always seemed to have such a struggle with it.

Pushing the door open, Jennifer found a set of uncovered wooden stairs behind it, leading upward. She took each step with great care; the stairs were old and the bare planks creaked and groaned each time she put her weight on them.

At the top was another door, this one of heavy steel, with a thick rectangular window set about two thirds of the way up it. As she neared the door a strange shift of the light inside the window struck her. When she got to the window and tried to look inside, she suddenly found herself face-to-face with a pair of anguished eyes staring out at her pleadingly. The eyes belonged to a little girl perhaps twelve or so years old, dressed in the very proper clothes of what a well-brought-up child of fifty years ago might have worn.

Breathing heavily, excitement colored with fear, Jennifer tried speaking to the little girl, who kept shaking her head and pointing at the window. Deaf, Jennifer wondered? For what reason did the Griggses keep a deaf little girl locked up here? The girl alternated between pointing at the window and putting a stained towel to her lips, behavior that at first confused Jennifer completely. Then, Jennifer solved both halves of her question at the same moment. The little girl was not deaf; her pointing to the window was to explain that she could not hear through it and, indeed, as Jennifer studied it she could see that the window was not just a single pane of glass, but several—thick enough to make it completely soundproof.

Apparently the little girl was trying to explain this by mouthing words for Jennifer, and each time she opened her mouth, Jennifer could see blood, which explained the stained towel. It also provided one answer to who the girl was—the one whose tooth Harriet had just pulled.

The little girl disappeared for a moment, then returned, carrying a small pad and pencil. Leaning against the door, she began writing some message for Jennifer and then held it up to the window for her to read. Almost simultaneously the girl's head turned sideways and an expression of fear crossed her face. A second later she disappeared from the window completely, and Jennifer could hear the sharp thuds and bangs of a scuffle hitting the inside of the steel door as the little girl and whoever it was who had brought that expression of dreadful fear to her face fought to keep what the little girl had written from being shown. There was nothing Jennifer could do, except try to keep her mounting fear in check.

Her heart thudding heavily against her ribs, Jennifer slipped downstairs, shut and locked the door behind her, put the key back on Harriet's dressing table, and fled back to her room.

Jennifer knew now that she would have to escape. The message the little girl had held up for her had been yanked away before Jennifer got to read very much of it, but she had seen enough to know that there was no alternative. "Get out of this house. Quick!" it had started. "Go get help for us and—" Then out of Jennifer's sight the little girl and someone unseen had had their struggle. From the violent bangings against the door, she knew it would not have been a pleasant thing to watch.

There was no more time for flattering Henry, for trying to manipulate him. Harriet was inflexible. Apparently both of them were dangerous. Peter would have to catch up with her at home; he would turn up. In the meantime, she could get her father under control again, and at least survive until Peter did arrive. Trying to calm herself, Jennifer sat down in the chair by the window—also, she noticed, made of steel mullions and Plexiglas and presumably only able to open six inches—and prepared her plans.

* * *

Downstairs, Harriet was playing the piano. Behind her stood Henry, listening to her play with a vacant, distant look in his eyes. The recital didn't last very long. On the wall beside the piano a small red bulb began blinking on and off, while a buzzer in the wall sounded an urgent warning.

Harriet stopped playing and threw a switch, which stopped both the light and the buzzer. She looked at Henry with a grim smile. "Well, that's it. Our little guest has left the third floor and unlocked the door. Is everything ready, Henry?"

At first Henry merely nodded, still in the grip of Harriet's piano-playing. She stared at him, a look of impatience and anger darkening her face. Finally he responded, but a little wearily. "Yes, Harriet. Everything's ready." He paused and appeared to shudder. "She's such a sweet little thing. . . ."

Harriet ignored his remark. "It's time, Henry. For this one, I left the key out in plain sight. To keep things moving along. I knew that that girl couldn't resist trying the key." Harriet gave a triumphant little laugh. "They never can."

With a shrug, Henry walked out of the living room and began fiddling with the front door; Harriet disappeared into the kitchen area. The downstairs suddenly took on a deserted look, the living room once filled with laughter, but tenanted now only by the haunted echos of Harriet's piano-playing.

In her room, Jennifer heard sudden silence descend on the house. Harriet must have gone back to her hammock—the sun was lowering, but there was still plenty of sunlight in the garden—and Henry back to his damn work with the trees and shrubbery. Jennifer didn't take time to pack; she was too anxious to get out of Blossom House. Precisely how, she was not yet sure. But somehow. Goddamn, she had to find a way.

Softly, slowly, Jennifer came down the great staircase. No one seemed to be around; the whole house was washed in silence. As she looked down the front hall she was surprised to see that the lock knob on the inside of the front door was back in position. Her original guess that it was out being repaired had been right,

Jennifer decided. Moving quickly, she slipped up to the front
door and turned the knob. It gave easily. Once again, as when
she had when she found the keys on Harriet's dressing table, it
all seemed a little too easy, but Jennifer was in no mood to worry
about it. Quietly she pulled the door fully open. Then she gasped.

Henry Griggs stood directly outside, staring her full in the face.
He didn't appear in the least surprised to see her. He smiled,
bowed toward her slightly, then pushed her back into the house
with a vicious shove.

Jennifer began to scream, but from behind her a huge hand—
Harriet's hand—clapped a moist cloth over her mouth. Instantly
she could smell chloroform. Jennifer thrashed and struggled, but
it was useless; Harriet held her whole body in a vise of steel.
Henry Griggs still stood in front of her, but the chloroform was
beginning to take effect, and he began to go in and out of focus,
sometimes seeming to be laughing, sometimes stern and angry,
sometimes becoming a completely different face—her father's,
Jennifer thought. Little by little her thrashing died down; she
could feel her muscles becoming involuntarily relaxed and useless.

"Peter. Oh, God, Peter," she mumbled into the gray void that
surrounded her.

CHAPTER NINE

Sometimes Henry gets upset about the unpleasant things we do to our guests. Well, if you analyze it carefully, you'll see that our guests bring an awful lot of it on themselves.

Take Jennifer's stealing the key from my room. And secretly—at least she thought she was being secret—unlocking the door she'd been forbidden to go near and creeping upstairs, anyway. Jennifer, like the others, simply couldn't resist prying into a place she'd been specifically told not to go. Curiosity. All little girls are nosy, I suppose, but at Blossom House, curiosity can be costly.

I can't pretend we don't program things to make pretty sure someone like Jennifer will do what we want her to; the missing lock knob on the front door always works, too.

I know Jennifer's type well. She's a born manipulator. Watching her go to work on Henry makes me sick—she's just as good at it as Henry's own daughter was.

Well, Jennifer's met her match in me. By the time I'm through with her, the only thing sweet little Jennifer will be manipulating is a mouthful of quicklime and dirt.

*Journal of Blossom House,
Entry, page 18—Harriet Griggs*

The first thing she heard was a distant roaring, like the sound of the breakers hitting the shore at East Hampton. It came in great waves, rushing at her like a freight train and then suddenly receding into the distance. Jennifer cautiously opened one eye to discover she was lying on an unfamiliar bed in an unfamiliar room. Slowly the roaring stopped, but her head continued to throb. Probably, she decided, the aftereffects of the chloroform. Jennifer's head wasn't too clear yet and she was having considerable difficulty focusing on any thought for very long, but this one she managed to hold on to. Strange. Why chloroform? Until the incident at the front door, the Griggses had been very peculiar people, but never actively physical about it. Now, apparently, the stakes had been upped.

She sat partway up to study the room. Over her head a starched white canopy ran around the four tall posts at each corner of the bed. She could see the window was framed in more of the same starched white material, pleated and gathered in the same way as the material of the canopy.

Trying to ignore the throb of her head, Jennifer tentatively put her feet over the edge of the bed and on to the floor, carpeted in a brilliant yellow shag. The sudden upward movement of her head made her dizzy, and Jennifer sat where she was, waiting for her body to reaccustom itself to being upright.

Looking around, one thing quickly became clear: This was a little girl's room, and really quite a pretty one. There were stuffed animals everywhere, and sitting on a little chair upholstered in a cheerful yellow-and-pink pattern, with the characters from *The Wind in the Willows* running through the design, was the stuffed peach she'd seen before. The peach had affected her strangely—as if it were a fuzzy satellite that gave off some kind of killer rays—and now she was sharing a room with it. Henry must have put it in there the day she saw him taking it up through the door at the end of the hall. A fuzzy satellite giving off death rays! A crazy and stupid thing to think, she told herself it was only a stuffed toy. But the logic of what she was thinking didn't stop a wave of shudders from surging through her.

Jennifer felt steady enough now to stand up again and begin exploring the room. The walls were papered in a bright, simply executed flower design; the flowers were huge and reminded her of American primitives she'd seen, or the drawings of children. Along one wall was a small, cheerfully painted desk, each edge painted with a chain of colorful winsome animals.

On the opposite wall was a simple white bookcase. Stacked on its shelves, Jennifer found numerous books about Nancy Drew, Heidi, and the *Bobbsey Twins*, as well as *Alice's Adventures in Wonderland*, and *The Little Minister*. Jennifer considered. Maybe the room had once belonged to one of Henry Griggs's daughters and had been frozen in time as a sort of memorial. Possible, she supposed. But why was *she* here?

The window, she found to be the most curious feature of all. Jennifer stood staring at it, trying to make sense out of it. On the inside was a heavy sheet of what appeared to be Thermopane. Beyond, Jennifer could see heavy stainless steel bars, the kind you might find in a prison. A prison. The word triggered a chain of associations that left Jennifer trembling. A few inches farther out, beyond the bars, was a screen of heavy wire mesh, and then, two more sheets, a few inches apart, of the same Thermopane as the inner window.

For a few moments she stood there, mystified by the elaborateness of the arrangement. The reasons behind it all suddenly clicked into focus, the relentless, final click of handcuffs being snapped into position on a prisoner's wrists after the death sentence has been pronounced.

The bars kept anyone from escaping; the wire mesh stopped anyone from breaking the Thermopane and screaming for help. The two outer layers of Thermopane made any cry for help from the inside useless. She had already discovered the same arrangement was used in her bathroom window. The room, so deceptively like that of a little girl's, was actually an escape-proof prison cell. Maximum security.

The door to the room was equally deceptive. It was painted to look like grainy, paneled wood, but the instant she touched it,

Jennifer knew it was made of heavy steel. In the upper center was a sliding steel panel, controlled from the outside, with a small glass-covered peephole in its center. Putting her eye against the peephole and squinting, Jennifer could see nothing of what lay beyond, except what seemed to be the wall opposite her room and the edge of another door. Maximum security, Jennifer thought to herself again.

Baffled and discouraged, Jennifer sat down in the little armchair and tried to make sense of it again. A little girl's room. But a little girl's room with a steel door and bars on the window? Could one of Henry Griggs's daughters have been so crazy and violent that she had to be kept locked up this way? And why would the Griggses choose this room to put *her* in? A sudden suspicion that somewhere inside she *did* know why began to torment Jennifer.

She tucked her feet up underneath her and looked around the room helplessly. The movement was largely automatic, but she felt stupid sitting there in her bare feet and dressed in the funny clothes they had put her in. She was wearing a short but loose nightie of some sort, made of white dotted organdy. Around the cuffs, the collar, and the hem were crocheted figures from the *Uncle Remus* stories; she could recognize Brer Rabbit and Brer Fox, but she had read the stories so long ago—or were they read to her?—that the rest of the characters escaped her. A little girl's nightie, yet it fitted her as if made for her— except across the breasts, where it was almost uncomfortably tight.

She got up and looked into the closet and checked the hooks on the inside of the bathroom door. Empty. The clothes she had been wearing, even her stockings and shoes, had all disappeared. Thinking further, Jennifer decided she must be on the third floor of Blossom House. She couldn't be sure, of course, because she had been unconscious when they brought her to this room. But the angle of the ceiling near the window sloped, telling her she must be up under the roof. Her window had to be set into a modified dormer of some special design. Technical details such as this helped her avoid what was really troubling her.

There was no rational reason to explain why she was here or why the Griggses should be doing this terrible thing to her. Face it: Henry and Harriet Griggs were plain crazy. An empty feeling crept into her stomach: crazy *and* dangerous. Out of this conclusion, though, an idea with a small ray of hope in it appeared. She prayed that the idea wasn't growing on her as firmly as it was, only because it *did* put a happier face on things, but she couldn't be sure. She went back to weighing her newest idea. Maybe, she thought, there was another cell like this somewhere on the third floor. Only that particular cell was decorated like a little boy's room and held Peter— God, wonderful, marvelous Peter. In spite of bars and steel doors and everything else, he will find a way to get out of his cell, come get me from here, and together we will escape this terrifying prison once and for all.

Jennifer suddenly laughed aloud, a laugh so loud and bitter, it startled Jennifer to realize it came from her. Whirling around in her mind suddenly were the accusations she used to hurl at her family. How badly they treated her, how they limited everything she did, how they virtually imprisoned her. A terrible realization struck Jennifer: She had escaped from one prison only to wind up in another one infinitely worse—and totally, terrifyingly mad.

Restlessly she walked around the room again, trying to find some spot she hadn't really explored. The room was neither that large nor that complicated; she'd already studied, probed, and put her hands on virtually every inch of it. With an unhappy sigh— almost a moan—she put her eye back to the peephole on the door. A shadow suddenly fell across it, like a cloud passing in front of the sun. A great eye, distorted by the glass, abruptly came into focus and stared into her own. She jumped back with a frightened gasp, feeling suddenly faint as the entire panel slid to one side with a sharp, slamming bang.

Filling the opening was the huge smiling face of Harriet Griggs. "Everything all right, dear?" she asked gently. "Anything you need?"

Jennifer stared at her in disbelief. "Anything I need!" she yelled. "My God, you can ask *that*? You're crazy—around the bend, bonkers. Both of you," she shouted. Her fury made the words come out unclearly. Her voice rose further. "Anything I need!" she repeated. "What I need is to know where the hell Peter is. What have you done with poor Peter, damn it? And I need to know—right now, for Christ's sake—why you've locked me up in this crazy hellhole. And I need to know when you're going to let me out. Jesus, what do I *need*? Only a crazy creep could ask a question like that. So when, damn it, damn it— when. When are you going to let me out?"

Not a muscle on Harriet's face moved; the smile appeared glued on the front of her head with epoxy. Very softly Harriet began speaking, as if Jennifer hadn't just been yelling at her with every ounce of her strength. "You will learn everything you need to know, dear—in good time." A small quizzical look appeared around her eyes; the smile remained fixed. "Just be patient, Olivia. Be patient."

Suddenly Jennifer began screaming, an unearthly scream with no top and no bottom; a scream that tore at the air and split atoms with its intensity. Harriet seemed not to notice, and the smile never varied. Jennifer leaned forward and used the only weapon she had: she spat directly into Harriet's eye.

The smile never left Harriet's face; it never even wavered. Calmly she wiped her face with a handkerchief. "That wasn't a very nice thing to do, Olivia. *Nice* little girls don't do things like that."

Harriet's calmness only made Jennifer's hysterical pitch grow higher. Her whole body was trembling with rage and frustration. "And for Christ's sake," she screamed at Harriet, "stop calling me Olivia. You know damn well what my name is. And it isn't Olivia, it's Jennifer."

Calmly, the smile touched with sadness, a sympathetic, determinedly helpful smile, Harriet slowly shook her head, as would a grown-up trying to be gentle in telling a child that no, *that* particular toy was just too expensive. Harriet sighed gently. "But, child, it *is* your name. I chose it myself because the name Olivia is a form of olive, and I just think the olive is an absolutely delicious little fruit. And you see, all of Mr. Griggs's daughters are named after fruits—fruits he grows—so how could it possibly be something like Jennifer? There's Cherry, Strawberry, Pippin . . . all of you."

The world exploded around Jennifer. Nothing made sense anymore. Maybe she had lost her mind. None of this was really happening at all. She shrieked uselessly, beating her fists against the steel of the door, crying for herself, because she was hitting the door so hard, her hands felt as if they must be bleeding.

Harriet smiled sympathetically, trying to calm her with "There, there, dear," and "Hush, child, you'll make yourself sick," and "Try and not take on so, Olivia; it's not good for a child to get as upset as this. . . ."

"Why?" Jennifer screamed, crying and sobbing. Her beatings on the door had become spastic slaps; she was too weak to hit any harder. "Why, for the love of God, why? Why are you doing this to me? What did you do with Peter? Where is he? Peter! Why are you keeping me locked up like this in this crazy house? Where is Peter? Who wants all these terrible things done to me? Who wants me to stay here like this?"

For the first time the smile left Harriet's face, and was replaced by a look of wonderment. She spoke as if the answer were so obvious, only a lunatic would have asked the question. "Why, your father, Olivia. You know that—"

"That's not true," Jennifer screamed. "My father wouldn't hurt a fly. And he's in New York, not here. Oh, God, let me go home . . . please, please let me go home. . . ."

"Your father's *not* in New York; he's right here, Olivia." Harriet's face took on a look of impatience. She pointed to the wall beside the window and grew annoyed as her eyes followed her own finger. "Oh, my. Someone has pulled the drapes out over everything. Push them back, dear, and you'll see how right I am. Your father is here."

Jennifer had become so angry and upset, she didn't even argue with Harriet's premise. Her bare feet thumped on the carpet as she stalked heatedly across the room and yanked back the curtain. Her eyes bulged in disbelief. The shock was so great, for a moment she thought she was going to be sick.

Nailed into the wall beside the window was a large framed photograph of Henry Griggs, smiling out at her, his white, Pickwickian fringe of hair looking more like a halo than ever because of the photographer's judicious backlighting.

Written across the lower right-hand corner, in red script and with a chinagraph pencil was his message for the day: "To his wonderful little daughter Olivia. With all my love—Daddy."

Behind her, Jennifer heard the sliding panel slam shut.

CHAPTER TEN

The one thing my father liked doing with me was hunting. I know, in a way, I was very much second choice, but I was the only choice he had. Henry, you see, couldn't stand the sight of blood. And the one time he went with my father, he threw up when he saw the duck all torn up and bleeding. He felt so sorry for it, he began crying, and my old man got real mad and called him a sissy and drove him back home in disgust.

I loved every minute of it. It took my father a while to get used to the idea, but he finally decided to let me come along. To me there was a tremendous kick in lying in wait for the creature— duck, pheasant, rabbit, fox—tracking it, sneaking up on it, and then, BOOM! you blew it to pieces. I was such a natural shot, my father grudgingly decided to make me his hunting partner. I was handy carrying his pack too, I guess. I never complained and thought I might really be making some headway with my old man. It was certainly about time.

Then, one morning, the whole thing fell apart. He'd brought down a mallard, and the damn bird had fluttered halfway out into the swamp. My father was yelling and swearing at that dumb bird for being so inconsiderate. I thought this really gave me a chance to score with him. Maybe we could even become friends.

*So I just waded right out into the swamp—I was fifteen, so I was
already huge, and the mud and the bugs and the sticky swamp
grass didn't bother me one bit—and brought that stupid damn
duck back to him.*

*It didn't work out like I'd hoped. He laughed . . . and said that
was pretty neat, all right, and maybe I should rent myself out as
a retriever. "Harriet, my giant bird dog," he said, and laughed
some more.*

*That really hurt. I got so mad I damn near used my 30-30 on
him. It was the last time we ever went hunting together. When
he'd ask me, I'd just tell him to go buy a bird dog.*

Maybe I should have used my 30-30 on him, at that.

> *The Journal of Blossom House,
> Entry, page 20—Harriet Griggs*

It took Jennifer quite some time to cool off. She kept pacing
back and forth across her room—cell, really—swearing sometimes, crying others. Once, when she was down toward the
window end of the cell, she abruptly came face-to-face with the
photograph of Henry and grabbed it by its frame, intending to
throw it against the door and smash it into pieces. The thing
wouldn't budge. Jennifer yelled and swore at it. The damn
hideous portrait was screwed right into the wall. Screwed—just
like she was.

Furious, she looked around the room for something she could
use as a hammer and break the glass, so she could rip the picture
out of the frame. No luck; she discovered there was damn little in
the room that wasn't nailed down in some way. Even her little
easy chair was fixed to the floor.

Finally an idea hit her; she remembered the little chromium
stool in the bathroom, brought it in, and threw it as hard as she

could against the picture, screaming in anticipation like a possessed demon. Nothing happened. The glass was still intact. Son of a bitch, it was bulletproof, shatterproof glass of some kind, and you couldn't have broken it with a bazooka shell at point-blank range. Those bastards thought of everything. Instead, she broke the only thing she could find to smash: the mirror.

Spent, she lay down on the bed, so frustrated, she wasn't sure whether to cry or scream. Was this how Peter felt down the hall someplace in *his* cell? Maybe, right at this very moment, he was lying on *his* bed unsure whether to cry or scream. Jennifer wondered if his room had a picture of Henry in it, too. No his would probably be of Harriet. Signed "Mummy"? Jennifer wanted to laugh but was too bitter. Even in a house as crazy as this one, she doubted if a brother and sister would marry one another. About half an hour later—Jennifer could keep track of time by the large Mickey Mouse clock set into the wall opposite her bed—she suddenly heard something making a noise outside her room. Gently the panel was pulled back.

Harriet's face appeared, still smiling at first, but suddenly looking quite concerned. "Oh, dear. You've broken your mirror somehow. That's seven years bad luck, Olivia."

In spite of a lot of things she'd like to have said, Jennifer remained silent. She felt enough bad luck had already been squeezed into the last few days to take care of at *least* seven years.

"I have your dinner for you, Olivia. I'm going to open this door a little and hand it in to you. Please don't try anything foolish, Olivia; it's always a temptation, dear, but, really, you won't accomplish anything."

There were the sounds of heavy bolts being slid back, and the turning of a key in a lock. Jennifer had advanced to just inside the door, ready to act. The door swung open, and Harriet, carrying a tray, filled the doorway with her enormous bulk, killing Jennifer's plan to dash past her and race down the hall to—well, she didn't know exactly where. Instead, Jennifer meekly accepted the tray, and then, as Harriet began to back out, threw the whole thing directly in her face. Soup poured down the front of Harriet's dress—beet soup, making her look a bit as if she'd just been shot; gravy and potatoes covered her face; pieces of meat, flatware, and rolls ran down her on to the floor.

Somehow she managed to nurture a vestige of her smile, shaking her head sadly from side to side. "Olivia, dear. That was very impolite. If that sort of thing ever happens again, you will be severely disciplined. This once, I'll try to overlook it. Learning to be polite is part of growing up; so is learning to accept a thrashing when you've done something bad."

The smile had finally vanished. Jennifer's act had put too severe a strain on Harriet's patience to sustain it any longer. Staring angrily at Jennifer, and using her foot as a sort of scraper, Harriet got as much of the mess on the floor as she could out into the hall. She stared at the sloppy remnants, half-ground into the carpet. "I'll bring you a dustpan and mop later. Use them. For the moment, your punishment will be going without supper. Later on, you'll discover that my program of punishment is far more extreme. . . ."

The heavy steel door was slammed shut with a shattering *thunk;* a moment later Jennifer could hear the bolts slammed into place with a vengeance.

Jennifer stared vacantly at the inside of the steel door. Sent to bed without supper. Her mother had tried that a few times when she was much younger, but Ingebord had always come to her rescue with a smuggled sandwich and ice cream or something. At the time, she supposed her mother had been puzzled at how little Jennifer reacted when sentenced to starvation but, as far as Jennifer knew, had never figured out the Ingebord connection. In a rough way Jennifer's punishment fitted the rest of the picture: she was spoken to like a child, she was rewarded and punished like a child, and she lived in what appeared to be a child's room. Only this time, there was no loving Ingebord to smuggle in contrabrand food. Why wasn't Ingebord here to rescue her now— not just from starvation, but from Henry and Harriet? Why wasn't *somebody* here?

Outside her door, she once again heard preparatory noises—the bolts being slid back, the key turning in the lock, the door's outer handle rattling as it was unjammed. Finally the door itself swung open. Harriet, pulling the door shut behind her with a finality that shook Jennifer, no longer was making any pretense of smiling. Her face was grim, her mouth set, her eyes intense. In one hand she carried Jennifer's suitcase.

Jennifer's heart leaped. Could that mean they were giving her back her clothes and letting her go? Over Harriet's other arm was a towel, and Jennifer could see that her other hand held a small aluminum bowl, some unidentifiable objects, and a safety razor. That didn't seem at all like things she would be given before a sudden release. Jennifer's soaring hopes went down as fast as they had gone up

Harriet went into the bathroom, returning with the bowl full of steaming water. This, the towel, and the other objects were carefully placed on top of the desk. Spinning, she advanced toward Jennifer and threw her down on the bed with one great shove. Jennifer tried to protect herself, throwing her arms across her breasts, not sure of what Harriet had in mind but deathly afraid it was either going to hurt or make her sick.

"Lie still!" commanded Harriet, the first words she had spoken since returning to the room. With one hand she reached down and suddenly ripped the nightie off Jennifer.

"Please, please, Miss Griggs, please don't . . ." screamed Jennifer helplessly. She had no idea of what she was asking Harriet not to do, but knew that, whatever it was, it would probably hurt.

Harriet seemed almost to snarl at her, the look of grimness on her face becoming more intense. Jennifer tried to wriggle off the bed, but when she turned over to escape—across the room, at least—Harriet smacked her naked buttocks a resounding slap so powerful, Jennifer could feel the breath go out of her.

"Lie still, I said," Harriet yelled at her. "Now, then, child, turn over on your back. Stop that wiggling. Quick, now!"

Embarrassed, Jennifer was too slow for Harriet in turning

over. Jennifer felt her arm nearest Harriet yanked hard, and then her whole body flipped over in one savage twist.

"Here," said Harriet, handing her the safety razor and a brush already lathered with shaving soap. "I want you to shave yourself. Everywhere below the navel. Take off the pubic hair—everything."

Jennifer looked first at Harriet, then at her pubic hair, then back at Harriet again. This was insane. This wild, savage woman made no sense. Shave herself *there*? Unthinkable. "No," Jennifer said flatly. "I certainly won't." She flipped herself back onto her stomach. Exposing her bottom to Harriet's powerful hands was putting temptation in her path, but far to be desired over having her naked body searched further by those glaring, probing eyes.

From behind her, Jennifer heard an impatient, irritated sigh, the frustrated moan of a mother whose child has rebelled. The yank tore at her arm again, and she was manhandled on to her back. At the same moment, all of the breath in Jennifer's lungs suddenly left her; to hold her in place, Harriet sat down heavily on Jennifer's upper stomach, her back facing Jennifer's head. "You're a very bad girl, Olivia. I'm ashamed of you. Lie still now, or you might to get cut by the razor."

Helpless, Jennifer tried to scream, but Harriet's great weight made it impossible. She tried to flail at her with her arms, but they beat the air uselessly; each time she managed to hit Harriet's back, Harriet would lean back and, without turning around, grind her free hand hard into Jennifer's face and follow this by giving her a free-swinging slap across the cheeks that stung and burned and brought tears to Jennifer's eyes. Her nose felt torn half off her face by the grinding action of Harriet's vengeful hand, her ears rang and ached, her cheeks were on fire. Jennifer stopped trying to struggle; Harriet was too big for her to argue with anymore.

"That's better, child," Harriet commented, noting the sudden stillness that had overcome Jennifer. "Just do what you're told, and we'll get along fine. Learning to obey is part of growing up, too.''

In silence, Jennifer felt herself lathered. The shaving cream was cold to her skin, and water from it ran down between her legs, but outside of a few involuntary shudders, Jennifer remained completely still. She could feel the razor smoothly remove all of her pubic hair in long, careful strokes. The towel was used to dry her, then more shaving cream went on and she could feel Harriet shaving her even closer, following the path of the razor with the fingers of her other hand to be sure all traces of hair had been removed.

Abruptly Harriet stood up, throwing Jennifer the towel to dry herself with. As she did Jennifer's eyes could not escape the sudden hairlessness of her body; she hadn't looked like this since she was about ten or eleven. Peter would laugh like hell when he saw it. Oh, God, oh, God, she hoped he would see it soon.

Harriet stood over her, a pair of scissors in her hand. ''Over into the chair now. Be quick about it.'' A little nervously, Jennifer moved over into the little easy chair, her eyes studying the scissors—they were really more like shears than scissors—with foreboding. Once she was in the chair, Harriet moved behind her, and Jennifer heard the noisy clicking of the shears. Her hair was being cut.

Why? Why in God's name would Harriet suddenly turn barber? A terrible thought struck Jennifer. Harriet might be cutting her hair to make it short enough for the *shaving* of her head. Jesus. Peter might not laugh like hell at a sight like that—a wife with a head as naked as a nun's and no pubic hair. Christ. Jennifer twisted herself around to face Harriet. ''What are you doing?'' she screamed. ''Leave my hair alone. It doesn't need cutting; I just had it done last week. It doesn't—''

Jennifer suddenly found herself unable to move or speak. Harriet had grabbed her by the long muscles of the neck, and her fingers were gripping them so hard, Jennifer was effectively paralyzed. ''Stop asking so many questions, Olivia, and be still.

Your hair has to be cut the way Mr. Griggs wants it cut. Turn around.''

Wearily Jennifer turned her head to face forward, and Harriet continued snipping away with her scissors. The hair was left fairly long in the back, but short in front, making a sort of pageboy out of it. When she was finished, Harriet handed Jennifer a set of brightly colored ribbons. ''For your pigtails,'' she said, a faint smile reappearing for the first time this visit. ''You'll remember how to braid them after a while.''

Without resisting, without saying anything, Jennifer accepted the handful of ribbons, unsure if she remembered how to braid pigtails or not. She was stunned to realize how easily you could slip into the acceptance of improbable things when under deep stress; one acceptance led to another, and pretty soon you no longer questioned anything. For instance, her automatic question when told she would eventually remember how to make pigtails should have been ''Why the hell does anyone want me—a seventeen-year-old—to wear pigtails?'' Yet she had not asked Harriet the question; she hadn't even asked *herself* the question.

Jennifer stood motionless before Harriet, dressed only in a large towel that Harriet had draped around her just before turning into Vidal Sassoon. Jennifer was acting, she realized, strangely submissive. In her head, she tried to analyze this sudden lack of resistance and decided it was the product of exhaustion. And fear. And hopelessness. The conclusions were not her own. Peter had told her once—he was deep into Psych II at Princeton—how captors could make their prisoners' wills crumble by inflicting extended periods of these states: exhaustion and fear and hopelessness. Until, in a zombielike state, the broken POWs would do just about anything they were told to without complaint.

Peter. Had they cut Peter's hair so it was now a little boy's pageboy cut? Had they shaved off his pubic hair and dressed him in neatly pressed short trousers? Had Harriet put him across her knee and spanked him when he was disobedient?

The thought of Peter sent a stabbing pain through her again,

Peter, somewhere down the hall, suffering the same dreadful indignities as she, so close to her, yet separated by enough concrete so that he might as well be a million miles on the other side of the universe.

"I guess it's time for this, dear." There was a chilling note to Harriet's tone, as if even she were embarrassed by the next step in Jennifer's transformation. Jennifer looked at the strange thing she held in her hands, a mixture of canvas strapping, belts, leather fasteners, and small brass loops.

"What's that? What the hell is *that*?"

"Shhh, child. Nice little girls don't swear. As for this, you'll see in just a minute. Raise your arms, please."

"No."

"Olivia, raise your arms this instant. You're becoming willful and naughty again. You know how I handle that sort of behavior, child. Raise your arms."

"No. I won't. Not until you tell me what you're going to do to me."

The slap from the flat of Harriet's huge hand seemed to come from nowhere and sent Jennifer reeling into the far wall. One hand rose to the side of her face, already sore, but now on fire. "Don't talk back to me, Olivia. Come back here this minute and do as you're told." Meekly—the POWs were always meek, Peter had said—she walked back to stand again in front of Harriet. Harriet watched her progress, and the smile—the events of the last hour had virtually erased it, but now it was back, as insincere, she suspected, as ever—covered her face. "That's a good girl, Olivia. You're learning, dear." Harriet patted her on the shoulder, retrieving the odd canvas contraption from the chair a moment later.

It baffled Jennifer how Harriet—how anyone—could smile so incessantly and speak so endearingly while doing such terrible things to the people she was smiling at and speaking to. Is that what POW camp commanders did? She didn't know.

"Raise your arms, child," said Harriet gently. "And turn around."

Jennifer tried, but at first her arms refused to move. There was still too much stubbornness in her to surrender this completely. She could feel small, involuntary muscles in her arms and throughout her body quivering, wanting to make her arms move upward, but the will seemed to be clapping the arms to her side, motionless, defiant, disobedient.

From behind her, she heard Harriet's voice again, still speaking gently. "I know it's difficult, dear, I know you're afraid of what will happen. But I can promise you: nothing bad's going to happen. As long as you do exactly what I tell you to. Now, dear, please, if you'll kindly"—there was a pause, a silence punctuated only by the sound of Harriet's heavy breathing behind her, a silence shattered when Harriet completed her sentence suddenly, bellowing at her in a shattering voice—"RAISE YOUR ARMS!"

The sudden change in Harriet's voice made Jennifer jump, her heart beating wildly, thumping against her ribs, her mind abruptly blanking out, unable to think or reason or consider. With surprise, Jennifer discovered that her arms had shot upward as if they had minds of their own, straining toward the ceiling, shaking, the fingers pointed as if they were trying to reach up and touch it.

"Fine, Olivia dear, fine." Harriet reached from behind her and, slipping it over Jennifer's head, fastened a strange canvas band across her breasts and around behind her. Holding more of the canvas contraption in her hands, Harriet moved around her, pulling the band tighter as she went, continuing until the breasts were flattened completely. Twice, Jennifer started to protest, but found she was too spent to resist further. The POWs again— exhaustion and hopelessness and fear.

Harriet went back and got an additional item from the chair. It was another canvas band, but this one seemed shorter and had two small brass loops set into its ends. Moving around her again, Harriet put this new band on top of the others, with the two loops winding up somewhere close to her backbone. Jennifer heard a faint metallic click and knew the whole device had been locked in place on her; she had seen the small, flat padlock in Harriet's hand.

Involuntarily Jennifer's right hand rose to explore what had been her bosom. It was gone. She was as flat as a twelve-year-old. "You've got damn nice boobs, Jen," Peter had once told her, staring at them appreciatively and wearing an expression that said he would like to do a lot more than just look at them.

"That about does it for now. Don't try to get that device off, dear; you'll get it twisted and out of kilter, and that can hurt. I'll take it off whenever you want to take your bath."

Jennifer stared at her numbly. She could feel tears building behind her eyes as she thought about her breasts; Peter had loved them so. She wondered if they'd bound up any part of Peter. No, she decided. *That* was a part of Peter no contraption in the world could make smaller, thank God.

"Everything you need is in your suitcase, dear. You'll want to start putting things away and then think about putting on something especially pretty. Daddy will be coming to see you later, and you certainly don't want to be sitting here wrapped in a towel. I'll be back before then to help you, Olivia." Harriet smiled broadly at her, a look of satisfaction covering her face. "You see how much better things go when you do what grown-ups tell you to, dear? I think we'll get along just fine." She gave Jennifer another pat on the shoulder and, after unlocking the door on the inside, closed it gently, locking it again from the outside. The bolts ground their way into position; the sliding panel was softly closed. Jennifer was left alone.

Jennifer eyed the suitcase with suspicion. Her own clothes? Well, probably at least *some* of them. She dreaded to think what any new clothes would look like. But it was better than being naked, she supposed.

With Henry wandering around this crazy place, *anything* was.

CHAPTER ELEVEN

One thing I could never understand about my father was how devoted he was to Henry. My father was the original macho man, long before anyone was using the word. Positive, strong, domineering—a dyed-in-the-wool he-man.

For myself, I liked Henry, of course, but always knew he was a very weak person. I don't mean he was a sissy or effeminate or anything, he was just very quiet and submissive. Shy, too. And always crying.

Hell, he cried when he hurt himself, he cried when some kid at school pushed him around, he cried when his wife died, and he cried when each of his daughters corked off, too. Weak. I'm twice the man Henry ever thought of being, but my father didn't seem to give a damn about that.

Those tears of his. Henry used to raise rabbits in a fenced-in area of the yard. Until the Day of the Rabbits. I went in there with a heavy stick and started to kill the mother and each of the little baby rabbits, one after the other. Pretty messy, sure. And about halfway through, Henry turned up and started screaming at me to stop, but I wouldn't and told him it was pretty stupid, me going out in the woods and shooting rabbits while he stayed back home raising the damn things. Henry screamed and begged and pleaded and threw himself on the ground in front of them, but I just stepped over him and kept right on going. Henry didn't forgive me for weeks, and I have to admit I missed him.

My father heard about it and just looked at me kind of disgusted and went right on liking Henry and hating me. That doesn't make much sense, now, does it?

It's funny. I was thinking how much those wounded rabbits reminded me of Olivia when I sat on her chest to shave her. Big wet eyes when they feel pain, rabbits and Olivia.

I wonder, can rabbits cry?

> *Journal of Blossom House,*
> *Entry, page 21—Harriet Griggs*

For a long time Jennifer sat on the edge of her bed, staring. The wall opposite stared back, refusing conversation. This staring contest quickly became so unsettling that Jennifer began to fidget. Ordinarily she enjoyed being alone, thinking about things—recently, mostly Peter—fantasizing, dreaming, letting her imagination run as wild as it wanted to. In this terrible little cell, though, being alone, wrapped in an unnatural silence, was a crushing force—squeezing her, compressing her, strangling her.

Not that she wanted Harriet to show up again. With Harriet, you didn't have conversations, you had listening sessions. Orders to be remembered. Observations on the wickedness of little girls to be absorbed. Homilies pronounced on the benefits of obeying what grown-ups said. For Christ's sake, didn't Harriet realize *she* was grown-up? A violent and sadistic woman, Harriet, her brain swimming with wild intentions and sick objectives. Only, unlike most insane women, Harriet was able to put hers into action. Jennifer shuddered and pulled the towel closer around herself.

She couldn't resist, after sitting there a few moments more, trying to get the damn canvas binding off her breasts. Harriet had been right; all she accomplished was to twist the thing a little at the top and make it bite into her flesh. It took several minutes of hard struggle to get the band back where it had been. The pain lasted even longer.

Jennifer also couldn't resist taking another look at her shaved body. In spite of her awareness of what had been done—and the one look she'd taken earlier—the sight came as a shock. The thought of a connection between the bound breasts, the shaved body, and the kind of room she was in passed across her mind, but Jennifer dismissed it—as much from not wanting to accept it as from logic. Instead, she went back to asking herself *why* Harriet was doing these things to her, *why* she was here, and where Peter was.

With a sigh, unwilling to pursue her questions further, Jennifer looked at her suitcase and decided it was time to get something on. Maybe her beige Chanel. Henry, Harriet had mentioned, was going to pay her a visit, and she sure as hell wanted more protection than a towel for that encounter. Those eyes of his; from the moment she'd arrived here, the eyes had devoured her hungrily. Just like her father's.

Here lay the secret of getting out of this place: She'd play up to Henry, flatter him, make much of him. That would put her in a position of being able to manipulate him, much as she had her father. Even without entirely meaning to, eventually Henry would provide her with the means of escape from Blossom House. Jennifer felt suddenly better, back in an area that came to her naturally—the manipulation of people. Henry was by nature much nicer than Harriet, and Jennifer felt she could swallow her pride enough to make her act convincing.

Quickly she got her suitcase and put it on the bed. If not the beige Chanel, perhaps the pale blue Bill Blass copy. The locks on the suitcase made a loud report when she pressed them. Confidently she threw open the suitcase. She wanted to scream; her breathing stopped.

Not a thing of hers was to be seen inside. She became frantic, throwing the strange clothes she discovered on to the bed, burrowing below to find *something*, at least, of her own. Nothing. Even her traveling reserve of cold creams, night creams, perfumes, and lipsticks was gone. Jennifer stared at what had been put in their place and almost cried. There were four or five little dresses, short, colorful, and starched. There were similarly starched petticoats and dirndls. She also discovered little nighties with benign sleeping animals stitched around their hems; plain white underwear without lace, without style, without anything except the memory of what Jennifer had worn as a child. Everything inside the suitcase, in fact, was what a twelve-year-old might wear—or at least what a twelve-year-old might have worn forty or fifty years ago. There were even two pairs of Mary Janes— black patent-leather shoes—and the long white stockings that traditionally went with them.

At first Jennifer could not believe what she saw. A few minutes later she did believe it, but had turned furious. She wouldn't wear this kind of kiddy crap. She'd stand there in her damn towel and flatly refuse to change into her new clothes, as Harriet had suggested. But then she remembered that Henry would be paying her a visit and that the towel was damn little protection from him. A few seconds after that Jennifer remembered that these were the kinds of clothes Henry was supposed to like, and that pleasing Henry to get him into the right frame of mind might very well be her only way out of this crazy place.

Disgusted, Jennifer held up each dress in front of her in the remains of her mirror, as if it were a Dior original. Each one was more dreadful than the last. Finally Jennifer picked one that seemed a smidgen less offensive and put it on. It was a pale blue dress, falling from her shoulders to above her knees in a completely straight line, a design that pretended her waist didn't exist. Alice in *Through the Looking Glass* would have found the dress faintly familiar. Around the white, starched collar was an elaborate design of crocheted figures from *The Water-babies*, done in pinks and yellows and reds to complement the blue of the dress. Clearly the dress represented a lot of work. The kind of work that seemed out of character for Harriet.

Almost the moment she had finished getting dressed, she heard the door being opened again. The timing was too neat. Had Harriet been watching through the peephole, waiting for the right moment to make her entrance? Jennifer boiled over but managed to bring herself under control. To manipulate Henry effectively, she had to try her damndest not to get Harriet working against her; it was the same philosophy she had had to resort to with her own mother, trying to avoid open arguments with her so that she could control her father more efficiently.

"My," said Harriet, back wearing her full motherly smile, "that dress looks almost as if it were made for you, dear." She didn't add that it *had* been; you have to ration the shocks you feed people, or they begin to lose their effectiveness.

"It's very—pretty," Jennifer said, faltering a little as she always did when she considered a lie too transparent.

Harriet's eyes moved past her to the bed. "But you must put your things away, child. Mr. Griggs is very particular about neatness, you know. And we do want to keep Mr. Griggs happy, don't we?"

Jennifer nodded, smiling to herself. Yes, she did want to keep Henry Griggs happy; he was her key to getting out. "I'm sorry, Miss Griggs," Jennifer said abjectly.

"That's all right, dear. Children always forget things like that." She walked around Jennifer again, muttering little sounds of approval. Suddenly she stopped, standing directly in front of her, smiling widely. Jennifer tensed. She wasn't sure which Harriet frightened her more—the frowning, wild-eyed Harriet who screamed at her, slapped her, and knocked her down, or the smiling Harriet, full of gentle words laced with terrifying implications. Jennifer decided that, while neither could be trusted, the smiling Harriet was the worst. No width of smile could hide the malevolent intent of the woman, and the malevolence was all the more sinister for being hidden behind a mask of pleasantness. "Is something wrong, Miss Griggs?'' she asked anxiously, upset by Harriet's staring at her so long.

"No, no, dear. But your hair. Can I help you with the ribbons?''

"The ribbons . . .'' Jennifer repeated vaguely before she remembered the handful Harriet had given her to make pigtails out of. "Oh, thank you very much, Miss Griggs, but I'm sure I can handle them myself.'' Jennifer hated herself for being so pleasant, but it was a necessary, if degrading, part of getting Henry Griggs into position to be manipulated. She didn't realize that each time she *was* pleasant, Harriet became more suspicious. That girl was up to something, Harriet told herself; the key question was *what*.

"All right, dear. If you're sure you can,'' Harriet said cheerfully. "Daddy will want to see you wearing them when he comes by, which should be any minute now.''

"I'm sure.''

"Good.'' Harriet paused, then looked at Jennifer again with an expression of warm intensity. "Now, when Daddy comes, child, remember to be especially polite. Your best party manners. Daddy is very particular about things like that.''

"I understand. Of course.''

"And when you're talking to him remember that your name is Olivia Griggs and that you're twelve years old and that he's your daddy.'' Harriet was neither the smiling nor the screaming Harriet for the moment; her face was filled with hopeful earnestness, desperately concerned that Jennifer perform as she was supposed to in front of her brother. "You can call him Daddy if you want; he would love that.''

Inside, Jennifer could feel herself begin to boil. She was damned if she was going to call Henry Griggs Daddy; she was damned if she was going to pretend that her name was Olivia; or that she was only, for Christ's sake, twelve years old. She decided that even manipulation had its limits as to what someone could be expected to do to achieve it. "Yes, Miss Griggs,'' Jennifer said in a small voice.

The latent rebellion against her instructions, while supposedly hidden, had not escaped notice by Harriet. She could see it in Jennifer's face. Harriet took a deep breath and reemphasized Jennifer's marching orders. "Your name is Olivia Griggs, you're twelve years old, and your daddy is coming to see you in a few minutes. You will be very polite, but not standoffish. He may ask you questions, or he may not. But I want you to understand, Olivia, if you vary the slightest bit from what I've told you, if you don't choose to act and say as I have instructed you to, you will be severely punished. Severely—and painfully. Good little children do as they're told."

Jennifer thought of saying something but did not dare speak; she was too filled with fury—a little of it directed at herself for having been so compliant, even though it was necessary. Her intended maneuver suddenly appeared weak and almost certainly doomed; Henry, in his own way, was probably just as demented as his sister. And just as dangerous. Walking across the room, she picked up the brightly colored ribbons and turned to look at Harriet with an expression calculated to tell her that the making of the pigtails was something she wanted to do only when no one was there to watch her struggle.

"Fine, dear, fine," Harriet said heartily. Her eyes fell on the bed. "Those clothes, dear. Do be sure to put them away before your daddy gets here."

Jennifer nodded and listened to Harriet go out the door, followed by the grinding and slamming of the bolts. Listlessly she struggled with the ribbons. You really needed longer hair than hers to make them come out well, but she was able to fashion rudimentary pigtails. Checking herself in the bathroom mirror, Jennifer decided she looked like a tomboy forced into a little girl's clothes for some special occasion; all she needed were red hair and freckles to complete the picture. Her eyes returned to the bed and the messy suitcase full of her new clothes; it should be taken care of—Harriet herself had mentioned it—but Jennifer couldn't face the idea of hanging those dreadful dresses in her closet and putting those terrible nighties, underwear, and stockings in the little bureau. It would be too final a gesture, an acceptance of her status here. She didn't want to give in to the fact that she was a prisoner in Blossom House for— For how long? Jennifer wondered. She didn't know. Christ, it could be forever. No, things like that didn't happen to people like her, not in this day and age, not ever. Even POWs got out eventually. And if she could work on Henry effectively enough, maybe not really too long at all. Or, hell, at any time Peter could turn up, looking ridiculous in a pageboy haircut and neat short trousers, but acting strong and assertive and efficient as only Peter could. That would make her sentence even shorter. Oh, God, where was Peter, anyway? Where did they have *him* locked up?

Behind her, Jennifer suddenly heard the bolts being slid back once more. Jennifer turned. Framed in the door stood Henry Griggs, smiling warmly. Again the timing seemed too neat: pigtails in place, Henry in her doorway. The peephole was a very effective spy.

Henry advanced into the room, softly closing the door behind him. "Just came in to kiss my little Olivia good night," he said with a saccharine smile. Jennifer would have liked to have thrown up; nausea is never around when you need it. "My, but you look pretty."

Jennifer found herself unable to speak. She might throw up yet. This man was going to be very difficult to play up to; he was too concerned with playing up to *her*.

"Pretty little dress, pretty little bows, pretty little girl. Wonderful, pretty little Olivia." A bell rang in Jennifer's head. She didn't have to play up to him; she *had* him. Without saying a word, she had him. Jennifer could tell by the smoldering glow in his eyes, the almost pleading sound in his voice. The most she did was allow a winsome smile to flicker briefly across her lips. Henry stood in front of her awkwardly, shifting his weight from one foot to the other. "I can remember, Olivia, when you were still very little, how you used to play choo-choo with me. Remember? You'd sit on my lap, and I'd make noises like an engine and then blow the whistle, and when we got to a station,

I'd all of a sudden open my knees, and you'd go sliding down my legs to the floor. Oh, my, Olivia, sometimes you'd laugh so hard, you'd wet your pants. Just laughing and laughing and laughing . . ." To Jennifer, Henry's suddenly misty eyes seemed to be disappearing into his head, lost in a private reverie of some other time with some other little girl. The man was mad. The realization of this made Jennifer increasingly fearful; there was no way of guessing what he might do next. In his own way, he was just as frightening as Harriet. "Would you like to sit on my lap *now*, Olivia?" Henry asked suddenly, his eyes fastening on her with some inner urgency.

Desperately Jennifer tried to think of something that would avoid answering this sad, but frightening old man's question. She was suddenly bathed in fear, thinking of what Henry could do. Through her mind ran those dreadful moments in her bedroom in the middle of the night, when Henry had sneaked in to "get some things out of the closet." It had scared her half to death then; now the recollection had come back uninvited, like the instant replay in a baseball game. Only Jennifer knew that Henry wasn't after the pennant, he was after *her*.

The small muscles beneath her skin began to quiver; she was aware of an involuntary twitching of her hands; she could feel an uncomfortable sweat collecting under the damn canvas bands flattening her breasts. Henry continued to stare at her with his incandescent eyes, the unanswered question still on his face. Divert, divert, divert! Jennifer could hear her brain screaming at her.

"Please, could you read me a bedtime story? *Please?*" she asked suddenly, going over to the bookcase and grabbing the first book she could fasten her shaking hands on. She brought the volume over to Henry and retreated quickly to the edge of her bed.

"The *Uncle Remus* stories," Henry noted. "Good book. Written back when you were still allowed to catch niggers instead of tigers by the toes." He ruffled through the pages, looking for one he liked. "Ah, here we are," he announced, looking up at

Jennifer. His eyes clouded again. "Don't you want to sit on my lap *now*, Olivia?"

Jennifer struggled not to let her dread become obvious. "Well, it's so comfortable there, I always fall asleep and don't get to hear the story."

A look of displeasure came into his face. He slapped the book shut with a frightening finality and stood up, frowning. "Very well, Olivia. No story. Some little girls don't deserve them." He looked around the cell, suddenly seeing the suitcase on the bed beside Jennifer and the mass of clothes sticking out of it. He was apparently determined to mask his irritation, abruptly turning his frown into a smile and pointing at the mess. "Daddy's shocked," he said with a strained little laugh. "You're terrible to be so messy, Olivia. Promise me that you'll put all those clothes and things away the moment I leave?"

"Yes," Jennifer answered. She knew the correct answer to please Henry and sew up her control of him would have been "Yes, Daddy," but she couldn't bring herself to that. "And I'm sorry I made you angry," she added; contrition was always a useful ally in the manipulation process.

She could see Henry melt. "You didn't, Olivia. I don't know where you got such a silly idea. You know how much your daddy loves you. Now it's time—past time, really—that you gave Daddy a big hug and a kiss, got into your nightie, and scooted into bed."

Jennifer began to tremble again; for some reason this idea was more unsettling than his last. She grabbed for another diversionary tactic, one she also hoped would answer the question that had been boring into her brain for days. "Can I ask you a question before I do?"

"You can always ask Daddy a question, Olivia. You know that."

Jennifer stared him right in the eye. "Peter. Where's Peter? Is he all right?"

Henry Griggs stared at Jennifer blankly. "Peter? I don't know any Peter. Is he a little playmate of yours from up the street somewhere?''

"Peter *Owen*. You know him. You mar—''

"You have so many friends, Olivia, sometimes I just can't remember them all. So no, I don't know where Peter is, because I don't know a little boy named Peter.''

Jennifer panicked. Henry's contention that he didn't know Peter had thrown her into a complete state of shock. She didn't know whether he really believed what he'd said or whether his comments were contrived. The effect was the same anyway. Henry's reaction made Peter seem suddenly intangible even to her. A sudden coldness crept up her body and settled in her stomach.

Henry shook his head, still wearing his benign stare and studying the lost expression on Jennifer's face with concern. "I'm afraid when you're my age, Olivia, all children look very much alike. Except my little Olivia, of course.'' Henry glanced at his watch. "Look at the time! Nightie, kiss, and into bed. Quickly, now!''

Jennifer had a horrible thought. Was Henry planning to stay in the room while she changed into her nightie? To forestall any possibility of this, she ran over, pecked Henry on the forehead—about as affectionately as you would kiss a python—and, forcing a giggle, grabbed her nightie and raced into the bathroom. Through the door, she could hear Henry calling good night to her, muttering a succession of "sleep wells" and "good dreams" and "don't forget your prayers,'' until his voice finally faded away, and she heard the bolts slam home.

Later, in bed, Jennifer was unable to sleep. She was still trembling; her few moments with Henry had so filled her with dread, she could not easily calm herself. A short time later the lights turned themselves out, apparently on the command of a master switch somewhere. Only a dim night-light remained, burning just outside the bathroom door. Because there was a bright moon, though, once her eyes accustomed themselves to the darkness, she found she could see quite clearly.

For about twenty minutes after her lights went out, a hidden speaker began playing softly, opening its peculiar program with the "Parade of the Wooden Soldiers," and becoming progressively softer and more restful, winding down to a choral arrangement of "Now I Lay Me Down to Sleep," and ending with a distant-sounding Brahms lullaby. All of this, Jennifer found herself thinking, seemed a very elaborate arrangement for three—she assumed it was three—Peter, the little girl she had seen, and herself—prisoners, even in an insane place like Blossom House.

Lying in the dark, dressed in a long white nightie trimmed with eyelet lace, she began torturing herself, wondering if Peter's lights had just been turned off, too. Or, because he was a boy, did he get to stay up a few minutes longer?

Suddenly Jennifer sat up in bed. In the dim moonlight she could see her open suitcase lying on the floor where she'd put it when she climbed into bed. Henry's orders—Harriet had given her the same caveats a little earlier—abruptly come back to her. Quickly she climbed out of bed and unpacked the suitcase, hanging up her dresses in the closet, and putting the other things in the dresser drawers. Feeling better, she slipped back into bed.

The second she lay down she caught herself feeling surprised. Harriet had said "Good little girls do what grown-ups tell them to." And Christ, that was exactly what she was doing: what the grown-ups told her to. She was already beginning to *think* like a twelve-year-old, a realization that stunned her.

Had this happened to Peter, too? Peter, oh, Peter. Hell, why hadn't he broken out of his cell yet? With an ingenious mind like his, that kind of escape should be a cinch. And why, at least, haven't they let her see him? They must have known she'd never buy a story like Henry's—that he'd never heard of a friend of hers named Peter. For Christ's sake, he'd *married* them, right here in this dreadful house.

She dug her fingernails into the mattress to force a feeling of concreteness back into her mind. She knew, she was sure, she was absolutely positive, that it was only a matter of time before Peter showed up—laughing, teasing, being sexy—to save her.

Even as she tried to convince herself, an ominous thread of doubt kept crossing her mind, a dark cloud that kept making her wonder if she would really ever see Peter again. Of course I will, damn it, of course.

Sailors are always respectful of dark clouds. It might have been better if Jennifer had been, too.

CHAPTER TWELVE

It beats me why boys are all so rotten—genetic?—that they've only got one thing on their minds: sticking it into some girl. I guess it is genetic. I never met a boy who thought about much else— Christ, they start having erections when they're only six months old.

Well, I suppose I have to be fair. There was one boy at high school who seemed to be different. Oppie Mannerheim. We saw a lot of each other. See, Oppie was just crazy about music and my piano-playing; unlike those other jerks, he went for stuff like Brahms and Beethoven and Mozart. The rest had musical tastes that didn't run any deeper than "I'll Never Smile Again" or "Juke Box Saturday Night."

He wasn't much to look at: runty, bad eyes and big glasses, and the kind of complexion that looked like it should be pimply. I guess, in a way, I kind of loved him, and I know he loved me back, too. But the furthest we ever went was to hold hands. Sometimes I wondered if maybe there wasn't something a little sissy about him.

The kids at school really went to town about Oppie and me. We did make a funny picture, I guess—me so damn big, him so damn small. The boys would hoot at us in the hall, making

*leering little cracks about him, like how did he like being smoth-
ered under Ape-Lady. He used to get mad when they said things
like that about me and get into a lot of fights, which he always
lost. That really made me like him.*

*Those conceited pretty-boy jocks finally wrecked the thing, though.
They got hold of Oppie one day and beat him up, took off all his
clothes, and painted his balls with red nail polish. That hurt so
much he screamed like crazy. Then, still naked and part red, they
shoved him into the nurse's office.*

*The story was all over school by afternoon, and Oppie couldn't
take it anymore. Somehow he made up with the guys; pretty
soon, Oppie, who didn't have a mean bone in him, was calling me
Ape-Lady and making fun of me like all the rest of those bastards.*

I wish someday Oppie would turn up at Blossom House.

> *Journal of Blossom House,
> Entry, page 25—Harriet Griggs*

The dark clouds of doubt that scudded across Jennifer's mind
were something Peter Owen could have told her all about. He
was under the darkest cloud of all. And had been ever since the
first night they spent at Blossom House.

It began with the drugged champagne he was given. His was a
powerful intoxicant and tranquilizer, but one chosen because its
effects were relatively short-lived. In combination with alcohol,
his system would be free of it at about three in the morning. An
estimate, of course, but a highly reliable one.

On the other hand, the sedation Jennifer was given after dinner
was slow-acting and longer-lived; it was estimated that hers
would wear off at about six in the morning, leaving her with
nothing more serious than a drug hangover and a case of badly
torn-up nerves.

All of this pharmacological expertise had been provided by Cousin Larry, the Griggses' relative who was responsible for Blossom House's third floor. At one point two years before, casting around for a steadier way to make a living, Cousin Larry had gotten about halfway through pharmacological school before abandoning it. Since his other ventures included narcotics sales, he had a ready source of raw materials to practice this sophisticated trade. The Griggses had told him the affects they wanted from their drugs; Cousin Larry had cheerfully provided them—for a fee that made Harriet's eyes bulge in disbelief.

The result of the drug program Cousin Larry provided was that just about the time Peter was coming out from under *his* dosage, Jennifer would be slipping into hers. Like trains thundering through the night, they would hurtle at each other from opposite directions but on different tracks, one going into and one coming out of a deeply drugged state. The drugs worked as scheduled; they always did. Cousin Larry might be expensive, but he was good.

"Peter, Peter, wake up. Wake up, Peter."

Peter Owen already had been stirring restlessly in his sleep, but the sound of Henry Griggs's voice was fuzzy, shouting at him as if from a great distance. Peter shook his head, resisting the sound. It was a dream, he told himself. More of that crazy dream he seemed to have been having for hours. He tried turning himself back into his pillow, but the grip of someone's hand on his shoulder, shaking him, made reality impossible to avoid; perhaps that distant voice was not part of a dream, after all. "Peter, can't you hear me, Peter? Come on, Peter, I'm sorry, but you have to wake up."

Tentatively Peter opened his eyes. He looked over at Jennifer; she still appeared to be in a deep sleep, undisturbed, apparently, by the voice that tortured him or the hand that shook him. He turned to his other side and saw Henry standing over him, one hand still on his shoulder. Griggs was wearing pajamas and a bathrobe and kept looking at Peter with a strange intensity. If Henry Griggs was still in his pajamas, Peter asked himself, why the hell was there such a fuss about his getting up? At the bottom of the bed, he saw the window still black with night. "What the hell?" he muttered, looking up at Henry Griggs.

"Sorry to wake you like this, Peter, but there's an urgent call for you. Downstairs. What a time for someone to call."

"There's been a mistake, Mr. Griggs," Peter said, beginning to pull himself together rapidly. He was suddenly conscious that he was not wearing his pajamas, but was dressed only in his shorts. Odd. But then, he couldn't remember very much about going to bed at all; last night was a blur. He frowned at Henry Griggs's information and shook his head. "There *couldn't* be a call for us. Nobody knows we're here."

"Somebody does. They said they absolutely had to speak to you right away." Griggs referred to a scrap of paper in his hand and looked down again at Peter. "Somebody named Hillary Crane, she said."

Peter swore to himself. Hillary. Under pressure, Jennifer had promised she wouldn't tell anyone, but Peter had guessed she'd wind up telling Hillary, anyway. Women were like that. But how the hell had Hillary tracked them down to Blossom House? Neither she nor Jennifer had known of the place themselves until they arrived. Another possible way of salvaging his sleep came to Peter. "She doesn't want to talk to me, she wants to talk to Jennifer. Hillary is *Jen's* friend."

"No, she specifically asked for *you,* Peter, and said please not to let Jennifer know she was calling. You can take it downstairs. . . ."

"Goddamn." Peter looked over at Jennifer and, in spite of Griggs's message, shook her anyway. With an old man like him, you can't expect messages to arrive intact.

"She said she specifically wanted to speak to you, Peter, not Jennifer," insisted Mr. Griggs, a touch of petulance creeping into his voice.

Shaking his head, part in anger, part in confusion, Peter Owen tried rocking Jennifer back and forth again. Hillary was *her* friend and she could damn well go talk to her. Jennifer sighed in her sleep but didn't wake up; her breathing remained untroubled and steady.

Henry Griggs stared at Peter. "The call . . . it's downstairs, Peter. . . . Are you going to take it, or do you want me to tell her Jennifer will call her back? To me, she sounded very upset, but then, of course, I don't know the girl."

Henry Griggs knew more about Hillary Crane than he was letting Peter know. Harriet and he had found Hillary's name in Jennifer's address book, underlined several times, with affectionate little footnotes about Hillary. From this, it was not hard to see how close Jennifer and Hillary were. The perfect person, Harriet had said, to interrupt Peter's sleep; the drug would make Jennifer impossible to waken, and Peter, whether he wanted to or not, would have to go downstairs and take the call. It had worked.

"Shit," Peter grunted, fumbling around the room. "Is Miss Griggs up, too? What I mean is, do I need a bathrobe? I can't seem to find the damn thing."

"No, she's still asleep. Everybody in the world is still asleep—except you and me and this very agitated Hillary Crane person. You won't need a bathrobe."

From Peter came another chain of oaths and curses. Where had Jennifer put his bathrobe? Harriet wasn't a problem, apparently, but he wasn't too fond of wandering around a stranger's house wearing only his shorts. Were they clean? Yes, clean the previous morning, he remembered.

With a defeated shrug, Peter threw his hands in the air and followed Henry Griggs down the stairs into the still-dark front hall. The house had a feeling of hostility that Peter could feel; he shivered slightly, although some of his shivers and shudderings, he decided, could have come from walking around in only his shorts, leaving so much bare skin exposed to the early-morning chill.

At the bottom of the stairs, Henry turned to the left and walked quickly down a long service hall that ran past the kitchen. "In here," said Griggs, and pointed through a doorway to a small room on the right. "I'm afraid some of our phones are in very inconvenient places."

Looking around, Peter was struck at what a curious room they were in. The only furniture appeared to be a low, flat-ended couch—the kind you might find in an old-fashioned country doctor's examining room. The floor had no rug of any kind and was cold against the soles of his feet. Covered with some kind of polyurethane tile, he decided, and shivered again.

Across the room and to one side, he saw the phone, sitting on a low plain table of unfinished wood; the phone was a bright yellow Trimline, and looked out of place in this dreary, empty room.

"Right over there," Henry Griggs said unnecessarily. There was a sudden coldness in his voice, which matched the coldness of the polyurethane; Henry was standing in the doorway with his arms folded across his chest, wearing a suddenly grim expression.

It was then that Peter saw it. The phone had a long wire, but when he'd picked up the receiver, he'd picked up the phone itself as well. With such a low table, he had had to. But the long wire went nowhere; he could see its end lying on the floor, torn and ragged, as if it had been yanked out of the wall.

Peter spun around to face Henry, a sense of dread that he couldn't explain sweeping through him. As he did he was vaguely aware of a sudden shadow moving behind him. Before he could put this into perspective, his body was seized from behind and he was thrown down on the couch by the weight of a body that had come out of nowhere. He found himself looking up at Harriet Griggs, a grim smile of satisfaction on her giant face. Henry Griggs moved over to the couch, a strange assortment of ropes in his hands.

"What—" Peter began.

Harriet Griggs slapped him across the mouth. "Shut up," she hissed. "Your days of pushing girls around are over. Now *you're* going to be pushed around." Peter struggled, but her weight was taking his breath away. As he struggled and thrashed to wriggle out from under her, she moved up and sat on his chest, almost smothering him with the force of her knees against his chest and diaphragm. She turned to one side. "Did you bring the slip ropes, Henry? Damn it, did you? You're always forgetting things."

"They're right here, Harriet. I brought them."

"One around his wrists, one around his ankles. Be quick about it, Henry."

Henry Griggs moved to Peter's head, and with Harriet's help, stretched his arms up over his head. A moment later Henry Griggs slipped a small noose over Peter's wrists and tightened it until Peter yelped in pain. Briefly, Griggs disappeared, and Peter felt the same process being repeated with his ankles. What the goddamn mother-fucking hell were these crazy people doing? Maybe it was a joke, only it wasn't a very funny joke. And that telephone connected to nowhere had a chilling feeling of premeditation to it. Still struggling, Peter again tried to speak. "I don't understand. Please, I—" he gasped.

"Shut up," repeated Harriet Griggs, and again slapped him hard across the face. Peter shut up. When Harriet Griggs slapped, the blow shook your head as if you'd just been hit by a hard-pitched baseball. Peter could feel blood running from his lip where her huge hand had connected with his mouth.

Once he was tied up, Harriet climbed off him. For a second she disappeared from his view. A second later he felt her hand slide under the waist of his shorts, followed by a ripping sound as she tore them in two down the front. She tried to pull them out from under him, but Peter resisted, automatically pressing down on the couch with his bottom.

"Raise your damn ass," yelled Harriet, and moved up toward him, the hand raised to strike. Peter raised his ass. Harriet Griggs pulled the ripped shorts out from under him with a jerk.

Peter began struggling again. There was something ridiculous and—at the same time—fearsome about lying buck naked in front of this Amazon.

Looking down, Peter felt a sinking coldness in his stomach. He saw Harriet Griggs staring at his genitals with a savage look, a strange twisted half-smile on her face. He couldn't shake the sensation that there was something lustful in her expression, and felt his balls shrivel at the horror of it.

"I don't know why that Jennifer girl is so riled up about you," Harriet said, and laughed unkindly. "Hell, I've seen better equipped six-year-olds." Harriet Griggs gave a mean, snarling laugh, joined by her brother, who appeared to find what she'd said terribly witty.

Peter knew he had to do something. The Griggses were absolutely, completely mad. While they were enjoying their insane joke, Peter suddenly swung his feet over the edge of the couch, hoping to be able to hop down the hall and yell for help. Or go out a window. Or maybe make enough noise to finally wake Jennifer. Or something—*anything*—to get away from this savage pair of terrifying lunatics.

The Griggses' laughter died quickly. Peter had only managed to hop halfway across the room before Harriet had seized him from behind and hurled him, facedown, onto the couch again. Peter twisted over onto his back and began thrashing to free himself from her grip, but Harriet put an end to this by landing on top of him, kneeling, her knees digging painfully into his chest. To make it more painful, she began bouncing up and down on him. Peter began to gasp and choke; the air was squeezed out of him and he couldn't breathe.

Harriet Griggs seemed to find this even funnier than her joke. Almost reluctantly she climbed off his chest so that Peter could begin breathing again. "Stupid," she said acidly. "A very stupid thing to try, young Mr. Owen. Around here, people who try stupid things are ordinarily punished. Although, in your case, you're due to be punished in the ultimate fashion anyway, so I can't think of anything else to be done beyond what's already planned." She stood, grinning, one finger raising to point at Peter's groin. "As for that little thing of yours, you shouldn't be embarrassed by my staring. Believe me, I wouldn't touch it for the world. That's all you damn young bastards want, anyway. For you, *Petey*"—she rolled his nickname around with relish, savoring it as you might a rare wine—"as for you, Petey, no more, no more. Today you get what you deserve. What all you fancy-pants, too-damn-attractive-for-your-own-good boys deserve. . . ."

A new wave of fear broke over Peter. Harriet Griggs couldn't mean?— Christ, that crazy damn bitch *could*. Henry too. They could do anything they wanted with him—slit his throat, shoot him, strangle him slowly. Harriet would like *that*. "Please," Peter repeated—still having trouble getting his lungs working after Harriet Griggs had kneeled on him—"Please. I've never done anything to you. Why are you doing this to me, for Christ's sake? I haven't harmed you, I haven't taken anything of yours, I haven't—"

The open hand of Harriet Griggs smashed across Peter's face again. This time it was so hard, for a second Peter couldn't see. Slowly his eyes refocused, although there seemed to be a grayish fringe running around everything in the room. "You don't learn fast, do you?" Harriet muttered. "When I say shut up I mean shut up until I tell you to speak."

Peter realized his mouth was full of blood and wondered if her blow had knocked out one of his teeth. Christ, he hoped not a front one. Hockey players at Princeton were always losing theirs and walking around looking like East European farmhands. His flight into pointless thinking about minor matters came to an abrupt end, and the dread rose in him once more. After being told something by his sister, Henry Griggs had opened a closet door and reemerged, carrying a low flat stool with some sort of blue metal square fastened to it. The low, square thing had a familiar look to Peter, but from where he lay, he couldn't figure out what it was. He was sure, however, that whatever it was, it was going to hurt.

The stool was placed in the middle of the floor. From a drawer in the plain wooden table, Henry Griggs produced another slip rope. Standing on the stool, he fastened one end of the rope to a large metal ring protruding from the ceiling; the other end—the end with the slip knot and the oval of rope—was allowed to hang down. Peter found he was being measured by Harriet, who held a tapemeasure and counted off the inches from his chin to his toes.

"Fifty-eight, fifty-nine, fifty-nine and a half. That should be about right, Henry. If it isn't, we can make up the difference at the top end."

"You forgot to allow for the stool and the plate," Henry noted.

Harriet Griggs flushed. "I didn't forget," she corrected him, angrily. "I was going to subtract it from the total. Fifty-nine and a half inches minus twenty-four. That makes thirty-five and a half inches, damn it."

"You forgot, Harriet," said Henry gleefully, adjusting the length of the loop of rope from the strange blue metal object's top. When he'd completed that he began moving the slip knot up and down the end of the rope, fiddling with it until it moved easily. Peter's heart stopped. Suddenly it was all very clear. The loop and the slip knot formed a noose; he was to stand on the low stool until they chose to kick it out from under him. They were going to hang him. Jesus Christ.

Peter's dread of Harriet's hand shrank before this new fear. "Listen," he screamed. "I can pay you. My family. They'll pay you not to hang me. I swear they will . . . they'll pay you anything . . . they have the money, I promise you, I swear to you, they'll pay. . . ."

A broad smile settled on Harriet Griggs's mouth. "Why, Peter Owen, you don't think we'd hang *you*, do you? Such a nice, handsome, sensual boy. Hang *you*? Don't be silly, Peter. You're going to hang *yourself*. . . ."

Peter began screaming, thrashing on the couch, throwing himself first to one side and then the other, wriggling, heaving, throwing his body in the air in a futile struggle to fight the inexorable.

Harriet Griggs picked him up as if he were a baby and planted him on the stool, which felt strangely cold to his bare feet. Henry adjusted the noose, allowing it to fall from the back of his neck.

"Why? Why? Why?" screamed Peter, his stomach still heaving from his struggle on the couch. "Why *me*? I've never done anything to you, I swear it." Even on the stool, Peter's body kept on twisting and thrashing violently. Twice, Henry Griggs had to reach up and steady him, or he would have fallen off.

"Not *done* anything?" asked Harriet sarcastically. "All young boys like you do terrible things to girls. We can't kill all of you, so you'll just have to do."

"Running off with innocent young girls," Henry threw in quietly. "Defiling their sweet, pure bodies, ruining them, sometimes even killing them. I had a daughter—"

Harriet cut him off. "Being cruel to a girl if she isn't one of those tiny little creatures with big, helpless eyes. Being cruel if she's a little bit bigger than the rest. It doesn't matter what kind of mind she has or anything else," Harriet added savagely. "You're all a bunch of cruel, stuck-up, sex-crazed bastards. Now you pay, pretty-boy. Now you pay."

No matter how he tried, Peter couldn't struggle out of the ropes they had tied around his wrists, so tight, his hands burned from a lack of proper circulation. Just before Harriet had put him on the stool, his hands had been yanked over his head and fastened instead behind his back.

"Miss Griggs," pleaded Peter, suddenly deciding there was no other course but to throw himself on their mercy. When would they kick the stool out from under him? Would it hurt? Would someone come dashing in at the last minute like they always did on TV? "Please, Miss Griggs, don't do this to me. Maybe I *have* done some lousy things, I don't know. But nothing very much, I swear it." His voice had started this approach in a subservient, almost gentle tone. But as Peter looked at what lay ahead of him, the voice began rising again, ending up more as a scream. "No. Don't. Please. You can't. Please, don't. For God's sake, you can't, not *me* . . . please, for the love of God, *please* . . ."

Harriet Griggs snorted and turned to Henry. "Turn it on, Henry. I can't stand this crybaby's drivel any longer."

Peter heard the snap of a switch, desperately trying to figure out what they had in mind for him now. Nothing happened. Peter was silent, baffled as well as terrified. Perhaps twenty seconds later he became aware of a strange feeling of warmth on the soles of his feet. Warm, and getting warmer. Twisting his neck around, Peter was able to see his feet briefly. The full horror of their plan hit him with staggering force; the strange blue box fastened to the stool he was standing on was an electric hot plate. The full implications of what Harriet Griggs had meant when she said, "Hang *you*? Don't be silly, Peter. You're going to hang yourself. . . ." became clear.

Desperately Peter began pleading, crying, screaming, cursing, offering money, shrieking at them, tears running down his face. It was a jumble of words, shouts, screams and logic. Harriet remained fixed to the floor as if deaf, a small, satisfied smile pasted on her face.

Quickly the hot plate he was standing on became uncomfortable to the soles of his feet. Peter began raising first one, then the other of them off of it. The heat rose. He began jumping up and down, trying to find the way that hurt the least. He tried screaming again, but it only widened Harriet's smile. As the plate grew hotter Peter could stand less and less time on it; he knew if he stepped off, he would be strangled by the rope. Each time he landed briefly back on the hot plate, the noose tightened; the slip knot prevented the rope from loosening to where it was before. Peter, crying and moaning, felt the rope cutting deeper into his neck, his breath coming in shorter and shorter gasps, his heart pounding wildly against his ribs. He was surprised to find himself suddenly tumescent and remembered reading somewhere that this was the inevitable result of slow hanging.

He tried to scream as the heat from the hot plate began searing his feet, making small sizzling noises each time a foot landed on it squarely, turning his feet so the plate would hit the sides of his feet instead of their already badly burned soles. It only made the knot grow tighter. Once again, he tried to scream, but the tight rope around his neck turned it into a strange gurgling sound. Through his gaspings for air, he managed to plead a little, but wasn't sure that anyone could understand him. "Jennifer. Don't do this to Jennifer." His body shook and twisted as the red-hot plate burned into his skin again. "Don't—not me—please. . . . Oh, God, please. . . ."

By now the rope had cut off almost all of his air, and Peter could see things around him becoming gray. He made one final, desperate effort for air, but the hot plate was now a glowing red, and he heard the strange singeing sound of his own flesh for the second he could stand it.

He heard himself coughing and gasping as he gave up trying to stand and let his body hang from the end of the rope, twisting around in a convulsive little circle, his toes banging against the side of the hot plate. Quickly he felt himself losing consciousness, the ceiling above his thrown-back head spinning above him. "Rah, tiger, sis-boom-bah" the men of Princeton had sung. They were unable to help him any longer.

The last sound the Griggses heard from him was what appeared to be Jennifer's name, but they couldn't be sure. His body twisted and jerked several more times, the toes pointing and unpointing in a death spasm, a sort of farewell orgasm to go with his valedictory erection. A series of small shudders, then stillness. Peter's mouth slowly dropped open.

Harriet's entry in the journal had been entirely accurate; Ape-Lady was laughing, almost hysterically, looking gleefully at Peter's bulging eyes, the tongue that swelled out of his mouth, and the bluish cast of his skin.

Finally Harriet brought herself under control. "Those rich kids certainly do make a fuss about things. Spoiled. Spoiled rotten." The ridiculousness of her own statement made Harriet laugh again but, suddenly, she turned serious. Quickly they cut Peter's body free from the rope. With a heave, Harriet threw his naked body over her shoulder and, with Henry following meekly behind her, dumped it into a shallow pit she had dug earlier that day, not far from one of the blossoming apple trees. Quicklime was added to it to speed decomposition. With a satisfied smile, she took Henry by the arm and led him quietly back to the house.

Chivers's Garden Club would have been considerably shocked to learn what Henry Griggs's "magic" fertilizer they wrote about so fondly actually was.

CHAPTER THIRTEEN

Sometimes I think this Olivia girl is going to give us a lot of trouble. Headstrong. Stubborn. Willful. A lot of young girls today are like that. With most of them, I suspect the strong-willed act is just that—an act. See, they've been exposed to the Gloria Steinems and the Betty Friedans and the Bella Abzugs, and they try to imitate those women—or Ms.'s or whatever they're calling themselves this week. Militant, hard, dominant.

Underneath, I think, they're still the way girls always were. Demure, dependent, waiting for the right guy to come along and protect and support them.

Olivia is different. In her, the willfulness isn't put on, it's real. You could see it the way she pushed that boy Peter Owen around—without his even knowing it.

Olivia is going to have to be broken. It's going to be a battle, but that strength of hers has to be knocked out of her fast—or we'll really have problems.

No better time to start than now. We'll put together a will-breaking program for her that'll either tame her or kill her.

Turn the screws down real hard. A little of that, and she'll come around.

Journal of Blossom House,
Entry, page 27—Harriet Griggs

The door panel slid open, followed by the hollow, menacing sound of the outer bolts being slid back. The key turned in the lock. Although the sound sent a wave of dread surging through her, Jennifer tried to affect unconcern, not looking up, and burying her head in the book she had been pretending—or maybe it was attempting—to read. *The Little Minister*. Overly sweet, cloying, but better than *Uncle Remus* or *Heidi*.

Out of one corner of her eyes, she saw Harriet fill the door briefly, then advance a few feet into the room, kicking the door shut behind her with one foot. When Jennifer continued with her pretend-reading, Harriet began breathing heavily; angry little wheezes came from her great bulk. "Olivia!" she said sharply. "Come take this tray. I'm not your maid."

"I'm not hungry."

"Take the tray," repeated Harriet. "You have to eat your breakfast. Take the tray now, child."

Jennifer buried herself deeper in her dreadful book. In three steps, Harriet walked across the room and, balancing the tray on one hand, sent the book flying into the air with the other. Jennifer could see that the hand remained raised above her and stared at it, remembering the painful blows Harriet could inflict with it. Sighing, Jennifer took the tray.

"That's better, dear," said Harriet warmly, the inevitable warm smile spreading across her face. "You mustn't let your strength run down, child. Breakfast is God's way of making little girls grow up strong."

"I'm not hungry." Jennifer listened to herself; she sounded like a frightened tape recording.

"*Try*, Olivia. Otherwise, otherwise—well, there are ways of *making* you eat, aren't there, dear?''

Above the fixed smile, the threat of painful violence brooded in Harriet's eyes. Her right hand twitched, as if readying itself to strike. Jennifer shivered, remembering the pain that hand could produce.

Listlessly she picked up her fork and began pushing the food around on her plate. The moment Harriet was gone, she'd dump the whole plate down the toilet again. It had worked yesterday, hadn't it?

Harriet appeared to be reading her mind. "And don't think you can fool me by putting the food down the toilet, Olivia. I have ways of knowing.''

Goddamn right she did. The peephole. Until now, though, Jennifer hadn't realized how much time Harriet must devote to watching her. "Yes, Miss Griggs,'' said Jennifer meekly. There was no point in getting beaten again for not eating, she decided. Besides, much as she hated to admit it—even to herself—she was hungry, and the food smelled good.

Without thinking, Jennifer reached for her coffee. Instead, her hand hit the coldness of a milk glass. The breakfast abruptly smelled dreadful. Every morning it was the same. There would be no coffee, only milk. One soft-boiled egg, already open, staring balefully up from its egg cup. On the same plate, two strips of well-done bacon. Instead of rolls, there would be a small bowl of either hot Wheatena or oatmeal. Only the orange juice would be familiar. Beside it would always be a single large apple, apparently either to be eaten with breakfast or saved for midmorning. Jennifer could hear a crazy rhyme begin going around in her head: "An apple a day keeps Harriet away. . . .'' Christ, she had been alone too damn long.

Stopping her fussing with the egg, Jennifer turned her face toward Harriet. "Miss Griggs? Could I ask you something?''

"Of course, dear. Asking is how we learn.''

"I was wondering, Miss Griggs, if instead of all this breakfast,

I could just have toast and coffee. It's what I'm used to, you see."

Harriet looked at her as if she were crazy. "*Coffee?* Little girls don't drink coffee, dear. There'll be plenty of time for that when you grow up."

Jennifer could feel the awfulness of her position push down on her again, trying to crush her with its sinister overtones of total insanity. She struggled with a sudden need to burst into tears. Not in front of this malevolent giant, she told herself, beginning to shake from the effort of not crying. In spite of her battle, Jennifer could feel herself beginning to lose control. Too much had happened to her too suddenly. Her voice shaking, she looked up at Harriet again. Her visible loss of control seemed to make Harriet's smile widen. "Could I ask something else, Miss Griggs?"

"Of course, dear."

"Peter. Where is Peter? Is he all right? Is he on this floor? Is he all right? CanIseehimcanhecomehereandseemecanIseehimrightawayohGodGodGod . . ." Jennifer's whole body shook, her thoughts as scrambled as her words, a knifelike pain cutting through her, her last vestiges of self-control rapidly crumbling.

Harriet stared at her blankly. "Peter? I'm sorry, dear, I don't know who you mean."

Like Henry before her. Harriet was denying that Peter existed. How could she, how was it humanly possible, to try to pretend something like that when she and Peter and Harriet and Henry had sat at the same table only a few days before? When it was Henry and Harriet who had performed the marriage ceremony? The network of fear that had been weaving itself around her insidiously began to strangle her. Jennifer knew it was about to happen, and it did. Her voice rose to a scream. "*Why are you holding me prisoner here? Damn it, why, why, why? I haven't done anything! Why do you have me locked up? For Christ's sake, tell me before I scream . . .*"

Harriet smiled, shaking her head sadly from one side to the other. "You *are* screaming, dear. And it's not very nice. You shouldn't yell like that at grown-ups. It's terribly impolite, Olivia."

"Jesus Christ," screamed Jennifer. *"Tell me—"*

Harriet stopped her in midsentence by holding up her huge hand. The gesture was sufficient. That hand held too much power within it to hurt. "I'll overlook your behavior, Olivia. Just this once. Nerves. It's what you get from not eating a regular breakfast. But please, dear, get those insane ideas out of your head. Heavens! You're not a prisoner, you know that. I can't imagine where you get such crazy notions. You're not being held against your will, Olivia, you know that. This is your home. Where you've lived all your life. We love you. No one's trying to do anything but bring you up right and turn you into a wonderful, gentle woman." Harriet suddenly laughed. "A prisoner! Oh, Olivia, sometimes you do say the strangest things."

Jennifer stared at Harriet, reason collapsing around her ears. Even if she'd been able to think of what to say, she doubted if she could say it. Without a word, Harriet picked up the tray and, still shaking her head in wonder at Jennifer's "crazy notions," walked calmly out of the room. Behind her, the bolts slammed shut, the lock turned, the panel in the door slid shut. Jennifer was alone.

The will-breaking program was in full swing. Jennifer could feel its ominous workings, even if not understanding it.

Today, as every day now, Jennifer was left entirely to herself. At first this had come to Jennifer as a relief. Harriet was such a threatening woman, she only had to slide back the bolts and Jennifer would start to tremble. After the second and third days, though, the loneliness became oppressive. Jennifer could sense the shift in her routine in a general way, but without really being able to pin down the specifics. Little by little, things were changing.

Harriet no longer waited around, even to criticize her. She would walk into Jennifer's little room—cell, Jennifer reminded herself—put down or pick up the food tray, and then leave, having said nothing. Twice Jennifer tried to get her to talk, once even being quite rude to produce some—*any*—reaction.

Harriet only shook her head, as if warding off a blow, turned around with the tray, and walked back out. Confused, Jennifer again tried to understand what was happening. Harriet was not acting like Harriet, and this fact must mean something.

She could find no explanation, and sat down in her chair, unable to face any more of the little girls' books on the shelf. Sat and stared. From the bathroom came a steady dripping. Funny, the tap had been dripping ever since she first woke up in this room five days ago. Then, she had barely noticed the sound. Now each drop of water hitting the basin sounded like a hammer blow. The anvil of hell. The dripping sound seemed to grow louder, almost deafening, a hammering that began to drill painfully in her brain, making Jennifer's whole body tremble. There was no way to shut out the sound; two days ago the door had been taken away. Instead, Jennifer covered her ears with her hands, feeling silly to be sitting in a chair with her hands holding on to the sides of her head. The device did not work anyway. The sound was so burned into her brain, she would have heard it if they'd wrapped her ears and stuffed them with wax stoppers. Even, Jennifer thought to herself, even if she were dead. The word startled Jennifer. She wasn't sure why, but suddenly there were too many sinister implications buried inside it, a sense of dread that made Jennifer's flesh crawl. Stupid, she thought. It was only a word.

At about eight that night, Harriet had wordlessly handed Jennifer her tray and just as mutely removed it. A half hour later Jennifer heard the sliding panel move back once again. Jennifer glanced up at the Mickey Mouse clock on her wall; it was time for Henry's nightly visit. His calls, as precisely timed as a rocket launch, were far less threatening than anything she experienced with Harriet. Henry seemed a gentle man, soft-spoken and always polite.

Jennifer knew that Henry, like his sister, was dangerously insane, and the fact was always at the front of her mind, but at least with Henry, you didn't have to worry that at any minute he might race across the room and split your face open with a hatchet the way you did with Harriet. Besides, with Henry, Jennifer had something to gain—if she played her manipulative cards right, a possible escape.

"Hello there, little Olivia," Henry said, advancing into the room with his usual broad smile. "So pretty . . . so pretty . . . I know I keep telling you that, and by now you must be tired of hearing it but, oh, Olivia, it's so terribly true. That dress is one of my favorites, you know. I'll have to see if we can't get some more like it—in different colors." Henry sighed. "Of course, these days it's very hard to get nice clothes for little girls. Most of what you find is trying to make little girls look grown-up. Terrible."

"It certainly is," Jennifer said sweetly, playing up to Henry. She had come perilously close to saying "It certainly is, Mr. Griggs," but had managed to stop just as the words took shape on her lips. She was damned if she would call him Daddy. Maybe when she had him completely in her control and needed some special thing from him to help her escape out of Blossom House, maybe then she would call him Daddy, not before. Instead of having been so pleasant when she agreed that little girls' dresses today were all wrong, she would have liked to spit in his eye and say something like "Listen, you old fart, you don't know a damn thing. You're crazy, you stupid old goat. Now get your ass over to the door and let me the hell out of this nuthouse."

Jennifer smiled to herself, thinking how good that kind of honesty would feel. But it would be a stupid honesty, since with it would go her only possible hope of escape. She smiled at whatever it was Henry had just finished saying—he had been talking about how good this kind of early warm spring weather always made him feel, like a kid, he'd added—and turned her deepest, charming look on him. "You're certainly not very old," she noted. "At heart, I suppose you *are* just a kid."

The effect on Henry was instant and dramatic. Jennifer could see Henry virtually shake with pleasure. He blushed, holding up one hand to indicate it wasn't, of course, true, but perfectly willing to be told it again. Any man is subject to flattery; Henry was a total slave to it. Jennifer recorded this fact in her mind; it could be useful later.

Henry promptly began fishing to hear the same compliment—or some variation of it—again. "Well," he muttered, his head shaking itself in a burst of self-deprecation. "Well, it's just that in deep winter I'm as grumpy as a hibernating bear. Sour. Unpleasant to be with. Terrible. Then, spring comes, and I change completely. You know—as happy and frisky as a new-born lamb."

Jennifer wanted to laugh. It was so obvious. Henry had set himself up for her to compliment him. The urge to put in the knife and twist it instead—saying something like "a fat, old, toothless, hibernating bear all year around, that's what you are, you stupid old man"—was hard to resist, but Jennifer fought hard and controlled herself. Henry's goodwill—his infatuation with her—was too important to her getting out of Blossom House. Then she could get the police, come back, and rescue Peter, who, she was still firmly convinced, was held a prisoner somewhere on this floor. She thought for a second, hoping Peter wasn't too worried about her. The sound of Henry's clearing his throat brought her back to what she had to do.

She turned toward him, laughing slightly, a bright little light playing through her eyes. "Oh, I think you're just being hard on yourself. I really do. I can't imagine that you're ever anything but that happy, frisky young lamb all year around. I mean that." Inside, Jennifer groaned. How could she say such things to this dreadful old man? When she'd manipulated her father, at least, she'd known he was basically a kind, good person. Henry was a doddering monster, mad as it was possible for a person to be, evil in his intentions and cruel in his behavior.

Henry, though, had been so pleased by her latest sally that Jennifer heard a strange suggestion of happy little grunts coming from him. As she looked at Henry a strange light came into his eyes, and she was terrified he would dart across the room and try to kiss her. Resisting him could raise havoc with her escape plan. She was almost relieved when she heard the sliding panel moved back from the outside.

The door opened, and Harriet came in, something she had never done before while Henry was with Jennifer. With her came a sudden chill breath, the sort of cold, damp, ominous smell you encounter when you open the cellar door of an old house. Harriet ignored her and walked up to Henry. "It's time, Henry. It's time for it to begin, right now."

A pleading look crossed Henry's face, and Jennifer wondered if he was going to cry. "Now?" he asked. *"Already?"*

"This minute, Henry. Come on."

Henry sighed and came over to Jennifer, taking her hands between his own and squeezing them. "Be brave, Olivia. Remember your daddy will be thinking about you the whole time. Don't let anything scare you."

Harriet cleared her throat impatiently; Henry shrugged and went out the door without looking back until the last moment, when he turned and gave her a sad little wave. It reminded Jennifer of the kind of wave families gave their children when they're leaving them at boarding school for the first time—trying to keep cheerful and tell the children how much fun they are going to have, but fully aware that the first six months will leave them miserably unhappy.

Outside, the bolts were slammed shut with an empty, final sound, the sliding door was closed with a slam, and the key was turned in the lock as if it would never be opened again. Jennifer didn't know what to make of what had just happened, but her instincts sent a faint shiver through her body. "Time for it to begin," Harriet had said. For *what* to begin? Didn't they consider locking her up in this prison cell as something having already begun?

"Be brave, Olivia," Henry had said. What terrible kind of things was planned for her now? Physical torture? Starvation?

Killing her? "Don't let anything scare you," Henry had also said. My God, how could anyone not be frightened just with things as they were? Now, to this, something new was about to be added.

The only thing Jennifer noticed that had changed that night was that she didn't hear the usual, macabre serenade of the "Parade of the Wooden Soldiers" and the Brahms lullaby. Just cold, empty stillness, a silence as suffocating as the grave.

CHAPTER FOURTEEN

There's nothing really new about brainwashing. The Germans used it in World War II, the Russians still use it today. I suspect our own CIA resorts to it any time it suits them.

Of course, centuries before this, the Chinese were already dabbling in the technique. When you think about it, the Chinese water torture is nothing more than a way of brainwashing so effective, you can cause incredible agony without inflicting any actual pain. It's a torture I'd love to try on Olivia, but Henry would never stand for it. Damn it, his attraction to Olivia could give us big trouble one of these days; I'll have to keep a close eye on both of them.

The object of any brainwashing, of course, is to reduce your prisoner to a state of mind where he will do anything you want him to, believe anything you tell him, and accept and follow orders without questioning. Great idea, in principle.

But I don't know how long treatment like that is going last with Olivia. As I said earlier, Olivia has a lot of genuine strength to her. Well, I suppose when I see the treatment wearing off, we can always put her through it again.

I wonder if the Chinese ever had to do that with their water torture. Whether, when they ran up against some particularly *strong-willed and stubborn prisoner, they had to keep repeating the torture at intervals. If they did, there must have been an awful lot of wet Chinese running around the countryside.*

Journal of Blossom House,
Entry, page 28—Harriet Griggs

At first, outside of the lack of the evening concert, Jennifer didn't notice any change. The deathly silence in the room, though, depressed her; even "Wooden Soldiers," Brahms, and "Now I Lay Me Down to Sleep" were at least sound of some kind. Her cell was so silent, Jennifer began hearing sounds she knew she had made up—rustlings, whisperings, and the occasional scurry of small feet across her rug. Mice? No, you couldn't possibly hear mice traipsing across a carpet.

The first major change in routine showed up the next morning. Her breakfast arrived—God, what she'd have given for a good, strong cup of coffee and a well-buttered English muffin!—on the dot of seven by her Mickey Mouse clock. This was the same time it had arrived ever since she'd been locked away there. But now, no one arrived with it.

Staring at the door, she realized there was another sliding door, this one horizontal and positioned quite close to the floor. When the slide was pulled back a sort of shelf extended into her room; on this, her breakfast tray was slid through the door. She saw no one.

The reasoning behind this arrangement baffled her. And disturbed her. Certainly, Harriet was no one she particularly wanted to see. Harriet was capable of anything; nothing was beyond her. But however frightening, she was at least another human being. A contact with the outside world.

Jennifer wondered if this same arrangement was going to be used in giving her her luncheon and dinner trays; she could not have explained why, but the prospect of this much isolation sent a shiver of dread through her. She realized she was probably supposed to put her tray back on its curious little shelf when she'd finished eating, but decided not to. This would force Harriet—even an outraged and angry Harriet—to speak to her. But even some hours later, nothing had happened, absolutely nothing. The tray remained uncollected.

After breakfast another small change became apparent to Jennifer. Her Mickey Mouse clock suddenly stopped running, its hands frozen at 7:35. A little later she was startled when something was lowered across the outside of her window, something opaque enough so that no light came through it. Without either the clock or the outside light to tell her roughly what time it was, she was adrift in a world without perimeters.

She told herself she would be able to get a rough idea from when her meals arrived. This solution to the timelessness of her world quickly fell apart. Until now, meals had been brought in by Harriet, following a strange, but meticulous schedule. No longer. She had been able to read only two additional chapters of *The Little Minister*—something she knew rarely took her more than twenty minutes a chapter—before the low door opened again, put out its tray holder, and presented her with lunch. By Jennifer's calculation, this meant it was only about eight-fifteen.

In spite of knowing exactly what was being done—but not why—Jennifer realized she now must live in a totally disoriented world. No way to tell day from night. No clock. Her meals served sporadically to avoid her using them as an approximate time fix. Good God, Jennifer asked herself, why *this* treatment? Why should they want to confuse her *this* way?

She had been asking all along why she was locked away and why Peter was kept so carefully separated from her; to this she now had to add questions about why Harriet—Henry, too?—should want to rob her of the one thing that up until now they had left her with too much of: time. Nothing of the new approach made any sense to Jennifer, and she began pacing the floor restlessly. She couldn't take any more of *The Little Minister;* later she'd try *The Swiss Family Robinson,* but she seemed to remember from her childhood that the book was written in very old-fashioned

English, and she'd had a hard time getting through it even when she'd been the right age for it.

Her pacing grew more frantic. The damn bands around her chest abruptly began to hurt, and she wondered if it was because she was suddenly sweating so heavily, it made the material chafe. Nerves. After perhaps twenty minutes or so of hard pacing, the bands hurt so much, Jennifer decided to sit down. Maybe not moving would lessen the sweating; Jennifer wasn't sure. She sat in her chair under the suddenly harsh glare of her ceiling light, staring emptily across the room. The sweating didn't stop, or even diminish; it must be some purely nervous reaction to the new restriction of her confinement. Were they doing the same thing to Peter down the hall somewhere? Today, though, even her thoughts of Peter turned depressing. Maybe these diabolical people had already killed him; maybe her steadfast belief that he was somewhere on the same floor was illusory. No, they wouldn't kill Peter. No one would. Like herself, he was a captive somewhere else in this vast house and eventually would come and rescue her. Damn it. Today, even her self-assurances had a hollow ring to them.

Putting her head back, she tried to rest. Her eyes fell on the photograph of Henry Griggs; she could swear his smile was broadening as she stared at him. Sharply she sat up, shaking her head as if there were water in her ears. She was not going to let herself go crazy. Damn it, she wouldn't let this brace of tacky criminals drive her to that. Maybe that's just what they had in mind too, locking her up in this hermetically sealed time chamber. No, damn it, no, she wouldn't let them get to her.

Jennifer stood up and began pacing again. She went to the bathroom and drank two full glasses of water. The luncheon stared up at her from the floor with reproach, but she couldn't bring herself to touch it, in spite of the voice of logic that whispered to her that luncheon and dinner might be as far apart as breakfast and luncheon had been close together. She poked at the meal a little and put it on her table. If she got hungry, she'd try.

As she walked back to her chair Jennifer again found herself looking at the framed photograph of Henry Griggs. As she looked his expression definitely changed, from its usual benign smile to an expression of deep concern. It was crazy. Photographs don't change their expressions to respond to things going on around them.

The idea hit her like a falling stone. Maybe she was already crazy. Hadn't she heard somewhere that the insane are always the last to realize it? Maybe she *was* only twelve, maybe her name *was* Olivia, maybe Blossom House *was* her home. Maybe that other life she remembered in New York was only a figment of her insanity. Maybe Peter Owen had never existed, except in her mind. Maybe Henry Griggs *was* her father.

On the wall, Henry Griggs's picture abandoned its worried look; it was replaced with his usual broad smile. Oh, Christ, Jennifer told herself, she was as nuts as the Griggses were. She threw herself on the bed, hoping she'd be able to fall asleep. She closed her eyes and waited. Nothing happened. She was too wide awake. Lying there—she could not have explained why—she could feel reality beginning to slip through her fingers. She struggled hard to keep a grip on it, but this noiseless cell, where time was an enigma, made feeling entirely rational very difficult.

Finally, without even realizing it, Jennifer did fall asleep. She had no idea, of course, for how long, but she knew that when she woke she was hungry. She attempted to eat the luncheon delivered some time earlier. As meals at Blossom House went, it was good, but roast beef in some kind of gravy and mashed potatoes covered in some of the same sauce tasted rancid and repulsive when cold. The ice cream in the dessert dish had, of course, long ago melted and become thick, chocolaty soup. Jennifer picked at the meal listlessly, trying to find some part of it at least marginally edible. The best she could do was a pair of Parker House rolls, which she lathered with soft butter and ate with relish. Still hungry, she went back and tried the roast beef; if you scraped off the gravy, it wasn't too bad.

It was a long, silent day. Some hours later the lower sliding panel of her door opened and dinner arrived. This time—she had lost all sense of hours and times now—Jennifer ate it right away, hungry or not, determined to avoid the terrible cold meal she'd had for lunch. The sound of the panel sliding open and closed was the last sound she heard in what she assumed was a day. Troubled, frightened, and afraid of losing her hold on reality entirely, Jennifer climbed into bed and finally forced herself to fall asleep. She had no idea whether it was late afternoon, late evening, or even morning. She had hoped Henry would show up, but he, like the hands of the Mickey Mouse clock and the thing covering her window that made night and day inseparable, seemed to belong to the corners of timelessness.

For the next few days Jennifer's routine was the same. Meals were delivered at random times, and the cell was steeped in deep silence that pressed in on her from the time she got up until the time she surrendered to her bed and tried to sleep.

Henry Griggs's picture kept changing expressions, something that troubled Jennifer deeply. She knew it couldn't be happening, and yet . . . it was. By the end of what Jennifer estimated was the fifth day, she was stunned to discover she was talking to herself out loud. She tried to stop, but couldn't. She talked to the picture of Henry Griggs, she talked to Peter Owen—a long, loving conversation held with a blank wall, asking him to for God's sake come and rescue her. There were similar conversations with her spiteful mother and her wonderful father, apologizing for the terrible note she'd left behind, and with Hillary Crane, asking her if she didn't think it was strange not to have heard from her yet. Why hadn't she told people so they could come looking for her? What surprised Jennifer the most about these conversations was her total acceptance that the people she was talking to were answering her back. She could hear them in her head, assuring her, scolding her, praising her. She would wait for their answer after she'd spoken to them, and then hear the voices begin to talk back to her.

When she was through, Jennifer had had an opportunity to put this new phenomenon into perspective, she realized how crazy it was. But the voices continued, all day and all night, talking to her, and Jennifer had no choice but to answer them.

It was just a little while after her breakfast was delivered—it could have been three in the morning or three in the afternoon—that they began. They took possession of her, terrifying her, making her scream from the agonizing dread of them, leaving her limp and unable to cope or respond. The hallucinations. Wild, irrational, terrifying—but as concrete as the bars on her windows and the thickness of her walls.

"That was a terrible note you left, Jennifer," her father growled, suddenly standing in front of the photograph of Henry Griggs and staring at her with a mixture of reproach and hurt. "A terrible note. It hurt your mother; it hurt me; I know you always had your problems with your mother, but I always tried my best to make you happy. . . ."

Mr. Delafield shook his head sadly and began to fade back into the picture of Henry Griggs again; the last thing Jennifer could see of him was his head shaking sadly from side to side. "Daddy!" she screamed, but the image was totally gone now, leaving only the photograph behind.

For a second Jennifer sat motionless on the bed, her whole body shaking from the experience. Suddenly she heard another voice calling her, and spun toward the metal door, her heart jumping wildly. "Jennifer, damn it, you're a spoiled brat. A selfish, spoiled brat. . . ." Peter stood there, naked, his finger pointing at her angrily. "I told you the other night we should never have gotten married; you're too much of a fucking baby. That's why I got the marriage annulled. I couldn't put up with your shit any longer. . . ."

"*No, no, no!*" Jennifer screamed. "*I love you, Peter. Don't—*"

"Always whining, always complaining," Peter snapped at her in fury.

She heard herself screaming "*No, no, no!*" as the battle of the other night, when he was drunk, replayed itself almost verbatim. She saw Peter beginning to laugh; he was holding on to his prick and peeing on her rug. His laughter grew wilder and his whole body shook with it. "Piss on you, you fucking little spoiled brat." The laughter had consumed him entirely. "I told you if you wanted St. Bart's, you shouldn't have run away with me. Now you know I was right. . . ."

Jennifer raced across the room to seize Peter, to grab him, to hug him, to make him tell her he was only kidding. But by the time she got across the room, he had turned and disappeared through the door, still laughing, his buttocks shaking from how funny he thought it was.

Neither her father nor Peter could have been real, yet they had been there. Had the Griggses succeeded in driving her crazy this easily and quickly? No, of course not. It was just her nerves. . . .

"Little girls do what grown-ups tell them, Olivia. Or they're severely punished," roared Harriet, suddenly appearing out of her bathroom.

"I'm not a little girl, damn it." Jennifer heard her voice screaming at Harriet, and for some reason the fact surprised her.

"Do what grown-ups tell them and never, never swear." Harriet came across the room and planted herself directly in front of Jennifer. "But you won't listen, Olivia, you just won't listen. Your name is Olivia, in spite of what you pretend. You're twelve years old, this is your home, and your daddy loves you, in spite of the awful things you try to do to his picture. You're a bad little girl, Olivia; sometimes, I just don't know *what* we're going to do with you. . . ."

"That's not true, any of it. My name's Jennifer Delafield—I mean Jennifer Owen—and—"

Harriet bellowed with mean laughter, holding her sides and rocking back and forth. "See, *you* don't even know what name to pretend is yours. A lying little girl on top of everything else. Your name is Olivia, you are twelve years old, and this is your house, and your daddy's name is Henry Griggs. You've lived here all your life. You may have to be punished very severely, Olivia, to get this terrible wild streak of imagination in you out of your system. Don't even know what name you pretend is yours . . ."

Harriet began laughing again and slowly vanished into the wall, clucking and threatening as she disappeared.

Jennifer didn't even know how to start getting a grip on herself. Harriet had gone, but returned a few minutes later, screaming at her again. All day long, every time Jennifer turned around, the woman seemed to be right behind her, towering over her, yelling and shouting and threatening. "Olivia. Twelve years old. Your daddy is Mr. Henry Griggs. You've lived here all your life. . . ."

Jennifer began screaming at her, pleading with her. The appearing and disappearing hulk of Harriet loomed over her, paying no attention to her pleading, but instead threatening her with more and greater punishments. "We can shave off *all* your hair, Olivia. We can tie you up and whip you until you bleed. We can starve you. We can shove a red-hot curling iron up between your sinful legs—wicked little girls like you are always playing up there with their fingers. We can put your head under water until you've almost drowned, Olivia. We can do any or all of those things unless you start being a good little girl and do what you're told. Do you understand me, child?"

Because of the stopped clock, the irregular pattern of meals, and the opaque material shutting off all outside light from her room, Jennifer had no real idea of how long the hallucinations— soul-racking, agonizing, terrifying—had been going on. Her mind had become so confused battling the creatures that kept invading her consciousness, she was incapable of making a sound judgment anyway.

Actually, it had been three days, and the brainwashing process was rapidly escalating in its effect on Jennifer. She was no longer able to sleep, even fitfully, adding exhaustion to her already considerable list of disorientations. Food she could no longer face. When she tried to eat, she quickly threw it back up. All through the endless nights and days, curled up on her bed in a semifetal position, she could feel the painted animals from her furniture crawling across her like an army of bugs; they stood just outside her reach, screaming at her. When she swatted at them, they disappeared. The giant stuffed peach bounced around the room, taking on an odd elliptical shape, and finally sat at the foot of her bed and hissed at her; beside it, the stuffed animals hooted and jeered at Jennifer, sometimes nibbling at her bare toes or trying to creep up inside the fullness of her nightie.

Under the covers or on top of the bed, Jennifer found she shook constantly, as if exposed to cold blasts of air; a few minutes later everything would change, and she would find herself sweating as if stuffed inside a sauna.

The hallucinations grew more vivid. The painted figures off the furniture were shaking their fists at her now, growling, screaming, and threatening her. Jennifer fled into the bathroom only to find Harriet standing inside; in her hands, she held the toilet bowl, which she shook at Jennifer, as if planning to dump the whole fixture over her head. "Good little girls do what grown-ups tell them, or they are severely punished, Olivia," she screamed at Jennifer. Jennifer began to back out of the bathroom, but a curious thing was happening to Harriet. As Jennifer watched, piece by piece, Harriet changed into Jennifer's mother. "Good little girls don't come to the table wearing jeans, Jennifer," Mrs. Delafield said reproachfully. "You know that. Why are you always such a problem to your father and me?"

"You smoke cigarettes when you think nobody knows about it, Olivia," Harriet scolded her in a voice that was a shattering scream. *"Olivia's stupid! Olivia's stupid!"* Harriet cackled, rocking with laughter.

Over the next few hours Harriet's and her mother's faces became so blurred and confused that Jennifer was never sure which of them she was talking to. They kept appearing everywhere. They would abruptly pop out from behind the curtains, they would step suddenly out of the closet as she passed its door. Once, Jennifer even discovered their faces staring down at her from the circular ceiling light fixture, their bodiless heads equipped only with a pair of arms that their heads rested on, malevolent cherubs on the vaulted arch of a church, peering down from either side of the fixture and screaming at her.

Gradually everything in the room became something it was not. The rug on the floor turned into a funeral blanket of flowers thrown over Peter's body; only his head was visible, smashed in as if by a shovel. Henry Griggs and the dirt-encrusted shovel he had the first morning Jennifer went looking for Peter materialized out of nowhere, Henry holding the shovel and standing over Peter, only suddenly it wasn't Henry Griggs anymore, it was her father, swinging the shovel around over his head and calmly explaining why he'd done what he'd done. "Peter, you see, Jennifer, never really knew what he was going to do with his life. He told me that once. Well, I made the decision about his life very easy for him. Don't ever say your father never did anything for you, Jennifer. . . ."

Jennifer pressed herself hard against the wall, trying, by standing on the bed, to get away from the army of insectlike animals that were crawling all over the floor. It didn't work. Seconds later she could see the tiny animals moving across the blankets and beginning to crawl up her legs. She swatted and scraped, but the creatures appeared unfazed.

From the end of the room the stuffed animals began screaming at her, crawling up on to the bed and shaking their fists at her. The dread began to suffocate. Across the room, Harriet and her mother were back changing places, although sometimes now both of them were visible at the same time, laughing at her, scolding her, screaming at her. The smiling photograph of Henry Griggs on the wall threw back his head and roared with insane laughter. Jennifer couldn't breathe. She fell from the bed to the floor in terror, screaming helplessly, over and over again. The room spun beneath her.

A cyclonic cacophony of sounds—howls, screams, animal grunts, distant wailings, and intimate whispered exchanges—whirled around inside her head faster and faster, growing louder by the instant. Her earlier difficulty in breathing transmogrified into suffocation; it was as if the full weight of the giant barn doors once used to crush witches was being pressed against her chest by the good citizens of Salem.

Jennifer, driven by the sheer exhaustion of the day, fell into a deep sleep on the floor, where she curled up tightly in a futile effort to protect herself from so hostile an environment.

It might have been half an hour later, it might have been half a day later, that Jennifer was wakened by the sound of the panel on the steel door being violently slammed open. Hopeless, terrified, Jennifer raised her head a little but remained lying where she was, frozen in fear.

PART II

CHAPTER FIFTEEN

Henry got very angry when I accused him of letting that worthless little rich girl wrap him around her finger. He denied it, of course. But I reminded him of how he'd countermanded my orders in Olivia's training, watering the whole program down, and of how he'd go all sad and mushy every night about the time he used to visit her. Sickening.

Sometimes Henry seems to forget that I make the decisions. That when someone like Olivia comes along, it's me who decides when it's time to begin the program, and me who decides when she's had enough.

Several times I made Henry peer through the peephole to see just how unattractive Olivia could look—my God, when that girl fell apart, she looked like she'd been torn into pieces by banshees— and made him listen to her cry and scream and talk to people who weren't there. He didn't say anything, just turned away and looked sad. Damn it, I knew that girl was going to be trouble.

Well, I can handle it. No spoiled little Park Avenue brat is going to beat me. I took care of Peter; I can take care of Olivia.

> *Journal of Blossom House,*
> *Entry, page 33—Harriet Griggs*

Outside her door, Jennifer heard the harsh sound of metal against metal, followed by a cluster of grindings and clankings. The suddenness of the sound tore at her—now what?—but she was so exhausted, she lacked the strength to move. From above her, she heard the Mickey Mouse clock whir and click and saw its hands spin until they came to rest at eleven o'clock. Jennifer stared at the clockface, transfixed. Eleven o'clock in the morning, or eleven o'clock at night? A few minutes later the light-proof material covering her window was yanked roughly upward and out of sight; a brilliant stream of blinding sunlight poured in. Eleven o'clock in the *morning*.

Jennifer blinked at the brightness and realized, for the first time, that she was still lying on the shag carpet. Crazy place to sleep, but then the whole world was crazy, and maybe she was the craziest person in it.

There was a metal *thunk*, and the panel in her door slammed open, the sound striking her ears like a painful giant hammer. Jennifer flinched, shaking badly.

Harriet's face filled the panel, smiling. "Good morning, Olivia." Jennifer didn't answer. She *couldn't*.

With her finger, Harriet beckoned Jennifer toward the door. Jennifer sat on the floor where she was, blinking at Harriet uncertainly. It didn't *seem* like part of a new hallucination. Still. . . .

"Come here, child," ordered Harriet, and once more waved Jennifer toward the door panel. Still unable to speak, suspicious, frightened—but even more afraid not to obey—Jennifer staggered to her feet and walked slowly and unsurely toward the door, one hand on the wall to steady herself. In front of the panel she stood face-to-face with Harriet—Harriet real or Harriet hallucinatory. The huge face studied Jennifer quizzically, her expression slowly changing to one of concern and alarm.

"Heavens, you poor child. Go wash your face or something. It always makes one feel better." She shook her head despairingly, the semblance of concern still pasted on her face. "You look like you haven't slept for a week. Scoot, child." Still afraid not to obey, Jennifer walked unsteadily into the bathroom and turned on the water.

Harriet had more than enough reason to know exactly how little Jennifer had slept the last week. Hour after hour, her face wearing an excited smile, she had watched through the peephole into Jennifer's cell and seen her thrash and writhe as the demons of madness tore at her. Hour after hour, through a hidden microphone in the cell, she had heard Jennifer shriek and scream and curse, had listened to her dialogues with the imaginary, had heard her beating her fists helplessly against the unfriendly walls of her cell. Even to herself, Harriet could not explain why she had enjoyed this spectacle so thoroughly, which seemed to fill some deep need inside her.

Jennifer walked back into the room. The splashing of cold water on her face, the fresh smell of soap, the ritual strokes of a comb through her hair, had made her feel a little better. The fear of another hallucination was gradually draining out of her. This Harriet was no hallucination, and although a monster, she was a real, not imaginary, one. Harriet's face still filled the door panel.

"Oh, my, yes, Olivia! That's helped a lot. Little girls always feel better when they've combed their hair and washed their faces."

She and Jennifer stood staring at each other for a moment, Jennifer still so unsteady, her body began to rock from one side to the other. "Are you *sure* you're all right, dear?" Harriet asked, frowning as she watched the face beyond the door moving from side to side.

"Yes, Miss Griggs." They were the first words Jennifer had spoken to anything but apparitions for days, and her own calm, rational tenor startled Jennifer.

"Good." There was a silent pause, punctuated every few seconds by the sound of Harriet fussing with something to one side of the panel. "Your breakfast will be along in a bit, Olivia," Harriet announced. "That will make you feel even better." Harriet smiled her broadest smile, adding: "I should probably also come in there a little later on and help you straighten the place up. I'm afraid it's a dreadful mess." Jennifer automatically looked behind her at the room; Harriet was right. "Yes, Miss Griggs."

"In the meantime, though, I have a little treat for you, Olivia. I'm going to leave the panel open and let you see how our little family at Blossom House lives. There's a Thermopane cover that swings over the panel opening; no one will be able to hear you, and I'm afraid you won't be able to hear very much of what's going on outside, either. That will come later—when you become one of the family." The shiny Thermopane cover was closed over the panel, and Harriet turned and walked away.

The sight outside her cell made Jennifer blink in amazement. The room beyond was huge, seemingly filling the entire third floor of Blossom House. Through her small, narrow window—its width made seeing the entire room impossible—Jennifer could count perhaps ten or twelve other girls in the room. Their actual ages were impossible to guess, since they were all dressed very much as Jennifer was—in what a little girl of forty or fifty years ago might have worn. At the moment they were sitting on the richly carpeted floor in a semicircle while Henry Griggs read to them from *My Friend Flicka*. Through the glass, Henry's voice was only a distant mumble, but Jennifer could see his lips moving.

Beyond this group, at the far end of the room—furnished in what looked like the comfortable furniture of a country house—was a highly polished dining table, carefully set with fine china, silver flatware, and dominated by two oversized silver candelabra that gleamed softly at either end of the table.

At each end stood chairs more massive than the rest; a wineglass was to the right of each of these two settings. The rest of the places had smaller, less impressive chairs in front of them, and a tall milk glass beside the plates and silverware.

Jennifer's eyes traveled back to the girls at Henry's feet. She wondered, already half sure of the answer, if the girls were as young as they looked, or were, in actuality, as old as she was.

Shivering, she decided they'd probably gotten here the same way she had—after a wedding.

Damn, she thought. This crazy Henry and his sister, Harriet, married people and then turned the brides into little girls. Somewhere—probably in other cells on this same floor—were their husbands. Jennifer's heart leaped at the thought. Somewhere on this floor, then, was Peter. She wondered if he knew where she was yet. She pressed her face against the Thermopane, trying to see down the wall her own cell was on, but she couldn't see very much of anything.

Her efforts were interrupted when she saw Harriet walk across the room and clap her hands. In a body, the girls on the floor slowly rose to their feet, curtsied to Henry, and began moving toward the table. Henry smiled back at them and disappeared out a door to one side of the huge room. Watching, still straining to see down her own side of the room, she saw Harriet marching toward her cell. To let her out? My God, she hoped so; she might catch a glimpse of Peter in *his* cell.

Her heart sank. Barely looking at her, Harriet slammed the metal cover of the panel shut, blocking out her view of the outside. She was alone again. And more confused and afraid than ever. Her lunch arrived through the horizontal panel in the lower half of her door. Only nibbling at first, Jennifer felt guilty to realize how hungry she was and ate until everything on her tray was gone. She hoped Peter was as hungry.

At five thirty by the Mickey Mouse clock on her wall, the metal cover of her window ground open once again, but the Thermopane cover remained in place. Harriet smiled at her through the glass, mouthed something, and vanished. Henry, she could see, was leading the girls in singing, waving his arms vigorously as they stood in front of him. Faintly Jennifer could hear the girls working on a round. Not a very sophisticated one—"Row, Row, Row Your Boat," to be precise. Henry, she could see, kept stopping them to point out where someone had gone wrong, as sober-minded as if he were conducting the chorus from *Aïda*.

A few minutes later the round was abandoned and the girls began "Frère Jacques" with apparent enthusiasm. For Jennifer, the song evoked memories of Chalmer's and happier, safer days before her world had gone mad. At the end of their last try at it, Henry looked at his watch and dismissed them. Once again the girls curtsied to him and broke into pairs.

Feeling strangely left out—her nose pressed against the window, as it were—Jennifer watched through the Thermopane as the girls arranged themselves at small tables and began playing Pick Up Sticks, checkers, Chinese checkers, and jacks. There was something so completely peaceful and normal to the picture they presented, Jennifer broke into a cold sweat. Is this what happened to you after you'd been a member of Blossom House's happy little family long enough? She shuddered.

It hadn't been very long—perhaps half an hour—when Harriet reappeared, sweeping into the room, dressed in a long maroon velvet hostess gown. Walking to the far end, she carefully lit the candles on the three-branched candelabra. Henry walked in, wearing an almost-matching velvet smoking jacket. The girls curtsied, the candelabrum glowed, and the growing mountain of dread in Jennifer grew. Looking neither to the right or left, Harriet marched over to Jennifer's door, smiled, and shut the metal door over the panel.

Jennifer felt like a bad little girl being punished for something—for what, she didn't know—and she sat down on her bed, once again alone, surrounded by overwhelming silence, and filled with an inescapable sense of madness that shrieked at her in the stillness.

Almost two hours later Jennifer again heard someone fussing with the panel. She had spent the time, when not eating, trying to restore some order to her room—not, she told herself, because Harriet had told her to, but because she herself could no longer stand the mess.

Smiling, Henry came in. The evening visits, apparently, were to resume. "Olivia, dear," he began, "in spite of everything, you look wonderful. I know it was a difficult period for you, and I hope you don't hold it against *me*. There were reasons. . . ."

"I didn't know what had happened to you," Jennifer answered, her native instinct for manipulation racing back into play. "I missed you." The statement was only partially a lie. Crazy as old Henry was, he was better than being left alone for a week in a timeless, claustrophobic void, skirting the thin edge of madness. Worse, Jennifer told herself, Henry's absence had kept her from working on him, preparing him, softening him up. If she was ever to escape, it would have to be with Henry's help—witting or unwitting.

Henry looked as if he might cry. Her loving little statement had touched him. "That's very sweet of you to say, Olivia. It goes without saying that I missed you, too. My God, I missed you. Every night at the regular time for my little visit, I ached to come up and see you, but, of course, I couldn't. You understand." Henry looked even sadder and muttered something Jennifer couldn't understand about "the program—the program doesn't allow it. . . ."

With a shy smile, Jennifer struggled to look pleased; she was relieved to gain new assurance that her spell was still working. But underneath the smile, a host of fears were continuing to grow.

At first she had been most concerned with what had happened to Peter; now, she more and more realized how helpless she was—and that she was in terrible danger herself. These people—strident Harriet and seemingly gentle Henry—could do anything they wanted to her, *anything*.

"Would it make you feel any better if you sat in my lap for a while?" Henry asked, his moist eyes questioning hers with an intensity that was terrifying.

Jennifer shook her head and sat down wearily on the edge of the bed. "I'm tired, so terribly tired," Jennifer sighed, desperate to avoid Henry's offer.

Peter. Oh, God, Peter, where *are* you?

CHAPTER SIXTEEN

Even though Henry and I had a great time together as children, I sometimes had trouble with him. Usually, there was very little question that I made the decisions. But every now and then I'd see a sudden streak of wanting to take over seize him.

Most of the time when it happened, it would begin over something quite small—and grow. By the time it had passed, he'd be arguing like crazy and asserting himself all over the place. To keep it from turning into a a real donnybrook, I'd have to play the game his way.

Henry still hasn't changed much. For the last day or so I've noticed that restless look on his face and suspect I'm in for some bad times, but like everything else with Henry, he'll forget about it after a while, and we'll be back to normal again.

I don't know why men always feel they have to prove something to themselves. Perhaps it's genetic. Although, thinking about it, I'm not really sure anyone could honestly call Henry a man. He's too weak.

Journal of Blossom House,
Entry, page 36—Harriet Griggs

"It's time, I tell you."

"Well, I'm not really sure, Henry. She strikes me as needing a few more days to adjust. The program worked quite well, I think, but the girl needs more time to fully accept who's in charge. Perhaps another week."

"You've never done anything like that to any of the other girls."

"And you've never spent so much time with any of the other girls." Harriet's smoldering resentment that Henry should spend so much time with Jennifer had finally come to the surface. Bitterly Henry laughed at his sister.

"So . . . that's what it is . . . you're jealous, Harriet."

"Don't be ridiculous. It's just that that girl's a bad one. I knew it from the moment I set eyes on her. She's using you, Henry. I don't know for what, but she's using you."

"Shut up, Harriet. I said it's time she came out with the other girls, and I meant it. It's time. Now, without any more nonsense about it, let's go tell her." Slowly they walked out of the kitchen.

Harriet threw her hands in the air and shrugged. There were moments it was not wise to argue with Henry, and this was one of them.

Jennifer was finishing her breakfast, avoiding the Cream of Wheat as if it were poisoned, but enjoying the toast, marmalade, and butter. She'd even eaten the eggs and bacon, something she couldn't remember doing since she was about fourteen. The milk, as always, she left untouched.

She was startled to hear the sliding cover on the panel and see its Thermopane window moved away. She glanced at her clock. In the rigorous timetable of Blossom House, this visitation was not on the schedule. Jennifer heard the bolts being slammed back and the locks turned. The door opened, and Henry and Harriet both walked into her cell. For a moment Jennifer didn't move. Then she remembered, and stood up to curtsy, receiving a curt nod from Harriet in acknowledgment. Unsure of what to expect from this unscheduled visit, Jennifer cowered inside. Now what?

Henry beamed at her. "I have some good news for you, Olivia—" he began. Harriet cut in, her harsh voice drowning Henry out in the middle of his sentence.

"We have decided it is time you become a regular member of our little Blossom House family." Jennifer was surprised to feel as if she'd just been accepted into an exclusive club. My God, *Blossom House*? Still, at least she would have other people her own age to talk with, and possibly, just possibly, she'd learn where they were keeping Peter. She let her mouth drop open, staring at Harriet and Henry in pretended pleasure.

Unaffected, Harriet barreled ahead. "I have canceled all the morning classes today so you can have a good chance to meet and get to know the rest of our happy little family." Remembering the rules, Jennifer curtsied, first to Harriet, then to Henry. "Very nice, dear," Harriet said, but there was an easily recognizable overtone of hostility lurking behind her words. "They're a very nice group, the other girls and—"

"I have something else to tell you," Henry said, speaking loudly enough to stop Harriet's run-on declaration. "It will take a little time to get used to but, in the end, you'll realize what an improvement it is." Harriet looked startled and appeared about to start talking herself again, staking out her position of dominance, when Henry went on before she could get started.

"From now on you're no longer Olivia. You are Peaches. *Peaches*. A much better name for you, you see. So I'm changing it. Peaches."

Stunned, Harriet stared at her brother openmouthed. Then she recovered a little. "Now, look, Henry. Her name's Olivia and—"

Henry laughed gaily, smiling at Jennifer with a conspiratorial look. "Don't you like it better? Peaches."

"Peaches . . ." Jennifer looked at Henry and knew manipulation demanded positive response.

"Henry, damn it—"

"She even looks like Peaches—my dear, sweet Peaches—don't you think so, Harriet?"

For some reason Jennifer couldn't understand, Henry's last

sentence had sent Harriet into a raging fury. Harriet should have seen this rebellion coming when he placed the giant peach in Jennifer's room. Her face turned red with anger, the small veins on her face throbbing luminescently. Harriet was so angry, she could only produce tortured, sputtering sounds.

"I think Peaches is a wonderful name," Jennifer lied. The soft, cuddly giant peach in her room—with all its sinister overtones—suddenly made some sort of crazy sense.

"Henry!" yelled Harriet. "You just can't—"

"I said her name is Peaches. That's final. I've decided it. So Peaches is her name. Period."

To Jennifer's surprise, Harriet's opposition crumbled. Until this moment she had not realized that Henry ever made any of the decisions. She was even more surprised to realize that in a contest of wills, Henry could bring Harriet to surrender. In some ways it was encouraging for her ultimate goal. Until now, she had believed all the evil of Blossom House was really Harriet's doing and was stunned to discover Henry had as much of a voice in things as he apparently did. The thought shook her. It made Henry as responsible for the evil as Harriet, and therefore as frightening.

"Very well, then," Harriet said crisply. "We'll give you a few moments to tidy yourself up, Peaches"—Harriet had even managed a weak smile as she said the name—"then we'll introduce you to the rest of the family." As she turned toward her brother, Jennifer could see the smile vanish, replaced by an ugly, drawn expression. "Come along, Henry," Harriet said firmly. "Leave the child to fix herself up."

At the door, Jennifer could see Harriet virtually push Henry out of the cell. If they argued outside, she never heard it. With a small sigh—meeting a whole new set of people always frightened her a little—Jennifer ran a comb through her hair, brushed her teeth, and straightened her dress. She couldn't help but remember the terrified feeling she'd had when her father and mother stood to one side, watching, while she was introduced to the other little children on the opening day of kindergarten.

They hadn't taken to her at first, either.

*   *   *

Jennifer, with Henry and Harriet walking behind her, came out into the middle of the vast room that took up most of Blossom House's third floor. There was utter silence, but Jennifer could feel twelve pairs of eyes boring into her, appraising her, weighing her—a mixture of curiosity, skepticism, and hostility. Harriet clapped her hands together loudly, moving out in front of Jennifer and Henry.

"Children," Harriet said in her loudest voice while Henry stood beside her, beaming at Jennifer. "Children, as I told you earlier, when I canceled this morning's classes, we have a new member joining our happy little family here at Blossom House. Her name is Peaches. Now, if you'll come forward one at a time. . ."

On a signal from Harriet, two of the girls had earlier carried her great high-backed chair from the dining table over to where Harriet planned to sit, facing them like an empress holding an audience. "Start, please, children. One at a time. Don't be shy."

A pretty, but vaguely unpleasant-looking girl scrambled to her feet and thrust herself toward Harriet. She curtsied, first to Harriet, then to Henry, turning to face Jennifer.

"Pippin. I can always count on Pippin. This is Peaches, Pippin. Pippin will make you feel right at home, Peaches, I'm sure." Pippin bowed slightly toward Jennifer, then curtsied again to Harriet. Quickly she turned to take her place on the floor again, but Jennifer had not missed the mean look the girl had flashed at her as she passed. It was a strange expression, one of distrust, dislike, and superiority all at the same time. Pippin, Jennifer could already guess, was going to be trouble.

Another little girl came forward and repeated the same ritual. "This is Cherry, Peaches. Sometimes a little disobedient, but a nice child."

As she turned to go back to her place, the girl named Cherry impishly stuck out her tongue at Jennifer while giving Harriet the finger with her far hand. Harriet bellowed at her to come back. "I saw that tongue of yours, Cherry. Always have to cut up,

don't you, child." Jennifer sighed in relief; Harriet had not see
the finger. "Pippin, bring me the ruler."

The girl named Pippin jumped to her feet, trotted across th
room, and returned with a wicked-looking ruler she'd taken fro
the blackboard stand. With a self-satisfied smile and a curtsy, sh
handed it to Harriet. Jennifer looked at her in bewilderment; fo
some reason Pippin was enjoying this. Most of the other gir
were shifting uncomfortably on the carpet, eyes averted. Eve
Henry had walked away, going to the far side of the room an
fussing with some things on the wall, his back turned to wha
was about to happen.

"Come on, Cherry," commanded Harriet. "You know wha
to do; you've been through it enough times." Harriet sighe
impatiently. "Hands out, palms up."

Cherry shrugged and extended her palms, her eyes shut. Yo
could hear the whistle, piercing and awesome, as the ruler slice
through the air, Harriet putting all the strength she had behind i
Jennifer winced, hearing the sharp crack as the flat side of th
ruler struck Cherry's palm. For the moment Cherry made n
sound, in spite of the pain she must have felt each time Harri
brought the ruler down on her palms. Trembling, Jennifer sa
Cherry's eyes open slightly to study Harriet; Harriet pause
the ruler still raised. Suddenly Cherry began to cry loudl
simultaneously slipping Jennifer a tiny wink. Jennifer smiled
herself. The tears were pretend tears—but they worked.

Harriet, satisfied now, drew herself up to face Cherry, st
standing stiffly in place before her. In her sternest voice, sh
spoke: "From now on, Cherry, *try* and be a good little girl. I hop
you've finally learned your lesson. All right, then, you're di
missed; go back to your place."

Cherry curtsied and slowly went back to her spot on the floo
She appeared cowed, but Jennifer could just make out the edg
of a triumphant smile at the corners of her mouth. Her big ey
rose to meet Jennifer's. The wink again. Cherry, Jennifer kne
was someone she was going to like.

One by one the rest of the girls were introduced, all, sh

noticed, named after fruits or nuts. Cherry, Pippin, Jaffa (as in
the orange), Bartlett, Strawberry, Melonie, etc., and, of course,
herself—Peaches.

When all of the introductions had been made Harriet remained
sitting sulkily in her imperial chair. A smiling Henry said something to her that Jennifer couldn't hear, but it didn't seem to
cheer Harriet up much.

The girls remained seated, waiting for Harriet to act. Jennifer
saw Henry whisper to Harriet again, and even tug at her sleeve.
Rising slowly to her feet, her great bulk seeming to fill the room,
Harriet shot a disgusted glance at Henry and clapped her hands
for silence.

"All right, girls, we're going to leave you now, so that you
can get acquainted with Peaches"—her voice still seemed to
creak a little whenever she had to say Jennifer's new name—
"without any grown-ups around to inhibit you. Be extra polite to
our new little girl and answer any questions she may have. All
right, children, your time is your own now."

As a body, all the girls rose to their feet and performed the
inevitable curtsy. Without even glancing at Jennifer, Harriet
marched out of the room, followed by Henry.

The moment they'd left, the other girls fled from Jennifer, as if
she carried a bad disease. It *was* the first day of kindergarten. Even Cherry disappeared, something which surprised—and also
hurt—Jennifer a little. A moment later, though, she saw Cherry
across the room talking urgently with someone, apparently continuing
some critical conversation that had been interrupted when Henry
and Harriet made their entrance. Even in this crazy world, she
supposed, life had to go on. Awkwardly Jennifer stood by herself
in the center of the room, waiting for someone to make an opening
move. She could see fleeting glances of curiosity covertly thrown
in her direction, but nothing more. Somehow, Jennifer told herself,
she had to escape the center of the room to someplace less
conspicuous.

The only girl to come over to her and attempt conversation was
the one called Jaffa. She was a strange-looking creature, some-

how appearing a bit older than the rest, although dressed identically. Behind a pair of oversize glasses, a pale, unhealth
complexion tried to hide from the world; she wore a somber
depressing expression that made Jennifer feel that the girl migh
never have smiled in her whole life.

"I should probably say welcome," moaned Jaffa, "but, give
the circumstances, that would be a travesty." Jaffa looked around
studying the other girls in the room. "Nobody seems terribl
anxious to speak to you, either. They avoid me, too. Som
bunch. Garbage."

For a moment she studied the floor, apparently uncomfortable
because she could see Jennifer's eyes wandering across the room
looking for something. "But I think we'll get along all righ
Peaches. I heard you were better brought up and educated tha
most of these creeps. I've got my M.A., not that that counts fc
much in here. In mathe—"

Jennifer finally saw them and put one hand on Jaffa's arm t
show her she wasn't running out on her deliberately. "Jaffa
please don't think I'm being rude, but there's something I have t
do. Just *have* to. Excuse me."

Jaffa started to say something, but stopped, apparently long
ago inured to people finding excuses to get away from her. Sh
watched Jennifer walk briskly across the room, and sighed th
sigh of the lonely.

Jennifer had indeed found them—what she had been thinkin
about all morning. The other cells. In one of them must be Peter
She raced down the long row. About half of the cells appeare
furnished for the girls; the other half stood empty. Jennife
almost cried, her whole body steeped in sudden coldness. "Goc
damn," Jennifer muttered, trying to overcome her disappoin
ment. She was baffled; slowly, though, the natural optimism tha
had sustained her for so long rose to the surface. Maybe ther
were cells someplace else in Blossom House—in the attic, (
possibly the cellar. That was it, she told herself. The husbanc
were kept someplace else, deliberately separated from their wive
Peter was here somewhere. She could *feel* it.

A crash and a scream spun her around. Two girls—she couldn't
see them well enough to know who they were—had gotten into a
screaming, hair-pulling fight over some slight, real or imagined.
Watching, Jennifer realized that one of the girls was Pippin,
something that only confirmed Jennifer's suspicion that Pippin
represented painful trouble—for everyone. The rest of the girls
ignored the battle, continuing whatever they'd been doing. Apparently, fights involving Pippin were not considered unusual
enough to bother with, although to Jennifer, it didn't seem much
in keeping with Harriet's description of a "happy little family."

For a moment the two girls separated. "Take that back, Strawberry," Pippin hissed. "I don't kiss crazy old Harriet's ass, and
you know it."

They were circling each other now, like jungle animals. "You
do, too. Christ, everybody knows about you and Harriet."

There was a sudden click, and a small knife appeared in
Pippin's hand. Her voice rose to a scream. *"Take that back, you
bitch. Or I'll—"* She suddenly lunged toward Strawberry with
the knife raised. Strawberry sidestepped and began frantically
groping behind her for something to defend herself with. The
flash of the knife had finally drawn the interest of some of the
girls, who stood at a safe distance and watched. Watched, but
made no move to interfere. Another yell from Pippin, another
scream from Strawberry. The knife sliced through the air again.
Another sidestep, but a closer call.

Jennifer was so horrified, she gave an unexpected and shattering scream of her own. Spinning, Cherry raced over and yanked
Strawberry to one side, inserting herself between the two girls. For a
moment Pippin was knocked off-balance enough for Cherry to
get an iron grip around the wrist of the hand with the knife.
"Drop it, Pippin. Drop it!" Pippin thrashed and struggled, almost freeing herself, yelling as loudly now at Cherry as she had
at Strawberry. When the diminutive Bartlett heard Cherry's sudden appeal for help, she grabbed Pippin's other arm, stuck out
one of her feet behind the girl's ankles, and pushed. With a
resounding crash, Pippin went over backward. Almost lazily, the

knife fell to the floor, well out of Pippin's reach. Between Cherry and Bartlett, they held Pippin down on the rug while she struggled and screamed and cursed and spat at them. When she seemed to have calmed down a little, they gradually let her up; Cherry kept the knife.

"I'll get you," Pippin promised Strawberry. "*And* you," she added, glaring at Cherry. "Miss Goody Two-Shoes." Still furious, she stormed off, shoving other girls out of the way to get to her room.

Cherry came over to Jennifer, laughing. "Want to buy a slightly used knife? For a moment there, I thought she was going to stick poor old Strawberry. Strawberry's not very bright, or she wouldn't tangle with that bitch." Cherry appeared to ponder a second. "Matter of fact, Strawberry's not very bright—period." She looked at Jennifer with a smile. "With all the people you had to meet, I doubt if you remember it, but I'm Cherry—disarmer of the wicked."

"I do," Jennifer answered quickly. "I loved the way you twitted Harriet."

"I'd shake your hand, but my palms are still a mite tender."

Jennifer laughed again. "I *bet* they are."

Cherry led Jennifer over to a small couch set against the far wall of the room. "You must have a lot of questions, Peaches. New girls always do. Shoot."

Jennifer suddenly realized she didn't know where to start, so she started with a minor point that had been troubling her. "Well, these names. I mean, I'm sort of surprised that when Harriet isn't around you don't call each other by your *real* names."

"Too confusing. We've tried it once, but then we'd get mixed up—at dinner or something, when Harriet was around—and use our real names in front of her. She blew her cork. Cut off our food for three damn days. So we went back to using *her* crazy names; in the end, it's easier."

"What about the girls? Who are they, how'd they get here? . . ."

"All of us got here the same way you did. Henry, the jovial justice of the peace. As to who they *are,* well, I know more about some than others. Some, like you, just got here this year; a couple have been around two or three years."

"Two or three *years!*" The world around Jennifer was collapsing, time falling in on her like houses during a typhoon.

Cherry looked at her appraisingly; Jennifer's sudden paleness told her that what you said to Jennifer had to be carefully edited and gently put. For a while, anyway.

Still shaking inside, Jennifer struggled to pull herself together to ask the one question uppermost in her mind. "The husbands," she asked, her voice strained. "What happens to the husbands?"

It was a question Cherry had hoped Jennifer wasn't going to ask, but had known she *would* ask. "The husbands," she answered vaguely. "Well," she lied. "Nobody really knows."

"What I mean is, are they kept in some other part of this damn place, or . . ." The word *or* dangled in space, an innocent conjunction, a benign connective in ordinary circumstances, but now suffused with what, to Jennifer, were hideous, unspeakable connotations.

"That's a big mystery around here," Cherry lied again. It was, of course, no mystery at all. Like a lot of the others, Cherry was well aware of what Henry Griggs's "magic fertilizer" had as a principle ingredient.

"Have you seen *your* husband since they clapped you in here?"

"Well, no. It's a long story, but he was an old man, see. I'll tell you the whole grim episode some other time."

"Have *any* of the girls seen theirs?"

Cherry shifted uncomfortably. "Not that I know of." She saw the look of panic sweep over Jennifer and tried to soften her answer. "I don't think Harriet likes the idea. Everything has to be separate. In her mind—if you can call it that—we're only twelve years old, remember. Too young to have a husband, and certainly too young to be getting visits from him. Anyway, there's all sorts of rumors about what happened to the men. Maybe they just run off somewhere.''

"It will be different with Peter," Jennifer assured her. "Peter will be back for me, I know it, I just *know* it."

Cherry was about to say more, but Strawberry had walked over to them. She stood, still looking frightened, and took hold of both of Cherry's hands. "Thanks, Cherry, for pulling that tiger off me. For a minute I thought I was about to be sliced up like bologna." She turned toward Jennifer.

Strawberry laughed grimly. "Bologna, fruits, nuts," she said with disgust. "But at least *you* got a name that sounds like a name. I knew a girl once everybody called Peaches. Nice girl, at that."

Jaffa had wandered over to them just in time to hear the end of the conversation. A grim look flitted across her face, and she turned her head away as if to make the whole matter of the name *Peaches* go away. From her reaction, Jennifer knew there was something unpleasant tied to her assigned name, something frightening.

Suddenly Jennifer felt very depressed. It was too much. "I hope nobody will mind, but I think maybe I'll go lie down in my cell for a few minutes." She felt she had to get away from this collectively gloomy crew; they were shattering her faith in her delusions. As she got up she ran into Pippin, who apparently had been standing on the edge of the little group.

Pippin carefully avoided looking at Strawberry; instead she stared at Jennifer with hostility. "That's just about what I'd expect. All you rich kids are spoiled and think you're too damn good for the rest of us. Shit."

Immediately Jennifer knew someone had been spreading unpleasant stories about her among the rest of them. Harriet, she supposed. No one here could have known her background unless Harriet had told them. To get out of the group, she virtually had to push Pippin out of her way.

"Go on, crybaby, run," Pippin taunted. "Go hide in your cell and pretend you're back on Park Avenue."

Jennifer turned to answer but saw Cherry shaking her head, warning her not to.

Her first morning with the happy little family of Blossom House had left her shaking inside—from anger, from disappointment, and from fear.

CHAPTER SEVENTEEN

Henry was in one of his male-dominant moods this morning. Christ. He went against me on a lot of things, but the worst was changing that awful girl's name from Olivia to Peaches. My God!

I can guess what's going on in his mind about the Peaches thing, and it's pretty sick. I had no choice but to go along with it; when Henry's acting like this, God himself couldn't do anything to stop him.

Journal of Blossom House,
Entry, page 37—Harriet Griggs

The unusual morning of free time had, instead of making things easier for Jennifer, made it worse; too much unoccupied time always gave the girls time to discover how little they really liked each other. Harriet was well aware of this phenomenon, counting on it to make things rougher for Jennifer.

"Usually," Cherry told her, "old Harriet stays right with a new girl when they put her in here—organizing games, integrating the poor kid, letting the old girls get to know her a little at a time and accept her into the group. It's a pain in the ass, having to put up with Harriet, but it works. With you, damn it, she's doing everything different.

"I think Harriet's hoping it'll make the other girls get the impression of you as an outsider. She's into a lot of psychological crap like that. And leaving you on your own this morning *is* going to make it harder for you to be accepted. Brutal. I don't think the lady likes you, kid."

Jennifer, who *knew* Harriet didn't—but not why—nodded in resigned agreement and looked directly at Cherry, who was sitting on Jennifer's bed. "She doesn't exactly seem fond of you either, Cherry."

"Talk back too much. One thing she can't take is talking back."

To nourish her effort to manipulate Henry, Jennifer knew she had to at least keep Harriet neutral. Maybe she should start buttering her up a little; certainly, she had to control herself and not talk back. She saw a strange look crossing Cherry's face and wondered if the girl could read minds.

"I guess I don't really have to say this," Cherry added a moment later, "but stay clear of Pippin. I can't prove it, but I think she's Harriet's spy. I *know* she's Harriet's favorite. Two of a kind, I guess. Anyway, Pippin does a lot of Harriet's dirty work on us in return for—well, I'm not exactly sure in return for what. Food, I know. Drugs, I suspect. But whatever else, she's bad news. Don't cross her, and don't say anything in front of her you don't want repeated to Harriet."

Jennifer shuddered. All those sweet-looking little girls, none of them seeming a day over twelve, curtsying and bowing to Harriet in their little starched dresses. Yet, underneath the starch and the ruffles, a squirming nest of intrigue. It seemed strange to Jennifer that so much backbiting and plotting and factionalizing could go on among so small a number of people yet, obviously, it did. "What about Jaffa?" Jennifer asked suddenly. "She seems like such a sad person." From the beginning, Jaffa had simultaneously fascinated and repelled Jennifer, and she wasn't sure why.

Cherry sighed at the question. "Jaffa *is* a sad person. The oldest girl here—almost twenty-four, I think—even if she doesn't look it. Got her masters in math—some weird kind of theoretical stuff, she told me—and married one of her professors. No one else understood what she was talking about, she said. I thought professors were supposed to be extra bright, but the dumb jerk picked Blossom House to get married in. You know the rest. So, she's back in a world where no one can understand what she's talking about. I guess that would make anybody sad.''

"Sad or not, I like her," Jennifer argued. "Besides, outside of yourself, she's the only person so far today who even tried to talk to me.''

Cherry shrugged. In the past, she'd tried to make friends with Jaffa, but the girl's determined, dull gloominess had proven too much for her to take. She smiled at Jennifer. "Okay, if you can stand her, be nice to her. She needs a friend.''

From outside Jennifer's cell—Harriet had told her they were to be called rooms, not cells—from outside Jennifer's *room*, there was a sudden snarling and screaming and the sound of bodies hitting each other. Cherry jumped to her feet and ran out into the main room, followed by Jennifer. Tangerine and Bartlett were having a furious battle—biting and kicking and spitting. When Jennifer found out what the fight was about, she had a hard time believing two adults could possibly get into a donnybrook over it. But as she watched—Cherry was in the middle of it, trying to stop the fight; Pippin stood on the edges, egging Tangerine and Bartlett on—she remembered reading that with any long-confined group, objects of no real value can suddenly assume vast importance.

"I found it in your cell, damn it," Bartlett yelled.

"You tore my cell apart, and took it," screamed Tangerine back at her.

"You stole it, you stole it, you're always stealing things," Bartlett shouted, shoving Tangerine so hard, she hit the wall with a terrible thud.

"It," in this case, was a simple comb. Bartlett's comb had disappeared, apparently, and Bartlett had decided the one she found in Tangerine's cell was her own.

"Look," said Cherry, staring down at Pippin and stepping in

between the two girls. "All of the combs in here are identical. The one you found in Tangerine's room could be hers or it could be anybody else's. How could anyone know for sure? It's a stupid thing to fight about, anyway."

The two girls seemed to calm down a little, but there were still muttered insults being thrown back and forth. Cherry tried to calm them down further. "If it's that important to you, Bartlett, I'll give you mine. For Christ's sake. And anyway, I don't know what you were doing messing around in Tangerine's room. Prying is just as lousy as stealing."

"Prying is just as bad as stealing," mimicked Pippin in a singsong voice. "You should have run a Sunday School, Cherry, instead of being a whore."

The savagery of Pippin's remark stopped the argument. It stunned Jennifer for a moment, but a second later she decided it was just Pippin being her usual, poisonous self.

Cherry had drifted away. Once again Jennifer made an effort to get some of the other girls into a conversation, but while not impolite about it, the girls kept the talks short and quickly moved on to do something else somewhere else, *with* somebody else. Jennifer stopped trying; she could understand how Jaffa must have felt her whole life.

Standing alone, she suddenly saw Jaffa heading toward her. Jennifer fled back to her room, feeling ashamed of herself as she did. But just now, in this troubled juncture of her stay at Blossom House, she couldn't bear the thought of a gloomy conversation with the girl.

Fascinated by Jaffa or not, it was too much to expect.

A little after the Mickey Mouse clock on her wall told her it was noon, the room outside became suddenly quiet. She stepped out, just in time to see Harriet sweep into the room. Her eyes immediately went to Jennifer.

"This is no way to get to know the rest of your family, Peaches. You should be mixing, talking, making friends, not sulking in your room by yourself. Sometimes I don't know what to make of you, child."

The other girls had lined up and were curtsying, although she noticed that Cherry barely bobbed. Jennifer curtsied properly, in spite of hearing a loud, derisive snicker from Pippin.

"All right, children, it's lunchtime. I hope you've been showing the new member of our family how well we can all behave." Jennifer wanted to hoot with laughter, and carefully avoided looking at Cherry, whom she knew would make some sly, droll expression that would break her up.

The luncheon was quite formal, preceded by grace, said by the tiny Bartlett. Jennifer began to perspire. How could anyone say grace in these frightening circumstances? Sneaking a look around the table, she saw all of the girls, their hands folded in front of them, looking angelic in their starched pinafores. It said a lot about the hypocrisy of appearances.

The food arrived on the same dumbwaiter that Peter had mentioned their first night there—something about a little girl calling down the shaft and warning them to get out of Blossom House while they still could. *That* was what they should have done. She should have listened to Peter when he first wanted to leave, but instead, she'd talked him into staying for a "little champagne." This whole mess was her own fault. Wherever Peter was, he must have realized this by now too and be silently cursing her. The thought almost made Jennifer cry.

Throughout the meal Harriet maintained her pose as the gentle but firm mother. "Sit up straight, all of you," she said at one point, taking the edge off her command with a gentle, understanding smile. "Nice little girls don't *slouch*."

The girls barely spoke to one another during the whole meal, and when they did it was so softly, Jennifer couldn't hear them. Talking across the table, Harriet reminded them that arguing was not permitted. "You have to yell when you do," Harriet reminded them. "And nice little girls don't do *that* either."

To Jennifer the meal was the Mad Hatter's tea party. Only

there was no looking glass for her to disappear through, and her principal reaction was not laughter, but fear.

After luncheon they returned to the regular Blossom House regimen. Three hours of classes, Jennifer learned, were scheduled, all of them led by Harriet. Oddly enough, Jennifer looked forward to them; using her mind might take some of the edge off worrying about the situation she was in, along with allowing her to escape her suspicions about what might have happened to Peter. Her mind was always stimulated by schoolwork—the excitement of hitting the right answers in calculus, or of expressing herself in themes on history, or of the challenge presented by interpretations of Sartre and O'Neill and Joyce.

Just as she was about to sit down at a pupil's desk with the others, Henry strolled in. "Peaches," he said, smiling at her broadly, "we're going to be doing your schoolwork over here."

Harriet, Jennifer could see, was fuming. "I don't understand. . . ." Harriet began weakly.

"I'm taking over Peaches's classes myself, Harriet. She needs special work, I think. Come on, Peaches."

Slowly Jennifer rose, following Henry to the other side. She had avoided looking at either Harriet or the others as she stood up to go; some of the girls appeared as annoyed by Henry's show of blatant favoritism as Harriet did.

With a satisfied sigh, Henry seated Jennifer in an easy chair, facing him. Throwing open a math book, he began. As Jennifer started to look through the book's pages, she couldn't believe what she saw; at best, the work was on the sixth-grade level. "Mr. Griggs," she complained, "this math is sixth-grader's stuff. It says so right on the front page. I'm much more advanced than—"

"I know, I know," Henry said, apparently very pleased with himself. "Aren't you lucky to be in the advanced group?"

Jennifer was stunned. "The advanced group! My God, Mr. Griggs, I—"

"Please, don't swear, Peaches; it's not at all nice." He paused briefly, apparently to remember what they'd been talking about.

Then: "Oh, my, yes, Peaches. The advanced group. Why, most of the other children are only working on fifth-grade material, and some of them, not even that."

Jennifer started to object again, but Henry didn't appear to hear her. Wearily she opened the math book. She flinched; there was something insulting about staring at a key math problem no more taxing than $112\frac{2}{17} \times 2$.

Three hours later Jennifer's head was spinning from the effort of trying to appear interested in primitive subjects she'd put behind her five or six years ago. If it were not for her need to keep Henry fascinated with her, she'd have taken all the textbooks and shredded them in front of his eyes. Henry suddenly slapped the history book shut. "Well, Peaches, you've done extraordinarily well, dear. I don't think you'll have any trouble keeping up with the advanced section's work at all."

"Thank you. You're a swell teacher." Jennifer hated herself for saying it, but knew that one of the secrets of effective manipulation was flattery that didn't sound like flattery. She forgave herself because it represented the light at the end of the tunnel: escape.

Henry beamed. "Not *swell*, Peaches; slang is impolite. *Good* would have been a much more fitting word for a child of your age to use." He glanced at his watch. "My, it's getting late; it's past time for calisthenics to start. Working with a receptive young mind always makes me lose track of the time."

Jennifer looked at the other girls, still with their heads buried in their books, writing tables on the student desks in front of them, being put through their paces by Harriet. Jaffa was ashen; if Jennifer had trouble accepting sixth-grade-level work, she could imagine how someone with an M.A. in theoretical mathematics must feel. The girl's eyes appeared half-closed.

"Jaffa," Harriet suddenly shouted at her. "Pay attention, *please*! You'll never get through long division if you don't pay attention."

Maybe, thought Jennifer, Henry had been right. She *was* lucky to be in the advanced group.

At about a quarter to four Harriet clapped her hands and began the calisthenics; fifteen minutes had been allowed for the girls to change into their gym bloomers—ruffled, trimmed with lace, and as antique-looking as all the rest of their clothes at Blossom House. Clapping her hands to keep time, Harriet put them through what she had described as a rigorous program. Jennifer smiled to herself: hopscotch, blindman's buff, stoop tag, and bean-bag races. On the edge of the group, Henry roared with delight at every race and sally, keeping score of each game himself and adding the figures to a giant chart he kept.

Bath time. Milk and cookies. Then quiet table games: a go-fish tournament and, for some curious reason, Mah-Jongg.

Just before dinner, decked out in the most formal of their little girls' dresses, Jennifer, as with most of the others, stood outside the door of her room, awaiting the arrival of Harriet and Henry so they could begin dinner. She was surprised when Cherry, breaking the rules as usual, slipped over and stood beside her.

"Peaches," Cherry said in a soft, tortured whisper, "I guess I ought to tell you something before someone else does. In a place like this, even the people who like you will tell anything bad about you they know. Anyway, back earlier—" Cherry seemed to be having trouble saying what she wanted to say; it was unusual for a girl who usually had trouble *not* saying exactly what she thought—"back earlier, what that damn little bitch Pippin said. I mean, about me being a whore on the outside. Well, it's true." Jennifer studied Cherry carefully; she had gone pale and was having increasing trouble controlling her voice.

"I don't know exactly how to explain it, Peaches. But see, I ran away from Culver Hollow in West Virginia, because there wasn't anything there for me. To New York. There wasn't anything there for me, either. I don't know exactly how it happened—I sure hadn't planned on it—but I met a guy, a pimp, I guess, and wound up working the Minnesota Strip. It was awful; you wouldn't believe how awful. But I guess it wasn't any worse than being pawed by my stepfather in Culver Hollow. I'm not proud of it, Peaches. Christ, I hope you understand how these things can happen. . . ."

Jennifer put a reassuring hand on Cherry's arm. To her, Cherry was talking of another world, a world she'd only caught a glimpse of in hastily hidden tabloids, a world she couldn't understand, a world so far from her well-ordered universe of Park and Fifth Avenues and boys from Princeton and boys from Yale, it was as if Cherry were talking about life on another planet.

"Of course I understand, Cherry," Jennifer lied. "Everybody, one time or another, does things and winds up in places they don't know how they got to." Although, it suddenly struck her, the particular place she'd gotten to at the moment was because she had enjoyed flirting with an ancient justice of the peace, Henry Griggs, in spite of all warnings from Peter and from inside herself that they shouldn't stay where they were a moment longer. Her words to Cherry had been inadequate, and Jennifer knew it. She tried to amplify them.

"And well, gosh, Cherry, it doesn't change what I think about you one bit. In the same spot, I might have done the same thing myself." Another lie. She hoped Cherry couldn't see through the hollowness of it.

"I don't know, Jennifer," Cherry sighed, using Jennifer's real name, showing how much the confession had rattled her. "Everybody always says something like that, but I sometimes wonder how much, deep-down, they really mean it."

"Well, screw the others. I *do*." Jennifer paused, pondering something that baffled her. "What I *don't* understand is how you wound up here. . . ."

"Married a customer. Nice, rich, old customer who wanted to take me away from all that stuff, he said. I figured, hell, he's real damn old, and when he dies, I'll pick up the loot and spend the rest of my life in a fancy apartment, soaking in a hot clean tub, looking out the window at night and wondering how things are going with the poor bastards on the Strip. Well, my nice rich old man did everything right but one thing: He chose Blossom House to get married in.'' Cherry pondered a moment, then laughed. "Shit. Maybe my pimp steered him here."

Jennifer laughed too, if a little uncertainly. Again, she began trying to reassure Cherry that it didn't matter, which, of course, at the moment, it did. "Oh, well, people get themselves into—"

"Children," Harriet said, walking into the room, wearing the same deep maroon hostess gown Jennifer had seen from her door-panel window. "We shall sit down for dinner in just a moment." She studied the room, her squinted eyes coming to rest on Cherry. "I don't understand, Cherry, why you simply refuse to obey the rules. You know perfectly well you're supposed to be outside your own room, not someone's else's. After dinner we'll have a little discussion, you and I, as to what we should do about your continual disobedience—one might almost say defiance."

Defiance, Jennifer thought. The Minnesota Strip, in a way, had been Cherry's ultimate defiance. To survive in a world rougher than she had ever known, perhaps defiance was the only way.

Dinner was a highly formal affair. She was seated to Henry's right, because, he said, it was her first night at the table and there might be things she didn't understand. His explanation fooled no one. Harriet's face grew stormy, and some of the girls' resentment started to show. The favoritism was too patent. Playing up to him during dinner only made things worse, as her playing up to her father had always infuriated her mother. In her life, history seemed to have a way of repeating itself. Now Harriet was infuriated by her playing up to Henry. Screw them both.

It was a meal quickly eaten, sometimes in almost total silence, except for Jennifer's chattering to Henry. Harriet glowered. Henry loved every minute of it.

After dinner the girls again gathered in a semicircle on the floor in front of Henry's chair. Raising and lowering his voice dramatically, he read to them from *Little Women*. They were about halfway through, Jennifer estimated, and the book read out loud was just as deadly as when you read it to yourself. While Jennifer was doing her best to appear enthralled, smiling at Henry whenever he interjected some comment of his own, she suddenly heard Cherry's voice whispering beside her. "You think *this* is bad? Some nights, as a special treat, they let us watch TV. Guess what: *Sesame Street* or *Mister Rogers' Neighborhood.*"

By 9:15, the whole lot of them were in bed. Lying in the dark, Jennifer struggled to sort out the day. Her device of playing up to Henry—at the moment the only way she could think of to engineer a possible escape—appeared highly workable, even if it did raise everyone else's hackles. Especially Harriet's, a dangerous woman to antagonize; Jennifer knew she was already an enemy.

Other faces flew across her mind. Jaffa—with the M.A. in theoretical mathematics, faced with coping with long division. Pippin—a treacherous, dangerous girl, a spy, picking up Harriet's lead and being as unpleasant as she could manage. Cherry—the Minnesota Strip confession shouldn't bother her, yet it did. Jennifer hoped she'd get over it quickly; Cherry was the only one here so far who had been kind to her, and the only one she really trusted. All in all, a frightening collection.

But most frightening of all—she'd caught herself on the edge of it twice today—was that the claustrophobic atmosphere of Blossom House—the clothes, the schoolwork, the books, the children's games, the language used to her by both Henry and Harriet—had made her almost believe, if only briefly, that maybe she *was* just twelve years old, that her name *was* Peaches, and that this *was* and *always had been* her home.

Doing her nightly rounds, Harriet's face suddenly appeared in Jennifer's door panel, softly lit and appearing to float in space, a bodiless ghost from another world. "Well, Peaches, dear. Sleep well. Good night. Don't let the bedbugs bite." Harriet laughed eerily and slammed the sliding panel shut.

Jennifer wanted to scream. More than ever, she suspected Harriet of planning something far more terrifying than even the most vicious bedbug could manage.

CHAPTER EIGHTEEN

If that little monster Peaches doesn't think I see what she's up to, she's crazy. Playing up to Henry the way she does—obvious, shameful behavior, a Park Avenue floozy's game. (Are there Park Avenue floozies? I guess there are; one street or the other is all the same to a prostitute.)

Worse, that senile old fool Henry doesn't seem to catch on to what she's doing. He laps it up. Every time I try to tell him, he just says I'm jealous.

I don't know what Peaches hopes to gain; he isn't going to let her get away from here any more than I am.

Playing up to people is something I've had trouble with ever since I was a child. I don't know why.

Journal of Blossom House,
Entry, page 38—Harriet Griggs

"Another day, another nothing," Jennifer said to Bartlett—her room was next to Jennifer's—as they walked out into the main room at breakfast time a week or so after Jennifer's introduction to the family.

"Yeah," Bartlett answered, giving Jennifer nothing more than a weak smile. A second later she had disappeared to talk with someone on the far side of the room. Jennifer was hurt and angry. Bartlett, tiny and bright, was someone she'd have liked to have as a friend, but every overture was shrugged off, not impolitely, but without any apparent interest on Bartlett's part in hearing what Jennifer had to say. She'd tried everything with all of them—except Pippin—but the response was a uniform indifference. Cherry tried to help—just about everyone seemed to like Cherry—but even she couldn't make much headway in getting the other girls to accept Jennifer. For the first time in her life Jennifer felt like a social outcast.

She knew all of the others resented her buttering-up game with Henry. Since she didn't dare explain the reason behind it, the resentment lay where it was, festering. She also knew that Pippin—standing in for Harriet—worked hard at discrediting her, making up conversations that had never taken place, in which Jennifer was quoted as saying things like the other girls were really quite beneath her; that they hadn't been well brought up; that "her education and background made her too refined a person to be thrown in with such riffraff."

No one, of course, believed very much of what Pippin *ever* said, but the impression of Jennifer as being a snob stayed with them.

Cherry's highly favorable reports on Jennifer were dismissed by Pippin; she'd overheard them talking, she said, and knew that Jennifer had promised Cherry enough money to get off the Minnesota Strip for good if she'd just be her friend. "After all," Pippin added as the clincher, "Cherry's very used to getting paid for friendship." This explanation was so preposterous, even Jaffa laughed. The laughter only made Pippin more furious; she was more determined to come down hard on Jennifer than ever. Harriet's instructions aside, she now had her own reasons for destroying her.

It was that afternoon that Pippin saw an opportunity to up the stakes in the game. Outside Jennifer's room, she had heard

Jennifer telling Cherry and Jaffa she was sure Peter, somehow, would come back to get her. It was only a matter of time, Jennifer added, perhaps trying to convince herself as much as the others. There had been a silence in Jennifer's room while Cherry and Jaffa struggled to find some way to tell Jennifer the truth without shattering her completely. They failed. Weakly, Jaffa had murmured that, well, one could never be sure in crazy messes like this, but that it was possible Jennifer was right, she supposed, and the best thing for her to do was just try and be patient.

Cherry was even less encouraging. She didn't want to lie to Jennifer, yet neither did she want to shake her completely by blurting out the painful, dreadful truth. There was a time for such things, and this wasn't it.

"Oh, I don't know, Peaches," she began. "I don't think *anybody* knows. Jaffa probably has the right idea: be patient, and just wait and see what happens."

A moment later Pippin watched Jaffa and Cherry leave Jennifer's room, escaping from a situation that had made them both extremely uncomfortable. At that moment they both hated themselves for being so spineless. Watching them disappear, Pippin knew her opportunity had come and she strolled into Jennifer's room, even managing to produce a small, understanding smile for her.

Seeing her walk in—something Pippin had never done before— Jennifer was startled. Maybe Pippin had finally accepted her. No, with Harriet calling the shots, highly improbable. Still, it was worth being as pleasant as she could manage. "Oh, hi, Pippin. Well, today wasn't too bad. Better than most, don't you think?" Pippin said nothing but continued to stare at her, the unsuitable smile still fixed to her face like a severe case of acne. Jennifer tried again. "What's up, Pippin? Is there anything I can do for you?"

The smile on Pippin's face vanished abruptly. "For me, nothing. For yourself, yes." The mysterious answer hung in the air for a moment, then Pippin pulled the trigger. "Those girls—Cherry

and Jaffa—hell, they were lying to you, Peaches, lying like
crazy. 'Wait and see,' they said. That's a laugh; it just made you
look like a jerk. Listen to me, Peaches, and listen to me good.
There's no point waiting around expecting to see Peter. You'll
never see him again. Because he's dead. Dead just like all the
rest of the husbands are dead. Including mine. Gone. Wasted.
Killed. Butchered by your sweet old big buddy, Henry. Grow up.
Face it. It's the truth.''

Inside, Pippin smiled. The look on Jennifer's face, the wheez-
ing gasp she had given, the suddenly ashen color of her skin as
the brutal facts were thrown in her face, was worth the price of
admission. However, Pippin had little time to enjoy the show.

Her entire frame trembling badly, Jennifer dove across the
room and began shaking Pippin violently with her hands. The
attack was so sudden and so extreme, Pippin felt helpless before
it. From about six inches in front of her face, Jennifer shouted
directly into it. *"It isn't true, that baloney you're spouting, no
for a damn minute it isn't. You're a lying bitch. A cruel, spiteful
lying bitch!"*

Jennifer swallowed hard, the harsh salt taste of tears welling
inside her throat, the enormity of what Pippin had said beginning
to sink in, the first real doubts beginning to hit her. *"You're
lying, damn it—lying,"* she screamed, her voice breaking and her
breath coming in strangled sobs. *"Listen to me, listen! It's not
true, I tell you, not true, not true, not true!"*

Even Pippin was rattled by the violence of Jennifer's outburst,
trying to cover the fact by smiling thinly. Jennifer had shaken
her; now she would shake *her*. "Not true?" Pippin laughed.
"You're fucking right it's true." With a lunge, she seized Jennifer's arm, her fingers biting into the flesh with the iron vise of
her hand, and dragged her over to her window. With one long
finger, she pointed down into the garden below.

"See that little mound of earth over there by the row of apple
trees? Newly turned over, wouldn't you say? *That's* where your
precious Peter is now—buried in quicklime and fertilizing Henry's crazy goddamn fruit trees. I saw them do it once, just like

that. Drugged drinks. A little trip downstairs on some pretext or other. And then, ZAP! Dead. Stuck out in the orchard with your mouth full of quicklime.''

Jennifer stared out the window at the mound of earth near the apple trees, her eyes vacant. She didn't believe it, she couldn't believe it Yet some part of her *did* believe it, and it was tearing at her insides, like the eagle ripping open Prometheus's guts as he lay chained to a rock in the gray vastness of the Caucasus Mountains.

"The mound a little farther to the left,'' Pippin said calmly, beginning to enjoy herself, ''—the one that already has grass growing over it and has settled down more into the soil—well, that was Jay Filmore, poor bastard. He's the one I watched them do.''

Slowly Jennifer turned toward her, eyes wild, unbelieving tears running down her face, mouth twisted into a grotesque mask. From inside her, suddenly, there came a cry, a scream, a shriek, an uncontrollable piercing sound that ricocheted off the walls of Jennifer's tiny cell and spilled out into the vastness of the living room, tearing at the air around it and making the walls seem to tremble.

From outside came the sounds of confusion. Pippin began backing out of Jennifer's room, hearing others running toward it. She backed straight into Cherry, hurrying through the door. Roughly Cherry spun Pippin around. "What the hell have you done now?'' she demanded, looking at Jennifer, who stood facing her, staring.

"She's flipped. Your little buddy's flipped.''

Cherry grabbed Pippin, slapped her face hard, and shoved her out of the room with every bit of strength she had. Then she went over to Jennifer and held her, trying to find out what Pippin had said. From Jennifer's condition, Cherry could guess.

For the first time since she'd come into the room, Cherry saw Jennifer's eyes focus on her. "You lied to me,'' she hissed between sobs. "You lied to me about Peter. He's dead. You lied to me.'' Jennifer burst into open tears, Cherry holding her tightly

in her arms, Jennifer's trembling finger pointing silently to tl
mound of earth beyond her window.

Neither Jennifer nor Cherry made it to the breakfast tabl
They'd both come down with something, Bartlett solemnly e:
plained to an unbelieving Harriet.

For several days Pippin backed off. It was not that she
yielded—Pippin never yielded—but her brutal treatment of Jenn
fer had stirred sympathy among the others, something Pippin ha
not counted on. It had made Jennifer a new friend in Bartlett. Th
diminutive girl, bright and almost always cheerful, had been in h
room—the next one to Jennifer's—during Pippin's dreadful recita
Bartlett had detected the enjoyment in Pippin's voice as sl
unfolded the facts, including Pippin's own frightening confessic
that Harriet had let her witness, step by step, the killing and buri
of Jay Filmore.

Filmore's name was one that Bartlett was quite familiar wit
he had been her husband. To Cherry and Jaffa, you could no
add Bartlett as a firm ally of Jennifer's. The reverse reaction ha
infuriated Pippin, but there was little she could do about it exce
sulk in her room and frantically work on new plots to destrc
Jennifer, with Harriet as a willing partner.

It took Jennifer almost three long days to recover from tl
shock of what Pippin had forced her to believe. Inside, she st:
did not yet fully accept that Peter was dead; they could be wron;
all of them; Pippin could be lying, making the whole thing up; a
of the husbands—including Peter—could still be locked up som
where inside this huge house, imprisoned rather than kille
Constantly Jennifer found herself torn by these two diametrical
opposed beliefs, wondering, searching, torturing herself. Reali
locked in mortal combat with hope, the essential battle of existenc

Pippin did not stay quiet long. In every private conversatic
Harriet would goad her. "You blew the last try, Pippin," Harri
would scold, "you'd better get cracking, girl. Those little 'f
vors' I do for you can stop any time I decide it. Or, a few wor

from me, and I could make the other children turn on you. If they knew some of the things you've done to them over the last year, they'd be delighted to get my permission to tear you in pieces. So move, child, *move*."

When Jennifer walked into Jaffa's room that afternoon, she found the girl adding the last painted touches to a weird-looking black object she had on the desk in front of her. "Jaffa, what in the world. . .?"

Solemnly Jaffa put the strange-looking black thing on her head. It was a Mickey Mouse Club hat. "It suits me, don't you think?" Jaffa asked her, as close to laughing as Jaffa ever got.

"It's really *you*," Jennifer answered with a giggle, thinking Jaffa was kidding.

Jaffa turned her sad eyes to her, taking off the hat and playing with it in her hand. "Peaches," she asked, "do you sometimes—well, ever—have the feeling that maybe you *are* only twelve? That a lot of what you remember about your life before Blossom House was a dream or something you made up?"

Jennifer looked at her in acknowledgment. She could easily imagine how much more acutely Jaffa, older and with the trained mind of a graduate mathematician, must suffer from the sensation of sometimes thinking like a little girl. "You bet I do," Jennifer answered. "All the time. It drives me nuts. And I don't even have an M.A. like you do."

"That's the part that bothers me most—those damn exercises in long division I have to plow through every day. I'm deathly afraid if I do it long enough, I'll really start to believe I *am* only twelve. My mind will go. It terrifies me, all day, every day, all night, every night."

Jennifer groped to find something, anything, that might reassure poor Jaffa, but a noise behind her made her turn around. Pippin had come through the door and was standing there with a grim-faced Tangerine. Jaffa immediately hid the Mickey Mouse hat with her feet; Harriet would not be amused, and if Pippin ever got a good look at it—she was already craning her neck to see what it was—Harriet would know of its existence in a matter of hours.

Pippin's sullen eyes moved over to Jennifer; Tangerine shifted her feet uncomfortably. "You stole Tangerine's stuffed doll, Peaches. I saw you coming out of her room with it. Poor Tangerine made that doll herself."

Jennifer gasped. The charge was so outlandish—and in itself so ridiculous, grown women fighting over a stuffed toy—her first instinct was to laugh. But seeing Pippin's solemn expression and the angry, accusing look that had crept over Tangerine's face once the charge had been made, Jennifer converted the laugh into outraged denial.

"That's crazy. I don't steal things. You know that, Tangerine. This is just some trick—"

Pippin stood her ground. "All right, if you're so high-and-mighty sure that you *didn't* steal it, let's go look in your cell, Peaches."

"Tear it apart if you want," Jennifer answered and followed them out the door as they headed for her room. From behind her, she had heard Jaffa's doleful voice calling, "Careful, Peaches. It's a trick. *Careful . . .*"

In Jennifer's room, Pippin began searching while Tangerine mostly watched, uncertainly. The closet was rummaged through, a lot of the things on hangers winding up on the floor. With a flourish, Pippin pulled the drawers out of the little dresser and dumped everything inside on Jennifer's bed, running her hands through the pile like a cannery worker sorting clams. The curtains were looked behind, the furniture looked under, and Jennifer's bathroom gone through, Pippin even checking inside the toilet tank to see if the doll might be floating in the tank water. It was a favorite place, she pointed out, for alcoholics to hide their bottles.

Back in the center of the bedroom, Pippin appeared stumped. Tangerine looked embarrassed. "Ah," Pippin said suddenly. "I bet I know where it is. Help me with this, Tangerine." On

Pippin's command, Tangerine helped her lift the mattress off the bed and drop it on the floor. There, in the center of the bedsprings, was Tangerine's doll. "See?" Pippin said triumphantly. "I knew we'd find it somewhere in here. Oh, poor little doll. It's head got all squashed and torn from the springs." Sadly she handed the remains of the doll over to Tangerine, who stood staring at it as if she'd just found her dog dead on the street, squashed by a fast-moving truck. Slowly her eyes rose to Jennifer's.

"So help me God, Tangerine. I didn't take it. Honest. I don't know how the hell it got there. Christ, maybe . . ." Jaffa's earlier words came back to haunt Jennifer, whispering into her ear: "*Careful, Peaches. It's a trick . . .*"

"Maybe Pippin put it there herself," Jennifer said to Tangerine suddenly. "To make you hate me the way *she* does. Maybe. . ."

Pippin hooted with laughter. "So it was a plant, *that's* how it got in your room? And I planted it there. Come off it, Peaches; you've seen too much television." From Pippin's throat came the dreadful laugh again; Jennifer's insides shriveled. She saw Tangerine, the doll hanging limply from one hand, coming across the room toward her, her face filled with fury. To Jennifer's surprise it was Pippin who held out a hand and stopped her.

"Don't, Tangerine. Not now. We'll get her. Later. We'll get her *real* good." The laugh again. "C'mon, Tangerine, let's go down to your room and see if we can fix this poor, battered little thing up." With Tangerine still looking at her ominously, they walked out of Jennifer's door. Not before, however, Pippin had gotten off a parting shot.

"So long, Peaches," Pippin said, smiling darkly. "Too bad these doors don't have locks on them. For nighttime. I think you'll be needing a lot of locks before *I* get through with you."

Just outside her door, Jennifer heard Pippin telling Tangerine: "Rich bitches are always like that. Can't stand anyone to have something they don't."

The remark Pippin had made about her needing a lock on her door at night confused Jennifer. But what terrified rather than confused her was not just Pippin—she could handle her, she thought—it was the realization that Harriet must have known all about the accusation of theft, the planted doll, and Pippin's sinister threat before any of it had happened.

She might be able to handle anything Pippin could come up with, but Harriet? No.

The story of the stolen doll was public knowledge by dinnertime that night. The others had trouble taking the doll very seriously—Tangerine, they had realized long ago, was very much of a flake—but the theft of something personal was something they *did* take very seriously. They all had small items, things they had made, things they had found, things they had been given, which were of enormous value to them. To steal such an object was like stealing part of a person's soul. At dinner, they studied Jennifer curiously, trying to see if a thief's hands looked any different than their own. Even Bartlett, Jennifer thought, seemed to be avoiding her. Later Cherry was able to reassure Jennifer it was her imagination—and convince Bartlett that the entire incident had been a rigged one. Tangerine, she would work on when she'd cooled off.

Jennifer and Cherry both agreed that it would probably happen again, only it would be something worse. "Maybe," Cherry suggested cheerfully, "Pippin will overplay her hand and plant so many things in your room, the other girls will realize how ridiculous the whole thing is and start laughing at her. I'll start preparing them for it now. It'll make it even more obvious if they're expecting it."

But Harriet's mind was far too devious for anything so simple. Nothing else was stolen, no more "plants" appeared in Jennifer's room. The fact was that Harriet was already planning something far more painful than stolen personal objects to turn the others against Jennifer. When Pippin first heard what Harriet was planning she roared with laughter. It was diabolical. The others would tear Jennifer apart, a thought that both Harriet and Pippin found enormously pleasing.

*   *   *

"As a special treat, children, you are going to be allowed to watch *Little Lord Fauntleroy* on television," Harriet announced. "In one way, it's part of your education. But it's also very well done, I understand. A moving drama. So please, children, be on your best behavior for the next few days; I don't want anything to spoil it for you."

To the girls the announcement was an exciting one. Outside of occasional glimpses of *Sesame Street* and *Mister Rogers' Neighborhood*, they had seen no television at all since they arrived at Blossom House. *Little Lord Fauntleroy* might not have been the show any of them would have chosen—"Why not *Three's Company* or *Quincy* or *Dallas*?" Bartlett had asked sadly—but at least it was television, with real grown-up actors moving around and talking in a story with a beginning and a middle and an end.

The next day, the television set was wheeled in and set up in the corner. The excitement among the girls rose as they stared at the large screen, set upon a high rolling stand that made it possible for them all to see it at once. Smiling, Harriet announced that the program was tomorrow night and that, instead of the usual formal dinner, the occasion would be honored by a sumptuous buffet laid out on the great table, and that she had planned some quite extravagant dishes for it.

The mere presence of the television set, the change in routine, and the promise of the program itself drove the excitement to a feverish pitch. For an outsider looking at the girls, there would have been something infinitely pathetic in the excitement that could be generated by such a small, simple event. Even Jennifer felt herself getting carried away a little.

The next day arrived, and the girls began to torture themselves with anticipation. Harriet found the atmosphere in her classes so keyed up, teaching was difficult; Henry gave Jennifer a long talk on the period depicted in *Lord Fauntleroy,* instead of his usual dreary meanderings through math and history and geography that Jennifer had already been put through years earlier.

During calisthenics, Jennifer noticed that the girls' nervous energy was expressing itself in a much higher degree of activity than was normal. Stoop tag became so violent, Harriet had to stop the game in the middle; she switched instead to blindman's buff, only to discover it too can be played so roughly, it becomes dangerous.

Jennifer looked at Henry, gleefully keeping score, apparently delighted in the heightened level of game playing. In his eye was a gleam of malevolence that startled Jennifer. If only her escape plan didn't depend so heavily on his unwitting cooperation, she would have put on a blindfold and pretended to stumble in to him so hard, Henry wouldn't get up for a week.

A tremendous push from behind her sent Jennifer reeling. She spun, to see Pippin smiling at her, a smile that was more of a leer than anything else. "Don't do that again, Pippin," Jennifer yelled at her and turned away.

"I can handle you anytime," Pippin answered, walking across the room and again catching her from behind with a brutal shove. Baffled, Jennifer planted her feet and stared. The leer was still in place, Pippin's eyes cold and challenging. She moved toward Jennifer and punched her hard in the stomach. "Crybabies like you, Peaches, need a little pushing around now and then. Rich bitches that steal stuff and then lie about it. You make me sick."

Looking around, Jennifer saw that Harriet, although pointed in her general direction, seemed not to have noticed. She found this strange, since Harriet usually caught any movement the least out of the ordinary; the talent had allowed her to stop many brewing fights before they really got started. Cherry, Jennifer could see, was on the far side of the room, absorbed in something.

From Pippin, Jennifer again heard the sound of short, excited breathing, almost animallike in its intensity. Jennifer knew she was going to have to fight. Pippin was spoiling for it.

In a last, futile effort, she tried to appeal to Pippin's fear of punishment, already suspecting the appeal would be turned down. "Look, Pippin, this is stupid. Harriet will—"

"Stupid. Stupid like your precious Peter was stupid. I hear he was a big fag, anyway. A *stupid* fag. I don't know why you bothered to—"

The shriek that came from Jennifer surprised even Jennifer. She dove toward Pippin just in time to receive a hard blow to her face that staggered her. In an instant Pippin landed on top of her, yelling, "Fag-lover, fag lover!" into her ear. Jennifer could feel her hair being torn out of her skull, nails tearing deeply into her face, and the horrible thump of her own head against the wall as Pippin banged her head against it, over and over and over.

Struggling, but at a disadvantage, because Pippin's counterattack had taken her by surprise and she was now on the bottom, Jennifer fought back as hard as she could, punching Pippin in the stomach and pounding her on the breasts, trying to get a grip on Pippin's hair so she could throw her off. "Peter was a fag, a big fag!" Pippin continued to scream at her. The words cut deep; they were outrageously wrong, Jennifer knew, but somehow their venom twisted inside her like a loose razor blade. The battle continued. Pippin was much stronger, Jennifer discovered, and more used to assault. At Chalmer's, the girls got furious with each other at different times, but somehow always managed to stop short of anything physical.

Above Pippin's screaming, Jennifer could hear Cherry trying to calm Pippin down; at the same time she roughly pulled at the girl from behind to try to get her off Jennifer. Pippin didn't budge. Finally Bartlett arrived and began yanking at Pippin from the opposite side, and Jennifer could feel the girl's grip loosening. Between them, Cherry and Bartlett—with the sudden, unexpected intercession of Jaffa—managed to heave Pippin entirely off Jennifer, dumping the screaming and cursing girl roughly to the floor. Pippin looked up in stunned disbelief.

While Cherry pulled Jennifer to her feet and began using her hankie to blot the scratches on Jennifer's face, Bartlett turned to Pippin, her hands clutched to her side, determined not to help. "I don't care if you *are* Harriet's favorite," Bartlett announced.

"You're going to catch it this time, Pippin. I saw what you did, I heard what you said, I know that you deliberately started the whole damn thing."

Pippin smiled up at Bartlett, one corner of her mouth turned up to show her contempt. "You just wait and see who catches it."

By then, both Henry and Harriet were on the scene. Henry helped Cherry lead Jennifer into her room and said he would be back with some antiseptics and lotions for her face. "Peaches," he asked her softly, "how did this happen, dear? I can't believe—I won't believe—that you started it."

"She did, too," Pippin screamed at him. "Ask anybody who saw it. For no reason, no reason at all, she just suddenly came at me. Yelling. I think she's crazy, Mr. Griggs, I really do. All I was doing was defending myself from her. . . ."

Harriet came out of Jennifer's room at the same moment. "You poor dear," she murmured to Pippin, helping her to her feet. "Just look at your face." Stopping Henry just before he got to the door, Harriet called after him with an announcement clearly as much intended to be heard by the others as by Henry. "Henry, it *was* Peaches's fault. I saw her attack Pippin with my own eyes. Without provocation. She just jumped on the poor child. And then, a moment ago when I was in her room, she spat in my face. Spat at *me*. Disgusting. Absolutely disgusting. She will have to be severely punished. Very *severely* punished."

Openmouthed, Bartlett listened from Jennifer's doorway. "She did not. She didn't come near you. She didn't spit at—" A glare from Harriet robbed Bartlett of her small reservoir of courage. She had tried to be brave, she wanted to be brave, but she had never been a strong person, she told herself, hating the fact but unable to change it, withering under Harriet's stare. "I mean, I didn't *see* her spit at you, Miss Griggs. Maybe when I was in the bathroom getting the water or something . . ." Her voice trailed away into nothingness. Defeated, herself the enemy, Bartlett shrugged and suddenly pulled back into Jennifer's room, beaten.

With a faint smile flickering across her huge face, Harriet

turned away, as if Bartlett had never spoken. "In a matter such as this, it's difficult to imagine what sort of punishment should be decided upon."

From Jaffa, whom no one had ever heard speak before when there were this many people to hear her: "She called Peaches's husband a fag, Miss Griggs. If that's not provocation, when everyone knows the man is dead . ."

Harriet's answer was simplicity itself. She smiled at Jaffa patronizingly. "Don't be ridiculous, Jaffa. Twelve-year-old little girls aren't old enough to have husbands. Someday, perhaps if—"

"Nuts." Cherry had spoken the word flatly and definitely. The room was hushed, as if someone had just died. Perhaps someone just had.

Harriet drew herself up. They had all walked into her trap to destroy Jennifer. "Very well, then. I now know what the punishment shall be," she said, her satisfaction at the solution appearing quite spontaneous. "I'm sorry, children. It hurts me, it really does. But since Peaches has been a wicked little girl, very wicked, and there are some among you who choose to defend her—a girl who spat at *me*, a girl who attacked a member of your own family, and a girl there are those of you who will lie for—I can see no other solution. No *Little Lord Fauntleroy*. That's final. No buffet. That is also final. You will go to bed in twenty minutes without your supper. Maybe then you will realize that it was all Peaches's fault, that I don't lie, and that Pippin was blameless. If you have any complaints, take them up with Peaches. The punishment is all her fault. Good little girls don't make such a fuss about things."

With one swift movement, Harriet turned and stalked from the room, slamming the door noisily and bolting it from the outside in a succession of thuds and crashes.

Her plan, however, didn't work as smoothly as the door. The girls were all disappointed, and some of them *did* blame Jennifer for what had happened to their very special treat. Others—the brighter and more knowing ones—saw through the scheme easily. Some wouldn't speak to Jennifer; others offered her their understanding and even helped out with ointments and salves. In classical military terms, Harriet, who had looked upon the intercession of Bartlett and Cherry and Jaffa as an unexpected added reason to cancel the television program and the buffet, had engaged in too obvious a case of overkill to be believable. The tearing apart of Jennifer never took place, because not enough people believed what Harriet had said.

Jaffa looked at the others as they slowly retreated into their rooms, sulking like little school children. The renewed sensation that maybe she *was* only twelve, that maybe in time her mind would desert her, sent her into her own room in a deep depression. Theoretical mathematics seemed very far away and long ago.

The next morning, Jennifer awoke slowly, but with a distinct feeling that things could only get better from here on out. She had faced Harriet, Harriet had tried to turn the other girls against her, but she had survived. After a mostly sleepless night this assurance suddenly made her feel able to face anything. The feeling was put to the test even before she had fully pulled herself out of bed.

From outside, she suddenly heard Bartlett screaming as if her heart were being roughly torn from her body. Another attack from Pippin? Jennifer didn't know, but she raced out the door.

Bartlett was standing outside one of the rooms, staring inside, looking at something with an expression of disbelief and horror. Jennifer raced through the main room to see what had happened.

From a pipe in the ceiling of the room, Jaffa's body swung slowly back and forth, her eyes wide open, the rope around her neck thrusting her head forward at an impossible angle. On her chest was a large paper sign, hand-lettered in Jaffa's familiar writing: GOOD LITTLE GIRLS GO QUIETLY.

In the most grotesque touch of all, Jaffa was wearing the black

Mickey Mouse Club hat Jennifer had watched her make. To Jennifer it explained everything: the fear of really turning into a twelve-year-old. Moving back and forth with the motion of Jaffa's body, the giant black mouse ears cast long and sinister shadows across the walls.

CHAPTER NINETEEN

Sometimes I think certain people lead charmed lives, like some mysterious benevolent spell followed them around and did marvelous things for them all the time. Take Peaches. That Little Lord Fauntleroy business should have finished her as far as the other girls went. Instead, she seems to have more friends now than before it happened. Whatever the spell that controls her life is, she damn well knows how to invoke it.

> *Journal of Blossom House,*
> *Entry, page 40—Harriet Griggs*

Like everything else at Blossom House, Jaffa's funeral was washed with madness. The morning after Jaffa's suicide, Harriet strode into the room at the time the day's lessons usually began. She clapped her hands loudly. ''Jaffa's funeral will take place in about half an hour. I know you will want to pay your last respects to your little friend properly, so I want you to get into your best dresses, put on clean little white stockings, and buff up your Mary Janes.'' Harriet looked at them all sternly. ''When you're finished, I want you to stay in your rooms and wait—doors closed, please. We'll be busy getting things ready out here. Any questions?''

None of the girls had any questions—at least none they dared put to Harriet. "Very well, then," Harriet said, and turning on her heels, started toward the outer door. As she reached it she remembered something and turned back to them. "Oh, yes. I almost forgot." She held out her hand to show them a dozen black ribbons. "Mourning bands. To tie around your pigtails. Pippin, will you see that each child has one?" Pippin took the ribbons with a look of utter disgust, the first time Jennifer had ever agreed with anything the girl felt.

Approximately forty-five minutes later—the getting ready apparently took more time than Harriet had expected—the girls, still in their rooms, heard Harriet return. The funeral was about to begin.

Harriet went down the long line of doors, pounding on each and calling out the occupant's name. The inevitable curtsy. On each girl, as she emerged, Harriet pinned a rosette made of more black ribbon.

Jennifer gasped at the sight outside. Harriet and Henry Griggs were dressed in solemn black; Henry wore a black tie, while Harriet was decked out in a black hat. Funeral wreaths hung on every door, and the entire area of the main room had been festooned with black crepe-paper swags. From the loudspeaker came a selection of dirgelike Brahms and other low-key music, all of it highly depressing. It was already the parody of a funeral.

Laid out in the center of the long formal dining room table was Jaffa. At both her head and feet stood two giant church candlesticks, each holding huge flickering candles, the soft glow of which played across her face and body. Her hair had been carefully brushed and spread out across the table in the shape of a fan, its golden color in sharp contrast to the black cloth that covered the table and fell to the floor to make a catafalque. Somewhere along the line, her usually pale face had been subtly made up, adding a slight touch of color to features that had never enjoyed it before. The sight, to Jennifer, was startling; Jaffa had never looked so alive as when dead.

The effect, however, was made completely bizarre by one small touch: on her head, Jaffa still wore the Mickey Mouse Club hat, the mammoth ears casting long, strange shadows when caught in the light of the flickering candles. She looked, Jennifer thought, as if she were trying to sit up; the white satin pillow her head rested on was too thick for the job, and tilted her head and neck forward too far.

Jaffa's hands were folded across her chest, resting on the white dotted swiss dress she was wearing. One hand held a tiny baby-blue teddy bear, the other clutched a small pink plastic calculator. Jennifer had never seen either before; certainly, they weren't among the effects she had had in her room.

Jennifer always had trouble not giggling at funerals; this one was so grotesque, all she wanted was to find some way to express her fury at the people who were responsible for it. Like punching Harriet in the nose, or kicking Henry in the crotch—anything that would restore a little down-to-earth sanity to poor Jaffa's farewell.

Harriet suddenly spoke out. Studying her, Jennifer thought how impossible her fantasy of punching this huge woman in the nose had been; she seriously doubted if she could reach it.

"Children," Harriet boomed, "I want you to stand very quietly in a circle around poor Jaffa. Join hands. Now, search your souls to think good thoughts about your friend. Jaffa was a nice little girl, but a sad little girl, all mixed up in her head, which is probably why she did what she did. She was never any trouble, though, and we shall miss her. We shall now stand in silence for ten minutes, thinking our good thoughts and hoping that we never become as confused."

Ten minutes, in ordinary circumstances, is a relatively short time. Jennifer, though, never realized how long ten minutes could be when you're standing in place, clutching the hands of the persons on either side of you, listening to solemn funeral music boom from a loudspeaker. She found herself swaying; she found herself sweating; she found herself desperately wanting to giggle. If Jaffa had been standing there herself, certainly *she* would have—and a giggle from Jaffa was like a bellowing roar of laughter from anyone else.

The tape played on endlessly, until it suddenly produced Grieg's funeral march. This piece, usually reserved for kings, heads of state, and high military leaders, was so out of keeping with a young girl wearing a Mickey Mouse Club hat that Jennifer found her stomach heaving violently in and out from the effort of not giggling. When she saw Harriet beginning to stare at her, she released one hand and wiped away imaginary tears so that Harriet would think she was sobbing rather than laughing.

Grieg ended abruptly. The tape, apparently, was an old one which had frequently been erased and used over before being pressed into service today, with its melancholy new repertoire of dirges and chants recorded for the occasion.

At one point, after the end of one piece and just before the beginning of the next, a brief section of what had originally been recorded on the tape suddenly burst from the speakers. What they heard shook Jennifer badly, evoking terrifying memories; it was the piano piece she had heard played downstairs the morning Peter disappeared—the weird Mozartian arrangement that Harriet had seemingly conceived herself—familiar, yet not quite recognizable. To Jennifer it was a frightening and bitterly ironic snatch of music; to the others it was merely confusing.

The ten minutes of silence was followed by the hymn, "For All the Saints Who from Their Labors Rest." At its end, Henry stepped forward and raised his hand like a priest, reading them the "Service for a Dead Child" from the *Book of Common Prayer*. Harriet then stepped forward and led the girls—most of them sullen, a few crying—in the Lord's Prayer.

"Ashes to ashes . . ." Henry intoned. Reaching for the hymnal again, he appeared to be about to call for another hymn. Harriet frowned; it was time for this solemn service to be over. Leaning forward, she seized Jaffa's body and threw it over her shoulder like a sack of potatoes. Staying only long enough to adjust Jaffa's body on her shoulders more securely, she started toward the door. "All right, children," she called over her shoulder. "Get back to your lessons. Spend your time studying. We will be taking tests this afternoon. Get going." She marched out of the room, slamming the outer door behind her with a crash as final as death itself.

In the "quiet" period just before lunch, Jennifer sat in her room, feeling suddenly very depressed. Part of it, she knew, was the death of Jaffa. In spite of her continual withdrawn gloominess, Jennifer had come to like and respect the girl. More important, Jaffa, along with Cherry and Bartlett, had been among the handful she really trusted at Blossom House.

Another cause of her depression, Jennifer knew—even if unable to understand quite why it affected her so—had been the brief burst of Harriet's piano playing. She had no proof there was any connection between the Mozartian arrangement and Peter's disappearance, but she could not separate the two in her mind.

To free herself from her mood, Jennifer walked over to the window and looked down into the orchard. Out of the house came Harriet, with Jaffa again thrown over her shoulder. Right behind was Henry, carrying the same strange-looking spade she'd seen him with in the kitchen the morning Peter vanished. The memory made her shiver. Along the line of apple trees, she saw that a new trench had been dug, not far from the mound Pippin had pointed out to her. Jaffa's body was dropped in, and Henry began shoveling quicklime in on top of her twisted body. A moment later Harriet began using another shovel to refill the trench with earth, patting it down into a small mound when she was finished. Once again the shiver ran through Jennifer. Was Peter out there under one of the other mounds? Was this how she herself would eventually wind up one day? The shiver had turned into a shudder, and Jennifer felt her whole body begin to tremble.

In New York, some other people were asking themselves questions, too. "Damn it. I don't *know* what to do," Townsend Delafield, Jennifer's father, said to her mother. His voice had an unpleasant ring to it, and Mrs. Delafield was not used to being snapped at like this. "First that note she left. Now, total silence. Given the note and the fact she knew we would truss her up hand

and foot if she had even suggested marrying Peter, I suppose I can understand Jennifer's silence.' . . .''

"You're always making excuses for her," said Jennifer's mother. "It's the reason she's such a mess, *I* think."

Townsend Delafield was too much beside himself to notice what his wife was saying. Through years of practice, he had learned, most of the time, to switch off his mind when she talked, anyway. "What I can't understand is Peter's not letting his family know he's okay," he continued. "I talked to Peter's father last week, and he said Peter left a very sweet note behind him, apologizing for running off, and telling his mother and father how much he loved them and that they'd be hearing from him as soon as they got settled."

"You didn't tell *me* that you talked to Ted Owen last week, Townsend." Mrs. Delafield made a face. "What else aren't you telling me?"

Mr. Delafield ignored her. "They must be settled by now, for Christ's sake. Jesus, it's been a month."

"Maybe there was an accident," Mrs. Delafield suggested.

"The police would have tracked us down and told us. Through his license plates. I checked."

"Well, perhaps Peter turned as mean as Jennifer, and they both want to make us worry—on purpose."

Mr. Delafield looked at his wife. It was remarkable how little she understood her daughter. For that matter, it was remarkable how little she understood him, too. "I'm going over to the Owens'. Ted Owen and I are going to talk it over again with the police. Damn it, there has to be *some* way of finding out where those kids are."

Watching her husband stand up and adjust his tie in the mirror, Jennifer's mother sniffed. Her maternal instincts had long ago been dulled by Jennifer's playing up to her father. "How sharper than a serpent's tooth . . ." she said to Mr. Delafield in the cutting little voice she knew always irritated him.

Townsend Delafield turned from the mirror to face her. "Oh,

shut up. For once, shut up." Breathing hard, he walked swiftly from the library and out the front door, slamming it hard enough to rattle the dishes in Ingebord's kitchen.

"I'm sorry, Mr. Owen, but our hands are more or less tied." Ted Owen shifted uncomfortably in the hard chairs the police inspector had seated him and Townsend in. "You see," the inspector went on, "they're too old for most states to classify as runaways. And they're probably married, you say, which makes it even harder to get the cooperation of other states . . ."

"But Jennifer's only seventeen," complained Mr. Delafield. "She's not legally married in New York. She didn't have our legal permission."

Leaning slightly toward the two men, the inspector looked at them with sympathy, but without too much understanding. "Mr. Delafield, you're a lawyer. You must know there are several states where they could get legally married, and neither you nor I could do a thing about it."

"Mr. Delafield's in corporate law," Ted Owen pointed out, apologizing for his friend's ignorance. "They don't get into things like this very much."

"Well, I'll do what I can, gentlemen," the inspector said, rising to his feet and leading them to the door.

"Thank you, Inspector, that's good to hear," Ted Owen said in farewell.

For several minutes the inspector sat quietly in his chair, studying the wall opposite him. He hoped to hell Messrs. Delafield and Owen would tell his superiors that they had thought what he said was good to hear. Between them, the two distraught parents appeared to have a great deal of clout; the commissioner himself had called him several times to ask if he was making any progress. At the moment, he couldn't really answer that he was.

Well, he would send out fliers to the departments in other states. He couldn't make any official requests, of course, but maybe someone in one of those departments across the country would come up with something.

Damn, why were the children of the rich always making so much trouble for everybody?

Among the people the children of the rich were making trouble for was Hillary Crane, Jennifer's best friend at Chalmer's. She alone had been sure of where they were—or at least where they had been—Chivers, Maryland. But, suddenly, everything had seemed to be wrong.

Jennifer had promised she would write or call her as soon as they were settled. It was a month now, and not so much as a word. Jennifer would have called her, of that she was positive, not necessarily so much for Hillary's sake as for her own. Since childhood, Jennifer had never been able to keep things to herself, particularly where Hillary was involved. She would have been bubbling over to let her best friend know exactly where she and Peter were and what they were doing and how great married life was. Those were the kinds of things Jennifer *had* to tell.

But nothing. No letter, no phone call. Just silence. An alarming silence that day by day bored deeper into Hillary; it was as if Peter and Jennifer had fallen off the face of the globe.

About a week ago, she had grown even more alarmed. First, Mr. Delafield had called her. "I don't want to upset you, Hillary. But I know how close you've been to Jennifer—since you were both very little—and I was wondering if you'd heard anything from her since she"—his voice began to sound simultaneously sad and agitated—"since, well—she left town."

"Gee, no, Mr. Delafield, not a word." Hillary struggled with how to say what she wanted to say without giving away that Jennifer had made her promise she would never tell anyone. "In fact, Mr. Delafield, I was thinking about calling you to ask the same thing. Jennifer promised she would write or phone the moment they were—settled—but I haven't heard a peep."

Townsend Delafield's voice suddenly took on a hard edge. "You *knew* they were eloping?"

Hillary was trapped. "She told me, yes, Mr. Delafield. We've been friends for so long . . ."

"I've been her father even longer, Hillary," snapped Mr. Delafield. "If she told you they were eloping, she must also have told you where they were getting married. Come on, Hillary. I don't want to do anything to her, it's just that I'm getting quite worried."

"She didn't tell me where, Mr. Delafield," lied Hillary. "I guess she was afraid that if I knew, I might tell someone."

On the other end of the phone, Hillary could hear Jennifer's father swearing at the heavens. He sounded desperate, being torn apart both by Jennifer's leaving and now her disappearance. Hillary wanted to say something that would make him feel better and, for a moment, considered telling him about Chivers, but was finally forced to decide against it. A promise was a promise.

"Hillary," Mr. Delafield said, trying to get back to talking to Hillary instead of yelling at her. "Listen to me, *please*, Hillary. I know if Jennifer asked you not to tell anybody, well, you're such a good friend of hers, you probably wouldn't. I respect and admire you for that. But, look, I'm terribly worried that something may have happened that we should know about. Wherever she is, she may need help. And I'm asking you as an old friend, someone who has always liked you and tried to help *you*, to tell me where Jennifer and Peter eloped to. I know breaking a promise is always tough, but for Jennifer's sake . . ."

Two days later, she received an almost identical call from Peter's father, equally distraught, equally convinced she was lying when she told him she didn't know where Peter and Jennifer had headed. Mr. Owen tried to be pleasant, but the call only frightened Hillary more. Maybe she should tell them both about Chivers; maybe Jennifer was lying desperately sick or horribly injured somewhere.

In the end, Hillary decided that if she hadn't heard anything by the weekend, she would go to Chivers herself. Her family would be furious, but she'd halfway explain it and be able to work on where Peter and Jennifer were without having to break her promise. Somebody in Chivers must have married them, somebody

there must have known where they were heading after that
Assuming, of course, they'd ever gotten to Chivers. That phrase
assuming they'd ever gotten there chilled her as it drifted through
her mind. It was like the taillights of Jennifer's car disappearing
up Park Avenue the night she left. Frightening, without reason.
Well, she *hoped* without reason.

CHAPTER TWENTY

I can remember my father's funeral like it was yesterday. The damn thing went on forever. Prayers, hymns, responsive readings—the works. Then, when we got to the graveside, old Reverend Starkers started all over again. Like my father owed him money or something and Starkers was afraid to let him out of his sight.

For a minute I thought Henry was going to pull the same stunt with Jaffa. He liked playing minister, and I could see he wanted to pile on more hymns and prayers. The Reverend Henry? I don't think so.

The only one of the girls who didn't behave right was Peaches. She thought she fooled me by wiping her eyes with a handkerchief, making out she was crying instead of laughing, but I saw through it real fast. Heartless little bitch.

Well, the next funeral Peaches goes to she won't find so funny. It's hard to laugh when you're about to get a shovelful of quicklime in the face.

> *Journal of Blossom House,*
> *Entry, page 41—Harriet Griggs*

"Oh, they'll show up sometime this afternoon. Every year I get excited just thinking about that tour. They bring a photographer and everything. The lady at the Garden Club told me over the phone that their tour here is one of the high points of their program."

Trying to smile and look interested, Jennifer saw the almost childlike excitement with which Henry anticipated the tour, the wonder and the praise. It seemed entirely out of character for him—as did his passionate delight in shrubs and flowers itself. "Well, you certainly *should* be proud; everything looks magnificent."

Henry nodded, his ebullience still running high. "One year, they even ran a color insert in their little publication, and sent it on to *House and Garden*. I guess they didn't run it, but the Garden Club said that's not too unusual; they get stuff from all over the country."

Jennifer and Henry were standing at the window of Jennifer's room, looking down at the orchard below. Although she knew she had to keep on trying to play up to Henry, Jennifer had a tough time being sweet and endearing when her eyes kept brushing the new mound of earth near the apple trees. The mound must be close to Peter's grave, if Pippin was to be believed. But getting out of this madhouse, she had convinced herself, was more important than any grave, and Jennifer treated Henry to a radiant smile.

"I wouldn't let that worry you. Magazines are like that. You have to know somebody, I guess. Anyway, maybe they'll run it *this* year."

Henry stared at the orchard with a worried look. "Their photographer will be getting here a little after the blossoms have peaked this year, I'm afraid, but there's nothing I can do about that."

"I think they look magnificent," Jennifer said, squeezing his arm. Henry smiled warmly. A moment later he squeezed her arm in return and left the room, muttering something about "a lot of things to be done before the tour began."

While he was talking an idea had been spinning a web around

Jennifer's mind. Ten days ago she wouldn't have dared suggest it to anyone but Cherry, but Jaffa's death, her fight with Pippin, and the Fauntleroy incident had all backfired on Harriet. The rest of the girls had slowly, hesitantly, and sometimes almost reluctantly, begun to accept Jennifer, along with Cherry, as the other of their two leaders.

Just before classes began Jennifer had a chance to explain a little of her plan to Cherry. The girl laughed loudly, and then turned to look at Jennifer, her eyes hesitant. "I think it's great, Peaches. But, look. It could screw up your game with Henry. We're all counting on that to get you out of here. Because if *you* get out, *we* get out."

Jennifer stared at her with amazement. "How did you know about that? I mean, playing up to Henry, and—"

Another laugh from Cherry, but this a very subdued one. "I know damn well you're not playing coy with that old bastard Henry—smiling at him all the time, flattering him, teasing the pants off him—because you've suddenly gone ape over the crazy old lech. Hell, don't forget what I used to do for a living."

Starting to laugh, but still bewildered that Cherry could see through what she was doing so easily, Jennifer started to answer, when Harriet strode in the door. "Lessons, children. Time for lessons." She looked at Jennifer with a hard, self-satisfied smile. "Mr. Griggs will be busy this morning, Peaches, so you'll have to join the rest of the group." A slow, unpleasant smirk crept over her face. "That is, of course, if you don't think you're too good for us."

The moment Jennifer sat down, Harriet began grilling them on their history assignment. Stridently a buzzer she had never heard before began ringing in the room, loud and insistent. Harriet swore, getting to her feet, a look of displeasure on her face. "No more classes this morning, children," she snapped suddenly. "Use the time to study. And, Pippin, be sure they stay quiet." Leaving them all a little startled, Harriet had hurried—she almost ran, Jennifer suddenly realized—out of the room.

To Cherry it was not, apparently, a new experience. "Another one,'' she said to the others, and ran toward her room. So did the rest of the girls. Jennifer looked in Bartlett's room and saw her standing at the window. Quickly Jennifer joined her.

"Poor kids,'' Bartlett sighed, pointing down toward the front path. On the curb, a young couple was standing, studying Blossom House, and talking, waving their arms a little, seemingly not agreeing on whether to come in or not. Jennifer blinked hard. It was almost precisely the same thing she and Peter had gone through before they made their fateful entry into Blossom House.

Bartlett began waving her hands and shouting; at their windows, she could hear Cherry and the others doing the same thing. Abruptly the lights went out. "It's to keep them from seeing our silhouettes if they look up, poor stupid bastards,'' Bartlett muttered. "It doesn't do any good, I guess—they can't hear us through the Thermopane and with the lights out, they sure as hell can't see us—but we always do it anyway, just in case. Stupid.''

The couple walked slowly up the path and, as if from another planet, Jennifer thought she heard the front doorbell ring. Thirty seconds later the young couple disappeared from sight, swallowed up by Blossom House. A simple but charming little wedding. Champagne. Lunch. And by tonight, Jennifer supposed, there would be the Mozartian piano piece again. A trench in the rear grounds, near the apple trees. A shovel. Quicklime. A new girl would be added to their family upstairs, a new boy added to the mounds beside Peter. Jesus.

About noon—luncheon didn't appear to be coming, and it was not hard to figure out why—Jennifer got her cool back and began talking to Cherry again. Between them, they expanded on Jennifer's plan. One by one Cherry talked to each of the other girls; Pippin was carefully excluded, although it was obvious she knew something was happening, poised on the other side of the main room, glowering at Cherry and the others, her hands twisting anxiously at her side. Finally she could stand it no longer and grabbed Cherry by the arm. It was exactly how Cherry had predicted Pippin would behave.

"What the hell are you up to?" Pippin demanded angrily.

"Up to?" Cherry asked, her face a mask of injured innocence.

"Damn it, I'm not *that* stupid. What's going on? Tell me, or I'll—"

"You'll what?" Cherry countered. "Tell your bosom buddy Harriet I wouldn't tell you what was happening? I think you got it wrong, Pip, old friend. As far as I know, exactly nothing is going on here. Downstairs, well, that's something else."

Pippin began to shake with frustration. "You stinking streetwalker. I'm going to get you if it's the last—"

Pippin never got to finish her sentence. From behind her, on Cherry's signal, Bartlett and Guava had grabbed Pippin's arms and twisted them behind her, pushing them so far up, Pippin yelled with the pain. Jennifer yanked a pillowcase over her head, tying it loosely around her neck, so that Pippin couldn't see who was doing this to her—and later identify the person to Harriet. Pippin struggled and thrashed, but a small group of girls wrestled her to the floor, tying her up, hand and foot, like a chicken trussed up for baking.

"She looks better that way, anyhow," Cherry hissed to Jennifer. "Come on, let's get her into her room and tie her to the bed." Not very gently, Jennifer and the others dragged her into her room, dumped her on her bed, and fastened her to it.

"You filthy bitches," Pippin screamed from under the pillowcase. "I'll get the whole bunch of you for this. Cherry and Peaches particularly. I know you're behind this, both of you. Harriet and I'll get you. But good!"

What had long been believed about Pippin had just been proved. She had damned herself by her own words. It came as no real surprise to anyone, but it was such definitive proof that none of the girls here would ever believe a word she said again.

"What time did he say they were coming?" Cherry asked Jennifer.

"He didn't. But I got the impression it must be right after lunch. He kept talking about how the sun had to be high for the photographer to get the full beauty of the blossoms. One o'clock, two o'clock, I don't know.''

Cherry laughed grimly. ''That must be raising hell downstairs. A real quickie marriage and murder. Minute rice for the bride and groom.''

Downstairs, in the hall outside the room where the young couple was patiently waiting for someone to come back and marry them, Henry was whispering urgently to Harriet. He had dragged her there just moments before the wedding was supposed to start. ''I couldn't help it, Harriet. They called and said they were sorry, but something had gotten screwed up and they'd have to be here a little earlier than they'd planned on.''

''Christ. How much earlier?''

''I don't know. Just earlier.''

''You should have told them to come another day, then, Henry.''

''They already had the photographer with them,'' Henry protested. ''I couldn't tell them that.''

''You're stupid, Henry. Jesus Christ, but you're stupid. This wedding—''

''We'll just have to get it over fast,'' Henry countered. ''That girl is the best candidate I've seen in a long time. Everything's perfect about her.''

''I don't like it, Henry. Rushing through things. Maybe we should forget the rest and just do the wedding.''

''No. Absolutely not.''

Henry's voice had a strange, firm ring to it, a familiar tone that told Harriet resistance was useless. She desperately wanted to argue but didn't. Once Henry had decided to assert himself this way, there was no appeal. What bothered Harriet was that he seemed to be slipping into this role more and more frequently ever since—the idea hit Harriet the first time with thunderous impact—Peaches had shown up. That awful little brat was making Henry feel his manhood. Staring at her brother, Harriet wanted to scream at him that she understood what was happening, that he was changing, and that she knew it was the effect of his seeing so much of Peaches. She played up to him, she flattered him, she made him feel like a man. Goddamn.

Instead, Harriet merely shrugged. It would have to be the fastest wedding/murder they'd ever staged.

"There they come," Bartlett announced. "A whole line of cars just stopped in front. A lot of old ladies are climbing out. We're on."

"Quick kids, line up over here," Cherry said, motioning the whole third floor contingent over to her.

"It'll take them quite a while to get inside." Bartlett laughed. "Two of them are on canes, and some of the rest look like someone should be carrying them."

A few minutes later Jennifer hurried away from her window and stood beside Cherry, facing the others. "The last one just came in. We can go anytime."

"It's your show," Cherry said and walked over to where the others were standing, facing Jennifer, lined up like a glee club.

"Everybody ready?" Jennifer asked. There was a chorus of nods. "Okay, first row lift your chairs up . . ." The front row had chairs from the dining room table, which, on Jennifer's command, they raised slightly off the floor with their hands.

Checking up and down the double line, Jennifer lifted her arms in the air, fingers extended, like a conductor. "Here we go. A-one, a-two, a-three—*Now*!" The effect was gratifying.

CHAPTER TWENTY-ONE

Sometimes Henry's love of gardening is a real pain in the ass. All right, I'll admit his flowering trees and shrubs are breathtaking; his little indoor greenhouse full of unusual orchids adds a nice touch of color in winter; his dried-flower arrangements are spectacular; and his bulbs and other plantings put on a show in spring that makes Blossom House live up to its name.

The trouble is, Henry frequently puts his gardening ahead of our primary business here. Anyone else would have told the damn Garden Club to come back some other time; Christ, they could make a mess of recruiting Jaffa's replacement.

Not Henry. He insisted on trying to do both, so we had to break our necks to get the wedding out of the way before the old bats of the Garden Club showed up. Then, Peaches—I know she was behind it—got in the act and almost made the difficult impossible.

What that awful little girl needs is a heavy spraying with a powerful insecticide, like some of the kinds Henry uses on his plants. One that knocks off pests for good.

I don't know any of them by name, but maybe those crazy damn ladies from the Garden Club could recommend one to me.

I'd get a kick watching Peaches go down in a blaze of chemical glory.

> Journal of Blossom House,
> Entry, page 42—Harriet Griggs

Perhaps three quarters of an hour earlier, there had been a frazzled sense of confusion downstairs. Henry and Harriet had had to speed up the young couple's wedding shamelessly. They were a pleasant young pair, the girl about sixteen and enormously attractive, the boy a bit older, and nowhere near as good-looking as she was attractive. Nose and ears too big, much too big. Understandably, they were both very nervous, and Harriet's frenzy rattled them further.

They had no way of knowing that behind her understanding smile, she was livid with Henry. All of the frills and little touches so dear to both of their hearts had had to be scrapped, something which depressed Henry as much as Harriet. Still, as Henry had told her, the Garden Club's write-ups of him, year after year, were too important to him to tell them to come back some other time; their annual visit was the high point of his year.

The ceremony had been raced through at such a clip, the couple was startled when Henry virtually insisted they stay on for a celebration drink of champagne out on the terrace. Like Jennifer and Peter, they had tried to beg off, but Henry Griggs and his sister made it impossible to refuse without appearing terribly rude.

A few minutes later the drugged young man had complained of feeling dizzy and ill, and disappeared into the bathroom. Harriet smiled to herself. So far so good. When he didn't return, his new wife—her name was Constance—grew increasingly anxious.

"Oh, I wouldn't worry, Constance," Harriet had said, and then repeated a statement that Jennifer would have remembered from her own wedding: "It's always the men who get upset a weddings, not the women. Men aren't as strong as they'd like to think. He'll be all right.''

After two or three minutes more Constance had grown insistent. "Please," she said. "I have to see if Choo-Choo is all right." Shrugging, Harriet rose to guide her.

Smiling benignly, Harriet gently shepherded Constance toward the bathroom. "Here we are," she said, and threw open the door with a flourish. There was a choking, unbelieving gasp from the girl.

Choo-Choo hung naked from a pipe in the bathroom ceiling, his body still writhing and twisting in a last frantic struggle for air. Constance, openmouthed and clutching at Harriet for support, screamed a scream that had no beginning and no end, assaulted her ears, and made even Harriet wince.

The girl spun around, first to plead with Harriet, then back toward the bathroom, unable to accept what she saw happening to her new husband. Calmly, still smiling, Harriet covered the girl's face with a chloroform-soaked cloth. Constance's struggles were brief. Only minutes later Harriet picked her up and carried her to the same isolation cell Jennifer had first been locked up in when she was moved upstairs. The girls watched her, until she disappeared into the isolation cell. From outside, they heard her body being dumped onto the bed, an echoing, empty sound, filled with the cold dread of hopelessness.

Behind Harriet stood Henry, watching it all with disapproval. This wasn't the graceful, well-ordered way he liked things done. He was about to say something to Harriet, registering his disapproval, but Harriet beat him to the punch. She was livid. Yelling, she put the whole blame on him.

"Christ, Henry, you jerk. That was the most disorganized, frantic one of these we've ever done. And it's all your stupid fault, damn it. You forgot half your stuff, you botched up the ceremony, you . . ." Henry decided not to say what he had planned to; his sister was in too foul a temper and would get back at him when the Garden Club arrived if he did.

Dragging a kitchen chair into the bathroom, Harriet, still mut-

tering at him, climbed up on it and was about to cut down the
late Choo-Choo. But she'd barely reached up with her knife
when the front doorbell rang. "Your damn Garden Club. They're
what's behind this whole mess. Jesus God, what a moment for
them to pick." Staring hard at Henry, she cursed the world, the
Garden Club of Chivers and Henry. "When I get you alone I'm
going to give you a piece of my mind that you—"

She halted in midsentence. The front doorbell had rung again.
Rattling around the unfurnished, uncarpeted back halls of Blossom House, the sound had a desperate urgency to it, as if it were
trying to tell them a man was still hanging in their front bathroom, and hurry, please, or that man would begin yelling and tell
the ladies of the Garden Club what actually went on in this place.
Harriet spun on Henry, dragging the chair out of the bathroom,
and leaving Choo-Choo where he was. No time, no time for the
cutting down and disposal of a no-longer-needed husband. "Go
answer the door, Henry," snapped Harriet. "I'll close the bathroom door; we'll just have to leave him there. Go answer the
door, Henry, for Christ's sake, before they think something's
wrong in here. They're your goddamn guests, anyway."

Listening to her muttering and cursing in the background,
Henry walked to the front door and opened it. He was wearing
the most ebullient meet-the-Garden-Club-ladies face he could put
on. "Welcome, dear ladies, welcome! Every one of my flowers
has been getting ready all morning to greet you!"

For a statement that was at best nauseating, the Garden Club
was surprisingly affected. They twittered. They giggled. Lace
hankies flew to wrinkled mouths beneath aging straw hats. To
them, Henry Griggs was not only a master gardener of awesome
proportions, he was also, as always, the most gracious, charming
gentleman on the whole tour circuit.

A tight smile pasted on her face, Harriet joined them in the
front hall. Her greetings were not as effusive as Henry's, but she
welcomed them with apparent enthusiasm, saying how much her
brother always looked forward to their annual visits. "He's been
getting ready, thinking and planning it out, for weeks now." The

ladies smiled, although a little uncertainly. Harriet was different from her brother, so different, one of them had mentioned it just before they arrived: "Poor man. There's something strange about that sister of his. Oh, well."

The whole group of them was just starting toward the orchid room when—*stamp, stamp, stamp*—a tremendous noise erupted over their heads. *Stamp, stamp, stamp.* Feet pounded on the floor, kept in unison by Jennifer's waving arms. Simultaneously the front row was bringing chairs down on the wooden floor in time with the stamping. Even downstairs the sound was overwhelming.

For a moment Harriet couldn't speak, staring up at the ceiling in horrified confusion. The ladies' eyes followed her upward.

Stamp, stamp, stamp. A panicked Harriet knew she had to say something—*anything*—that would explain the racket. *Fast.* Hastily she improvised, gathering enthusiasm as she spoke. "It's those workmen again," Harriet said wearily. "We're doing some quite extensive remodeling on the third floor, you see, and the men seem to be hammering and pounding from morning until night." Studying the women, Harriet couldn't decide whether they believed her or not; they looked more curious than convinced.

Stamp, stamp, stamp. "Henry," Harriet said suddenly, deciding that no amount of explanation was going to do much. "Why don't you go upstairs and talk to the workmen? Ask them to hold it down for a little while; we have important guests down here. I can show the ladies your orchids myself, and if they have any questions—and I'm sure they will—you can give them the answers when you get back."

Stamp, stamp, stamp. Reluctantly Henry walked slowly out of the room, pausing to look back at the members of the Garden Club with a wistful expression. Damn Harriet. She was robbing him of his moment of glory, a moment he looked forward to all year, every year. Even disappointed, he still had to agree with her. Those girls had to be stopped somehow.

"This way, ladies," Harriet said over the din, and with her

arm showed them toward the orchid room. A small but insistent voice stopped her.

"I'm terribly sorry, Miss Griggs. But I was wondering if you could show me where the bathroom is. I just finished my morning tea before we left for here, and you know how tea . . ."

Harriet turned pale. My God, some crazy old lady had to pee. Swell. When she went into the bathroom the first thing she'd see was a naked young man hanging from the ceiling, eyes bugged, tongue bulging out between his lips. More improvisation. "I'm terribly sorry—it's very awkward and embarrassing for me—but the same awful construction people that are making so much noise upstairs turned off all the water in the house this morning. It's terrible. They're working on the plumbing up there too, you see, and they had to turn everything off all over the house. I'm sorry . . . I don't know what to suggest, but—" The lady blushed and left it at that.

Stamp, stamp, stamp.

The sound of the bolts on the outer door of the main room was heard inside, even over the crashing and stamping; the girls had been making a game of it, but their enthusiasm shrank a little when they knew someone was coming in to deal with them. Harriet, probably; all of them were afraid to one degree or other of Harriet.

Bartlett, standing on the hinge side of the door, looked through the wide crack and mouthed a silent "Henry."

The others breathed more easily, raising their stamping back to full volume. Harriet would have panicked them. Henry they could deal with. Cherry and Jennifer exchanged glances. To salvage Jennifer's escape plan, appearing to be a "good little girl" was important; it could destroy her favored status were she to be discovered leading this group of stampers and crashers by Henry. Quietly Jennifer slipped into her room while Cherry took over her place in front of the glee club.

"Children," Henry yelled as loudly as he could. "Stop that! Right now, stop that!"

Stamp, stamp, stamp.

He was ignored; the stamping continued, the girls pretending Henry wasn't there. The fact that these rude, evil children were spoiling his moment in the sun with the Garden Club infuriated him. He was aware of an anger he rarely felt growing inside him. Finally it exploded.

"Stop it!" he roared again, walking quickly over to Guava and slapping her hard across the face. The behavior was so unusual for Henry, the girls were stunned. So, for that matter, was Henry. But, as if driven by some force over which they had no control, the prisoners of Blossom House went on with their stamping. To further upset Henry, Guava reacted to the hard slap by smiling sweetly at him.

Stamp, stamp, stamp. *"Damn it, stop!"* Henry bellowed, now frustrated as well as furious. He strode over to Bartlett and slapped her so hard, she was knocked down. From the floor, Bartlett too managed a sweet smile. She even contrived not to put a hand to her face, which burned where his palm had struck with surprising power.

Cherry received the same kind of shattering blow, only one far more powerful. Henry had always disliked her, but when Pippin had gone public with Cherry's former occupation, the dislike turned to loathing. On Henry's list of those who were to be disposed of, Cherry was at the top. He was considerably thrown when Cherry reacted to his blow by curtsying deeply—almost gratefully.

Henry was stymied. This kind of mass disobedience was something they'd never run into at Blossom House before. It was as if the whole bunch of them had been unionized and were using their strength of numbers to overcome their individual grievances. Henry hated unions.

Stamp, stamp, stamp. The crashing of feet on the floor continued unabated, but there was a new sound to it. The girls were beginning to move slowly toward him while stamping. From them rose an ominous chant in time with their stamping. "Dad-*dy*, Dad-*dy*, Dad-*dy*," they chanted, staring at him grimly. Henry began to feel the sudden grip of fear. He was outnumbered.

Peaches, he noticed, wasn't there. Briefly Henry felt better
At least his wonderful Peaches wasn't party to this terrible
insurrection.

"Dad-*dy*, Dad-*dy*, Dad-*dy* . . ." The fear seized him again
The girls, the pretty little girls ordinarily so gentle and sweet
looking in their little starched dresses, were stamping their way
closer to him, their expressions frightening, closing in on the spot
where he was standing. There suddenly seemed to be so many of
them, Henry thought, their faces carrying expressions of vio
lence he'd never seen them wear before. They could overcome
him easily and, if they chose to, literally tear him to pieces.

The vise of fear tightened around his heart. Henry began tryin
to back out of the room slowly, hoping to preserve some sem
blance of dignity, but one of his feet crashed into somethin
behind him and tripped him. He fell backward against the door
frame, one hand groping frantically to find the door handle.

A terrible cry came from the girls, their arms outstretche
toward him, their hands clutching at him like talons, trying t
seize him and rip him open. The cry rose to a scream fc
vengeance. It was too much for Henry Griggs. All his preten
sions of dignity crumbled. He fled.

For a moment the girls stood silently, awed by their ow
power, but giggling and laughing at the same time. "Our Henr
is sure a mountain of strength. Start the stamping again, kids,
Cherry commanded, laughing herself.

Stamp, stamp, stamp.

When Henry walked into the orchid room he heard Harrie
pointing out to the ladies of the Garden Club the various wonde
of each plant. He knew she was probably getting about half th
names and all of the facts wrong—she always did—but was to
shaken to let it bother him. He could still feel the fear inside hi
from upstairs, and now, added to it, was his fear of what Harri
would do when she realized he had failed completely.

Stamp, stamp, stamp. Harriet's eyes rose to meet his, starin
at him with venom. "I'm sorry, ladies," Henry said in a voice s

shaky, it still bore the mark of his experience, "those workmen are very stubborn. Muttered about contractual agreements and scheduling problems and their awful union. They won't be through for an hour or so. I couldn't do a thing with them . . . they wouldn't stop."

Drawing herself up, Harriet stared angrily at her brother. She had gotten his coded message. "Very well," she snapped, "I'll go handle them myself. Women are always better at these things," she added, giving the ladies a put-on smile. "You take over here, Henry. At least you're good with flowers."

The ladies tried to pretend they hadn't heard Harriet's rude attack on Henry, and turned to him, smiling, prepared to learn more about the wonders of the orchid before being led outside to view the gardens. "What a bitch," hissed one of the young members to the lady beside her.

The lady, unused to this kind of language, pretended she hadn't heard. But to herself, she had to agree.

The fun of the stamping was beginning to wear off. Cherry and Jennifer kept urging the girls on, kidding them, pushing them, encouraging them. Several times Jennifer jumped as high as she could, managing to land in unison with the beat. Still stamping, they gave her a hand. The crash of sliding bolts brought their eyes to the opening door. Jennifer's heart froze.

This time it was Harriet, but it was not Harriet alone that frightened her. In the woman's hand was a shotgun, a sinister, gleaming double-barreled 30-30. A single blast could take care of one or several of them at once, blowing them into small pieces and scattering their flesh around the walls.

"Stop that racket!" Harriet screamed, the gun traveling up and down the line. Her eyes burned with a malevolent hatred more violent than Jennifer had ever seen in her. A wave of fear swept through her.

"Stop it, damn it, or I'll . . ."

One by one Jennifer and the others stopped. Unlike Henry, Harriet meant what she said. The idea of taking one of them as an example and blowing her into a thousand pieces was not in the least beyond her. Heads lowered in defeat, the girls allowed themselves to be herded back into their rooms, suddenly more cell-like than ever. Outside, each of them heard the lock turned, the panel slammed shut, and the iron bars shoved across their doors. Almost immediately the rooms' loudspeakers crackled into life, and Harriet began speaking, her voice cold, harsh, and unable to conceal an almost irrational fury. It was only the second time Jennifer could remember the PA system being used for a message.

"You have all been bad children—disgusting, wanton little girls. Evil, wicked, and unpardonable. You might as well resign yourself to severe punishment. Among other things, no food for three days. When you are out of your cells—for lessons, say— there will be no talking among you. You are not to speak to one another under any circumstances, nor to Mr. Griggs or myself when we choose to speak to you. Lights out by eight P.M. every night. That, I should tell you, is only the beginning. We will not tolerate outright disobedience at Blossom House—ever." The speaker clicked off.

A few minutes later Jennifer heard the sliding panel in her door slide open—gently, so as not to make any noise. "I know you were behind this whole thing, you little bitch," Harriet hissed. "And I know you think the game you've been playing with Mr. Griggs will protect you. It won't. I have ways, very unpleasant ways, of handling people like you. By the time I'm finished you'll wish you were never born."

The panel slid back shut, this time with a more audible *thunk.* Harriet apparently so livid, she was unable to shut it quietly and keep her visit a secret.

Jennifer stood staring at the closed panel. Harriet, she could guess, would keep her promise. To keep Henry from knowing he would be told of some mysterious accident. Another funeral in the main room. The thought made her tremble. Harriet and Pippin, between them, would devise an accident that was not only terminal, but agonizingly painful. A torture of the damned.

It would come soon, probably during one of the next three days, while the rule of silence was still in effect. The rigidly enforced lack of communication would make the disposal that much simpler; Pippin would be part of it, of course, enjoying the chance to satisfy her long-standing hatred of Jennifer.

Until now, Jennifer had been looking at her escape almost abstractly. The playing up to Henry had been part of a long-term effort, with no fixed date for setting it in motion. No longer. If she didn't get out of here quickly, she would never get out—except out to a mound in the earth near the apple trees. If her effort to escape didn't succeed now, Peter would shortly become a widower, although—and it was a hard realization to accept—she herself was probably already a widow.

The lights abruptly went out. Eight P.M., she supposed. In the eerie stillness she heard a laughing coming from Pippin's cell. "Bye-bye, Peaches. If Auntie Harriet says you'll wish you never were alive, she means you'll wish you never were alive. And pretty soon after that you won't be. Oh, dear, I hope it doesn't hurt *too* much. Of course, I'll do my best to see that it does. Nighty-night, now."

The laughter again—brutal, frightening, evil.

CHAPTER TWENTY-TWO

I can't prove it, but I'm damn sure Peaches was behind that thing with the Garden Club. Half of those old bats probably can't hear much anymore, but the racket from the third floor was so loud, you didn't need ears.

I suppose Peaches's idea was to get them curious, hoping one of them would say something to the police. Fat chance. If any of them had looked the least bit suspicious, I'd have planted the whole lot out in back with the others.

I was never big on flowers like Henry, even as a kid. Manure stank. The hose never reached the faucet. Bugs, rabbits, and dogs flattened them. And just when maybe you'd finally grown a few decent flowers, WHAM! The first frost knocked them on their asses. All curled up and wilty, like Henry when he's been swimming in cold water.

Peaches is no flower, but I'm going to make damn sure she gets her fill of big, slimy bugs and vicious dogs before I turn her into fertilizer.

And I don't plan to wait until the first frost.

Journal of Blossom House,
Entry, page 43—Harriet Griggs

The three days without food was going to be hard on all of them. By the morning of even the first day, they could feel their stomachs complaining bitterly—rumbling, growling, demanding to be fed. At home, Jennifer had never eaten very much, but at Blossom House food had assumed dimensions of a far greater importance, largely because eating was something to look forward to, something to do. Her appetite had risen accordingly. She was afraid all this eating might have made her gain weight; maybe this enforced dieting would help her lose some. Besides, she wasn't precisely going hungry, anyway.

The night before, about an hour after Harriet had locked her in her room, she had heard the bolts of her door slide back, this time so quietly done, it didn't make a sound. From the rattle of his breathing, Jennifer immediately knew it was Henry. "Shhh," he whispered unnecessarily, "not a sound. I've smuggled in a little something for you, Peaches; I couldn't bear the thought of you lying up here hungry." He handed her a large paper bag that surprised her with its weight. "There's some for the morning too, and lunch," Henry explained. "I'll bring you up some more tomorrow night. I know you weren't one of that rowdy group that spoiled the Garden Club's visit, and I think it's stupid to punish you as if you were."

Jennifer could feel him sit down on the edge of her bed, and she shifted nervously. This man might be the key to her escape plan, but there were some ways she was damned if she'd use to pay for it.

Henry breathed out heavily. "If you want to start right in, go ahead, Peaches. I won't mind."

The master manipulator's computer clicked to "on." "Oh, thank you, but I'll wait and enjoy it after you're gone. I bet it's delicious. But I don't want having a full mouth to interfere with our talk. I love the conversations I have with you, you know; I look forward to them all day."

"That's very nice of you to say, Peaches," Jennifer knew that in the dark Henry was aglow with a pleased smile and probably blushing. That a grown man could fall for such obvious drivel proved to her that he was incredibly naive, but then, her father had always fallen for it too, and the last word anyone could pin on him was *naive*.

"Well, dear Peaches," said Henry in a sad voice, "I'm afraid our conversation tonight is going to have to be awfully short. I don't want to be missed by—anybody." Henry stood up and leaned over her bed. "I have something to ask you, Peaches. *Please*."

Jennifer felt her muscle tense. Good God, he wasn't going to suggest— No, of course not.

"Please don't let anyone know I was here, Peaches. *Please*. Or that I brought you food." Jennifer, knowing she had been silly, almost laughed in relief. "It would only cause trouble," Henry continued. "So just keep quiet about it, all right? Not a word to the other little girls or my sister." There was a pause as Henry considered something. "*Especially* my sister . . ."

Slowly, turning back to her as he neared the door—something Jennifer could tell by the sound of his whisper—"I hope you like what I brought. I'll do it again tomorrow."

"Good night," Jennifer whispered in his direction. Then, remembering she was supposed to be manipulating him: "And thank you an awful lot. It's wonderful."

There was a whispering sound of metal on metal, the lock was thrown, and Henry was gone. She fished around in the paper bag to see what he'd brought, more out of curiosity than anything else. In amount, it was prodigious; in selection, it was imponderable. A loaf of bread, okay. Margarine, okay. Jam, okay. But little cans of anchovies, of quail eggs, of smoked *octopus*? Obviously Henry had not raided the refrigerator; his theft had been from shelves loaded with delicacies and specialties.

Jennifer sighed; there was enough of everything to keep more than herself well fed for some time. Cherry. She would share it with Cherry. Cherry wouldn't spill it to anyone else. The others? Well, there wasn't much she could do about them. The food might stretch farther, but it would raise the danger of talk, and with Pippin wandering about, word might get back to Henry that Jennifer had broken her promise not to tell anyone.

She made herself a double sandwich of jam and margarine and thick, sliced bread, filling her stomach for the first time that day. The meal made her feel self-indulgent and greedy. She knew Cherry and the rest of them must be suffering from empty stomachs. There was no way to get some to Cherry tonight; her room door was locked from the outside. But thinking about it, Jennifer knew that, in spite of a natural instinct not to risk exposure by sharing the food further, she was going to have to. In the morning, somehow with Bartlett and Guava and Strawberry and Melonie and Tangerine and Honeydew and Casaba— all of them. Sharing the food this far would leave all of them still pretty hungry, but there was enough to at least take the edge off their punishment. Her original plan to share the stash with only Cherry suddenly appeared selfish.

Lying in bed, chewing contentedly away, Jennifer was surprised to realize the different way in which her days at Blossom House had made her think. It was a startling change; back in New York, the concept of sharing with others had been unknown to her.

Almost immediately something else suddenly surprised her. The jam—pure, concentrated sugar—had just discovered a new cavity in her teeth. Damn. Jennifer's teeth had always been a problem—kept cosmetically perfect by an orthodontist, but genetically vulnerable to cavities. The twinging ache made her wince for a second, then it disappeared. In New York, Dr. Fletcher would have been as relieved as Jennifer was.

A sudden new thought struck Jennifer. What *did* they do about teeth at Blossom House? They couldn't very well take any of the girls to the dentist; having a dentist come here was even less likely. A sudden recollection of the girl at the window of the third-floor door, a bloody towel pressed to her mouth, came back to haunt Jennifer. Along with what she remembered seeing came a recollection of the soul-shattering screams she'd heard coming from above her before she'd gone through the forbidden door to the third floor. A spasm of dread ran through Jennifer's body. *Harriet* did their dental work for them.

She struggled to dismiss the memory. It was too awful even to think of. Besides, the twinge had disappeared, hadn't it? Pulling the covers up tightly around her, Jennifer, lulled by the soporific of an unexpectedly full stomach, fell soundly asleep.

The next morning, Jennifer discovered that distributing the food to the others was not going to be easy. The rigidly enforced silence would have made it difficult enough, but at the beginning of the morning's classes, Harriet had added a new twist that would make it even tougher. "You understand, of course, children, that because you are not allowed to speak to one another, there will also be no visiting between rooms during the quiet period or your free time. You are all wicked little girls, and I'm quite aware, once out of my sight, you would begin to talk."

That pronouncement destroyed Jennifer's first scheme. She and Cherry decided that note-writing would do the job for them; only delivery remained a problem. It was while they were exchanging these little slips of paper that near disaster struck.

"I'll take that." Harriet loomed before them like Godzilla, snatching the note Cherry had just handed to Jennifer. There was a smile of satisfaction on Harriet's face; she had them. Slowly the note was examined on the outside, Jennifer praying that Cherry hadn't written something that would compromise their food supply and its source. With elaborate care, enjoying every moment of the suspense, Harriet slowly unfolded the note and began to read it aloud. "Smoked octopus?" she read. "Better we should smoke Harriet and eat *her*. Fat and blubber are good for you . . ."

Harriet's voice trailed off; the note was clearly stronger than she had expected. The other girls struggled not to laugh, knowing that laughter at her expense would only make Harriet angrier when she came to punishing Cherry and Jennifer. Pippin knew this so, and laughed uproariously.

Jennifer's heart sunk. If Harriet knew her delicacy shelf well,

she'd catch the octopus reference, and know not only that Jenni
fer was getting food, but precisely who was providing her with it

Harriet, however, seemed too preoccupied with the insult t
worry about that part of the note. "Very funny, Cherry. I sup
pose it's the kind of thing that amused your customers back i
New York." Jennifer blinked in disbelief; it was the first suc
reference to the Minnesota Strip she'd ever heard Harriet make
Cherry, she could see, was thrown, blushing deeply, probabl
struggling to keep herself from saying something Harriet woul
make her regret.

Spinning around, Harriet marched across the main room and
moment later returned, the ruler in one hand, the other han
hiding something behind her back. Without understanding, Jenn
fer saw a long black cord of some sort, running from behin
Harriet across the entire room. The arrangement mystified her.

"Hold out your hands, Cherry, palms up. By now, you kno
the routine well enough." Wearily Cherry extended her hand
Dropping the ruler, Harriet seized one of Cherry's wrists an
brought the other hand out from behind her back. Gaspin
Jennifer screamed, suddenly realizing what Harriet had in min
In Harriet's hand was the little play-iron the prisoners of Blosso
House were encouraged to use for their starched dresses; it w
red-hot. Before Cherry could react she had turned away, towar
Jennifer, when her friend had screamed—Harriet brought the ir
firmly down on Cherry's upturned palm. There was a sma
sizzling sound, a sudden whiff of something one would smell at
hamburger stand, and an ear-splitting shriek from Cherry. Jennif
felt faint, leaning against Bartlett, who was standing beside he

Harriet let go of Cherry's hand and brandished the iron in t
air. "You next, Peaches. Step forward and hold out your rig
hand, palm up, please. Come on, don't dawdle, Peaches. Ta
your punishment like a big girl."

Biting her lip, Jennifer stepped foward, eyeing the iron wi
dread. "Your hand, Peaches, your hand. If you don't, there
always your face." Suddenly Harriet appeared to reconsider.

was not by chance; another ploy to make the girls turn savagely on Jennifer had just occurred to her.

"No, Peaches. Don't. For a moment I forgot. Mr. Griggs would become highly disturbed if he knew I had damaged his favorite little girl. Instead of burning you with the iron, then, we'll just extend the no-food rule by another day." She turned to the others, still standing frozen in front of her, appalled by what she had done to Cherry. "Children, that extra day without food you can thank Peaches for. It's only Mr. Griggs's favoritism that stops me from giving her the punishment she deserves. So you'll all have to suffer in her place."

Pulling herself up, Harriet started toward the door, stopping just as she reached it. "And Cherry, if you want to find out how much of me is blubber and how much is muscle, just try me. Pippin, write down the name of anyone who talks."

Jennifer was helping Cherry to her room—the burn on her hand was a deep, brilliant red, but not as bad as she had originally expected—when she heard the door slammed and bolted from the outside.

From somewhere down the line of cells, Jennifer heard Pippin laughing her sinister laugh. "Okay, kids, who's going to be the first one to try talking? I've got my pad and pencil all ready." The question was met by silence, the others turning to stare at Pippin with loathing. They had seen through her trap: even the most agreeable answer to her question would involve speaking—and their name being put on the list for Harriet. Suddenly Pippin, doing a bizarre burlesque of a dance, broke into *The Mikado*. "As some day it may happen that a victim must be found, I've got a little list—I've got a little list. . . ." The laugh again, challenging and evil.

Jennifer looked at Pippin in disbelief. She was unsure why, but it stunned her to discover that Pippin could sing at all, much less sing something as light and fragile as Gilbert and Sullivan. It was like uncovering evidence that Lucrezia Borgia hummed the Dr Pepper jingle in her sleep.

*　　*　　*

"You didn't tell anyone?" Henry asked anxiously, putting down a new bag of food beside Jennifer's bed.

"No one," Jennifer lied. "You asked me not to, and I didn't."

"That's a good little girl. I put some ordinary things in the food bag this time; Harriet will never miss them."

Jennifer wasn't so sure this was true but mumbled in agreement anyway. Anything to keep old Henry happy. Well, *almost* anything.

"Everything else going all right?" Henry seemed desperately anxious to please her tonight. He had slipped into her room as he had the night before, silently, after lights-out—still eight o'clock sharp—and everything he asked her, even his presence here indicated to Jennifer that her continuing manipulation of him was paying off. Jennifer decided it was time to lay the groundwork for her first try at escape.

"Oh, about the same as usual," Jennifer answered after a long pause; given the circumstances, sounding melancholy came easily.

"You don't sound very happy, Peaches. Maybe the food I'm bringing isn't—"

"No, the food's fine. I just miss things. You know, crazy little stuff. Silly things like watching people walking on the street, seeing the lights in store windows, hearing people talk to each other . . . dumb things like that. If I could just . . . Oh, well, I shouldn't bother you with *my* problems."

Henry stood up. In the dark Jennifer couldn't see him except as a dim shadow, but she imagined that he was trying to look firm and powerful. "You *should* bother me with your problems, however silly you think they are, Peaches. That's what a daddy for. You're his favorite little girl, and to me, nothing that troubles you is silly."

"Well, what I was wondering was"—Jennifer knew she had to approach this idea with great care, testing the waters gingerly until she could catch the drift of his reaction—"if maybe you could take me out some night and let me see some of the things miss so. You know, with you right beside me. Look in the store windows, see the lights, and, say, maybe"— Jennifer made h voice sound suddenly excited, playing it as if the idea had just occurred to her—"maybe we could stop in at a bar and have a drink or something. You know, just have fun together."

Jennifer discovered she'd made a terrible mistake; Henry's voice had a deeply shocked, almost unbelieving sound to it when he answered her. "A bar! Good Heavens, Peaches, little girls aren't allowed in bars. You're much too young. In another six years or so, when you're eighteen—but *now*? Oh, Peaches, what a crazy, impossible idea! Maybe a soda fountain . . . or an ice-cream parlor . . . There's a wonderful one on Gulliver Street; some days they even have a clown there for the children. . . . Or there's an old-fashioned one over on Peters Avenue, with real old-time ice-cream-parlor chairs and little marble-topped tables, and they have seventeen kinds of sundaes, can you believe that? Or on Hubble Lane there's . . ."

Jennifer knew she had won. Henry was even crazier than she had thought. He wasn't talking about the recklessness of the idea; he was already thinking about where they could go together.

"You'd have to stay right with me, of course, Peaches. But you'd want to, anyway, I suppose. And it will all have to be figured out very carefully, so that no one ever finds out about it." Henry seemed lost in a private world, his voice growing dim and lilting, as if he were half asleep. "Oh, there's so much I'd love to have you see, Peaches. There's a little Ferris wheel near the edge of the town and—"

A step had to be taken, and grimacing in the darkness of her room, Jennifer took it. "Oh, I'd love *that,* Daddy. It sounds wonderful. A Ferris wheel!"

For a moment there was a pause. Henry was absorbing her use of the word *Daddy;* creepy as it made her feel, Jennifer knew it would cement the sale. She had been saving the word for just such a moment as this.

For several minutes more they talked about nothing. Henry seemed to be pretending that he'd put the outing from his mind; Jennifer knew better. Finally he decided he had to leave. "Good night, Peaches," he said happily, leaning down to peck her on the forehead.

"Good night, Daddy."

Oh, Christ, Jennifer said to herself. How low did she have to stoop?

The next morning dawned brighter than any morning since Jennifer had arrived at Blossom House. A chance to get out, a chance to be free again, and a chance, perhaps, to find out what had happened to Peter. The police. The first thing she would do was go to the police, get the others freed, and then start the search for Peter.

Suddenly Jennifer wondered why Hillary Crane hadn't gotten worried by now and sent people looking for her. That damned promise she'd extracted from her. Didn't Hillary realize that by now that promise no longer held, that something had to have gone wrong somewhere?

She dismissed the idea quickly, so it wouldn't spoil her feeling of expectation. A trip to the ladies' room at the old-fashioned ice-cream parlor with the seventeen kinds of sundaes. A premature hop from the Ferris wheel and a race off into the darkness. Easy, so terribly easy.

She spread some marmalade—a new item, from Henry's second CARE package—on her bread, a lot of it. Substantial, like her new feeling of hope. Then the trouble started. It came again without warning. A piercing, throbbing ache in her tooth where yesterday there had only been a momentary twinge. This time, it didn't go away. It throbbed and ached and tortured, boring, it seemed, directly into the bone of her lower jaw, pulsing and throbbing like the still-beating heart torn out of a living human body. No one must know about it—except maybe Cherry. No today.

That morning before classes, keeping her mouth mostly shut so that air couldn't get at the cavity, she told Cherry of her success with Henry. Cherry was ecstatic. "Hey, if *you* get out, we *all* get out. Tremendous!"

Then Jennifer told her of the toothache.

"Jesus," Cherry said. "Don't let Harriet find out. Painless Parker she ain't." Cherry sighed. "It must be feel-bad day. I got a pain in my gut that's killing me. And I'm all sweaty and feel like shit."

But Harriet did find out. Pippin heard more than she let on; she had decided more was to be gained from listening in to whispered conversations than writing people's names down. Anything of interest she reported to Harriet. It was only a matter of time.

Pippin taunted her gleefully. "Drilling's always a barrel of fun with Harriet at the controls, Peaches. And in your case—with Harriet so fond of you, and all—there's always the possibility of the drill slipping and slicing up into your gums, or even up into the roof of your mouth. Harriet would love that. She's really very skillful with her drills—when she *wants* to be. Oh, she's certainly going to be amused when I tell her about your tooth." Pippin's eyes, always narrow and mean-looking, shrank down to virtual slits. "And tell her I will, kiddo. Good luck, Peaches."

At lessons that morning, Henry seemed not quite there, thinking of other matters, or daydreaming or something. Suddenly he leaned closer to her, facing her across the student desk and resting his arms on the far edge. "Tonight, Peaches. It's tonight. Harriet will be all tied up, watching a rerun of *Brideshead Revisited*—she's seen them all about eight times already—so it'll be easy. Wear your best clothes and just pull a blanket up over you. I'll be up for you by nine."

The shock of success ran through Jennifer like electricity; she knew her heartbeat must have sped up too, because she could feel the pulsing in her aching tooth, faster and much stronger than before. "Oh, that's wonderful, Daddy." She looked around to see if anyone had heard her call him that; it made her feel as sick as the toothache did. "I didn't realize it would be so soon," she said. "I thought you'd need more time to plan things."

"Not where my little Peaches is concerned," Henry said, settling back into his chair. "Don't worry about how it's done;

just concentrate on which ice-cream place you want, and think about the Ferris wheel. I'll take care of the rest.''

At lunchtime, Jennifer took a chance and gave Cherry the news that it was that night, standing in her doorway and whispering it to her. Cherry was lying on her bed, looking awful. She tried to be enthusiastic about the possibility of Jennifer's escape but had trouble mustering the energy. ''Goddamn, Jennifer''—using Jennifer's real name was something she only did when she felt scared or desperate—''Goddamn, but I feel awful. I asked Bartlett to tell Harriet I was having cramps. Bad ones. Harriet's used to that. But, Jesus, I ache all over and feel like I'm going to throw up any moment.''

''It's probably some bug,'' Jennifer said reassuringly, looking at Cherry's ashen face and not feeling very reassured herself. ''As soon as I get you out of here, we'll get you to a doctor. I mean, if you still feel that bad. You probably won't. Those bugs don't hang around long. You'll probably be at the nearest bar guzzling it down.''

Trying, Cherry smiled weakly. ''Or on the nearest street corner, looking for some john to pay my plane fare home. Usually *they* don't hang around very long, either.''

As soon as a starvation luncheon of bread and water was over, eaten in the eerie silence Harriet had mandated, knives and forks sounding like hammers against anvils in the stillness, Harriet stood up and looked directly at Jennifer.

''I understand you have a bad toothache, child. There's only one cure for that. A filling—or if we have to, an extraction.'' She started for the door but turned to look back and saw Jennifer with her mouth open to speak. ''Don't argue about it, child. All little girls hate having to see the dentist. They'll lie and say the tooth's stopped hurting or anything they can think of, just to avoid a little dental work. Silly. At Blossom House, though, we're good little girls and face up to what has to be done—bravely.''

Harriet unlocked the door, reached outside, and rolled in an old-fashioned country-dentist's chair. Originally its drill had been turned by foot pedals, which were still there, but it now boasted a high-speed electric motor for the drill. Harriet looked commandingly at Jennifer again. "Don't hang back like that, child. Come sit down, right here in the chair. Stop stalling. The chair—*now*."

As Harriet began advancing toward her the phony smile gave way to a grim look. Jennifer's first instinct was to back away from Harriet. She suddenly felt Pippin behind her, blocking her path and pushing her forward. Harriet's great hand grabbed Jennifer's wrist and yanked her toward the chair, pushing her roughly down into it with a grunt. "You're making things difficult, Peaches. But then, I should have expected that; you always cause trouble."

All along Jennifer had known there was no point trying to resist someone as powerful as Harriet. She squeezed her eyes shut and tried to think of some positive way to accept the inevitable. The tooth had to be drilled, anyway, she told herself, or the excruciating pain in her jaw would only grow worse. It might hurt a little, but not even Harriet would deliberately make it more painful than necessary; Pippin's stories were probably just that—stories. She was startled when Harriet and Pippin suddenly tied her wrists to the metal arms of the chair.

Harriet's veneer-thin smile had returned. "Just a precaution," she explained. "Little girls sometimes get frightened. Just relax, and I'll fix your"—the pause seemed interminable as Harriet widened her smile, rapping the drill against the palm of her hand with an ominous, hollow sound—"I'll fix your—tooth—in no time." The pause again, while Harriet widened the smile even farther and leaned down, letting her huge face fill Jennifer's whole field of vision. "Barring accident, of course."

There was the overwhelming smell of garlic breath; the expanding smile; the ratchet sound of Harriet's breathing. "Open wide," Harriet said cheerfully. "This will hurt."

CHAPTER TWENTY-THREE

For a while, when I was in high school, I started smoking cigarettes. Somewhere in the back of my mind I thought if I smoked enough, it would stunt my growth. Stupid and, when you think of it, funny.

What wasn't funny was that one day Ginny Simmons—a really mean girl in my class—ran across me down in the basement, puffing away like crazy. I pleaded with her to stay quiet but, damn it, Ginny went right ahead and told my teacher. I've hated squealers ever since.

Take Pippin. Okay, she gives me a lot of information. And does what I tell her to with the other girls. It used to be a very effective way of handling them. But between Cherry and Peaches, it doesn't seem to work anymore.

Pippin doesn't work for free, either. I have to pay her off in six-packs, an occasional jug of Scotch, and for Christ's sake, even Quaaludes. Damn, but I get mad when Pippin rips me off like that. It's nothing but old-fashioned blackmail. Today's young ladies are just a bunch of scheming bitches.

Sometimes I wish Blossom House were infested with a pack of vicious, hungry rats. I love the picture of that little crook Pippin having her toes nibbled away one at a time.

That would stunt her growth.

Journal of Blossom House,
Entry, page 46—Harriet Griggs

In her room, Cherry lay on her bed, still unable to find a position that didn't hurt. Twice in the last hour, she'd staggered into her bathroom and thrown up; something in that crazy food Henry was giving to Peaches must have gotten to her. Her stomach ached, she could hear her heart beating against her chest, and she kept having sudden fists of heavy sweating. "Just a bug," Peaches had said. Some bug.

Cherry knew she should be out in the main room with Peaches, but she was afraid that she'd throw up again—in front of everybody—if she moved. She had heard the drilling start and knew her place was beside Peaches, reassuring her, telling her everything was going to be all right, trying to calm and comfort her. Tonight was the night for her escape attempt, and Peaches would need all the cool she could muster to pull off a tricky maneuver like that.

An ear-splitting scream suddenly came from Peaches. Cherry groaned and tried to go out and help; she got as far as her own door but had to stop. Inside herself, she knew she didn't have the strength anymore. Her head was spinning, her legs weak beneath her. Unsteadily she stood in the doorway, her face ashen, swaying back and forth.

Harriet had struck a nerve—literally—in Jennifer's aching molar. Another scream. "Please, please, Miss Griggs," Jennifer pleaded, "can't you give me something to deaden the pain? Honest, I've never felt anything like it. Please, Miss Griggs. You *must* have something."

Genially Harriet laughed, pausing in her drilling for a moment. "I have lots of things I could give you, but only good little girls get *them*."

"She's talking too much," Pippin said. "Do you want the jaw vise?"

"Good idea, Pippin. It makes the drilling easier, too." Pippin handed Harriet a weird-looking chromium device, which Harriet held in front of her. "Pull her head back and hold her mouth open," Harriet commanded. Wearing an expression of pleasure, Pippin did as Harriet told her. Jennifer could feel the vise go into her mouth, forcing her jaws wide open. With a grunt of effort, Harriet jammed the vise so far into the back of Jennifer's mouth, a trickle of blood oozed from either side, running down Jennifer's chin. Then Harriet reached forward and tightened two sets of screws to keep the vise in its wide-open position. Harriet was wiping the drill itself, blowing on it to remove bits of enamel and tooth still clinging to it.

Standing in her doorway, something had just struck Cherry for the first time. In the wrong hands, a dentist's drill could be a lethal weapon. It could easily be guided up into the roof of Jennifer's mouth, through it, and directly up into her brain. Would Harriet dare? Cherry answered her own question: she would—and later tell Henry that it had been a sad and tragic accident. Trying again, Cherry made a final effort to go out and help Jennifer, but her knees buckled and she had to crawl back to her bed. She was helpless. Jennifer would have to fend for herself.

Jennifer was aware of another piercing shriek that had come from somewhere inside herself. Harriet was apparently deliberately moving the drill around to grind into the exposed nerve. She heard her own screams once more, a series of piercing shrieks, as the drill hit the ultrasensitive nervous system of the tooth. Her whole body was twisting and struggling against the ropes that tied her to the chair. When one of her feet managed to kick Harriet, Pippin quickly tied her legs to the chair as tightly as her arms already were. The drill bored in, then slipped, cutting into the soft, inflamed gum tissue around the tooth. "So sorry, Peaches," said Harriet with a benign little smile. "These things happen, you know." The drill ground on, blood spurted from the gums, and Jennifer began shrieking again. She wasn't sure which was worse: the racking torment of the drill as it ripped into the exposed nerve, or the shattering realization that at any moment

Harriet, if she chose to, could drive the whirring drill up through the roof of her mouth into her brain. Independently, she had come to the same conclusion as Cherry. In the wrong hands, a dentist's drill could be a lethal weapon.

There were shrieks again, which kept surprising Jennifer by coming from her own mouth; Harriet, apparently, was deliberately ravaging the nerve.

"Hang on, Peaches, it'll be over in a minute," a gentle voice said to her, and a hand reached from somewhere and squeezed hers. The voice and the hand, Jennifer realized, belonged to Henry Griggs. For the moment the drilling had stopped. "Be a little gentler with her, damn it, Harriet. Didn't you give her any Novocain? Look, the poor thing's got tears running down her little face."

"Some kinds of drilling have to be done without painkillers, Henry. So you know where the drill is," Harriet snapped at her brother. "Anyway, it's all over now, except the filling."

"I still think you could have given her something," Henry complained.

"All right, Henry. If you're such a great dentist, next time Peaches gets a toothache, *you* fill it."

A few minutes later Jennifer felt some sort of puttylike substance being pressed into the hole made by the drill. The ache in the molar had disappeared. With Henry's arrival, standing close beside her, Harriet's chance to do anything to her had ended. The ropes were untied, the jaw vise removed. "There. That should feel better, Peaches." There was a pause, then: "Usually, good little girls say thank you, Miss Griggs."

Jennifer, out of the chair, tried to curtsy, but she almost fell over. Henry had to grab her to keep her from falling to the floor. Suddenly Jennifer found herself laughing helplessly. "I just thought of what my dentist in New York will say when he sees that filling." She laughed again to reassure Henry that she was in good shape for the secret visit to the ice-cream parlor and the Ferris wheel that night. The laugh was only on the surface; inside, Jennifer had already added, "*If* my dentist in New

York ever sees that filling. It all depends on you, Henry, old chum, my artfully handled, sick-in-the-head secret lover."

To Jennifer nine o'clock—the hour Henry was supposed to pick her up and stealthily slip her out of the house to drink in the delights of dazzling downtown Chivers—seemed as if it would never come. At Henry's insistence, she had been excused from the rest of the day's activities. Harriet had muttered and grumbled, but the firm tone in Henry's voice had subdued her. Oddly Jennifer wished she hadn't been let out of the games. Watching the hands slowly move around on her Mickey Mouse clock made time pass with agonizing slowness; just when she wanted him to go as fast as he could, Mickey was dragging his feet.

Twice she slipped in to see Cherry; the girl's deathlike pallor, the sweat gathered on her forehead, and the pains that kept racking Cherry's stomach were symptoms that even Jennifer could diagnose. A friend of hers at Chalmer's, Boo Boocock, had told Jennifer of them after she was discharged from Lenox Hill to recuperate from an emergency appendectomy. What the hell did they do at Blossom House if someone came down with appendicitis? Did Harriet switch from playing dentist to playing surgeon? No, not even Harriet would try that. They would just let her die, Jennifer supposed.

It occurred to her that if she could escape tonight, it would mean more than just her own freedom; it might be saving Cherry's life, something suddenly terribly important to Jennifer. They made an odd combination, Jennifer and Cherry, a warm collision between Park Avenue and the Minnesota Strip. It was a combination that worked; Jennifer had quickly overcome her initial shock at Cherry's occupation and replaced it with curiosity. Cherry had told her of the machinery and the hazards of the Strip, of her stepfather in West Virginia, and of poverty. Jennifer, in her turn, shared tales of coming-out parties, of people with homes everywhere, of a casual attitude toward the poor, because poverty was so far removed from their own existence, it was incomprehensible. The exchange of life-styles was something the two of them could talk about for hours.

Just before lights-out and the locking of her door, Jennifer chanced it and again slipped in to see Cherry. No improvement, but neither was she getting worse; for the moment, a medical standoff. "Hang in there, Cherry," Jennifer whispered. "If this works tonight, we're all out of here *fast*."

Smiling weakly, Cherry held Jennifer's hand briefly. "Good luck, Jennifer." Cherry was obviously terrified. And if Jennifer's diagnosis was right, she had every reason to be.

She smiled uncertainly, blew Cherry a kiss, and fled quickly back to her own room to get ready. Only an hour to go. Damn it, Mickey, move your ass.

On the dot of nine o'clock Henry slipped into Jennifer's room. "All set, Peaches?"

"I've been all set for hours, Daddy." In the darkness of the room, Jennifer felt it was safe to stick out her tongue at him the instant she had said the word.

"Stay right behind me, Peaches. Not a sound, now. And don't be frightened; Daddy will be just a step ahead of you. I know how badly an old, dark house at night, creaking and groaning and everything, can scare a little girl." What a posturing bastard Henry was, Jennifer thought; the person who was probably scared the most was Henry himself.

On tiptoes, they went out of the main room, down a short hall, and out into the large hallway that Jennifer remembered so well. Her first bedroom couldn't have been more than twenty-five feet from where she stood. Through Harriet's door they could hear the opening music of *Brideshead Revisited;* Harriet was apparently enjoying her fourth rerun precisely as Henry had predicted.

Still on tiptoes, they soundlessly went down the carpeted grand staircase. At the bottom—Henry seemed to know exactly where he was entirely by the feel of the walls—they turned to the left and down a long narrow hall into the kitchen area.

"The back door's straight ahead, Peaches," Henry whispered.

"Hold on to me and don't even breathe." In the silence, as Henry's hands fought to open the lock without making any noise, Jennifer could hear a thousand sounds. Rats or mice scurrying ahead of them; strange creakings from the walls; the groans of dusty, cobwebbed rafters; the moaning of wind down unseen chimneys. Jennifer could feel her heart beating; to her its pulsing seemed so thunderous a sound, she was sure Henry must have heard it.

"There," Henry hissed. "It's open. Shhh. Come now. I parked my car around the corner."

Slowly Henry pulled the door open, and the two of them stepped out into the blackness of night. It was the first breath of free air Jennifer had taken in well over a month. She was going to make it. My God, she was going to get away!

In the warm, dark air the two of them paused, drinking in the black stillness that surrounded them. "Well, Peaches," Henry said, still whispering. "You see, there was nothing to be afraid of; the only thing that heard us was the wind."

A blinding burst of light forced their eyes shut; Jennifer gasped, Henry groaned. From the blackness behind the light came a familiar voice, considerably more agitated than usual. "It's exactly what I've been expecting of you, brother Henry. That vixen's been working on you for weeks; now you were going to turn her loose. Well, you *aren't,* Henry Griggs."

Recovering from her shock, Jennifer was getting ready to run off on her own. Harriet, though, had not lost her talent for reading minds. "No, you don't, dear. I've been expecting that, too." A hand with the grip of a bulldozer seized her right arm so tightly, Jennifer yelped. With a disgusted sigh, Harriet shoved her brother back through the door and stepped after him herself, dragging a helpless Jennifer in behind her.

Henry seemed to be recovering. "I was only taking her to Lemmon's—you know, the ice-cream parlor downtown. And maybe the Ferris wheel. The poor child was feeling so depressed and—"

Harriet rocked with laughter, her mammoth breasts flopping together as they shook from the movement. "The ice-cream

parlor! The Ferris wheel! Henry, I always knew you weren'
much of a man—more of a eunuch, I'd say—but I would neve
have guessed you were a *stupid* eunuch. Sweet little Peaches her
would have been gone so fast, you wouldn't have known what hi
you. A trip to the ladies' room—and out the other door. Th
police. The end of everything. Prison.'' Harriet paused, appar
ently out of breath from her bellowing and her shattering laugh
ter. Recovering, she looked at Jennifer and shook her head. ''A
for you, I don't know exactly what sort of punishment could b
even remotely adequate. We'll have to study that. But you ca
count on me, child, to come up with something that will teac
you not to try anything like this again.''

Henry drew himself up, although beside Harriet he still ap
peared tiny. ''It's not Peaches's fault. The idea was mine. Peache
didn't even want to come along, but I sort of forced her into it.'

Jennifer stared in wonder. Possibly the last person in the worl
she had thought would try to take all the blame off of her and pι
it on himself, was Henry Griggs.

''You just *think* it was all your idea, Henry. Our little Peache
here is very skillful getting other people to do just what she want
them to. The punishment, Peaches, the punishment . . . Oϊ
there are so many possibilities!''

Henry's voice abruptly changed tone; it took on a hard, dee
quality that Jennifer had only heard once or twice. Each time, sh
remembered, Harriet had seemed to shrivel before it. ''There wi
be no punishment. No punishment of any kind, Harriet. I aι
telling you that, and I mean it. It was not Peaches's fault; it wε
mine. If you so much as yell at her, you'll hear from me.
Jennifer watched as Harriet took a deep breath to control hersel
and even without Harriet's saying a word, Jennifer knew tha
once again, Henry had won.

''And another thing, Harriet. It's time this nonsense abоι
nothing but bread and water was ended. And the no-talkiι
thing. All of that is very unhealthy for little girls. Do yc
understand me?'' Henry spun on his heels without waiting fϵ

an answer and disappeared into the darkness of Blossom House's labyrinth of hallways and tunnels.

In New York, Hillary Crane had made her decision. It was Friday, and Friday was the outside date she had set as a deadline. Something was definitely wrong. Still not a word from Jennifer or Peter. It was not like either of them. Staring out her window, she pulled herself away from watching the cars racing back and forth up Park and faced the reality. She had to go to Chivers and start nosing around for herself.

She had called Mr. Owen again—Townsend Delafield always ended up shouting at her—and asked if he'd heard anything yet. "No," Ted Owen answered glumly. "Not a word from either of them. We don't know where to start looking, either. As far as I can tell, the police have done nothing, and I'm at a dead loss about what to do next."

"Oh." It wasn't much of an answer, and Hillary knew it. Ted Owen seemed to know it, too.

"Hillary, I just can't believe that Jennifer would tell you that they were eloping without saying where they were going to get married. I'm sure you made some sort of a promise, but I would think by now you would realize something, somewhere, has gone wrong. Don't you owe it to us, Jennifer, to *yourself* for that matter—I understand she was your oldest and closest friend—to tell us where?"

Mr. Owen almost made Hillary give in in spite of herself. But the promise—she had made a solemn promise and, damn it, just this once, she was going to keep it. "I don't know where they went, Mr. Owen. I really don't know."

Ted Owen sighed, then mumbled something, then hung up. Hillary was pretty sure she'd heard him beginning to swear and decided he'd probably hung up abruptly to avoid having her hear him.

She felt sorry for Mr. Owen, she felt sorry for Mr. Delafield, but she felt sorriest of all for Jennifer. What could have happened? People—people *she* knew, anyway—didn't just fall off the edge of the world like that. She even felt sorry for herself, having to defy her parents and vanish into some distant void. She would leave a note for her family, a sweet, loving note, explaining as much as she dared. They would be furious. Mr. Delafield would be furious. Mr. Owen would be furious.

She packed quickly, working on how she'd manage when she got to Chivers. Hurrying, so she would be gone before her family got back, she threw a few things into her small overnight bag. The Yellow Pages would list the JP's in Chivers and, one by one, she'd go to each of them until she found the one who had married Jennifer and Peter. Whoever he was, he must have gotten some clue as to where they were heading next. It would be hard, exhausting work, but Jennifer was worth it, to find out where they'd gone to after Chivers or, Christ, discover what awful thing had happened to them.

Two hours later, her bank account raided, her mouth set firm, Hillary Crane, best friend and confidante of Jennifer Owen, née Delafield, was on a jet to Baltimore. There she would rent a car and drive on to Chivers. To look, to probe, to search—or to find out—what had gone wrong.

Staring out of the jet's window at the twinkling little lights below that were suddenly rushing up at the plane Hillary felt a growing sense of dread creep over her. Were those lights guiding the jet to the runway, or were they the outline of an arrow pointing toward Jennifer and Peter's doom?

CHAPTER TWENTY-FOUR

The first, the real Peaches, almost destroyed Henry; now there's a second, ersatz Peaches trying again. Before the whole mess started—oh, maybe twenty years ago—Henry was a talented, sometimes brilliant lawyer, a full partner of Ewing, Coxe, & Bradlee, one of Wilmington's most prestigious firms. He was on his way to the top, everybody said.

Until the accident. His daughter Peaches—her real name was Pamela, but Henry had nicknamed her Peaches when she was a little girl, and it stuck—was killed in a dreadful automobile accident, poor thing. The blow of Peaches's death was too much for Henry; he simply fell apart, never a strong man to begin with.

With time, he began acting more and more peculiarly. Ewing, Coxe, & Bradlee tried to be patient; Henry was a valuable asset, and they knew how much Henry had adored Peaches. It didn't work. Henry began making weird legal mistakes in court, non-sensical errors; the kind of thing that infuriates clients. Little by little the firm began edging Henry out; it was sad, but I guess they had to protect their clients—and themselves. In law, memories are short, and compassion has narrow limits. In the end, Ewing, Coxe, & Bradlee settled a good pension on Henry and pushed him out entirely. Henry never got over that, either. I can't really blame them, though.

At home, Henry became barely rational. He talked to himself all the time, muttering and staring into space. In fairness, over a pretty short span of time, he'd become a widower, his older daughter had killed herself, and his younger daughter, Peaches, the one person in life he really loved, had been killed in a crash. On top of all these blows, he'd been thrown out of a top job, one that he reveled in. Reeling, his mental troubles seemed to get worse instead of better as each day went by. He was terribly confused.

No matter what I said, I couldn't convince him that Peaches wasn't killed eloping to Chivers with some boy named Dykes. She wasn't. She was killed running from her father—hurt and confused.

I've always known the whole story, of course. Apparently, the afternoon before Peaches fled to Baltimore, Henry had been out drinking with two of his clients. He never could handle booze, Henry couldn't. And when he finally got home and saw Peaches, he went after her. That's pretty sick, I guess, but Henry had done the same thing several times before, once when Peaches was only twelve, I remember, and a few times when she was even younger. It was the first time, though, that Peaches was old enough to understand what her father was trying to do to her, and she did the only thing she could think of: run like hell.

Poor Henry didn't remember any of it, neither the afternoon that caused Peaches to take off, nor the earlier times with her. He'd blocked the whole thing from his consciousness, I guess, because it was so terrible. So he pretended the elopement caused her death to explain the whole thing to himself. He believed it too, my God, but he believed it.

I'm afraid I'm guilty of using all I know to control Henry. But it's worked, damn it, it's worked.

So it's time—it's past time—I got rid of Peaches for good and all. I'll enjoy hearing that spoiled little Park Avenue brat scream- ing and shrieking and begging for mercy.

There's nothing so satisfying as watching the rich suffer.

> *Journal of Blossom House,*
> *Entry, page 50—Harriet Griggs*

Henry Griggs and his sister, Harriet, sat in facing chairs, the last light of the afternoon sun filtering in boldly through the library windows. Every few minutes Henry would abruptly stand up and begin pacing the room, anger etched into his face by the stark light from outside, which made him look like the bust of a furious Zeus. Their argument was bitter, with much of Harriet's side of it hidden behind subterfuges and meant to accomplish things for far different reasons than she said. Leaning forward in her chair, Harriet waved a piece of paper at him.

"It's a list of girls I think have to be replaced, Henry."

The bust of Zeus turned and fixed her with a stare. "Replaced? Replaced *why?*" It was not so much a question as a hostile inquiry.

"Causing trouble. Continually disobeying the rules. Stirring up the others. You know the kind of thing that gets into some of them after a while. Others, well, others just start off as a disrup- tive influence."

It was obvious to Harriet that Henry had a pretty good idea of at least one person whose name was bound to be on her list. She would have to edge her way in, slowly, maybe even taking a matter of days.

But Henry seemed determined to make an issue of it right now. "I don't see anything wrong with the group as it stands at this moment. You're up to something, Harriet, and if you don't think I know it, you're crazy."

Harriet started a long way from Jennifer; it would make her

name seem more acceptable when she finally got to it. "Well, take Tangerine. Tangerine is very sulky. She keeps everybody upstairs on edge with her moods. And she doesn't contribute anything."

Henry shrugged.

"Or Bartlett. She was very much in evidence during that little display of bad manners before the Fauntleroy fiasco. And again, during the floor-stamping when the Garden Club was here. That did your standing with the Club a lot of damage, I think, Henry; I doubt if they'll call again next year."

In spite of Harriet's trampling on one of his most sensitive subjects, Henry remained impassive. Again, he merely shrugged.

"And, of course—I know how fond you are of her, Henry, but we have to run this operation practically—and, well, it saddens me of course, but—"

"There's Peaches." Henry virtually spat out the name. He had known from the beginning that Peaches's name was where Harriet would wind up, and it annoyed him to think Harriet considered him so dumb.

"Well, Henry, you know there's very little question she was behind the whole Garden Club thing. And those fights she keeps having with the other girls. Rich children always think they're better than anyone else and should get the best of everything—automatically. Maybe she was trying to spoil the Garden Club tour just to spite you. Who knows?"

Henry could feel the anger make his blood run faster. *"I* know that when I went upstairs to try to stop the stamping, Peaches wasn't even in the room. How could she be leading the whole thing if she wasn't there, for Christ's sake?"

"She probably put the other girls up to it and then went into her room, so she wouldn't be blamed. You've got to remember she's a very devious and scheming little girl, Henry. Like that thing she talked you into—going to the ice-cream parlor and the Ferris wheel. An obvious trick to make her escape."

"I notice you haven't mentioned your own precious Pippin, Harriet," said Henry, studying her carefully.

"All right, if that's what you want. She's a big help to me, but maybe you're right; *she's* a bit shifty, too." Harriet began making little check marks beside the names on her list. "Pippin . . . Peaches . . ."

Henry stopped pacing abruptly. "No Peaches. Pippin, all right." He was a little surprised that Harriet could abandon her ally so cavalierly just to eliminate Peaches; getting rid of her must be terribly important to his sister, and Henry had trouble understanding why.

Harriet decided it was time to play her last card. "Henry," she said severely, "did you know—Pippin told me this—that behind your back Peaches laughs at almost everything you say or do? Or that she calls you that old fart, Daddykins?"

"Peaches, no, Pippin, all right." Henry repeated it like an automaton; even though he doubted Peaches had ever said anything of the kind Harriet had just quoted, it still shook him considerably, possibly because it was how, in his most private thoughts, he would have described himself.

"But Henry," Harriet protested angrily. "A girl who says things like—"

As he spun around, Harriet was startled to see how red her brother's face had gotten, a dark, unhealthy crimson, almost glowing with fury. "You don't listen, Harriet. You don't ever listen to me. I said Peaches will not be on your damn list. Period. Pippin *ought* to go—a junkie, for Christ's sake. But that's up to you; you decide about Pippin. Bartlett and Tangerine, well, if they're a problem, pick one or the other, but not both. You decide that, too. But this is my final word about Peaches; I don't even want to hear you mention her name again. Understood?"

Numbly Harriet nodded. Henry was in his macho phase again, and resistance was useless. Muttering, Henry walked firmly from the room. To Harriet the confrontation had been a setback. But somehow she would get—she had to get—Peaches. In the most painful, agonizing sort of finale she could come up with. Harriet wasn't at all sure how to go about it yet, but the germ of an idea was already rattling around inside her head. A plan, a scheme, a plot that would end her troubles with Peaches once and for all. And simultaneously, end Peaches. Maybe she could think of a way to turn Henry against Peaches. Maybe she could harness him, Peaches's most avid protector. Maybe . . . Oh, hell. A solid, workable way would come to her eventually. For Harriet, one always did. All it would take was time. Meanwhile Harriet knew there were immediate, pressing decisions she had to make.

Pippin she would cross off the list; Henry had given her that option and, while Harriet had never really trusted the girl, she could still be useful. She had nothing against either Bartlett or Tangerine, another option Henry had given her. Maybe she would forget the whole proposal, or maybe she'd pick one of them to use as an example to the other girls.

Sometimes, Harriet told herself, running Blossom House was a terrible trial. At the moment, Peaches was making the trial almost unbearable for her. In time. In time, Peaches would be taken care of, laid out in a trench beside her husband, covered with quicklime, and then serenaded by her personal Mozartian arrangement at the piano.

Things on the third floor of Blossom House were back to normal, if such a word is applicable to being locked away, and treated and dressed like a twelve-year-old. The one exception to that return to normalcy was Cherry. To Jennifer's eye she appeared to be getting worse by the hour.

"Oh, Peaches," Cherry moaned, her eyes bright with fever, her face bathed in sweat. "Even the Strip didn't make me feel this bad. I don't know what—" Cherry stopped, hugging the blanket around her as a sudden fit of chills seized her. Jennifer was at a loss; motioning to her from the door, Bartlett looked as worried as Jennifer felt.

"How is she?" Bartlett asked Jennifer in an anxious whisper.

"Worse, I think. The fever seems higher, the chills are coming more often, she's throwing up every half hour—I don't know how; there can't be anything left inside her—and she keeps telling me how much it hurts." Jennifer considered for a moment. "The way I see it—I know I told you this before, but I'm surer now—it just *has* to be appendicitis."

Bartlett turned her face away. "Damn. I kept hoping you were wrong. But about half an hour ago I was talking to her, and I pressed on the right side of her stomach. She screamed. I saw in a movie once that that was how you could spot appendicitis for sure."

Jennifer nodded glumly. "I know. I did the same thing."

"Do you think Harriet would bring in a doctor?"

Jennifer laughed bitterly. "No more than she would bring in a dentist. She can't, I guess, and not go to jail."

"Jail, jail, who's going to jail?" Harriet had come into the room, unheard, and was standing behind them, one eye on them, the other on the bed with Cherry in it.

"It's Cherry, Miss Griggs. Bartlett and I both think she has appendicitis. Acute." Harriet looked at Jennifer angrily, as if she resented her interfering in an area where she, Harriet, was presumably responsible.

"Why wasn't I told of this sooner?" Harriet demanded, walking over to Cherry's bedside. "Where do you hurt, child?" she asked, wearing an expression that said she held Cherry personally to blame for being sick.

Cherry had looked up at the first sign of Harriet's voice, shrinking down farther into the covers. "It sort of moves around. It was a dull kind of pain at first, but it's gotten sharper now."

Harriet made a face and, like Jennifer and Bartlett before her, put both hands on Cherry's stomach. Suddenly she pressed down hard. Again, Cherry screamed. Twisting, she tried to struggle out from beneath Harriet's hands, hitting at her arms with her fists. "I'm sorry, Cherry," Harriet said gently. "I just wanted to see something, dear."

Harriet's apology worried Jennifer more than any diagnosis born of the movies. It meant that Harriet concurred.

As Harriet started out the door Jennifer walked up quickly behind her and stopped her. "Miss Griggs, it *is* appendicitis, isn't it?"

"I'm afraid so. I'm no doctor, of course, but there was a girl here a couple of years ago who had the same thing. . . ."

"Well, that's what she needs. A doctor."

"Impossible. You know that, Peaches."

"She *has* to have a doctor," Jennifer insisted.

"Don't talk back to me," Harriet snapped. "I said a doctor was impossible. We'll just have to let nature take its course and hope for the best."

"That other girl you mentioned. What happened to her?"

Harriet floundered, something unusual for her. "She died."

Jennifer boiled over. "And that's what you plan for Cherry? To let her die? You've got to get a doctor, damn it. What you're doing is outright murder."

"I should have been told earlier," Harriet countered defensively. "Pills, antibiotics, might have worked then."

"A doctor. Cherry has to see a doctor."

"That's not even a matter of consideration, Peaches, and you know it."

"You bitch. You murdering old bitch." For several seconds Jennifer and Harriet stared at each other, then:

"I'll overlook that, Peaches, this once. I realize Cherry is a close friend of yours. But this time only. Understand me? I can't understand why you're getting so worked up over a common whore, anyway."

It was too much for Jennifer. She grabbed Harriet, screaming. The slap hit her across the face so hard, Jennifer crashed into the wall behind her. "I said one time only, Peaches," Harriet hissed. "Shape up now, child, or you'll wish all you had was an infected appendix." Without looking back, Harriet marched out of the room and slammed the outer door behind her.

The spot on her face where Harriet had slapped her was already on fire; Jennifer was rubbing it gently when Bartlett came out of Cherry's room. "My God, she really belted you," Bartlett noted. "Your face is going to swell out like a pumpkin by morning. Are you all right?"

Jennifer nodded. "She let me have it. Really gave it to me. Maybe I shouldn't have called her a murdering old bitch."

"You didn't get anywhere with the doctor thing?"

"She didn't budge an inch. I guess I didn't really expect her to. But if Cherry doesn't get a doctor's help, that appendix of hers will burst, and she'll die. Even Harriet agreed about that."

"Damn." Bartlett groaned. "There's not a single thing we can do about it, either."

"Yes there is. Escape."

Harriet Griggs sat in the rocking chair in her bedroom, staring out the window and brooding. Earlier, she had returned upstairs with a bucket of ice cubes and a small pile of face towels, and given them to Jennifer and Bartlett. "Make ice packs and keep them pressed against the right side of Cherry's stomach," she directed them. "I looked it up in my medical book, and it said that that can bring the inflammation down, and that sometimes the appendix cures itself. You see, with a little help, nature's own defenses can work wonders."

Jennifer had looked at her, not even trying to hide what she felt.

"The only wonder that can save Cherry is a doctor."

Harriet snorted. "Don't be tiresome, Peaches. We can only do what we can do here. Why, the ice packs may fix that appendix up by itself. You'll see."

Harriet hadn't believed her own words any more than Jennifer had.

Fidgeting, Harriet left. Left to go downstairs to her bedroom and rock. Damn, she didn't want Cherry to die. Not because she held any affection toward the girl, but because Henry would assume Cherry's death was somehow her fault. She would show him the medical dictionary, she would tell him of the ice packs and her own personal involvement, but Henry would still believe it to be her fault. Damn Peaches; this kind of thing had never happened before she arrived at Blossom House. And these next few days were a time she particularly needed Henry's cooperation, albeit unwitting.

For sitting where she was, earlier, rocking absently, a new scheme had crept into her mind about how to get rid of Peaches. Until now, she'd gone about it all wrong, she decided. Trying to set Henry against her was impossible; trying to convince him that Peaches was using him was unworkable; trying to get him to believe that Peaches considered him a repulsive old fool, out of the question.

Earlier in her rocking, Harriet had already decided to reverse her field. To work at convincing Henry—a man very susceptible to flattery—that not only did Peaches like him as a person, but was drawn to him physically, secretly worshiping his mature attractiveness.

At that point it would be the end of Peaches. And it couldn't happen to a nicer person.

It would work. She knew Henry. Rocking slowly, a smile split her face, ear to ear.

CHAPTER TWENTY-FIVE

Early this morning—I had barely gotten up—Cousin Larry called. His voice alone rattled me. Said he was coming to visit us. I'd have told him we were going away somewhere, but it turned out he was already in town and—suspicious little bastard that he is—he'd have driven over and checked out my story. There's nothing to do but let him come; he knows too much to get him mad at us.

I just hope he doesn't ask to see what the third floor he finished up for us looks like today. He put a lot of time into that, and I suppose even Cousin Larry has some pride of workmanship in him. All the bars and mesh on the windows up there, the triple-thickness Thermopane, the inner doors and sliding panels, the "bugs" in the cells, etc., were his doing. Funny, he never asked why we would need cells like that, but I'm sure he was—and still is—curious about them.

Well, curiosity killed the cat, and maybe it's about time it did in Cousin Larry.

We have no further need for him.

Journal of Blossom House,
Entry, page 51—Harriet Griggs

"Is everybody sure of what their job is? I mean, *really* sure."

"I've been through every detail with each of them twice. If they haven't got it now, they never will."

In the hall outside the cells, Jennifer had been nervously going over the details of her escape plan with Bartlett; the balloon went up that day during lunch. The scheme would require participation of all of the others—except Pippin—and the whole group had accepted it with great enthusiasm. Small wonder. To them the idea of anyone's escaping from Blossom House was both exciting and encouraging, but even more encouraging was the realization that if Jennifer made it, they would all soon be free themselves. Courtesy of the police.

Bartlett had done that morning's missionary work with the girls to avoid Jennifer's being seen doing it; the task involved going from girl to girl and checking over the details in a brief and earnest conversation. If Jennifer had done the same thing, it might have raised Pippin's hair-trigger suspiciousness. Bartlett, since she was no particular enemy of Pippin's, could get away with it far more easily.

In her room, Jennifer went back to brooding over the plan, probing the scheme for possible places it could go wrong. Tricky, complicated, dangerous, but it might just work. It *had* to work. If it didn't, Cherry would die of a burst appendix. She herself would die—Peter? It was unfair. All the wonderful times they could have had together, all the wonderful things they could have seen, all the wonderful love they could have shared—pushed to one side by her own blindness.

She swore to herself and went back to the escape plan. She was running out of time; lunch was in fifteen minutes. She wondered aloud if God would take exception to a short prayer for it to work. Without waiting for Him to answer, Jennifer went ahead and prayed.

Slowly the others began pulling up to their assigned places at the dining table. Jennifer could see the same tenseness in them that she felt in herself; they all shared a giant stake in whether she made good her escape or not. Today, Harriet was late to arrive, which only made everybody—particularly Jennifer—grow more on edge. To Jennifer it felt as if she were being pulled at from several different directions by mystical forces: there was a sudden vacuum in her head, the kind of vacuum she used to notice as part of her stage fright just before she stepped out onto Chalmer's tiny stage; from somewhere she heard a strange buzzing—faint, but loud enough to make hearing what anybody said difficult.

Finally she heard the outer door being unlocked; Harriet was about to enter. As soon as she was in her place, the plan would burst into full operation.

Jennifer gasped. Instead of Harriet, it was Henry who came through the door. Jennifer was completely thrown. Nowhere in their contingency plans were there provisions for this unlikely switch.

"I'm sorry, children." Henry smiled as he drew himself up at the end of the table. "But your mother will be a little late in arriving today. I'm filling in for her; we are not to wait. She is downstairs having a long talk with your cousin Larry." He studied the faces around the table and suddenly laughed.

"Of course, I forgot. You've never met your cousin Larry, so, to you, he's just a name. Well, he finished the entire insides of his room and your rooms—the woodwork, the sound system, and, naturally, your marvelously efficient doors and windows. A very gifted person, your cousin Larry. You must meet him someday."

It stunned Jennifer that Henry could bring up their "marvelously efficient doors and windows" with a straight face: bars, heavy mesh, and triple Thermopane to keep any sound from reaching the street . . . or any person. Looking at him with wonder, Jennifer struggled to regain her composure. She hadn't counted on Henry's being here; she hadn't counted on Harriet's being downstairs; she hadn't counted on Cousin Larry at all. He would throw a monkey wrench into the whole maneuver, unless he was ignorant of the girls' presence on the third floor. However, as she studied the idea further, she realized he must have known; he had designed and built it as a prison, and for there to be a prison, there had to be prisoners. Sadly she decided there was no point in trying the maneuver until tomorrow at lunch. Cherry, she told herself, could last a little longer. Oh, God, please let her.

Discouraged, she gave Bartlett the signal not to act now, and watched her deviously pass the message on to the others. All of them looked horribly let down. She would try to pump Henry tonight during his visit, to see what they would have to do to neutralize the added peril of a mysterious cousin Larry.

From his end of the table, Henry began speaking. "We shall all be eating in a few minutes, children, but first, there is some business to get out of the way." He stood up and began moving his index finger slowly around the table, aiming it first at one, then another, of them. Through the main door—he'd left it open when he came into the room—came the sound of Harriet's piano, playing the peculiar Mozart variation on something none of them could ever quite recognize.

The finger abruptly came to rest. "Tangerine," Henry said softly. "It is time. Come with me, dear, please."

The others groaned, although some secret part of each was relieved the finger had not stopped on *them*. They all knew what was coming; Harriet's weird piano arrangement was played only to mark either an imminent execution, or to celebrate the burial of someone in the trench near the apple trees. The others groaned again, thinking about it.

Tangerine did not moan, she screamed. Horribly. A terrified shriek. She could not know that her selection was the random product of a deal made between Harriet and Henry and that the choice had been between herself and Bartlett. In retrospect, it would not have mattered much to her, anyway. She began running around the table, trying to get away from the advancing Henry. Henry was muttering to himself as he followed her. Damn it, why didn't Harriet handle this sort of thing? He loathed it. Instead, she was downstairs talking to that damn blackmailing Cousin Larry.

Twice Henry was able to get a grip on Tangerine as she fled before him, twice Tangerine twisted free, still screaming, her ace ashen, pleading with the others to help her. At first the other girls had been frozen in their chairs, too stunned to move. ennifer and Bartlett had been the first to come to themselves and were doing their best to trip Henry as he continued his pursuit round the table, knocking over the empty chairs to make his rogress more difficult. All of the others were on their feet too, oing their part; Guava had even broken a plate over his head as e passed. Henry, surprisingly agile and powerful for someone so enign-looking, had shaken his head like a wounded bull, then ken up the chase again, hating every second of it.

Harriet's music had stopped a moment before; now she suddenly appeared at the door, carrying the same 30-30 she had rought out the day of the Garden Club's tour. "I'll use it, nildren. I think you know that; I'm a little more direct in my methods than my brother."

Stung, Henry tried to recover his appearance of power. "Sit own. Sit down this minute, children. You're being very bad ttle girls."

Harriet brandished the shotgun, one hand slapping the stock menacingly. "Do what your daddy says and sit down. Right w," Harriet added, enjoying both her brother's discomfort and e look of terror stamped across Tangerine's face. One by one e girls sank into their chairs, wearing expressions running from elplessness to fury. The 30-30 was enough to intimidate any of em, and the fact somehow made them feel guilty.

Only Tangerine, too stunned to move, remained on her feet. ently Henry Griggs took her by the arm. "Come along, child. m sorry, but this is the way it has to be. There's no point fighting it."

Aghast, the table watched as Henry began to lead Tangerine ward the door. She looked at him in bewilderment and, stumbling, asked: "Why, Mr. Griggs? Why?"

Henry only shook his head and kept leading her toward the or. Every step or two, Tangerine would look back at the girls

around the table, pleading with them to help her. With Harriet's
shotgun still pointing in their direction, the others could do
nothing except lower their heads or hide their eyes or stare at her
wondering how the presence of death must feel.

At the door, Tangerine began screaming again, struggling to
free herself as Henry pulled her out the door.

"Luncheon will be a few minutes late, children. Please si
where you are quietly," Harriet announced with a slight smile
Then she hurried out the door after Henry, the shotgun a guaran
tee that there would be no further struggle.

The rest of them remained in their chairs around the table, too
shaken to speak. Bartlett cried, Jennifer cursed. Even though hi
heart had clearly not been in what he had had to do, it stil
surprised her that Henry was capable of playing so evil a role in
the affair.

From far down the table came Pippin's laugh. Parodying Henry
she moved her finger slowly from one of them to the next. He
finger stopped at Jennifer. "You're next, little girl. And lik
Daddy said, there's no point in fighting it." Then the awfu
laugh again.

"It's only put off for a day, Cherry." Jennifer could see from
Cherry's expression that someone who was in the amount of pai
Cherry was didn't measure time the same way others did. Twenty
four hours to her was an eternity. Jennifer tried again. "W
toyed with the idea of going through with it tonight at dinner, bu
both Henry and Harriet would be there, and that would almos
guarantee failure. Then, downstairs, just to complicate things
there's this young cousin of theirs, Cousin Larry. He built th
place up here."

Cherry tried to pretend the delay made no difference. "Don
know the gentleman. And if he's young, that's surprising. He mu
be a wimp." Both Jennifer and Bartlett laughed louder than wa
called for; they could see what Cherry was trying to do.

"How *do* you feel now, Cherry?" asked Jennifer. It was
stupid question, she supposed.

"Oh, the throwing up has lessened, but the pain seems worse. I can't really tell you much more than that."

"Just hang on, Cherry," Jennifer said.

"One more day, Cherry," Bartlett threw in. "Then it's the hospital. The operation's a snap, you know. Happy gas, slice-slice, appendix out, and you're home free."

"Just keep hanging on," repeated Jennifer. "Hang on . . . hang on . . . one more day."

Bartlett seized Jennifer's arm in concern as a new wave of pain swept through Cherry. Cherry could not reply to Jennifer and Bartlett's encouragement, only groan, clutching Jennifer's hand and pleading with her eyes.

Out in the hall, Jennifer leaned against the wall. She had no idea how long it would be before Cherry's appendix burst. After that, Cherry would have only a few hours before peritonitis set in. Unless tons of antibiotics were pumped into you immediately, as she remembered hearing it, you were dead.

Tonight, during Henry's usual visit, perhaps she could get more of a line on Cousin Larry, which room he was in, what he did all day, etc. For all she knew he could already be gone. If he wasn't, her escape effort became twice as dangerous. But for Cherry's life, she was surprised to find she was willing to take any chance, make any sacrifice.

The change in her attitude from the days at Chalmer's was so dramatic, it shocked even her.

"You have a fan, you know, Henry." The two of them were sitting in the library. Harriet was doing petit point; Henry was rereading *Captains Courageous* for what was probably the fifth time. Cousin Larry was out somewhere in his car; neither of them knew exactly where. "It doesn't really make much difference, anyway," Harriet had complained about half an hour earlier. "He'll come home in the small hours, full of liquor, stumbling and swearing and shouting at chairs. Terrible boy." Almost reluctantly, Henry's head rose from the book, and he blinked at Harriet.

"I'm sorry, Harriet, I didn't really hear you."

"I said you had a big fan, Henry." Harriet studied his face as she launched the new reverse approach that had come to her sitting in her rocking chair. "Peaches." Harriet could see Henry struggling not to smile with pleasure. "I thought at first—you know, when it got back to me from some of the other girls—that it was the normal sort of affection you'd expect to find in any girl toward her father. But now . . ."

Harriet could see that Henry was embarrassed but pleased, and that he was having trouble pretending to shrug the whole thing off. The new approach was working. My God, how could her own brother be so stupid? She escalated the level of the stories. "It worries me a little. Bartlett, I think it was, or maybe it was Tangerine, I can't remember which, said that Jennifer had told her she had always been attracted to older men, and that she found you increasingly—well, more and more, that is—appealing to her. I don't know how much there is to it, but it *does* worry me."

"Oh, nonsense, Harriet." Harriet was delighted to notice that however much he might deny the report, his breathing was coming faster, his face was turning pinker.

"Nonsense perhaps, Henry. But I would hope," Harriet added slyly, "that you'd have the decency—I know you do, actually—to resist any sort of possible advance Peaches might make. It isn't quite fair, you see. Girls her age are so vulnerable to their own half-formed sexual impulses."

Henry laughed loudly, but Harriet could see by the nervous twitch to his hands that her brother didn't really consider any of this in the least bit funny. It intrigued and excited him—precisely as she had planned it to. Poor Henry, she told herself. Most of the time he was such putty in her hands.

Henry suddenly looked at her sternly. "You shouldn't even think such things, Harriet. The stories are insane, anyway. School-girl gossip. She's only a child. I wouldn't touch a child, you know that."

Harriet nodded solemnly. No, that wasn't what she knew at

ll, but this was no time to argue the point. When she looked in
his direction again, he appeared deeply involved in *Captains
Courageous*. Only he never turned a page. In his head, she
knew, a fantasy was taking shape, growing, gaining control of
him. A few minutes later his eyes rose from the book again.

"Peaches isn't going to make any advances toward me, you
must know that, Harriet. That's a crazy thought you had back
here. She likes me, yes, but that's all. Of course, there *is* a type
of girl that finds older men . . . Heavens, I . . ."

Harriet nodded once more, smiling inside.

The ground had been prepared.

The seed had been planted.

It would flourish.

CHAPTER TWENTY-SIX

I think my troubles with Peaches are about to come to an unpleasant end (for her) and a highly gratifying one (for me). Sometimes Henry is so easy to push around, it makes me ashamed to be his sister. Today was one of those times.

He didn't want to drag Tangerine out of the dining room with everybody watching like that—especially his precious little Peaches— but I shamed him into it. Easy.

He didn't want to kill Tangerine either, but I kept reminding him of his agreement, and he caved in on that, too. Also easy. I was afraid he would lapse into one of his macho states and refuse, but I guess the new approach has his head spinning so fast, he couldn't.

All he did was disappear for a while, saying he was going out to pick up some magazines and stuff. That's Henry's way of saying he's going to McClanahan's Bar to get sozzled.

It's going to work, goddamn it is. I'm sure of that now. And afterward Henry will hate Peaches as much as I do—maybe more.

By the time the two of us get through with her, Peaches will wish she had a McClanahan's to go get sozzled at.

Posthumously.

> *Journal of Blossom House,*
> *Entry, page 51—Harriet Griggs*

The tourist office of Chivers, MD, was, Hillary Crane discovered, enormously eager to please. The office had provided her with a map indicating with little red dots where each JP held forth, his rates, the extras, and the other amenities. Besides the map, the tourist office had also given her an alphabetical list.

After thinking about it awhile in her motel room, Hillary decided to depend primarily on the alphabetical list rather than the map; the list would avoid missing any of them—Chalmer's had schooled her well in the "methodical approach to research," and it had stuck—and she could then use the map to help find where they were. This procedure would mean a certain amount of backtracking geographically, but it would ensure meticulous coverage.

It was slow, discouraging work. At the very first one—a Clayton Aaronson on Spring Street, JP and host—she began the approach she had decided to use with all of them. "Excuse me, sir," she began with a man she assumed was Justice of the Peace Clayton Aaronson, "I'm doing an article on different kinds of weddings for *New York* magazine and I wondered if I could talk to you for a few moments. The tourist office said you were one of the best-known JP's in town."

Mr. Aaronson, at first a bit stunned, grew increasingly friendly as he thought both of the publicity and the tourist office. Until now, he had never dreamed the office even knew he existed. "Come in, come in," he said warmly.

Hillary asked a few minutes worth of questions about his business and how it worked, and then moved quickly on to the kind of patrons he served. "You must get some celebrities every year, even if they're using their real names instead of their stage names so you might not recognize them. And I was wondering—"

It was only with difficulty that Hillary managed to stop Mr.
Aaronson from telling her of all the celebrities masquerading
under their real names he might have married over the years. You
could sense something special about certain people, he told her.

"Well, for instance, Mr. Aaronson, would you have any
record of having married a Jennifer Delafield and a Peter Owen?
It would be within the last six weeks or so."

Mr. Aaronson studied her suspiciously. "Celebrities, huh? What
are their stage names?"

"I'm afraid I can't tell you that."

"I see. Well, I'll check." Hoping he would find the names—
what if he'd married two movie stars and never realized it? The
publicity about him could still be very good for business—Mr.
Aaronson walked to a file case and pulled out a drawer. "Owen,
Owen, Owen . . ." he muttered to himself. There was no Owen
here, damn it. "I'm afraid not. No Owen at all," he said,
sighing.

"Of course, they may have used some other name," Hillary
suggested. "Some of those people do that. Did you ever see
either of these people here?" Hillary handed him photographs
of Jennifer and Peter and studied his expression.

"Well," Mr. Aaronson said, still trying to keep himself in the
publicity race, "they *do* look a bit familiar, but I can't be sure
. . . they're a nice-looking pair of young people, but I'm not
sure I ever remember seeing them in the movies."

"Stage." This was an easy out for Hillary. She picked up the
pictures and her note pad full of scratchings, thanked Mr. Aaronson,
and left.

"Hope you find the place they got married," he called from
his front steps, waving good-bye to her forlornly.

So did Hillary.

It went that way all day. Hillary had taken several shortcuts in
her line of patter, but the interviews still struck her as taking far
too long. Doggedly she kept going down the alphabetical list of
P's, none of whom had any record of marrying one Jennifer

Delafield to one Peter Owen, and showed no flicker of recogni
tion when Hillary showed them the photographs. She would close
her notebook, take back her photos, thank the man, and be off
to the next one.

Ironically, at one point, turning off Main Street and heading
for a JP on Eros Lane, she drove directly by Blossom House. She
saw the sign saying that it too had a JP, and came very close to
stopping and going into her routine. But her Chalmer's training
made her decide to stick to the alphabetical list; she would come
back to the Mr. Griggs described on the sign outside the house
when she got to the *G*'s. Wearily she continued down the list. The
"methodical approach to research" she'd been taught had some
serious shortcomings.

Staring at the ceiling of her room, Jennifer was beside herself.
Henry Griggs was not at dinner—Harriet had reigned over the
meal by herself—nor had he showed up for his usual nightly visit
with her. Damn. She desperately needed to know whether Cousin
Larry had left yet or was still in the house, whether he knew of
their existence on the third floor, and what sort of person he was.
It could make a great difference in how she handled her escape
attempt tomorrow at lunchtime.

From down the hall she could hear an occasional moan from
Cherry as she suffered another seizure of pain, a sound that made
Jennifer's whole body squirm in sympathy. Earlier she had once
again tried to convince Harriet to get a doctor for Cherry—it was
becoming a matter of life or death, she had explained.

Harriet laughed at her. "Everything in your world is always a
matter of life and death, isn't it, Peaches? It must be something
the rich amuse themselves with. Well, Cherry may die, or Cherry
may not, but whichever it is, she'll have to do it without a
doctor."

It was a bitterly cruel thing to say; worse, the woman actually
seemed to be enjoying Cherry's losing battle to stay alive.

Groaning herself, Jennifer pulled her little white nightie up far enough to make herself comfortable, turned on her side, and tried to sleep. Nothing happened; she stayed wide awake.

The closest she came to sleep was a fuzzy, floating collage of the day's events—a sort of drifting, half-conscious nightmare: Henry dragging Tangerine toward the door; Tangerine screaming and pleading with them to help her; Harriet's sudden appearance at the door with the 30-30; her own silent signal to the others that the attempt to escape would have to be postponed until tomorrow; Cherry's intermittent groaning and crying, her eyes telling Jennifer tomorrow might be too late; the sight out her window as she saw Harriet carry Tangerine's body out into the garden and dump it into a trench near the apple trees; Harriet and her curt, repeated refusal to get a doctor for Cherry, and her laughter. The review of all these events left sleep impossible.

A little past midnight her ears strained to make sense of a curious sound that kept intruding on her consciousness. It drew closer and then stopped moving, apparently just outside her door. There was a faint scratching and rattling, as if someone were trying to put a key in a distant lock. In the dim glow of her night-light the room was dark, but she was suddenly aware of a rectangle of brightness; her door had silently swung open. Jennifer clutched at the covers, her whole body beginning to tremble, as fear swept through her in a great dark wave. "Yes?" she asked the blackness in a faint voice. *"Yes?"*

There was no reply. Jennifer's eyes told her that the door was again closed, but she wasn't certain whether anyone had come through it or not. At this hour, who would? My God, Cousin Larry? *"Yes?"* she asked again, panic edging her voice. For a moment longer her question was greeted only by sepulchral silence, then:

"Shhh, Peaches. It's me. Daddy. Don't make any noise, Peaches. It's Daddy."

Jennifer felt abruptly relieved. Henry Griggs. The man she had been waiting for all evening, so she could pump him about Cousin Larry. "Oh, Daddy," she said, her lips tightening at having to use that dreadful name with him. But she wanted something from him. That he was in her room at such an hour was strange, but was there anything about Blossom House that *wasn't* strange?

"I'm sorry, Peaches, if I frightened you. I *had* to see you. I didn't get home from the office until late, you see, and I wanted you to know that I took the new picture of you into town with me today. That picture of you on your little swing—you know the one—well, I tell you, Peaches, everybody just loved it. The partners, the junior lawyers, the secretaries—*everybody*—and they all said how pretty you looked and, my God, they were just flabbergasted to see how big and grown-up you've gotten."

Picture of her on a swing, the office, the partners, what the hell was crazy Henry talking about? It made no sense to Jennifer at all. It *did* make her uncomfortable, or was that because Henry had suddenly sat down on the edge of the bed, the sweet-sour smell of bourbon drifting toward her like Kentucky fog. "What—?" she began, and then stopped in horror. Henry Griggs was stroking her hair, running his fingers lightly along her neck, stroking the side of her face. Jennifer could feel herself panicking.

She was relieved when Henry Griggs suddenly stood up. Maybe her nightmare—or was it *his* nightmare?—was over. He made no move to leave, though, and Jennifer could hear some strange kind of rustling sound coming from the darkness where he was standing.

"Remember, Peaches," the voice in the darkness said warningly, "remember it has to be just like last time. Not a word to your mother or Kitty. Neither Mummy nor your sister would understand. . . ."

This statement made no sense either. Kitty? Had Griggs's daughter had a sister? One named Kitty? Henry Griggs was crazy—she'd known that all along—but usually coherent. Tonight his words were totally baffling—strange, rambling, insane. It was as if he were talking in some other, earlier life, talking to people long dead. She wasn't sure what any of it meant.

But, somehow, in what Henry was saying, she decided, lay the secret of Blossom House and the reason behind all of them being

eld prisoner inside it. A nameless fear clutched at her, as
shadows of what it could be surrounded her. She didn't really
want to understand . . . she couldn't . . . she wouldn't.

The full meaning fell into place like a black stone sinking
through cloudy water—dim and ominous and inescapable. With a
faint sigh, Henry sat down on the edge of her bed again, his
hands traveling up her body, trying to feel her beneath the
covers. At the same time the strange rustling sound she'd heard
earlier explained itself; it had been Henry Griggs taking off his
clothes in the dark. He tried to put one naked arm around her, but
Jennifer squirmed out of his reach. As if in a nightmare, she
heard him mumble, "Oh, my, Peaches. But Daddy loves you *so
much* . . ."

Pressed hard against the wall on the far side of the bed,
Jennifer struggled to stand up and climb over him. She heard a
confused whine come from him; a split second later, he had
grabbed her by the nightie and pulled her roughly back down
into the bed.

"No, for God's sake, no!" Jennifer yelled at him as loud as
she could. "Mr. Griggs, stop it, *no!*"

For an instant Henry Griggs seemed to pull back in confusion.
"You never called your daddy anything like that before," Henry
Griggs said reproachfully. "I don't know what's wrong with you
tonight, Peaches." On the far side of the bed, she could feel him
reaching over and beginning to run his hands up and down one of
her legs. She shrank against the wall, as far away as she could
get. *"Please* . . ." Jennifer moaned, trapped and almost in
tears.

"You never objected to anything Daddy *did* before, either,
Peaches. Ever. You're Daddy's favorite ten-year-old in the whole
world. Now, give me your hand and—"

Jennifer began to scream at the top of her lungs. But Henry
Griggs, maybe because of the bourbon or maybe from confusion
or maybe because her struggling infuriated him, seized her by the
waist and threw her roughly down on the bed. His breath coming
in gasps, he rolled over directly on top of her, simultaneously

sobbing and fondling her. She could no longer scream, becaus
his wet, unshaven mouth had completely covered hers.

Jennifer had taken an extra course—after hours—at Chalmer's
teaching her what to do in moments like this. She drew one kne
sharply up between his naked legs. There was something tha
sounded like a crunch, followed by a howl of pain. She coul
hear him groaning in agony and heard him fall off the bed in hi
writhing. Quickly Jennifer scrambled off and shrank into a cor
ner; maybe in the dark he wouldn't notice her there.

The pain of her knee in his groin seemed to have brough
Henry back to the present. She could hear him muttering abou
the third floor and Tangerine and Harriet and swearing at himsel
and them and the world. Stunned, Jennifer realized that in hi
semistupor, when he attacked her, crazy old Henry had though
he was back with the real Peaches, his daughter, years ago whe
she was only ten.

Tonight was what Henry Griggs had regularly done to his ow
daughter? Pressing herself harder into her dark corner, Jennife
had difficulty controlling the gasp inside her that struggled to ge
out. Had he still been doing it to the real Peaches when she'd ru
away—eloped, Henry had always told her—and was killed? Wa
it *why* she had run away? Another flash of insight struck Jennife
with blinding brightness.

It was Henry Griggs—over Harriet's violent objections—wh
had originally changed her name from Olivia to Peaches. They'
had a big argument about it, but Henry had won, something tha
at the time had surprised her. All along, then, to Henry, she ha
been Peaches. The *real* Peaches, his daughter. In Jennifer's min
she had always referred to him as crazy old Henry; the referenc
was not a whimsical one, it was an accurate description of th
man.

Henry Griggs must have been reading Jennifer's mind. "You'r
not the real Peaches, you're not my daughter," he yelled at her
In the dimness of the night-light Jennifer could just make out hi
outline, pulling his clothes back on, stumbling and fighting wit
them to get the pants and shirt over uncooperative arms and legs.

"You're not my daughter," he repeated, still yelling. "And you're going to pay for it."

Turning away, he stalked out of her cell, muttering and cursing. Her cell door closed with a crash behind him; the locks turned; the bolts slid noisily home.

"My God, my God," Jennifer heard herself say to the darkness beyond the dim glow of her night-light. Now she had both Harriet *and* Henry determined to destroy her. Still shaking, Jennifer went into the bathroom and drank a glass of water. Somehow all of her planning had gone wrong. All of her manipulation of Henry had backfired. She searched her mind to see what she might have done differently, but could find no fault in her effort. More philosophically, she comforted herself with the conclusion that the insane were too unpredictably dangerous to attempt rational manipulation.

Jennifer, of course, had no way of knowing that tonight's debacle had nothing to do with her own manipulations, but were the product of Harriet's scheme—to get Jennifer in a position where Henry would turn against her in fury.

It had worked. Harriet knew—as did Jennifer—that Henry was no longer her protector, but her adversary. Jennifer now, in her desperation, would try to escape. That Harriet was sure of. She would even help her a little. For the effect of Jennifer's getting out of Blossom House was planned to be far more hideous than anything Harriet would have dared try with Jennifer while she was still inside. The trap was set; Jennifer would walk into it. She and Cousin Larry—and in his way, Henry—would do the rest. Harriet shuddered with delight.

Jennifer was indeed walking into Harriet's trap. The escape plan was to be attempted the next day—at lunchtime—assuming she was still alive by then. The escape to Jennifer was critical. Not just for Cherry's survival, she concluded grimly, but for her own.

Her whole body still trembling, Jennifer climbed back into her bed. She would have liked to change the sheets; somehow they seemed profaned and soiled. As she lay there Jennifer began realizing something else. All along, while she thought she was manipulating Henry Griggs, it was Henry Griggs who had been manipulating *her*. It was Henry Griggs who had conceived of Blossom House, it was Henry Griggs who had shut them away up here, seeing in them the pale ghosts of his own ravished daughter. Harriet only *thinks* Blossom House was her idea, only *thinks* she is in charge, something Henry probably allowed because it served his purpose.

A macabre echo of her own battles with her mother drifted across Jennifer's mind. Maybe, from the beginning, her father, like Henry, had been the real force, too, like Henry, letting her mother think she was in control of things, but in the end, controlling them all—her mother, herself, Peter Owen, everything. Crazy.

No matter how hard she tried, sleep didn't even come near Jennifer for the rest of the night. Too much had happened. Too much depended on what happened at lunchtime the next day. Escape.

Saving Cherry's life. Saving, for Christ's sake, her own life. Saving *all* of their lives.

Once again, Jennifer prayed.

CHAPTER TWENTY-SEVEN

...e moment I came down for breakfast this morning, I could tell ...mething was wrong. Henry was already up, unusual in itself. ...atching him drink his coffee, I couldn't help but notice how ...dly his hand shook—that must have been some session he had ... McClanahan's Bar last night.

...hen I mentioned something nice about Peaches—my new re- ...rse approach, you see—he slammed down his cup and walked ...t of the room. For a moment I wondered if he might not have ...ready succumbed to what I'd said about Peaches. And that ...aybe he'd slipped upstairs and gotten slapped in the face by ...aches. Or worse.

...o, that's too much to ask. My tactics are good, sometimes ...illiant, but they don't pay off that fast.

...nnifer's time will come, though. The trap is baited and waiting ...r Henry. Then, between Henry and myself, we'll get rid of that ...le troublemaker once and for all.

...men.

Journal of Blossom House,
Entry, page 52—Harriet Griggs

Waiting for lunchtime was even harder that day than it ha~
been the day before. So much more was at stake; Jennifer knew i
was only a matter of time before Henry descended on her in ful
fury. Twice, as she lay sleepless the night before, she had hear~
noises outside her cell and been convinced that it was Henry an~
Harriet coming to get her, 30-30 in hand.

This morning, when she went in to check on Cherry, she foun~
her much worse. It seemed as if her stomach, cleared out by now
of any food, must be throwing itself up. Putting on her warmes~
smile, Jennifer had tried twice after breakfast talking to Harrie
about a doctor for Cherry; she had been met with indifferen~
shrugs. "I'm getting tired of you asking that, Peaches. I'v~
already told you we're not going to, and that's all there is to it.'

Carefully Jennifer had studied Harriet's face to see if she coul~
uncover any change in attitude because of last night's struggl~
with Henry. She could detect none—Harriet was her usual, un~
pleasant self, snapping at her, putting her down, brushing he~
off.

But then it occurred to Jennifer that Henry was not apt to hav~
told his sister what had happened; it was one of those things an~
man, even Henry, would want no one to know about.

Henry did not show up during lesson time. In one way
Jennifer felt relieved; when a man has tried to rape you, yo~
don't particularly want to face him—outside of a police lineup
On the other hand, she now had no source to tell her wheth~
Cousin Larry had left yet or not; he remained the unknown in th~
escape-plan equation.

"Today," Jennifer whispered to Cherry. "At lunchtime. Th~
time I'll make it." Cherry was too sick to do anything more tha~
clutch Jennifer's hand, staring at her face, her eyes pleading f~
the help Jennifer had promised her. As Jennifer went out th~
door, though, she heard a croaking voice come from Cherry
bed. "Good luck, Park Avenue, good luck . . ." Cherry's voi~
trailed off into nothingness.

She would need it, Jennifer thought. With Henry and Harri~
both separately out to get her, with the unknown quantity ~

Cousin Larry lurking downstairs somewhere, she was going to need considerably more than luck to make it out of here. Toward lunchtime she could see Bartlett again making the rounds of the other girls repeating their individual instructions, clarifying any gray areas in the roles they would be playing, and encouraging them by repeating her litany that Jennifer free was all of them free. And yes, it could be pulled off, she was sure of it.

Back in her room, Jennifer again prayed. Prayed that Cousin Larry had left, prayed that Henry Griggs was out shopping or something, prayed that Harriet didn't keep the shotgun *too* handy somewhere on the third floor, and even prayed that Peter, for Christ's sake, would choose this moment to reappear and mow down Henry and Harriet with a machine gun. Jennifer had been doing a lot of praying lately, but this, she grudgingly admitted to herself, was the most she'd ever asked from God in a single prayer.

Promptly at noon Harriet strode back in and took her place at the head of the table. All of the girls curtsied, some of them a little shakily, worried, probably, by what was coming next. The final step in Jennifer's plan had only been put into place the previous afternoon; before that, there had still been one important missing element she would have had to improvise on. But during that traumatic scene with Tangerine—one poor girl struggling with Harriet and Henry and the 30-30 in furiously disconnected moments of wild confusion—she had seen something that stuck in her head. At first it had not seemed much, but as she thought about it, it suddenly made the plan whole. Jennifer would be using it today. In a strange way it meant that sad, tragic Tangerine was as much a part of the escape as any of them were.

Jennifer felt her muscles tense; it was almost time. Around the table she could see the others' faces staring at her, waiting for her to give the signal to begin, while filling the time with idle chatter for Harriet's benefit. It was like a cage full of nervous tigers.

After looking up and down the length of the table—a pro center checking the linesmen on either side of him before snapping the ball—Jennifer suddenly gave the signal.

It all seemed to happen at once. Bartlett and Strawberry, on Jennifer's cue, started it. "You pig, Bartlett. You didn't pass me any butter."

"Have some," Bartlett said, laughing. "Here," she added, and lobbed a pat of butter across the table at Strawberry with her spoon.

A cry of angry warning exploded from Harriet. Neither Bartlett nor Strawberry paid any attention. An apparently furious Strawberry screamed at the top of her lungs, "You're always doing things like that, Bartlett. Selfish, mean, awful things. I've had all I can stand." Leaping to her feet, Strawberry hurled her butter plate and roll at Bartlett. "If you won't give me the butter, take the roll and the plate and everything else!!"

The others had joined the yelling and throwing, producing pandemonium. Harriet had gotten to her feet and was screaming at everyone to be quiet and sit down or they would be severely punished. "Back in your places, back in your places!" she yelled. "You're already in enough trouble. Right now, I say. Sit down. Be quiet. This minute!" Slowly they took their places.

Looking cowed, Bartlett began whining. "Strawberry started it, Miss Griggs. It was Strawberry."

Strawberry answered by standing up again and throwing a full plate of soup across the table, some of it hitting Bartlett, most of it splashing over Harriet.

The table dissolved into preplanned bedlam. The other girls began racing around the table, shouting and yelling insults back and forth, throwing things at each other, and carefully expanding their circles around the table to take in most of the room. Harriet was shrieking at them, slapping them, grabbing them, trying to corner one of them at a time.

When Harriet had to go down to the far end of the room to stop Guava and Casaba from tearing the selection of games into tatters, Jennifer slipped under the table and crawled across the floor until she was just inside the hopefully unlocked main door. This was what Jennifer had noticed yesterday during the seizure of Tangerine; when Harriet was in the main room, she apparently

id not lock the outer door. Jennifer reached up for the handle,
eeping the rest of her body as low to the floor as she could. Her
eart sank. The handle wouldn't turn. Damn, it was locked.

She tried again, and the doorknob turned; it had been stuck,
ot locked. Great, Jennifer told herself. Through the crack she
ade by pushing the door open a little, Jennifer began slipping
erself out of the room. Seeing where she was in her plan,
artlett and Strawberry raced down to the end farthest from the
oor, beating each other over the head with a broom handle and
ne of the candelabra to draw Harriet's attention to themselves.
uickly Jennifer crawled the rest of the way out, silently closing
e door behind her. Inside, the din had become unbelievable.

Jennifer found she was in the small hall at the top of the stairs
at ran from the third floor to the second. In her mind she had
constructed as much of the layout of Blossom House from her
orted outing to the ice-cream parlor with Henry. Moving very
eedily, but struggling not to make any noise in case Henry or
ousin Larry were anywhere close-by, she started down the steep
airs, desperately searching her mind for more details of her trip
ith Henry. Somewhere downstairs there would be a door to the
tside. Or if worse came to worst, she could break a window
d scream for help, hoping someone was around on the street.
nce out on the street herself, she would stop a car somehow and
ce to bring back the police.

As soundlessly as she could manage, Jennifer crept out the
or of the second-floor landing. It was a door she remembered
ell. A door with a giant brass padlock. A door Harriet had once
rbidden her ever to go near. A door at the end of the hall where
r and Peter's bedroom had been that first night. Struggling, she
shed the memories from her mind. It was no time for sad
lections.

Upstairs, she could hear the thundering noise of the mini-riot
ll continuing. Bartlett and the others were doing one hell of a
od job. Later she must tell them— Again she fought herself to
ce that idea out of her mind, too; it was no time to think about
er. Listening carefully, trying to shut out the racket from

upstairs, Jennifer could hear nothing downstairs—no sound or voices or clatter, nothing—and decided it was safe for the moment. Softly Jennifer crept down the carpeted stairs and made her way to the first floor.

A sudden silence startled her, and she looked upward. Her heart sank. The banging and crashing on the third floor had abruptly stopped. Sooner than planned. The goddamn 30-30. Harriet must have had it hidden somewhere in the hallway outside the third floor's main room. Damn.

Moving more quickly, Jennifer began to look for a door—any door—through which she could get out of Blossom House. Another new sound made her heart contract violently, and Jennifer drew herself flat against the wall of the foyer. With ear-shattering loudness, some sort of an alarm bell had begun ringing, ripping apart the comforting quiet of the first floor with its strident terrible ringing. From somewhere down one of the halls she heard men's voices talking excitedly. Henry and Cousin Larry, she supposed. Christ, the cousin *was* still here. First the premature end of the riot upstairs, then the unexpected alarm bell, now Cousin Larry and Henry. Everything was suddenly—and perhaps fatally—going very wrong.

The voices drew closer. In panic, Jennifer searched the lobby with her eyes until she found it: the door in the semicircular wall of the main entrance hall. It was the coat closet; she remembered it from those days when she'd been allowed the run of the house before being chloroformed and dragged upstairs. Stepping out of her Mary Janes, Jennifer raced across the hall and slipped into the closet, for the moment leaving the door open a crack so she could hear. Doors closing. The sound of two pairs of heavy shoes walking into the hall. Voices again—Henry's and someone else's—Cousin Larry's, she guessed.

"The damn alarm bell. Someone's probably set it off again by mistake," she heard Henry tell him. "There's a turn-off switch here somewhere." The alarm stopped.

But there was no switch to stop Harriet. From the landing of the floor above, Jennifer could hear Harriet screaming at her brother. "What do you think the alarm's for, Henry? Goddamn, when you hear it, you come *running*. Not sauntering along like some streetwalker. Do you understand me, Henry?" Jennifer, pulling the closet door almost shut, could still hear Harriet running on, her voice furious, taking her own carelessness out on her brother. "One of the girls is missing. Got out somehow. That damned Peaches. I told you a long time ago, Henry, to get rid of that girl, but you wouldn't listen. Now she's out. Your fault, Henry, your fault!"

"For her to get out, you had to have left the door unlocked again, Harriet. So don't go blaming it on *me*. It's what you always do." In his own way, Jennifer thought, Henry sounded as angry as Harriet. Recollections of last night's debacle with her were probably tearing at his equilibrium. She heard his voice suddenly become quieter, perhaps for Cousin Larry's benefit. "Besides, Harriet, she still has to be in the house somewhere. She can't have gotten very far. We'll find her."

In an almost whispered aside to Cousin Larry, Jennifer heard Henry add a grim final footnote. "We'd *better* find her. I have my own score to settle with that lying little bitch."

"Let's go," she heard Cousin Larry say. "Where do we start?"

"We'll give the downstairs front a fast going-over. But my own notion is that she'd probably head for one of the back rooms off the kitchen to find a door she could use. I'll go there. You start up here."

Jennifer pulled the door completely shut, but it was a thin door, apparently, and she could make out sentences and noises from the outside. There was a lot of door-opening and swearing, and finally the sound, faint but unmistakable, of someone heading toward the back of the house. Twice Jennifer was convinced by other footfalls that someone was about to yank open the closet door and find her. Her heart was pounding so loudly, she was convinced they must be able to hear it, and would home in on the sound as if it were a submarine's sonar blips. The sound of feet came closer, the sound of feet receded. Finally there was no sound at all.

If she could just make it to the outside . . .

Gaston, Gendry, Gray, someone named Griggs. Hillary Crane stared at the names, her eyes so tired, they kept blurring things. She'd known a boy in New York named Griggs, she thought. Total nerd. Picked his nose all the time, even at nineteen. She glanced at the list again; she was getting down the alphabet all right, but slowly, so terribly slowly.

Something about the name Griggs drew her eyes back to it, as if it were speaking to her in silent, pleading words. For reasons she couldn't understand, a shudder passed through her body. A result, she decided, of this exhausting routine of going from one JP to the next all day long, pretending to be with *New York* magazine, acting like a reporter, asking questions, producing her pictures, and lying, lying, lying. Exhaustion, along with a gnawing worry about Jennifer, she supposed. The combination was beginning to drive her up the wall; it made even the names of strangers take on sinister overtones.

With a sigh, Hillary searched the house numbers of Diana Street until she came to number 322, where she turned into the modest driveway of Mr. Avery Gendry, J.P.—DIGNIFIED WEDDINGS PERFORMED 24 HOURS A DAY. She didn't know how long it was until she reached the ominous Mr. Henry Griggs—two names farther down the list from Mr. Gendry—but perhaps then she would discover why his name had such an unsettling effect on her.

Not far from the closet, Jennifer could hear Harriet and Henry and Cousin Larry going over their options. Harriet sounded calmer, Henry Griggs sounded angrier, and Cousin Larry sounded merely confused. "Well, she still has to be in the house somewhere, that much I'm positive of," Harriet announced in a rock-sure voice.

"The back doors . . ." Cousin Larry offered it as a way to

explain where Peaches might have disappeared to. But as suddenly as Cousin Larry had brought the possibility up, Harriet shot it down.

"Impossible," she snapped. "I've already checked all the back doors. They're still locked from the inside. No, she's still somewhere in the house."

"Upstairs?" Cousin Larry's voice sounded as if he were determined to be helpful but already knew that his latest suggestion would be shot down as firmly and finally as his first.

"I've searched every room thoroughly," Harriet answered, sounding annoyed that a relative stranger like Cousin Larry should be inserting opinions and suggestions into something that really wasn't any of his business.

"It's a hard house for one person to search thoroughly," Jennifer heard Henry offer; there was a trace of contempt in how he said it.

"The really efficient approach," Harriet snapped, ignoring her brother entirely, "is for all of us to first tackle the second floor again. Tear apart every room, every hallway, every closet, until we find her. All I've come across so far is a family of squirrels living in one of the back bedrooms and a lot of mice."

Henry's opportunity to be as unpleasant to Harriet as she had to him finally arrived. "Not a very sound proposal, Harriet. While we were all upstairs searching there, Peaches could already be downstairs. All she has to do then is get to one door, and that's it. Or break a window and scream. They're fixed so no one could get out of them, but she could do a lot of yelling for help."

There was a pause, then: "Generally, Harriet, you're not so sloppy in your thinking."

Even through the door, Jennifer could feel Harriet bristling at him. "All right, Mr. Sherlock Holmes, think of something better. You're always very big knocking things down, now *you* suggest something for once."

Cousin Larry's voice intervened again. "Why don't the two of you—you know the house, I don't—search the second floor? I'll station myself down here on the first with the shotgun—to keep her from trying any doors or windows." Both Henry and Harriet sounded as if they were arguing with each other *and* Cousin Larry at the same time. Cousin Larry's voice rose above theirs, with its unpleasant nasal ring; the voice of a mean little boy who glories in his own unpleasantness.

"I'm almost sure," Cousin Larry continued, the idea growing on him, "that with the shotgun, I can take care of all the exits. It's a cinch. I'll sit down the hall near the kitchen, where I can cover all of them. *And,* if she tries anything back in this direction, well, I'll hear that before it happens, too." Cousin Larry laughed, obviously enjoying himself. "I'll nail the little broad; count on it." His thin, nasal laugh came through the door again; Jennifer shivered.

"Makes sense to me," Henry Griggs said. "Let's get started." As they walked away from the front hall to get the shotgun for Cousin Larry, Jennifer heard Henry offer a cryptic suggestion; she strained to catch all of it, but their voices were fading rapidly. "Just in case," Henry said, his words becoming even more distant, "just in case Peaches *should* manage to get out of Blossom House itself, we ought to think of some way that would keep her escape under our own control. . . . What if we . . ." They were too far away now for Jennifer to make out anything more. Their voices had become a blur . . . then silence.

Slowly Jennifer's heartbeat fell back to below the panic level it had maintained the entire time Henry Griggs & Company were out in the entrance hall. To Jennifer the closet suddenly seemed unbearably hot and stuffy, as if her own sense of dread had vacuumed up its entire supply of oxygen. Soon, she thought, soon.

Patiently she waited until she heard Henry Griggs and Harriet going up to the second floor to begin their intensive search. For the moment that left her with only Cousin Larry to deal with down here. As she thought about it she remembered that he was armed with Harriet's shotgun, so that dealing with Cousin Larry could easily be the most dangerous part of her whole escape. But there was no point in putting it off any longer; whatever his other talents, Cousin Larry simply wasn't just going to vanish.

Her heart pounding again, Jennifer eased the door open a crack. From what she could see of the hall through the narrow space of the crack, there was no trace of Larry. Listening intently, all she could hear was the blood pounding in her own ears. No one, it seemed, was out there. At the moment, anyway.

Taking a deep breath, Jennifer pushed the door open a little wider, then fully open. Nothing. Suddenly the floor beneath her feet plummeted into nothingness.

Staring at her was a strange man. Cousin Larry. She could tell by the shotgun he held loosely in one hand. For a moment they stared at each other in unbelieving silence.

Jennifer moved first.

CHAPTER TWENTY-EIGHT

No time, no time at all. I have failed you, Journal. I meant to get back to you and finish up that last entry of mine—to add to and embellish it—but this place has been a madhouse today.

That little bitch, Peaches, thought she was so damn smart. Thought she had an escape plan that would work. Only I manipulated her every step of the way, so I guess she's not as smart as she thinks. I set the trap and watched her walk into it. Bye-bye, Peaches.

By sundown, we'll have her planted in the orchard. Relaxing in a nice, cool quicklime grave. With the hot weather we've been having lately, I hope she appreciates how cool she'll be.

Somehow, though, I doubt it.

Journal of Blossom House,
Entry, page 53—Harriet Griggs

Head down, Jennifer charged straight into Cousin Larry's middle. The last thing he'd expected was to have anyone come out of the closet, so he was badly off-balance when Jennifer tore into his stomach. The blow came as *such* a surprise, the wind was completely knocked out of him, and the force so great, he was knocked over backward onto the floor.

Jennifer could see Cousin Larry's nostrils flare in disbelief and hear the rattling crash of the shotgun hitting the floor. Without pausing, Jennifer kicked it away from him and raced down the nearest of the back halls she could find. Damn, why hadn't she *taken* the shotgun? Damn, damn, damn.

Behind her, Jennifer was aware of Cousin Larry yelling for his aunt and uncle, some shouting back and forth between floors, and the heavy pounding of their feet as Henry and Harriet came hurrying downstairs.

"She was in there," Cousin Larry told them, still panting from the wind having been knocked out of him. "She was right there in the closet, damn it, right under our noses."

Angrily Harriet yelled at him in disbelief. "And you let her get away? With a shotgun and everything, you let her get away?"

"She was a wild woman, I tell you. She barreled out of that closet before I—"

"Oh, shut up. Christ, you're as bad as Henry."

There was a hurried conference of some sort, but again, Jennifer was too far away to make out what they were saying. Harriet was ordering Cousin Larry to do something, Henry was objecting, and Cousin Larry was interjecting his own modifications on whatever it was Harriet was telling him to do. Not daring to stay where she was much longer, Jennifer was aware that Cousin Larry's voice seemed to suddenly disappear, and heard what she thought was the sound of a distant door slamming.

Jennifer began to slip deeper into the hall, trying to keep herself headed for the back door, but also trying to pick halls and turnings—the rear area of Blossom House was a maze of disorderly contradictions—she didn't think they were apt to search until later. At the end of the hall she was in, she came to a small storeroom instead of the back door she was searching for. Inside, it was cramped and incredibly dirty, obviously a place seldom bothered with.

Floor to ceiling, the room was stacked with wooden boxes,

cardboard packing cartons, and pieces of old, broken furniture. Over everything, including the floor, was a layer of dust—soft, thick, and deep. Every step she took raised clouds of the stuff and made the urge to sneeze overwhelming. Quickly Jennifer began backing out of the room, one finger pressed against the side of her nose to keep any sneeze from shattering the silence of the service area. It would echo loudly through the uncarpeted walls and alert Henry and Harriet.

"Henry, damn you. Henry, get over here in this direction," she heard Harriet yell at her brother. "There's a whole bunch of halls back here she might hide in."

Henry's voice, when he answered, sounded put-upon and distant. Quickly Harriet countered. "Don't be such a big baby," she taunted. "Come here, I tell you."

Jennifer's first instinct was to move away from the storeroom door and try one of the other hallways. But she could hear Harriet's voice muttering a string of insults at Henry, and the sound of Henry's inadequate replies. They were getting closer. It was no time for untested explorations; she might come around a corner and walk straight into them—BOOM!—and that would be that.

Trapped, Jennifer retreated into the storeroom and softly shut the door behind her, trying to stir up as little of the nose-tickling dust as she could. Even through the door, she could hear the voices becoming louder.

The sudden sound of Harriet's heavy footsteps stopping outside the storeroom made her go rigid. "It's the outside doors we have to really worry about." There was more conversation, but she couldn't make out the words; they were almost whispering. Had they heard something? Did they suspect something? The dread coursed through Jennifer's body until she began trembling visibly; she could see her own hands shake, as if someone else were controlling them.

Failure or success could depend on whether they searched this room, and whether they searched it carefully enough to uncover her. Her nose began twitching. In panic, she heard the sound of

the doorknob being turned, and someone taking a few step
inside the storeroom. Her whole body began to shake with spasm
as she struggled to overcome the sneeze building up inside her.

"No one in here that I can see," Henry bellowed. There was
coughing noise. "Christ, Harriet, this place is filthy; there'
more dust in here than on Mount Saint Helens. You ought to ge
to it someday."

From outside, Harriet's voice, angry again: "Shut up, Henry
If you don't like the way I keep house, go hire yourself a maid.
Silence for a few moments, then: "The brat's not in there
right?"

"Well, I haven't had time to take the place apart—what a pi
of junk—but just looking around, I don't see her. If you want—

"Let it go, let it go," Harriet commanded, apparently stayin
well out in the hall. "It's the outside doors I worry about."

For the moment the urge to sneeze had left Jennifer. Instea
she was listening to her own heart, sensing the adrenaline pum
through her circulatory system, and shaking uncontrollably.

"Harriet," Henry suddenly called, "you ought to see what
found. That little toy Victrola that—"

Harriet exploded. "Come out of there, Henry. We've g
things to do, or that miserable little bitch is going to disappear c
us. Come out now, damn it!"

Jennifer heard a sigh and the metallic noise of some ancie
toy being put back on top of one of the broken pieces
furniture. A moment later she heard Henry's receding footste
and the sound of the door being closed loudly. A cloud of du
immediately mushroomed from the floor, and the compulsion
sneeze again seized her, but by squeezing her eyes shut tight a
pressing both sides of her nose hard, she beat it back.

Softly Jennifer tiptoed across the room and stood just insi
the door, her nose still twitching—but under control. Outsid
she once again heard Henry's footsteps approaching. Damn,
was coming back. To get the toy Victrola, perhaps? Unable
make it back to the packing cartons, Jennifer froze where s
was. The footsteps came closer, and then, a new sound: Hen

riggs was whistling. Jennifer wanted to swear but couldn't. The
azy bastard was whistling. The footsteps stopped just beyond
e door, which mystified her. Can you hear somebody *not*
eeze, she wondered? No. Ridiculous.

Out in the hall, there was a strange burst of noises. Metal on
etal. Henry was busy with something she couldn't identify. As
nnifer stood, frozen in position, a strange tickling attacked her
ft foot. Jennifer looked down. In the dim light coming through
small, barred window high on the far wall, Jennifer could see
undulating mass of small, furry somethings crawling across
r bare feet. Her heart stopped; she was unable to risk shaking
em off her because of Henry Griggs's silent, malevolent prox-
ity. Mice. Jesus Christ, mice. She'd been scared to death of
em since she was a little girl. Or maybe worse—it was too dark
see clearly—*rats*. Leering pink-eyed rats waiting to begin
ewing on her toes. Every instinct in Jennifer made her want to
eam, to kick, to run, to cover her ears and shriek her brains
t. It was a gray, furry nightmare, a thousand bad dreams from
ildhood returning to batter themselves against her mind.

Suddenly Jennifer heard Henry Griggs's footsteps fading again
he walked away from the storeroom. With a sharp intake of
eath, Jennifer kicked her feet wildly, sending the mice or rats
whatever they were back into hiding behind the boxes and
k, racing away from her with little squeaks of terror. Jennifer
ew how they felt, as she was more frightened than they were.
e quickly pushed the door open and stepped softly out into the
l. Far in the distance somewhere, she could hear Henry and
rriet again arguing about something, doors being slammed,
rs being locked, doors being unlocked.

After brushing the dust from herself as best she could, Jennifer
ted down the hall, but in the opposite direction. Another
dest entrance to a small hall suddenly appeared on her right.
e entered it and found that while this hall was a dead end,
re was another small one giving off to the left of that.

As she reached the turn and looked down the short hall,
nifer's heart almost stopped. At its far end was a door.

Heavy. Planked. Roughly finished. It was the same door she an
Henry Griggs had used the aborted night of the ice-cream parl
and the Ferris wheel. She couldn't believe it.

It was too much to hope for. Beyond the door lay escape, th
outside world, freedom. That word meant so many differe
things, some big, some small. Slowly, almost afraid to try b
cause she wasn't sure she could face another disappointmen
Jennifer turned the inner lock and tried the handle. My God. M
God!—it turned, it opened. She'd done it.

Outside, she stood in the last warm rays of the lowering su
blinking. She'd done it! It was hard for Jennifer to accep
Shaking herself out of the disbelief—staying that close to Blc
som House was inviting trouble—she looked around. To one si
of her was what appeared to be a well-kept flagstone path. At t
end of it she could see the street—the street and freedom.

She had done it, she had done it, she had done it! Oh, you
have been so proud of me, Peter! If you could only have be
here to see me do it. Oh, God. My God, Peter, where *are* yo

CHAPTER TWENTY-NINE

Checking her notebook, Hillary Crane saw she had finally worked her way down the list to the mysterious Mr. Henry Griggs. His place was on Valentine Street, but she had trouble finding it on her map; the daylight was fading fast, and the inside light in her rented car was of little help.

She battled with the tourist office's map, folding and refolding it, trying to find where the street was; the names were hard to make out in the dimness. There, there it was; she had finally found it.

A day earlier Mr. Griggs's name had made her feel uncomfortable. For some reason the name now demanded urgency. This job of finding where Jennifer and Peter had gotten married was affecting her brain, Hillary decided. A name was just a name, not something that could fill you with dread one moment and a compelling need for speed the next.

She discovered she was talking out loud. Shaking her head, she went back to tracing the shortest route to Mr. Griggs's home on the map; two blocks straight ahead, left turn, right turn, and she should be there. She started the car and, blinking at the darkening twilight, heard Mr. Griggs's name again whispering to her, telling her to hurry.

It shouldn't take her any more than five minutes, she told the whispering name, and then swore at herself.

Worry, Hillary Crane decided, can do awful things to your brain.

*   *   *

In her ears, Jennifer could hear the blood pounding furiously
So close, oh, God, so close. Quickly she hurried down to the end
of the path—it ran down the center of an alleyway between
Blossom House and an empty-looking building on the other side
shuttered, silent, dark—and leaned against the wall a moment
She needed to rest to pull herself together—her whole body was
still shaking—and to study the street for possible pitfalls. None
as far as she could see. There were a handful of people walking
on the sidewalks, but they seemed either to be talking to one
another or completely lost in thought.

Then she saw it, staring at it with disbelief. Pulled to the curb
a little to the left of Blossom House, was a car, its front door
open and sagging out over the sidewalk. Even from where Jennifer stood, she could hear the soft hum of its motor running. The
car's owner was stupid; in New York, anyway, a parked car with
a running motor was pleading to be stolen. But perhaps Chiver
wasn't that sort of town; perhaps—with the exception of Blossom
House—people around here didn't even lock their doors.

Trivia, Petty speculation. Crazy details. She scolded herself
But after so long as a prisoner, making so few if any decision
for herself, she had almost forgotten how to separate the impo-
tant from the unimportant.

Taking a deep breath, Jennifer looked at the car again. Apparently no one was anywhere near the little Ford; its owner mu
have gone back inside one of the houses along the street to ge
something he'd forgotten.

He wouldn't be happy when he came back out to get into h
car. The picture disturbed Jennifer. All right, technically, sh
was about to steal a car. But after hearing her story would anyor
say she shouldn't have? No.

Jennifer, still equivocating, found such sudden good luck aft
so much bad hard to accept, but—well, maybe those prayers. .

Damn it, stop stalling, she told herself. Jennifer swallowe
hard and shot across the pavement to the car. To make as litt
noise as possible, she pulled, rather than slammed, the car do

ut. Her jaw set, Jennifer slammed the little Ford into "drive," d slowly began moving down the long, shady street she had en for the first time six weeks before.

Gradually Jennifer picked up speed. She was free, my God, e was free! Her whole body shook with happiness as she spoke e word and considered the fact. *Free*.

So much to do, Jennifer thought, suddenly pulling rein on her citement. First, find a policeman. Tell him. Explain the secret Blossom House. He would look at her a little strangely—it s a weird story to absorb easily—but the clothes she was aring, the urgency she would put into her voice, and an pression of being on the edge of tears would bring him around ckly enough.

Tell him about Cherry. Have him call a hospital. She would bably have to go with him to the station house before they uld call out the troops and race to free the others, but she'd get t out of the way quickly. A sudden shadow fell across Jenni's mood. She must tell them about Peter, too. So they could rt looking for him. Was he dead—that was what the other girls kept saying—or was he still alive, as she kept believing self? It was time to find out.

Very soon, though, the rushing waves of happiness were sweep-across her once more. All that had happened in the last few utes was almost too incredible to accept. She, Jennifer afield—no, damn it, Jennifer *Owen*—had done it. Fantastic, elievable, awesome. Done it all by herself. Without any help m her mother or father. Without any help from the police. thout any help from her friends—some friend that damn Hillary ne had been; she hadn't lifted a finger. Without help from one, *she* had done the impossible.

A small noise behind her made Jennifer turn partly around in seat. Jennifer gasped, feeling the blood drain out of her body. m the floor of the backseat, Cousin Larry rose like some nster from the deep, a dripping menace, a thin, condescending le pasted across his sallow face.

Frantically Jennifer struggled with the wheel. It couldn't be

happening, not after getting this far. It *couldn't* be; it wasn't fai
Jennifer began swerving the car from one side of the street to th
other, blowing the horn, trying to draw attention to herself.
policeman, a policeman, there had to be one somewhere . .
She jammed her foot on the accelerator, sending the car roarin
forward, side to side, the horn blowing . . .

"You're going awfully fast, Peaches," Cousin Larry sa
smoothly. "Where's the fire?"

Jennifer began to scream.

Slowly, deliberately, Cousin Larry lifted a can of gasoline or
the seat back and poured it over the screaming Jennifer. T
smile never left his face. Bending over slightly, he snapped op
his Zippo, spun its little wheel, and then tossed the flami
lighter onto the front seat beside her. "Why, the fire's right he
that's where it is. . . ."

Jennifer exploded into flame—her clothes, her hair, her sk
all of her. . . . For a second Cousin Larry listened to her shrie
of agony and shrugged. Confidently he reached for the rear do
handle to jump out of the careening car. It came off in his har
Suddenly panicked, he pulled on the handle of the door opposi
The same thing happened. In the front seat, flailing at the flam
and screaming, Jennifer discovered the door beside her simila
had a handle that pulled off when you tried to use it. She brac
her feet against the steering column and kicked at the door. T
flames continued to sweep over her, and her screams turned i
shrieks. In the backseat, Cousin Larry began screaming himse

None of this was by accident. Before Henry had brought
car around in front for Larry, he had carefully removed
screws holding the door handles on. The thought had pleas
him. A just end for one devious blackmailer, combined with
fitting punishment for one ungrateful child. Gratifying symmet

The car, completely out of control at this point, shot throug
stoplight and out into the heavy traffic of Main Street. No
was steering. Cousin Larry was screaming and choking, a
flames were shooting from windows that would not go do

more than a couple of inches. The entire inside of the car was on fire.

What the roaring flames inside left unfinished, a speeding trailer-truck coming down Main Street completed. There was a hideous, grinding crunch as it plowed into the blazing car, bursting into flames itself as burning gasoline sprayed across it. In minutes, the entire street was jammed with police cars, fire trucks, and half of the horrified citizens of Chivers, Maryland.

In the fast-descending darkness the thick, oily smoke of the fire at times almost obliterated the jungle of neon. The signs still flashed on and off, but their Day-Glo reds, greens, and purples were visible only dimly—distant demons, glowing in hazy, sickly hues through the billowing smoke of the accident.

At the moment, there were no takers for free photographs— free!—for genuine keepsake albums, or for the promise of complimentary organ music.

Organ music? Only Harriet's weird Mozartian arrangement of "Yes, Sir, That's My Baby" could properly celebrate the grim victory of Blossom House.

Hillary's eyes were bothering her worse than ever—aching muscles, vision slightly blurred, a dull pain behind them. For a moment Hillary Crane wondered if she might not need glasses— an appalling thought to her—but quickly decided her eyes were merely suffering from overuse and exhaustion.

Squinting hard, she finally saw the name of the side street she was looking for, and turned into what appeared to be a very narrow alley. At its end, one more turn and she should be just about abreast of Henry Griggs's house on Valentine Street.

As she came out of the alley to make the turn, however, she had to jam on the brakes so suddenly, the steering wheel was jammed into her lower chest. To Hillary, it seemed incredible that she hadn't heard them coming, but she'd had the radio turned up loud, trying to lighten the dullness of her mission. Watching them, she shuddered. Another few feet, and she would have been crushed by the platoon of trumpeting fire engines that

were barreling down the street at right angles to her alley.
Patiently she waited for them to go by.

Reaching forward, she turned off the radio—the incident had
jolted her composure—slowly pulled out into the street, and
turned left. Almost immediately she found herself halted again.
A second wave of emergency vehicles forced her almost up onto
the sidewalk: police cars, a fire chief's car, two ambulances, a
paramedic van, and an oversize tow truck with a miniature crane
mounted on its rear deck. On the heels of this fast-moving
convoy came a scattering of press and television cars and trucks.

Almost timidly, after the last of them had passed her, Hillary
pulled out into the street again. She was startled to see—several
intersections farther down the same street—what the focus of all
the fire and police departments' activity was. A car, apparently,
had run the stoplight and plowed into a trailer-truck; both were
still blazing. Surrounding them, firemen were struggling to put
out the flames. From the wreckage rose a column of oily, black
smoke—like the pictures she'd seen of funeral pyres in India.

As she watched, a white-coated paramedic gingerly withdrew
his head from the shattered window of the car and turned to the
men around him, his face an expression of terminal grimness.

Hillary shivered. It always troubled her the way violence could
strike one down anytime. With no apparent reason, the hand of
God would suddenly reach out and smite you. It was an unsettling thought. She could not explain why, but the same thought
had led her mind directly back to Jennifer's disappearance. Crazy.
She shivered again.

For a few more minutes she watched the frantic activity, and
then parked in front of Henry Griggs's house. She could see his
name, lettered very inconspicuously, on the sign above the
words—BLOSSOM HOUSE. Looking at the house, Hillary Crane
decided Henry Griggs, J.P., L.L.B., certainly lived well,
far better than any of the other JP's she had so far visited.
Perhaps that came from his being a lawyer as well as a justice of
the peace, a combination that baffled her. The house itself was
magnificent. The plantings and flowers around it were lovingly

manicured—and staggering in their beauty. The reason behind
the mansion's name now became obvious. This man, in spite of
the ominous effect his name continued to have on her, was gifted
with a love of perfection and beauty.

She had no way of knowing that the same apple blossoms she
saw in the front of Blossom House were also falling off more
apple trees behind it, drifting onto Peter Owen's grave like
blown winter snow. She had no way of knowing that the same
Mr. Griggs who so loved his perfect blossoms was the man
behind the blackened, burned body of her best friend, Jennifer
Delafield. Nor would she have understood, even if she *had*
known, that Jennifer had been set ablaze inside a car, perform-
ing, ironically, what was quite possibly the first truly unselfish
act of her life—getting desperately needed help for a stricken
friend, a New York City prostitute incongruously named Cherry.

All she knew for sure was that Henry Griggs came next in the
alphabet on her list, and it was now time for her to interview
him. Rubbing her eyes briefly to soothe them, she picked up the
envelope with Jennifer's and Peter's pictures inside and walked
slowly up the path to Blossom House, again admiring the hand-
someness of both the house and the flowers around it.

The doorbell took a long time to produce any reaction. So
long, Hillary Crane had almost decided that no one was home
and had turned to leave. As she did the door behind her suddenly
opened. Inside, stood a pleasant-looking little man with a pinkish
face and a fringe of snow-white hair. He was not at all what
Hillary had been expecting. "Mr. Griggs?" She looked at him a
second, then: "The justice of the peace?"

"Mr. Henry Griggs. Correct, dear. You probably want—" His
pale-blue eyes took on a puzzled look as they searched the space
around her for the groom who should have been standing beside
her.

"I'm from *New York* magazine" explained Hillary quickly,
using the same gambit she had with all of them. "We're doing an
article on modern trends in marriage, and I'd like to ask
you a few—"

Mr. Griggs had stiffened, his face quite grim. "You've come at a bad time, I'm afraid. Tomorrow, perhaps. You see''—he waved vaguely toward the inside of the house, where, on the terrace beyond, Hillary saw an absolutely huge woman pouring the last of the champagne for a young couple—"we've just done a wedding, and now we're having a little celebration on the terrace. If you could manage tomorrow, dear—and maybe you'd like to bring along a photographer. The blossoms on the apple trees are all falling off now, but there're plenty of other things. . . .''

Hillary nodded and assured Mr. Griggs she would be back—yes, of course, with a photographer—tomorrow. With another smile and a faint wave, Mr. Griggs retreated again into Blossom House.

From the doorway, Henry smiled, watching Hillary walk down the path, then turned to join the young couple on the terrace. With Jennifer dead—burned to a cinder—neither he nor Harriet saw any reason to stop their operation. If anything, the death of Jennifer seemed to have whetted their appetites.

Hillary wasn't really so sure she *would* be back the next day. Her father, over the phone, had told her in no uncertain terms that it was time for her to come home. Yes, he understood that Jennifer was her best friend, but—well, this was a job for professionals, and he understood that both the Delafields and the Owens had hired private detectives to do the searching. They would want, of course, to talk with her. But right now, the important thing was for Hillary to come back to New York. . . .

Slowly a discouraged Hillary walked down the path away from Blossom House. Halfway down it, she stopped, puzzled, and turned around. From the house came the sound of someone playing the piano. It was a weird-sounding piece, redolent of Mozart, but nothing she could recognize. Yet it was unquestionably familiar, something she could remember from somewhere, a bittersweet melody that, for some reason, made her acutely uncomfortable. She shrugged and checked her list again, climbed into the car, and started the motor. Gunderson, Harvy . . .

Her eyes ached.

*   *   *

On the third floor of Blossom House, Bartlett heard the music, too. Down the row of cells, she heard Cherry moan, but her cries were becoming increasingly weak. It would not be long now.

A little earlier she had seen the young couple coming happily up the path toward Blossom House, smiling at one another, their eyes bright with hopes and dreams and plans.

Bartlett wanted to cry. Their smiles, along with their hopes and dreams and plans, had died with the last notes of Harriet's piano piece. Bartlett squirmed helplessly. After the last week's events there were so many cells to fill. . . .

L'ENVOI

"Well, here we go. The very final procedure. It's the last time you'll have to go through this, which should make you feel pretty damn good in itself. It shouldn't hurt, but—hell, I don't have to tell *you* this—removing the bandages always pulls a little. Ready?" The girl nodded, and the plastic surgeon reached down to where she sat in a chair and began cutting off the adhesive strips that held the long bandage to the left side of her face.

"Just think of it, darling. After this, no more bandages ever again. This is the very last one," said the other man, also a doctor, a GP named Oliver Bronson. Bronson took her hand and squeezed it warmly, watching anxiously as the plastic surgeon began tugging lightly on the bandage itself. Gently he was able to pull it down a little, moving very slowly so that the bandage wouldn't hurt her as it was separated from her face.

"Ouch," she said, her body stiffening.

"Sorry. Almost there," the plastic surgeon said encouragingly, still pulling gently on the bandage.

"After this one your face is on its own," Oliver Bronson noted, squeezing her hand harder. "That ought to make you feel pretty damn good."

"There." The plastic surgeon cut the adhesive strips from the bottom of the bandage and pulled the bandage completely off her face. Standing back a little, he studied his work, a pleased smile crossing his face. "Peaches," he said, "you're a very beautiful girl. The graft took perfectly; there isn't even a tiny crease where it joins the rest of your facial skin. Damn it, I'm pretty proud o this job." He turned to his old friend, Dr. Bronson, smiling broadly. "Well, Oliver? What do you think of your Peaches now?"

The girl, who had been running her hand over her face lightly as if testing the graft, suddenly sat bolt upright in the chair "Please stop calling me that, Doctor," she snapped at the plastic surgeon. "It's not my name." She blinked at the doctor, startled by her own vehemence. "I'm sorry," she added lamely.

The look exchanged between the plastic surgeon and the man she loved—Oliver Bronson—did not escape her. Well, damn it it *wasn't* her name. Yes, it was the name she'd given Oliver tha day over two years ago when he'd yanked her, clothes and hai still smoldering, off the street and into his office, but that wa because it was the only name she'd been able to think of. She must have had a real name before the fire, but everything in he past before that moment was now only a vague, distant blur. She didn't know who she was, where she was from, or even what he real name had been. It was only natural, she supposed, tha Oliver would call her Peaches at first—after all, it wasn't a name he'd made up, it was the name she'd given *him*—but every time he did, a shudder of dread she couldn't explain would run through her, and she'd finally made him stop. "It isn't my name," she'd kept trying to tell him, over and over again.

These days, he called her only one thing: darling. He'd fallen deeply in love with her, retrograde amnesia or not, stayed beside her, supported and helped her, and done everything humanly possible for her during the two years of endless plastic surgery. He'd had to fight other doctors and unsympathetic hospital administrations, uncooperative plastic surgeons, and overly curious hospital staffs bent on finding out who she really was. They never did, he never did, she never did.

In the process, he'd had to put up a lot of his own money, and worse, had had to put up with the pettiness and backbiting of his own profession of medicine, whose members sometimes acted as if the Hippocratic Oath was license for a conspiracy to obstruct.

Struggling against all of them—the plastic surgeon working on Jennifer right now had been one of the few helpful exceptions—Oliver had battled long and successfully to restore Jennifer's face and body, changing it from a grotesque, charred parody of a human being into a girl who literally could take a man's breath away with her beauty.

For her part, Jennifer was very much in love with Oliver. With the past reduced to a fleeting, occasional flash of recollection, he was all she could count on: he was her beginning, he was her present, and as their love deepened he had become her future. Before Oliver, nothing existed. Gone was any memory of Peter Owen, or of her family, or of Blossom House. His kindness, understanding, and obvious feelings for her had been all that had kept her going during the early, dark days of her recovery. Such was the depth of his understanding that he'd even gone along with her insistence that he stay away from the police and not try to discover who she had been before the terrible fire, which had erased everything about herself from her mind.

Jennifer could not explain, even to herself, why she was so desperate not to know who she had been, but her past, like the name Peaches, was somehow filled with a fear she could put no name to. Even thinking about it as she sometimes did, lying sleepless in her bed, would make her break out in a clammy sweat. The past was left unexplored—by her own adamant passion not to know. As if from a great distance she heard the plastic surgeon's voice asking her a question.

"Don't you want to take a look at yourself?" he asked.

Jennifer blinked at him, only slowly coming back to reality. She saw the surgeon was standing in front of her, a medium-size rectangular mirror held in his hands. Behind him, wearing a big grin, stood Oliver.

"Go on, darling, take a look. It's quite a sight."

Numbly Jennifer took the mirror and held it up to her face. A stranger stared back at her, a stranger not without beauty, but a stranger nonetheless. She had seen her face before, of course, as the plastic surgery progressed; this was the first time, though, she

could view the total effect—finished, completed, without ban
dages or burn scars of any kind. Knowing what the surged
wanted to hear, Jennifer rose to the occasion, laughing a little
"Wow," she said, forcing herself to sound as delighted as she
could. "Wow. She's some looker. I don't know who she is, but
she's got one hell of a face."

Oliver could guess what was troubling Jennifer. Turning to the
surgeon, he asked a question he hoped would resolve her fear
"Bert, isn't that pretty much what she must have looked like—
before, I mean?"

The surgeon furrowed his brow and gestured helplessly wi
his hands. "It's hard to tell without a picture. As for the bon
structure—naturally, nothing's changed there. The face—well,
has to be pretty much as it was, possibly a little different he
and there, but on the whole the same."

"See, darling, you've *always* looked like that. You just can
remember how beautiful you were—and are again."

Jennifer turned toward the plastic surgeon, touching his han
lightly. "Thank you, Doctor. Thank you for giving me bac
myself. Whether my face is the same, or a tremendous improv
ment on the original, thank you for everything." Jennifer gav
the surgeon a warm smile, knowing that the man was beamin
with pleasure as he put the surgical gear back in his doctor's bag

While Oliver and the plastic surgeon were downstairs, standin
by the front door and chatting, Jennifer crept noiselessly acro
the room and stared at her face in the large mirror hanging ove
her dressing table. The reflection was a beautiful one and, con
sidering what she had looked like when Oliver had found her o
on the street, was almost difficult to believe. Whose face was i
Hers; they said. Even this small question probing the past cause
a shiver to run through her again. Jennifer sighed and turne
away from the mirror, preparing a wide smile with which to gre
Oliver, whom she could hear climbing the stairs, whistling.

A week later the newness of the face had stopped botherin
her. It was as if the face had always been hers, staring back

er from the mirror. Jennifer and Oliver were sitting in the living
oom, having a drink before dinner. In the kitchen Jennifer could
ear the housekeeper rattling pans and banging things, reminding
hem she was there, and trying to hurry their entrance into the
ining room so she could finish up and be through for the day.

Oliver looked up at Jennifer suddenly. "Darling," he said, an
nusually serious tone to his voice, "We might as well face some-
hing. The last of the plastic surgery is over. You look like a
nillion bucks. More important, I love you very much, and I think
ou love me. Hell, why don't we cut out the kid stuff and get
narried?"

Jennifer's heart leaped. There wasn't anything in the world she
anted to do more. Yet, even as her face lit up with a smile of
adiant happiness, she felt a sudden wave of the old, familiar
read sweeping through her. That was stupid, she told herself:
liver's proposal had no connection with a forgotten past, it was
n event from her new life. To battle the fear inside her, Jennifer
ound she was stalling with nonsense reasons why what Oliver
ad just suggested was impossible. "I'd love to, Oliver. My
od, there's nothing on the face of this earth I'd rather do more.
ut—" She stopped, unable to explain.

"But *what*?" Oliver demanded, looking at her curiously.

"Well, you don't know anything about me. I mean, about who
was or where I was from or what sort of person I was. And I
an't help you, because I don't know either. You can't marry
omebody as full of riddles as that; it isn't fair to yourself."

Oliver laughed and came over to where she was sitting, plant-
g himself on the arm of her chair, and holding both of her
ands in his. "Look, darling, I probably know more about you
an I have about anyone else I've ever known. Screw the past. I
on't give a damn whether you came from Guam or Anchorage,
- if you were a society lady or a bank robber, or anything else
om your old life. The girl I love is the girl I know *now*, not
ome ghost from the past. I'm thirty-six and I've never wanted to
et married before; now I do. To you. And it's as simple as that.
ow about it?"

The dread inside Jennifer was slowly receding, but it stil clutched at her with its fingertips, holding on to part of her as i desperate not to let her go. To Jennifer, though, there was onl one possible answer to give Oliver and, swallowing hard to hol back the shadowy fear that still tore at her, she gave it: "Oh Oliver, how could I ever hesitate? Of course I will."

Three days later Jennifer was getting ready, putting the las touches of makeup on, studying herself in the mirror to see hov the new dress she'd bought for the occasion looked. Perfect. Th sense of dread she'd felt initially had gradually receded into th background; she could still feel it tugging at her sometimes late a night, but quickly learned how to keep it pretty well out of he mind. She had never been, she decided, happier than she wa now.

Oliver had been wonderful—gentle, considerate, warm—bu then, Oliver always was. They had discussed getting married i the chapel of some church—it would allow them to invite handful of the people closest to them, like the plastic surgeon an some other old friends of Oliver's—but had finally decided again it. They both wanted a very private ceremony. "A justice of th peace, I guess," Oliver had said. "Most of the places aroun town are pretty dreadful—wall-to-wall neon—but there are a fev really nice setups. One just down the street, as a matter of fact. go by it every day on my walk. Very chaste-looking and beaut fully kept up."

Slowly they left the house and walked down the street, turnin right at the first corner. "There it is," said Oliver excitedly pointing at a beautiful old Georgian set back from the street som distance. "God, look at that planting. Somebody really works c the grounds. A beautiful place to get married—doesn't look lik a justice of the peace's place at all."

Jennifer had stopped dead in her tracks, and Oliver, who ha been holding her by the hand, had had to stop too, studying he with a troubled look. Everything about the place was sendir ominous warning signals through Jennifer; she looked at the sign reading BLOSSOM HOUSE and felt her knees go weak.

"Nervous?" Oliver laughed. "My God, I can feel you trembling."

"Not nervous," Jennifer forced herself to say, hearing how unsteady her voice sounded. "Not nervous, just excited." She was lying; every fiber of her body was shaking, screaming out inside her—the wild cry of the Furies as they closed in on their doomed and helpless victims.

"Nervous," corrected Oliver, laughing again. "Brides always are. Don't let it throw you."

A smile that Jennifer didn't feel was produced and stuck on her face. Lagging behind, she allowed Oliver to pull her down the path toward the front door. Jennifer wanted to scream, to cry out, to run as fast as she could, but somehow managed to keep wearing the phony smile and allowing herself to be moved inexorably toward the huge front door with its shiny brass knocker.

Confidently Oliver led her up the steps. "Darling, this simply has to be the happiest moment of my life. God, you're wonderful," he said, turning slightly in her direction.

Numbly Jennifer watched him press the large doorbell. Suddenly the smile faded from her face. It all closed in on her at once. A man standing at that same door, holding her hand, ringing that same bell, herself blissfully happy standing beside him, just as she now stood beside Oliver. Going into Blossom House. Terrible things happening, vague, distant perimeters of disaster. Shrieks, screams, the cold of death. Déjà vu? Jennifer didn't know. All she was sure of was that she mustn't go through that door, and panic enveloped her, pressing down on her with the full weight of shuddering terror.

She grabbed Oliver's arm, staring at him wild-eyed, her face, her whole body, trembling visibly. "No, no, no," she hissed at him. He turned from the door to stare at her, completely baffled. "What—" he began.

Jennifer suddenly found she was crying. "I'm not sure, I'm not sure . . ."

Oliver's expression progressed from confusion to irritation
"It's one hell of a time to decide that."

"I don't mean you, Oliver. My God, I don't. I want to marry
you more than anything else in the world. It's this house. I'm no
sure, I'm not sure, but there's something terrible about this hous
that—"

The door suddenly opened. Jennifer screamed at the sound i
made. Standing in the doorway was a man so thin and tall, h
must have had to bow his head every time he walked beneath
lintel, looking at her curiously because of the scream she ha
quickly stifled. A little behind him stood a jolly-looking plum
woman he would later introduce as his wife. Oliver glanced a
Jennifer, squeezed her hand warmly, and laughed. "I tried to te
you about nervous brides, darling . . ."

Turning from her, he began talking to the justice of the peace
a man named Victor Hollingbroke. Yes, they would like to ge
married. Yes, they had the necessary identification papers—
Jennifer's had been neatly phonied by a friend of Oliver's in th
hospital's clerical records department—no, no one else would b
attending, and yes, they'd like to get married right away.

As they walked in all of the terror suddenly drained out c
Jennifer. She could not explain it. But the sight of the Hollingbroke
had somehow erased all the dread she'd felt about Blosso
House.

It made no sense, she knew that. What *did* make sense wa
that she was marrying Oliver, a man she loved deeply and wh
loved her with the same intensity. Twenty minutes later Jennif
stared into Oliver's eyes and heard Victor Hollingbroke pr
nounce them man and wife. The groom, he added, could kiss th
bride. Oliver appeared to need no urging. Fifteen minutes lat
they walked hand in hand out of Blossom House and turne
down the street to go back to Oliver's home.

For the first time in over two years Jennifer felt complete
free of fear; for the first time she could remember, she fe
completely happy. Let the past remain dead, she told herse
Today and tomorrow were all that counted. The two of the

walked quickly. Very soon they turned the corner and with that, lost sight of Blossom House—forever.

Almost every afternoon around four, the fog rolls into Big Sur, California, with the regularity of a well-oiled grandfather clock. The young couple hesitated outside the door of an unusually handsome house for this part of the country, then rang the front doorbell.

For a long time nothing happened, and they almost left, deciding no one was home. Suddenly the front door opened, and a huge woman filled the doorway. "Oh," the woman said after studying them for a second, "you probably want my brother." She turned and called up the stairs, motioning the couple inside behind her. "Henry," she called, "a young couple to see you. I think they"—she turned back to the couple, her eyes twinkling merrily—"want to get married."

The young girl laughed, the boy blushed. "My name's Harriet Garvey," the big woman said, smiling at them understandingly. "My brother, Henry, will be right down. He's the justice of the peace, you see."

Upstairs, the couple could hear someone moving around, preparing to come down. In the awkward silence the young girl tried fill the vacuum. "You certainly have a magnificent place. I've never seen such magnificent trees and shrubs."

The woman smiled. "Yes, Henry really dotes on his gardening. Spends hours turning over the earth, irrigating and fertilizing. It shows, I guess."

A few minutes later they were introduced to Henry Garvey, the huge woman's brother. They chatted for a little while, and very quickly all the papers necessary for the wedding had been produced, the register signed, and the young couple positioned for the wedding itself. The paperwork in California was different from that of Maryland, but everything else was very much the same.

Harriet and Henry had moved here a little less than two years ago, selling their house with some anguish. But while at first

they had felt completely safe in Chivers—Peaches, after all, ha
died in the automobile fire—they began hearing stories tha
someone had seen a little girl running down the street with he
clothes on fire. They became nervous. And when her body wa
not discovered in the burned-out wreck of the car, they knew sh
must be alive somewhere. It was time to get out; God alone kne
what she would tell people about them. Police, lawyers, cour
prison.

"I pronounce you man and wife. . . ." Henry Garvey said
smiling broadly at the newlyweds. Half an hour later the music
Harriet's piano floated out of the house and into the gatherin
fog. It was a curious piece she was playing, familiar, yet playe
in the style of an unfamiliar piece by Mozart.

Nothing had changed but the coast. As Harriet had told Henr
one day, "Someday we must put up a sign, Henry. Blosso
House West, I suppose."

For a second the two of them stared at each other. Then the
began to laugh, rocking back and forth with the ridiculousness
the idea, howling with exuberance, laughing until the tears ra
down their cheeks. . . .

It was impossible to know precisely what they found so funn